THE
LONG
FOREVER

Also available in the trilogy
THE SIGN OF ONE
INTO THE NO-ZONE

THE LONG FOREVER

EUGENE LAMBERT

First published in Great Britain in 2018 by Electric Monkey,
an imprint of Egmont UK Limited
The Yellow Building, 1 Nicholas Road, London W11 4AN

Text copyright © 2018 Eugene Lambert

The moral rights of the author have been asserted

ISBN 978 1 4052 7737 2

59776/1

www.egmont.co.uk

Typeset by Avon DataSet Ltd, Bidford on Avon, Warwickshire
Printed and bound in Great Britain by the CPI Group

Stay safe online. Any website addresses listed in this book are correct
at the time of going to print. However, Egmont is not responsible for
content hosted by third parties.

Please be aware that online content can be subject to change and websites
can contain content that is unsuitable for children. We advise that all
children are supervised when using the internet.

Egmont takes its responsibility to the planet and its inhabitants very seriously. All
the papers we use are from well-managed forests run by responsible suppliers.

To Paddy and Maureen,

to Kyle and Sky,

to my wonderful readers,

and last but not least,

to all my fellow identical twins.

PART ONE
EVASION

1
FEELING GRIM

'Is your friend no better?' one of the other prisoners asks.

'What's it look like?' I say, real short.

I shouldn't be bad-tempered. The girl was just asking. But Sky's getting sicker so fast she's scaring me. That, and I'm light-headed with hunger and choking with thirst. My skin is sore too, horribly prickly, almost as if it's trying to crawl off. It's like that healing itch us nubloods get when we're recovering from an injury, only loads worse.

Which is weird, because I'm *not* injured.

A dozen kids are stuck in this caged-off part of the star freighter's hold with us. All idents, nubloods like myself. They've got the skin-crawling thing too, but you'd hardly know looking at them. They're ident camp veterans, the toughest of the tough, and well used to suffering.

'Why haul us off-world only to let us starve?' I mutter.

Sky's green eyes are sunk into her face. She stifles a cough. 'Relax. They'll feed us. We're worth less dead.'

I hope she's right. We haven't seen our captors since we were loaded aboard. How long ago was that? At least three days, to be gnawed at by hunger so bad. One thing's for sure, we're not on Wrath any more. We're off-world. In space. Tunnelling through the big cold empty.

Where to? Guess we'll find out when we get there.

I lick my dry lips, imagining what I'd see if I could look back the way we've come. A scatter of stars, one of them the sun I squinted up at for sixteen years. Even if this freighter's drive is as shagged as the rest of it looks, we'll already be a good few light years on our way; too far to see the brown speck of Wrath, our barren little dump world.

Did I do right by coming with Sky? Don't know.

All I know is that with every breath I take, I leave Colm further behind. If my twin's still alive. By now he'll have led the attack on the Slayer spaceport we found hidden in the heart of the No-Zone. Knowing him, he'd be fool enough to lead from the front and get himself wasted.

At the back of the cage a pipe drips water into a little plastic beaker. When it's full the girl watching it so intently will drink it down. It's her turn and fairer than passing it around. Some kids take bigger gulps than others. Must be getting close too, because she licks her lips and nods to the waiting youngsters to get ready. While she drinks, they get to cup their hands under the pipe so no drops are wasted. I'm after the redhead lad. Three more beaker-fills between me and a few mouthfuls of brackish water.

At the rate the pipe drips it'll keep us alive . . . just.

Sky says it's set like that on purpose, to keep us weak.

I squeeze my eyes shut and try to forget how thirsty I am. Flashes of light spark on the back of my eyelids, in time with the vicious prickling of my skin. Somehow I end up thinking about that Peace Fair I went to, where this all began. Seeing idents for the first time. Wondering which one was evil. Missing the Cutting ceremony, but watching the Unwrapping in the middle of a baying crowd. Everyone straining to see as the bandages came off. Which twin would show the impossibly quick healing, the telltale sign of the nublood monster? The sickening executions that followed. Nooses around children's necks. The bang of the trapdoor as it fell open. The drop. A bar-taut rope twitching as a young life kicked itself away. Never for one moment suspecting that I was an ident myself. Worse still, that I was the one with the monster nublood pumping in my veins.

Now we know the hangings were faked so the kids could be spirited away afterwards. Like the ones in here.

I open my eyes and the redhead lad is next for the cup.

For maybe the thousandth time I reach inside my jacket, making out like I'm having a scratch. Feel the cold and reassuring metal of my snub-nosed blaster. When we were loaded aboard, the freighter crew couldn't be bothered searching us. They'll have figured their Slayer buddies would've taken care of that. Didn't even find Sky's leg brace, which would have taken some explaining.

'Don't!' she hisses. 'What if they're watching?'

'I'm sick of this,' I whisper. 'I say we bust out now. If we wait any longer, you'll be too sick to back me up.'

She shakes her head, sending her white dreads flying.

'No. We wait. I'll be fine.'

'You keep saying that; what if you're *not*?'

That's my big worry. All us nubloods feel like crap, but we're not getting worse. Sky *is* though. I grew up with a healer for a mother, so I know ill when I see it. Sky won't admit it, but whatever's hurting us is hurting her much worse. See, she's only pureblood and weak already from the darkblende poisoning that's slowly killing her. And that boiled buzzweed she takes for her lung pain doesn't seem to help with this, so how much more can she stand?

'We stick to our plan,' she snarls.

Our plan? Hers, more like. Sky's betting that we'll be taken to the same place they took her sister, Tarn. Her plan is to keep our heads down until the freighter lands and unloads us, before shooting our way clear. Yeah right. Me, I'm for busting out the first chance we get, jamming my blaster in the pilot's ear and making him take us some place safe. And this way we could give these other nublood kids a chance too.

But Sky won't have it. Says they aren't our problem.

'I don't like the way you look,' I whisper.

'Find someone cuter then.'

'That's not what I meant, and you know it. You –'

A violent lurching sensation shuts me up. My seeing goes all strange. Everything around me streaks away, smeared out to an impossible distance. For one heart-stopping second I swear our star freighter has slammed into something. But a few frantic blinks later everything snaps back. Something *has* changed though. That awful prickly feeling scratching at my skin is gone.

Sky lets out a sob of relief . . . so it's not just me.

'What just happened?' I gasp.

'Whatever it was – I'll take it,' she says.

The other kids are swapping startled looks when a loud

metallic *snick* jerks our heads round. It's followed by a soft sucking sound and then a soft breeze that's there one second and gone the next. Beyond the thick mesh caging off this part of the cargo hold, a rust-streaked hatch set into the forward bulkhead slides slowly open. Two men clamber inside through it, hauling a large dark something between them.

That something . . . is a man.

Slumped, unresisting, his head hangs down, hiding his face from me. But I see the matt-black uniform.

A Slayer!

Sky stays sprawled where she is, squirming to see past kids in the way. 'Are they bringing us food?'

'No, another prisoner. A Slayer. In a right state too.'

The black uniform is torn and filthy and he's clearly taken a fierce beating. His legs kick feebly as the crewmen drag him closer before dropping him. His head hits the deck with a loud *thwack*. Slayer or not, I can't help wincing.

One of the crewmen unslings a killstick and waves it at us. 'Back up, away from the cage door.'

'You heard him,' the other growls. 'Shift yourselves.'

Sky and me, we're already at the back of the caged area. Kids nearer the door haul themselves slowly and grudgingly to their feet before shuffling back towards us. The unarmed crewman unlocks the cage door and swings it open.

'Won't get a better chance than this,' I whisper to Sky, slipping the words out of the side of my mouth.

'No!' Her cold claw of a hand clamps round my wrist.

While the guy with the killstick covers him, his buddy grabs the Slayer by his heels and drags him inside the cage. The man's head leaves an ugly red smear behind on the deck plates. I'm raging, but Sky's still got hold of me. The crewman dumps the Slayer, retreats and clangs the cage door shut again. Gives it a tug to check it's secure.

'Some company for you,' he jeers.

'What we need is food,' somebody calls out.

'Eat this guy then,' the crewman says, and laughs.

They both clear off, and the hatch shuts behind them.

Sky lets go of me at last.

'Great!' I thump my head into the hull behind me.

Meanwhile, the nublood kids gather round the face-down Slayer. I see clenched fists and angry looks. One mean-looking lad growls something about it being time for payback and kicks the guy in the ribs.

I hiss out a breath and clamber to my feet. 'Hey! Quit that!'

Growler boy sneers. 'What do *you* care?'

'Yeah, back off,' a tall girl with a pox-marked face snarls.

I don't need this. Twelve of them, only one of me, and I'm supposed to be keeping my head down. But now I get my first good look at the Slayer. I see the way-too-long-for-a-Slayer blond hair, matted with blood.

'Oh, no way. It can't be!'

I barge past the kids, drop to my knees and roll him on to his back. Stare in disbelief at the battered face.

'What the frag are *you* doing here?' I hiss.

2
CHANGE OF PLAN

Murdo! Still in the captured and patched Slayer gear he wore the night he marched us over to be thrown inside the loading cage. But what's he doing here? We left him behind on Wrath. Unless they caught him? Crap! Does this mean they're on to Sky and me too? Nah. Can't be. The crewmen didn't even glance at us when they threw him in.

I'm working on winding my gob shut when growler boy grabs hold and hauls me to my feet.

'Mate of yours, is he? This Slayer?'

I'm collecting hard stares from the rest of the nublood kids too. And now that lurch thing happens again. We all stagger. By the time my eyes quit playing the fool again, the prickly skin feeling is back with a vengeance.

The kid holding me seems unfazed; he shoves his face at me. 'You and your sick friend over there – who *are* you?'

We haven't told them yet, or why we tricked our way into the cage and off Wrath, in case somebody squealed. Early on, one kid asked us where we'd appeared from. Sky told him a made-up ident camp name. And lied about us being shipped into the No-Zone weeks earlier to slave away on fetching and carrying inside the Slayer dome, until it came time to ship us off-world. Since then we've kept ourselves to ourselves and our mouths shut.

'What do you mean?' I say, stalling.

He's half a head shorter than me, but much broader and stockier. And I'm pretty sure his name is Cam. The way he carries himself tells me he knows how to use his fists; the harsh look on his face says he likes using them.

He jerks his head at Murdo, who still hasn't moved.

'You *know* that Slayer, don't you?'

'How about you let go of me?'

'How about you tell me why you're mates with a Slayer?'

He shoves me a step backwards, and his mates crowd round too, peering at me suspiciously. Behind them, I catch a glimpse of Sky struggling to stand up.

'You're asking for it,' I snarl. 'Let go of me, or –'

'Or *what*?' Cam gives me a harder shove that slams me back against the bars of the cage, rattling them.

That does it. I've had enough of being pushed around.

I crouch, which pulls him closer. Fists together, I burst upwards and lash out to break free. Before he can react, I've spun and hip-thrown him on to his back on the deck. He stares up at me, mouth open, winded and shocked. I'm guessing nobody's ever body-slammed him before.

His mates look gobsmacked too. Good.

It's tempting to be all sneery and '*I-did-warn-you*'. Instead, I hold my hands out in front of me to show him I don't want to fight. And I go for my most reasonable look.

'Okay, you're right, I *do* know the guy. His name's Murdo Dern. But it's not what it looks like. He's no Slayer. He's just wearing their gear and pretending.'

Even to me it sounds lame, heading for unbelievable.

I step back. Cam picks himself up, glaring at me the whole time. 'Pretending? Why would he?'

'It's a long story,' I tell him.

'And not one we want shouted out loud,' Sky says. She's up now, but it looks like it's costing her.

'So get telling then,' Cam growls.

'It'd better be good,' the pox-marked girl says.

Now I'd rather be finding out from Murdo how in hell he's wound up in this star freighter's cage with us. But, short of pulling my blaster, that'll have to wait.

'Tell them, Kyle,' Sky says. 'But keep it down. Okay?'

'Fine.' I whisper the telling in as few words as I can manage, starting with Sky, Murdo and me being ident resistance fighters. Their eyes go wide. People fighting *for* them instead of against must be hard to take in. Skipping the bad stuff – that we were making our last stand out in the No-Zone – I bang on instead about the Facility raid and the hundreds of nublood kids who were found there and brought to safety. At least for a while anyway.

One of the younger kids cheers, but I shush her.

I move on to how we stumbled across the Slayer spaceport. 'That's how they smuggle their mined darkblende off-world. And nubloods, like you guys.'

Cam recoils, like I'd punched him. 'We're *off*-world?'

'They didn't tell you?'

'No. We're just beasts to them,' the girl says. 'We thought we were being moved to a new camp.'

Sky's scowl slips. She looks almost sympathetic. 'We don't know where we're being taken, but it won't be on Wrath. This is a starship, not a windjammer.'

I see and hear the shock at our news. Fair play though, nobody wails or cries. Like I said, toughest of the tough.

The lad shakes himself. 'Were you captured then?'

'Huh?' I say, confused.

'You're in this cage with us. How come?'

'Oh yeah. I mean, no, we weren't captured. That's why Murdo's wearing the Slayer gear. We scavved it off troopers we'd killed. He walked us to the cage like he was our guard. Two prisoners, late for loading. The guards didn't ask any questions. Why would they? They're more worried about you guys busting out, not us breaking in.'

Cam looks like his head will explode. He's not alone.

'Knowing you'd be taken off-world, you got yourselves chucked in this cage?' he says, his voice climbing.

'Why would you *do* that?' pox-girl says.

Can't help it – I glance at Sky. She narrows her eyes.

But what can I do? I've a dozen mean-looking nublood kids glaring at me. I have to give them something.

'We got in,' I say. 'And we can get ourselves out.'

Slipping my hand inside my jacket, I flash my blaster. Just enough that they see what it is before I tuck it away again.

I see lots of eyes light up with hope.

Cam darts a look at Sky. Scowling, she nods. But makes no move to show them that she's carrying too.

'Well, what the hell are we waiting for?' he snarls.

Yeah, good question! Before I can answer him though, a groan reminds me that Murdo's still lying at my feet. I look down and see one of his blue eyes is open. The other looks like it'll be swollen closed for a while.

'We *can't* wait,' he croaks. 'It's bust out now, or never.'

'Who asked you?' Sky snaps.

Clutching his ribs, Murdo struggles to sit up. I help him to lean against the bars. He spits into his hand loudly and bloodily, fishes a tooth out of it, curses and chucks it away.

'How are you even here?' I whisper.

'Tell you later,' he whispers back. And then, so that everyone can hear: 'You don't get it, Sky, do you?'

'Don't get *what*?' Sky says, scowling down at him.

Murdo shows her his blood-framed teeth in a grimace. 'Feeling sick, Sky? Guts twisting themselves inside out? Skin crawling? You look like death, you know.'

'You don't look so great yourself,' she hisses.

Murdo just glances past her at the watching kids. 'Yeah, even you lot will be suffering.' He jerks his head at the hatch he was brought in through. 'There's a big red sign on the other side of that. It's a warning. Says this hold is unshielded. Which means that while they've got this tramp freighter's leaky old drive going, you're all being zapped. No big deal for nubloods – you heal fast enough to take it or they wouldn't carry you back here. But Sky and me, we'll be dead long before we make planetfall.'

Sky snorts. 'Bullshit!'

'Is it? You'll have felt them kill the drive before they dragged me in here. Why do that? So they didn't get zapped, that's why.

And they were hardly in here any time at all. What's that tell you about how lethal it is?'

Feeling as crap as I do, I don't doubt it's the truth.

'Fine,' I say. 'We bust out next chance we get.'

A glance at Cam and the others and I don't see anyone shake their head. They look well up for it. Sky, trembling visibly with the effort of staying on her feet, shoots me her darkest look, curses and nods.

'We've no choice,' I say.

'Story of my fraggin' life,' she says.

Growing up in the Barrenlands of Wrath, I'm no stranger to seeing people on the receiving end of beatings. Murdo's looks worse than it is. A cracked rib or two; a lumpy, battered and bloody mess for a face.

'You'll live,' I tell him.

Fishing with a finger inside his torn mouth, Murdo glares at me out of the one black eye he can still open.

'Only if we get out of here.'

'Yeah, yeah. We heard you the first time,' Sky says.

'So come on, Murdo,' I say. 'How did you end up here?'

But he says that telling can wait until after we've busted out. We're all crammed up against the bars of the cage now, as far from the drive compartment as we can get, with us nubloods shielding Sky and Murdo from whatever crap the freighter's drive is leaking out. That was Anuk's suggestion, the girl with the pox-scarred face.

Sky says it helps, but she's clearly still suffering.

'What are we up against?' Cam asks.

'There's only five crewmen aboard,' Murdo tells us. 'Two gave me my kicking, another three watched.'

'Good odds,' I say. Especially with us being nubloods.

'So we wait until they bring us food, then you pull your blasters and make them open the cage?' Cam says.

'Or shoot them, then blast the cage open,' Sky says.

Murdo shakes his head. 'Bad idea. See that hull? It'll only be a few mils thick. A stray blaster shot, even on low power, will punch through it like a hot knife through lard. And that's vacuum the other side. One hole and it's goodbye to the air in here. We'd be sucking on nothing.'

I groan. 'You mean we can't use our blasters?'

Sky curses. 'Course we can. We don't miss, that's all.'

Murdo rolls his eyes. 'No! You don't *need* blasters. There's loads of us, five of them. And they won't have energy weapons either, just killsticks or blades.'

I picture the guys who brought Murdo in. And it's true – neither carried a blaster.

Sky snorts, clearly unconvinced.

'You spring us out of this cage, we'll take care of the crew for you,' Cam says. And cracks his knuckles loudly.

His hard-eyed mates nod behind him.

'Should we blast the lock?' I ask Murdo. 'To get ready?'

'No. Could be alarmed. Best wait until they show up to feed us. We'll know they're coming when the drive shuts down.' He winces. 'With luck, I'll still be alive.'

I glance at Sky. Will she last that long? I'm sure she's thinking the same dismal thought.

Next thing I know, she's hauling out her blaster.

'Uh, Sky,' I say.

Before I can stop her, she squirms round and snaps a crackling shot off through the bars of the cage. My skin was crawling off me; now I nearly jump out of it.

'Are you crazy!?' Murdo hisses.

'No. Just sick of being fried, that's all.'

Her blaster round has hit one of the wooden crates stacked further up the hold. Flames lick at the blackened and splintered hole. I smell the choking stink of smoke.

'Oh great,' I moan. 'So now we get to burn to death!'

A siren starts to wail . . .

3
BUSTING OUT

Red lights flash. Everybody jumps up, shouting. Not that I can hear them over the wail of the siren, but I see the fear in their wide eyes, their scared mouths working.

I pull my blaster, but Murdo snatches it off me.

'I'll sort the lock!' he yells into my ear. 'The alarm will bring the crew running. Get the kids ready.'

And then he's gone, scrambling towards the cage door.

Cam's nearest. I grab hold of him and shout into his ear, telling him to get his mates ready to bust out. And he might be sullen and hard work, but he's no fool. He shoves me away and starts frantically passing the word on.

Sky tries to get up again, but slumps back down.

I go to help her, but she waves me away. So I run to see if Murdo needs a hand. He doesn't. I see a flash, hear a bang. The cage door flies open. Murdo pulls it closed again, its rusty hinges screeching. A second later I feel that lurching sensation again and my skin stops crawling off me as the freighter's drive shuts down. Cam's got the kids ready. Too ready. They're all eager and poised, eyes flashing.

I wave at them. 'No, no! Act scared.'

Anuk gets it. She rattles the cage's bars and starts yelling and screaming. 'Help! There's a fire in here!'

More kids join in. Just in time, as a man's wide-eyed face appears at a porthole in the forward hatch. Next thing, it's opening. A crewman wriggles inside; two more follow close behind. By now the crate is really blazing. The first guy curses and shouts orders. The other two pull red tube things off the bulkhead. They scuttle as close to the burning crate as they dare and start spraying the flames with a white foam.

Murdo shoves the cage door open. 'Get them!'

Cam's first out, Anuk right behind him. The guy giving the orders sees them coming. His hand dips for something at his belt. Too slow. Cam's already on him, drops a shoulder and knocks him flat. More kids scramble out, getting in my way. They hurl themselves on to the backs of the crewmen battling the fire. I see a girl snatch a packing strap off a crate. One end is a big metal ratchet. I finally make it out of the cage and help myself to another, leaving an arm's length to swing.

'Kyle!' Murdo shouts. 'The hatch!'

It's sliding closed again. I get there when there's only a crescent left open. Without thinking, I throw myself into the gap, brace my back and shove as hard as I can.

No chance. Its hydraulics are way stronger than I am.

All I can do is make one last desperate effort, wriggle through and throw myself out the far side. The hatch slams shut behind me. I'm picking myself up when I smell sour sweat and hear a breath being sucked in.

'No you don't!' a voice growls.

An iron bar cuts viciously through the air at me.

But I'm already ducking and somehow make it miss. The big crewman swinging it curses, off balance. And I don't give him a second chance to brain me. I sweep my strap around, putting everything I've got into the swing. The buckle end catches him high on the right side of his head.

He grunts, and collapses at my feet in a boneless heap.

I poke him with a boot, but he doesn't move. I make that four crewmen down, one to go.

And he doesn't look much of a threat.

At the far end of this corridor is an open hatch. A skinny little guy rushes through it, sees me and stops in his tracks. Pulls a killstick from his belt. But he's shaking so much that he fumbles and drops it.

I sneer. Can't help it. The guy looks so frightened.

But there's no point taking chances.

The closed hatch behind me has a flat plate on the bulkhead beside it that's covered in greasy handprints. A dead giveaway. I slap my palm on to it, hard. It flickers and something hums. The hatch starts to slide open. When I look round, the crewman's weapon is back in his hand. Much good it'll do him. With the alarm still howling its head off and flashing lights bathing me in red, I walk towards him. I make sure to clatter the buckle end of the strap off the deck, once, twice, so he sees what he's got coming. And it works. Before I'm halfway to him, his killstick hits the deck again. This time it's no sweaty fumble. He chucks it away, rather than take me on.

'I give up, okay? Please don't hurt me!' he whines.

Pitiful. But that's that. In almost less time than it takes to tell it, we bust out and take over the star freighter. And Murdo was right. Five crew, that's all. We hunt high and low, but find nobody else. Anuk waves a blade at skinny guy and he swears blind that's all there were. Only three are left alive now. I didn't mean to kill the guy who tried to brain me, but my blow must've caved his skull in. Nobody's crying about it, least of all me. The guy that shouted orders zapped two of our kids who jumped him. Killed them both stone dead.

The guy who did the killing is dead too. His crewmates have been thrown into the cage. They might live, but they're so messed up I doubt their mothers would know them.

'Can somebody shut that siren down?' Sky yells. She's on her feet again, outside the cage, her back against the mesh.

Murdo grabs skinny guy off me.

'You heard her. Where's the off button?'

'Flight deck.'

'Show me.' He drags him away, out of the hold.

I head over to Sky, skirting around the foam-splattered crate. The fire is out, but a few wisps of smoke still curl up.

And that reminds me – I'm angry with her. 'What if the alarm didn't go off? Or the crewmen hadn't got here so fast? We'd have burnt to death. You think of that?'

'Worked out, didn't it?' she says.

Sure. If you're not one of the dead kids. But I bite my tongue, knowing there's no point arguing. And I'm rewarded with one of her blink-and-you-miss-it smiles.

'You should've seen your face,' she says, poking me.

'One day you'll get us killed.'

'Yeah, yeah. You worry too much.'

The red lights quit flashing and the siren's wail chokes off. The silence that follows is kind of shocking, but it's a relief too. My ears adjust, my heart stops thumping. It's not the crisp silence like you'd get outside our cabin on a calm night after the birds had settled. Instead I hear background hums, the hiss and sigh of air pumps doing their thing. Keeping us alive. We stare at each other. And I guess that's when our heads catch up with what we've done.

'We've busted out,' Anuk says, her scarred face softening, her eyes shiny. 'Can you believe it?'

Next thing, everybody's whooping and jumping up and down, pumping fists and trading hugs.

'We're free, we're free at last!' a freckled girl chants.

Sky shrugs at me. 'Their whole lives they've been caged.'

I'm grabbed and hugged and have my back slapped. A tall girl spins me round gleefully, laughing as I stumble. All this with the dead bodies of their friends lying only metres away. Feels weird. Soon as I can, I slip away to rejoin Sky.

'Leave them to it?' I say.

She nods. We make for the hatch out of the hold.

But Murdo's back, shoving skinny guy ahead of him. He's holding the crowbar the dead guy tried to take my head off with and bashes it on the bulkhead.

BOOM! BOOM! BOOM!

Everybody shuts up and looks around.

'Save it for later,' he calls out. 'We've got work to do.'

It goes deathly quiet in here. Delight fades from faces. Mouths lose smiles and pull down into harsh lines. My guess is that Murdo's forgotten he's wearing matt-black.

'We're done taking orders from Slayers,' Cam snarls. He steps towards Murdo, fists clenched.

'Stop!' I call out, shoving between them. 'He's no Slayer, just wearing their gear. I told you, remember?'

Cam slowly lowers his fists.

'So you did,' he says, and looks disgusted. 'Pity. All my life I've wanted to rip a Slayer's head off.'

Murdo swallows so noisily I think we all hear him.

We're in the corridor, stripping the guy I killed so Murdo can wear his clothes. Murdo grunts and points. 'Look.'

Dead guy has no little finger on his left hand. Like me. And Sky. And the rest of the nublood kids. They all had them hacked off as soon as they were born. Mine, I traded to that sicko Answerman in the Blight, to find out I was the Saviour's long-lost son.

I shiver. 'Do you reckon he's an ident?'

Murdo shrugs. 'Could've lost it in an accident.'

I try to picture the guy's attack on me. How fast was he? Hard to say. Not fast enough.

For sure, the dead guy doesn't look like any nublood I've ever seen. He's a big slab of fat. So much so that his work clothes hang off Murdo. They're made from some material I've never seen before and look hard-wearing. Lots of pockets. Reinforced knees and elbows. I definitely need to find some for myself.

'This guy'll start stinking soon,' I say. 'So will the other bodies. What'll we do with them?'

'Stick 'em in the cage for now,' Murdo says. 'Space 'em later.'

He yells for somebody to give us a hand. Two kids, Ravi and

Pol, come out. They help us wrestle the dead guy inside the hold and into the cage. Skinny guy's already there.

He twitches big time. 'Is he dead?'

'What if he is?' I snap.

The guy sticks his head in his hands like it was his mother lying there, cold and stiff. And groans loudly.

'What's with him?' Sky growls.

The guy's head snaps up. 'Shank was our pilot!'

The silence that follows is ugly. And so is Sky's scowl.

4
MURDO'S STORY

'I didn't mean to kill him,' I protest. 'I just lashed out.'

Heads are shaken. I hear grim mutters.

'Great. What do we do now?' a youngster says.

My heart sinks. Thanks to me, we've traded our small cage for a bigger one hurtling through space with nobody at the controls. I daren't look at Sky, so I glance at Murdo. To my astonishment, I see his battered mouth twist into a grin.

'You think this is *funny*?'

He shrugs. 'Relax. It's not a problem.'

Cam curses. 'Are you deaf, or stupid? Your mate killed the pilot. Without him to fly this thing, we're screwed!'

Murdo loses the grin, trading it for a wince as he pushes himself away from the bulkhead he's leaning against. 'Wind your neck in, kid. I'm a pilot too, so we're *not* screwed.'

Out of the corner of my eye I see Sky start.

No kidding. We both know Murdo can soar a cobbled-together windjammer along Wrath's ridges like a bird, but this is a shift-stuff-between-the-stars spacecraft. Can he fly it? Like hell he can.

But I keep that doubt off my face. He's saying this to calm things down. And it's working. Sky's face is scrunched-up and sceptical, but the nublood kids are letting out held breaths and swapping happy looks again. Banged up in ident camps all their lives, what do they know?

They shoot a few questions at Murdo, but he waves them away. 'Later. I don't know about you guys, but I'm so hungry I could eat a fourhorn, horns, tail and all. How about we find food and fill our bellies?'

That gets a massive cheer. My stomach, which doesn't seem to care that we're still doomed, rumbles loudly. Murdo suggests they haul skinny guy out of the cage to show us where the food is and how to prep it. He's not keen, but Cam soon persuades him with a killstick.

All the nublood kids stream noisily out after them.

Anuk stops in the hatch. 'Aren't you coming?'

I say we will, but first we need to secure the prisoners.

Sky pokes Murdo in the chest. 'So you'll do the flying, huh?'

'Quit that,' he says, swatting her hand away.

'You don't really think you can fly it, do you?' I say.

He looks me in the eye. 'Just watch me.'

'Look, how the frag are you even here?' Sky growls.

Murdo's grin widens. 'I hid amongst some crates while they loaded them, ducked out of the hold and inside an escape craft off the crew compartment. Thought I'd stay there until you guys busted yourselves out. But time goes by and nothing happens. And the pod's life support must be faulty. It gets so cold I can't take it any more. In the end I figure I'll bust you guys out instead.' He winces and feels his battered jaw. 'Only when I opened up the pod's hatch, I ran straight into two of them. I could hardly walk, let alone fight. The rest you saw.'

I shake my head at him. 'Okay, but why?'

'Why not? The Slayer crackdown is making it damn near impossible on Wrath. Anyway, a life out there is only half a life. I belong out here. And –' he struggles over to the nearest wooden crate and slaps his hand on it – 'there's this. No marks on it, but we know what's inside, don't we?'

He laughs, all his aches and pains seemingly forgotten.

'Darkblende's worth a fortune. Sell this load here and we're not just sorted, Sky, we can go anywhere and do anything we like. Live so fine you won't believe it. We'll make the Saviour and his lot look like peasants.'

Sky's scowl stays put. 'You're mad, you know that?'

'Am I? We'll see. Hey, Kyle, do you think you could secure that cage again?'

I give myself a shake. 'Yeah, sure.'

'Do it then. I'll be on the flight deck, checking things out.'

With that, he lurches stiffly out of the hold.

Sky leans against a crate and sighs. 'Well, either he's mad, or he knows something we don't.'

'Seems awful sure of himself.'

'Doesn't he always?'

In cargo holds there's always some rope lying around. I find a heavy-duty strap that'll do. The cage's lock was some fancy electronic thing. After Murdo blasted it, it's melted slag. No problem. Growing up out in the Barrenlands, you learn to make do. I strap the cage door to its frame, lead the tails of the strap round a stanchion a few metres away, and use its built-in ratchet to cinch it as tight as I can.

Ugly. Effective. They'll never undo that.

The two dead kids lie by the charred crate. Somebody's thrown an old tarp over them, but their feet stick out. Inside the cage, one of the knocked-out crewmen stirs.

'You've no idea who you're messing with,' he snarls.

'Neither do you,' Sky snarls back.

We clear off through the hatch and slam it behind us. Through its porthole I watch the guy struggle up to wrench at the cage door. It holds. He slumps back down.

'If Murdo does get this ship's drive going again, they'll get a taste of their own medicine,' I say.

Sky grins. 'Hah. I hadn't thought of that.'

I'd raced through the freighter's crew compartment when we were hunting for crewmen. It looks much smaller now, with all the kids jammed inside. The lucky ones are curled up on two clusters of seats over by the walls. Others sprawl on the deck, or perch on anything they can find. Some stare around, their eyes big and curious. Most only have eyes for an alcove to the right. Cam, Anuk and skinny guy are pulling packets of crunchy-sounding stuff out of lockers that seem frosted up inside. Food, I reckon, from the eager looks on their faces. Light shines from a small clear hatch with something turning slowly inside it, and my mouth starts watering at the smell of warming food.

But I can't help seeing how filthy and tired it is in here. Which is weird. All my life I'd heard off-world stuff is slick and shiny compared to Wrath's rusty old crap.

Sky starts picking her way through the kids, heading for the hatch that leads forward to the flight deck.

'What about the food?' I say.

'It can wait,' she says.

My stomach growls, but what can I do but follow?

We're almost at the hatch when she suddenly staggers like a drunk. I lunge and hold her up.

'You need rest and food. Murdo can wait.'

'Don't be a gom. Help me.'

'Okay, okay.' I duck under Sky's left arm so it's over my shoulder, slip my arm round her waist and take her weight. She was never heavy, but now she's scary light.

We carry on through the hatch, along a companionway and up a few steps on to the flight deck. As we lurch inside, another hatch hisses closed behind us. It's brightly lit in here, and I have to squint. Two complicated-looking pilot chairs face forward, away from us. Murdo's to our right, sitting in front of flickering lights and several powered-down screens. When he sees us he rotates his seat and struggles up.

Sky pulls free, limps over and collapses on to it.

'What d'you think?' Murdo says, grinning his fool head off, eyes shining as he gestures around.

We both stare at him.

'You *do* know this is a spaceship,' I say.

'Not just some crappy old windjammer,' Sky says.

'Watch and learn, kids! It's been a while all right, but it's coming back fast.' Murdo slides into the left-hand pilot seat and fiddles with stuff. The panels in front of him all light up together. He laughs triumphantly.

'You can switch a screen on,' Sky says. 'Big deal.'

'Check this out then!' He taps at one screen confidently.

I'm in the middle of throwing myself into the seat beside him, but somehow I miss it.

And now I'm . . . floating in mid-air.

'Murdo!' I howl, flailing to grab on to something.

'Sorry,' he says, pawing frantically at his panel. 'Switched off the synthetic gravity by mistake.'

I crash back down.

From somewhere behind me, Sky yells curses.

'Been a while,' Murdo says again, cool as you like. 'Now then.'

The lights inside the flight deck dim to darkness. And suddenly I'm gazing out through forward canopy panels at a blizzard of stars. More than I've ever seen before, even on the clearest Wrath night. All of them scattered like sparks across a blackness so deep it sucks at my eyes. It's a good job the seat's there to catch me. I fall into it, amazed.

'Beautiful, huh?' he says quietly.

I have to force myself to breathe. 'That's . . . wow.'

We sit and stare, lapping up the view. When Murdo turns the lights back up to bright, I'm gutted.

'We'll have more time for stargazing later,' he says. 'Want to see where we were headed?'

'What d'you mean, *were*?' Sky says.

But Murdo's already playing with yet another panel. A column of green light shoots up in the space between the pilot chairs. It spreads out quickly to form a dimly glowing cube of green mist. Scattered throughout are thousands of white dots. A curved blue line arches between two of them. At its nearest end, a large red dot pulses. There's a few chunks of text too, but the whole display flickers and shimmers so much that I can't make them out.

He fiddles with the panel, can't fix it, and curses.

'Okay, so this is the star map for the Vulpes sector. Red dot's where we are. Blue line's our heading, so that's Wrath's system being left behind us and –'

Murdo reaches for the far end of the line in the mist, closes and opens his hand. The display zooms in to the line ending in a small cube, showing two suns inside it and some wriggling text. He leans closer and peers at it.

'I reckon that says Enshi Four.'

Sky levers herself up from her seat and limps closer to lean on the back of mine. 'What's Enshi Four?'

'A crappy little dust-bowl world, fourth out from a binary sun. They mine stuff there, but I forget what exactly. Only one settlement to speak of, up near its north pole.'

'Why would we be going *there*?' I ask.

'My guess is to sell the darkblende to the mining outfit based there. D'you remember Haggletown? Enshi's polar settlement is like that, someplace you come to trade your goods for whatever you can get. Some is legit, but mostly it's bootleg. Dark market. You can sell your contraband there and buy anything, with no questions asked.' He smiles around at us. 'It's my kind of place.'

'Do they deal in slaves?' Sky croaks.

'Absolutely. Big illegal market in slaves out here in frontier space, beyond the reach of the Core worlds. Mining worlds have loads of dirty and dangerous jobs no sane person would do. Slaves can't argue and don't need paying. Bigger profits that way. Nubloods like your sister would fetch a premium. Faster, stronger, quicker to heal. Already skilled miners. Yeah, they'd fetch big creds.'

Sky flinches visibly. 'You sound like you approve.'

I jump in before this gets nasty. 'How the hell do you know all this stuff, Murdo?'

Murdo stretches. 'This is where I come from.'

We both stare at him.

'Okay, real quick,' he says. 'When you guys were still sucking your thumbs, I was marooned on Wrath.'

'Ma-whatted?' Sky says, all incredulous.

He sighs. 'Can't this wait? I've got loads to do.'

'No!' Sky and me shout together.

'Okay, okay. No need to make my ears bleed. Back then, I was second pilot on a transport like this. It was called the *Never Again* too, just like my old windjammer. Sometimes we carried freight, mostly we smuggled stuff. Anyway, me and the skipper had a bust-up. Bastard dumped me on Wrath, with nothing but the clothes I was standing up in.'

'Why didn't he just waste you?' Sky asks, suspiciously.

'The woman we fought over wouldn't let him.'

'Wasn't Wrath off-limits?' I ask.

'That's *why* he dumped me there. No visiting starships, so no way off again. If he couldn't kill me, he wanted to be sure I was stuck there for the rest of my days. And before you ask, we knew nothing about the Slayers' darkblende mining operation, or that they were shipping it off-world.'

'Why didn't you tell us this before?' I say.

'It's none of your business. I'm only telling you now so you'll stop whining about who's going to fly this crate.'

'So you *can* fly it?'

'How many times do I have to tell you? Yes! Anyway, between the stars, this crate flies itself. It's got an AI brain like your old robot pet, Squint, only way bigger and brighter. All I do is program our go-to, and when I fire up the drive it does the rest. Orbital merges, ascents and descents, in-space dockings, it can do all that too. Or give me assist if I fly it manually. But for surface take-offs and landings, that's when you'll need me hands-on. Especially the kind of hang-outs we'll be dropping in on, off the beaten track.'

Sky's face hardens. 'So we don't need the crew?'

Murdo shakes his head. 'Nah, I say we space them, along with the bodies.'

'Sounds good to me.'

'Hang on!' I'm not sure I like the sound of this.

But Murdo's not listening, busy playing with the controls on the panel again. The flickering star chart zooms out. The blue line that shows our freighter's track starts blinking.

'What you doin'?' Sky asks, sharply.

'Changing course,' he says.

Sky pulls out her blaster. 'The hell you are!'

5
DECISION TIME

Murdo gawps at Sky. So do I.

'What's your problem?' he snarls.

'Leave the controls alone,' Sky says, teeth gritted. 'The course we're on will do just fine.'

'Are you mad? Put that fraggin' gun away.'

He shoots me a do-something glance, but what *can* I do? Maybe I could snatch the weapon out of Sky's hand, but what if it goes off? I remember his earlier warning about stray shots breaching hulls. No thanks!

'Sky, come on. Can't we talk about this?' I say.

'No. Nobody's changing course. That's where they took Tarn, so that's where we start looking.'

Wrath knows what would've happened next, but there's a banging on the flight deck's closed hatch. Anuk's muffled voice calls through it, asking what's keeping us.

I shout to her that we'll be along in a minute. Then I lower my voice. 'Let's all cool it, okay? If we keep on as we are, how long till we reach this Enshi place?'

'A standard-month, give or take. But so what?' he says.

'So there's no *rush* to alter course, is there?'

He takes a deep breath, and sighs it out. 'Guess not.'

BANG, BANG, BANG! Anuk's getting impatient.

Muttering stuff, Murdo presses something on the panel. The blue line stops flashing. A moment later, the misty green star map fades away, leaving me blinking.

'Happy now?' he says to Sky.

She pockets the blaster. 'Wasn't so hard, was it?'

Murdo stiffens, but lets it slide. And I can breathe again as he hauls himself up and out of his pilot seat.

'Let's get some food then,' he says.

'Sounds good to me,' I say, scrambling after him.

At the hatch he pauses to give me a sly wink. 'And we can see what those other kids want to do, can't we?'

He slaps a pad on the bulkhead and the hatch slides open again. Anuk is standing there, arms folded.

'What kept you guys?'

'Pilot stuff.' Murdo steers her along the companionway. 'How's the food coming? Found any booze yet?'

I make the mistake of looking at Sky and frowning.

'What?' she snaps.

'I didn't say nothing,' I protest.

The hot-food smell hits me again as we duck back inside the cramped crew quarters. A red-cheeked younger kid lets me have his place behind a drop-down table, and slides me a steaming bowl. The contents look like pigswill, some greasy white stuff floating in it, but I'm hungry and others are slurping it down happily enough. And it tastes better than it looks. Between mouthfuls, I ask where the skinny crewman is. Anuk tells me they stuck him back in the cage.

I'm starting on my second bowl when I think to make sure Sky's getting fed too. She's at the table nearest to the flight deck. Figures. Wouldn't want Murdo to get past her and back on the controls. Can't say she's guzzling the mush down, but she *is* having a peck at it.

With everyone chatting away it's loud in here. I look around at flushed, excited faces, eyes shining with relief and wonder. Hear a few cautious laughs too, like they're trying them out. And why not? These kids have gone from caged and helpless to their first taste of freedom. No more looking out through bars. No Slayers cracking whips and ordering them about. They can be kids, not prisoners.

Only . . . where's Murdo gone?

Then I see him, climbing up from the lower deck.

'Look what I found,' he yells, brandishing a gleaming cylinder. I've never seen anything so shiny.

'What is it?' Cam calls out.

Murdo tells us we'll need cups or glasses. Kids dash to the tiny galley kitchen and fetch them. Meanwhile, Murdo pops the tube open and sniffs whatever's inside.

'Mmm, I feel better already,' he mutters.

He pours sparkling golden fluid into a glass he's handed. Wisps of vapour rise to dance above it. He shuffles around, splashing some into our glasses, although not as much as he had. I'm not complaining though. Just the smell of the liquor almost burns the nose off my face.

We're all on our feet by now. I go and stand by Sky as

she sniffs at her beaker, only to jerk her head back.

'Oh crap, he's going to make a speech,' I whisper.

Sky groans. 'Kill me now.'

Murdo waves and shouts to get everybody's attention, a big grin splitting his battered face.

The kids quit their gabbling and watch him.

'This is best drunk cold,' he announces, 'so I'll keep it short. We got off to a bad start with me wearing the Slayer black, but Kyle's told you why that was, and now that we've bust out you must know I'm on your side.'

He pauses, as if hoping for cheers.

Doesn't happen though. The kids just stare.

Murdo clears his throat.

'Look, I know you must have lots of questions. Between me, Sky and Kyle we'll do our best to answer them. But first I think we should celebrate our escape.'

He raises his glass and glances at me, eyebrows arched.

I raise my glass. 'To . . . having a future at last!'

'Maybe,' Sky mutters, so that only I hear.

Anuk catches on fast. She raises her glass, to Sky first, me next and then Murdo. 'And to you guys for saving us!'

This gets them cheering at last.

Saved is a bit strong, I reckon, but the liquor is stronger.

Murdo knocks his glass back. I do the same. And regret it, because it's like swallowing fire. The next few minutes are filled with watery-eyed kids spluttering and pulling disgusted faces, while laughing their heads off at each other. If the freighter crew got out now, we'd be helpless. But they don't. And there's enough in the flask for a second round. Mysteriously, it slips down easier this time. The burning gives way to a delicious warmth, like someone's wrapped a soothing blanket around the inside of my head.

'Good, huh?' I say to Sky.

'Beats the gut-rot we had in the Deeps,' she admits.

I slip my arm around her. 'It'll all be okay. We'll work things out with Murdo and go find Tarn.'

She looks at me, her eyes solemn. 'Think so?'

But now we're swamped by kids firing rapid-fire questions. Gemini? Ident rebels? When did you guys meet? Do you know my brother/sister? We do our best to answer them in a way that makes sense. But the question we get asked more than any other is 'What now?'

And there's only so many times we can duck it.

Cam, his broad face flushed from the drink, holds his hand up for quiet and eventually gets it. 'Busting out's all well and good, but what happens next?'

'Tell them, Sky,' Murdo says. He leans back and folds his arms. Not sneering exactly, more like he's amused. 'It's only fair.'

'Fine,' Sky says. Maybe without realising, her hand seeks out the teardrop tattoo inked under her left eye. 'Kyle and me, we're here to go looking for my sister. Tarn was shipped off-world about a year ago. We figure she's been sold as a slave, like you lot would have been.'

Silence greets this. Some dismayed looks too.

'How do you plan to find her?' Murdo asks, all innocent.

I worry Sky will reach for her blaster again, but she just scowls defiantly. 'They were taking us to the Enshi system, probably to the same place they took Tarn. I say we still go there. Murdo can put us down near the main settlement. Then Kyle and me will take a scout around.'

I swallow hard, and hope she doesn't notice.

'What about us?' Anuk asks.

'Without me and Kyle, you'd all still be stuck in that cage, on your way to be slaves,' Sky snaps. 'Or worse.'

A fair point, but I wouldn't have said it.

And she's not done yet. 'I figure you owe us.'

Cam and Anuk swap looks, neither of them happy. Other kids mutter. Nobody likes to be reminded of a debt.

'What Sky means is we'd welcome your help,' I say.

Murdo chuckles. Sky glares daggers at him, but he's not bothered. He waits until everyone's looking at him, then spreads his arms wide.

'So now you know what Sky wants to do,' he says. 'But what do *you* want to do? The way I see it, we should all get a say in what our next move is. It seems only fair.'

Sky's scowl darkens, but what can she say?

The kids look confused, some anxious even. And it's not hard to see why. Their whole lives will have been about doing what they're told, without question.

'We . . . get to choose?' one kid says, uncertainly.

Murdo holds his hands out to them, like our old preacher used to back in Freshwater. 'Course you do. That's how things work when you're free. You've got rights.'

They stare at him, transfixed.

'Sky wants to chase after her sister,' he goes on. 'And that's fine by me. If I can help her, I will. But a landing on Enshi Four is fierce risky. No way am I signing up for that. Neither should you guys, if you want to live.'

Sky looks like she'll explode. Not for the first time I wish she didn't have that blaster.

'What's so risky about it?' I say, quickly.

'Everything! Sneaking a landing on a world isn't like sticking a windjammer down in a field. Whoever sent this freighter to Wrath, they'll be big-time operators. They won't take kindly to us grabbing their ship, so why would we go running back to them? It's plain mad.'

'We make sure we don't run into them,' Sky growls.

'Best way to do that is to steer clear of Enshi Four!' Murdo snaps back. He winces, clearly still hurting, and looks at the nublood kids. 'Look, I'll be straight with you –'

'You don't know how!' Sky says.

'Don't I?' His gaze never leaves the kids. 'Listen, I stowed away on this crate to get back off-world, and because chances like this don't come along twice in one lifetime. And it worked out. Take a look around. Here we are in control of a star freighter, with me to fly it wherever we want, a cargo bay full of the richest mineral in the galaxy and a ready-made crew in you guys. I have to pinch myself to make sure I'm not dreaming.

'You should too. Think about it: you guys have gone from nailed-on doomed to being able to do whatever you want! Why the frag would you risk that?'

I roll my eyes. 'You've got a better idea, huh?'

'Damn right I do. We've got a month before we're due at Enshi. A month before we'll be missed and anybody will come looking for us. I say we use that time to flog our darkblende cargo. Even if we only get half what it's worth on the dark market, that's still a fraggin' fortune. We could trade up to a better ship, one nobody's looking for. Set up as a legit free-trader, smuggle bootleg stuff on the side. It's that kind of money, with plenty to go around.'

Sky's lip twitches. 'And I should forget about Tarn?'

Murdo sighs heavily, like he's offended.

'Did I say that? No. I just figure we should get ourselves sorted first, and then we can *all* do what we like. With your share, you could buy yourself passage to Enshi. That way nobody would see you coming. You'd have creds to loosen tongues and get answers. You could pay some of these kids to come with you as backup, if they were up for that.'

I'm liking this better with every word he says. Sky must see this on my face, because I get glared at big time. But being glared at is better than being dead.

'Maybe Murdo's right,' I say.

The nublood kids watch us, their tough faces not giving much away. I wish I could say the same about Sky.

'Every second we waste,' she spits through her scowl, 'something awful could be happening to Tarn.'

Murdo throws his hands up. 'You don't know that. And I'll tell you something else, Sky, your sister won't be on Enshi Four. Not a chance. She'll have been sold and shipped out soon after she got there. She could be anywhere in the sector by now. You've seen the stars – that's a whole lot of anywhere. If you want to find her, your best chance is to ask the guys I'll be trying to sell the darkblende to. If anybody can help you track her down, it'll be them.'

Sky goes to snarl back at him, but starts coughing.

'Okay, Murdo, we hear you,' I say. 'But would this freighter have any med supplies?'

'I'll be fine,' Sky croaks.

Murdo hesitates. 'Bound to. Somewhere.'

'Can you find them?' I say, crossly.

'Sure. Soon as we sort out what we're doing. We need to elect a captain and a quartermaster, so we might as well get that done too while we're all gathered together.'

He explains this is how crews on free-traders have organised themselves since the days of sail back on Earth in the Long Ago. Everyone gets a say in big decisions, like where to go and what to do. The captain leads when there isn't time for discussion, like in a battle. The quartermaster has the same day-to-day authority as the captain, but looks after the crew's interests. He or she keeps order and settles any disputes. Captain and quartermaster get two shares of any profits, the rest of the crew get one. Either can be voted out at any time if the crew is unhappy.

'Don't tell me,' Sky says, when Murdo's done rattling through all this. 'You figure on being captain.'

He grins at her, then around at the nublood kids.

'Sure. I'll be throwing my name into the hat. Don't forget, I'm the only one who can fly this freighter. And only I have the contacts to sell the darkblende to!'

The nublood kids huddle and swap whispers.

Sky shoots a disgusted look at me. But what can I do?

'Okay,' Murdo says. 'If you want me as your captain, stick your hand in the air to be counted.'

Pretty much all the kids hoist their hands. I'm tempted, but don't. Sky just sneers and folds her arms.

Murdo grins and treats us to a stiff little bow.

'Thank you. A sound choice, if you don't mind me saying so. Now then, who shall we have as our quartermaster?'

I worry eyes might slide my way. They don't. Cam calls out that he'll do it. But Anuk gets shoved forward to stand against him, and collects way more hands. She looks as pleased about this as if she's been shot. Cam looks gutted. There's loads of good-humoured shouting, so it takes Murdo a while to get them to listen to him again. Beside me, I feel Sky stiffen.

'One last thing to decide before we go back to celebrating,' he yells. 'I say we look up my old contacts, flog the darkblende and get ourselves settled. Sky says we risk our necks to hunt for her sister. What do you guys say?'

'That's not fair,' I protest.

Murdo ignores this. 'Who's with me?'

Hands are slower going up this time, but up they go until he grunts with satisfaction. It's a big win for him.

'Anybody for Sky?'

Anuk sticks her hand up. So do two others. I raise mine too, but only so that Sky sees.

Her lip wrinkles. Bleak-faced, she stomps off down to the lower deck and the sleeping quarters. Truth is, I'm glad the vote went the way it did. But I hate seeing her raging.

I take a deep breath and go to follow her.

Anuk stops me. 'Maybe you should leave her be.'

'There's no *maybe* about it,' I say.

Halfway down the steps I hear her cursing, as well as loud smashes and bangs. Murdo winks. I continue on down.

'Hey, Sky,' I call. 'It's only me, Kyle.'

A half-seen something flies towards my head. Sky's blaster. I have to use all my speed to dodge. It clatters to the deck. I snatch it up and pocket it.

I guess I should be glad she only threw it . . .

6
DIVERSIONS

'Party's over,' Murdo growls. 'Let's get down to business.'

Rich, coming from a guy who's only just got up from snoring his drunk head off. Meanwhile, Anuk has had the rest of us hard at it for hours, cleaning and tidying. Our cramped quarters are way more liveable now.

'What d'you want us to do?' I ask.

Red-eyed and clearly suffering from a head-banging hangover, Murdo flinches. 'No need to shout, is there? We should have to space those bodies, and then I'll alter course.'

This last bit he says with a glare at Sky. She meets it, eyes narrowed, face like stone.

It's cool in the hold, but the stench of death is already nasty. Inside the cage we find more bodies than we'd expected. One of the two beaten-up crewmen is stiff and gone to the long forever. His gobby mate shouts threats at us until Cam sets his killstick to stun and shuts him up.

Skinny guy wisely keeps his mouth shut.

Murdo has him show us where the airlock is, in a small

compartment beneath the hold. After he's done taking Murdo through the lock's controls, I sling the guy back inside the cage. Then three of us wrestle the pilot's body down. He hasn't got lighter by being dead and we're blowing hard by the time we've shoved him into the airlock. Murdo taps at a grubby screen beside the inner airlock door. It closes, sucks inwards and seals.

Above us, a red light starts strobing.

'Warning, illegal override,' a machine-voice chants.

'Yeah, we know!' Murdo slaps the screen again.

The warning chokes off. He mutters something over his shoulder to us about opening outer doors with pressure still inside, so the body will be blown out.

As he does, I feel the slightest of thumps.

We take turns gawping through the clear-view panel set into the inner airlock door. Beyond the open outer door, the pilot's body tumbles slowly away from us against a backdrop of stars. I'd heard stories that if you ended up in space without a pressure suit it would be messy. But he doesn't explode and his blood doesn't boil out of him.

I can't decide if I'm relieved or disappointed.

The two dead kids, Mav and Kaya, we leave until last. Somebody's gone to the trouble of wrapping them up in canvas tarpaulins, a sort of makeshift burial shroud.

'Anybody want to say a few words?' I ask.

At first all I get is eyes flicking uneasily away from me, but then Cam surprises me.

'They died fighting . . . so we could be free,' he says.

Anuk repeats it. Next thing, they're all at it. I glance at Sky, expecting her lip to curl. Not a bit of it: her eyes are shiny and she chants it as loud as anyone.

Two more soft thumps and the red light quits flashing.

'Least they didn't die in a cage,' she says to me.

We clamber back into the hold and start making our way back to the crew compartment, while the machines that allow us to breathe start scrubbing away the stench of death.

'Hey, not so fast,' Murdo says, sticking his head up from the floor hatch. 'Bring the prisoners.'

'You're not serious?' I say.

Sky rolls her eyes. 'They're slavers. Serves them right.'

'No! Please don't!' skinny guy whines.

Murdo laughs, real ugly, and tells us there's an escape craft down below with four empty stasis pods. 'Stick 'em in there and it'll save us watching and feeding them.'

When we look dumb, he curses and grudgingly explains what stasis pods are. Seems they work by slowing your body down into a sort of super-hibernation. Deep-space escape craft have them so occupants can survive until they're found, which can take years. Whatever. I'm just relieved he's not going to space the prisoners in cold blood.

Sky mutters we should leave them in the cage to be zapped. But Murdo's captain and gets his way.

Curious to see the escape craft, I help carry the man Cam stunned. Skinny guy doesn't look thrilled, but climbs down himself and keeps his gob shut.

It's accessed through a second airlock. Disappointingly, the inside is a small compartment, with two recesses in the walls either side, one pod above the other. Murdo and Cam wrestle the unconscious guy into the upper left. When they're done, they step out to make room and I shove skinny guy ahead of me into the cramped interior.

'Upper right,' Murdo orders.

Skinny guy hesitates, shaking. A shove from me gets him moving though. He clambers up and rolls into it.

Murdo hits a switch. 'Sweet dreams.'

Translucent panels swish downwards to close off the two occupied pods. A dazzling blue light fills them. I smell that sharp stink you get when electrics short out. And jump back as skinny guy's hand, fingers spread wide, slams the inside of his panel. The blue light fades away, but the hand stays planted. Frozen.

That does *not* look like fun.

'Let's go,' Murdo says, already shuffling his way out.

Back in the hold, we crowbar open all the wooden crates that were loaded aboard on Wrath. Nestled inside each is a small unmarked metal chest. I worry darkblende's not stamped on them, or its tech name – promethium. Murdo says I'm a gom for thinking it would be. Screens on the chests list the weight of their contents. Twelve crates, with five hundred kilos in each.

Whatever it's worth, Murdo bloodshot eyes go greedy.

Minutes later, with the crates hammered closed again, he's back in the pilot's seat with as many of us as can squeeze inside the flight deck watching him. Sky's *not* here. She stayed in the crew compartment, busy sulking.

'Where are we going?' I ask him.

'Shanglo.'

'What's there?'

'An old contact. Deep pockets. Doesn't ask questions.'

As his fingers tap and slide on the control screen, Murdo tells us Shanglo is the moon of a planet orbiting a half-dead sun. At max drive speed it'll take seven standard-days to get there. Our curved blue course line shifts inside the glowing star map to point at a closer bit of space. The map zooms in and a new destination star pulses red. Looming over it, as if about to pounce, is what looks like an orange dust storm shot through with wisps of yellow and green.

'What the hell's that?' Cam asks.

'Some kind of nebula. Dust and gas, that's all.'

With a flourish, he stabs at his screen. I feel the lurching sensation as the freighter's drive kicks in. The stars in front of us seem to smear themselves towards us. But the flight deck's shielded, so that's as bad as it gets. Until the view ahead snaps to a sudden dark nothingness, like a cleverbox screen that's been powered down.

Nobody whimpers exactly, but I hear shocked curses.

'Hey, where'd the stars go?' I say, startled.

Murdo slumps back in his seat with a satisfied sigh. 'Relax. They're still out there. We just can't see them through the dee-emm, now that we're shifting.'

Dee-emm. Shifting. I've already passed on the little I know to the other kids. Like how suns are so far apart even light takes years to travel between them. How our dee-emm drive 'shifts' us into something called dark-matter space so we can go faster. Murdo calls it a sneaky short cut, a clever way of going behind the back of regular space.

'I see weird stuff out there,' a boy called Taka calls out.

Me too. Mostly it's darkness so deep it feels as if it's sucking my eyeballs out of my head. But there's something else. Oily and slippery, it oozes around the edges of my seeing. Look straight at it though and there's nothing.

'What the heck *is* that?' I ask Murdo.

He glances around. 'Spacers call it "seeing the spooks". It's to do with the way the dee-emm drive operates. And why we leave the flight-deck lights switched up when we're shifting, so we can't see outside. Spend too much time watching them, you end up going crazy. Some say –'

He hesitates, then flicks the lights back on.

'Tell us,' I say, catching his eye.

He grimaces. 'They say spooks are alien life forms. Monster space fish who swim around in dark matter.'

'What do *you* say?'

'I say we've plenty to worry about already,' he growls.

Life aboard our star freighter takes getting used to. The crew compartment would've been cramped for five, and there are thirteen of us. But the hardest thing is there's no day and night, which makes it tough to sleep.

Murdo's feeling better though, and loving life.

He says we have to wean ourselves off Wrath-time and onto the standard-time spacers use. Standard-hours are about the same length, but there are only twenty-four in a standard-day! We all moan like hell, feeling cheated, but he just laughs at us. Says standard-months have more standard-days in them, so what's it matter anyway?

Well it turns out it does matter!

He re-calculated our ages in standard-time. I'd been looking forward to turning seventeen in two Wrath-months; now I'll have to wait six more standard-months.

The only person more fed up than me is Sky. She was seventeen, now she's back to being sixteen!

With bog all to do, we count the days down to Shanglo. I teach the others stupid games I played as a kid. They teach me some of theirs. By far their favourite thing is to get me or Sky or Murdo to tell them stories about our adventures. They never tire of listening. But three standard-days out of Wrath we hit our first snag. Anuk put Stitch in charge of the food because he'd done cooking duties back in her camp. Now she drags him in front of Murdo, a face on her like thunder.

'Tell him!' she rages.

Shame-faced, Stitch admits we're almost out of food.

'He couldn't be arsed to check,' Anuk says.

I figure Murdo will go off on one, but all he does is shrug. 'Just as well we're only four days out from Shanglo, not a month out from Enshi Four. Isn't it, Sky?'

Sky gives him a spike-eyed glare, but says nothing.

Anuk says we'll manage, but it'll mean short rations and going hungry. Been there, done that, but it's still bad news. Murdo reassures us we'll be able to load up with food at Shanglo.

Everybody settles back down.

But when nobody's looking, Murdo whispers that I should meet him outside the cargo hold. Before I can ask why, he slides off in that direction, real furtive.

I tell Sky. She says she'll come with me.

The few kids that aren't sleeping are playing games or taking it easy. Anuk's in the galley, chewing Stitch's ear off about the food, so nobody notices as we stroll out after Murdo. At the far end of the main companionway, we catch up with him. He's outside the hold's closed hatch, by the big red warning sign about the lack of shielding.

When Sky goes to say something, he shushes her.

'Keep it down,' he hisses. 'There's something I have to do, but I'll need Kyle to help.'

'What with?' I whisper, suspicious.

Murdo glances past us, but we can't be seen back here because of a dog-leg in the corridor. His lived-in face is less battered by now, but he looks uneasy.

'These dark-market contacts of mine,' he says. 'They're all chancers. With promethium being so valuable, there's a risk they'll just try to take it off us.'

'Let them try,' Sky mutters.

Murdo grins. 'All the same, I'd feel better if we had insurance. We should stash some of the cargo. That way, if we have to run for it, we won't have lost everything.'

Sounds reasonable to me. 'Where would we hide it?'

'In that escape craft, with the prisoners.'

Sky sniffs. 'Oh yeah, nobody would look there.'

But Murdo's no fool. He tells us that after we've loaded a couple of crates aboard, he'll launch the escape craft. It can float about until we come back to retrieve it.

'But what about the guys in stasis?' I ask.

He shrugs. 'What about them? Won't do them no harm.'

'And you're sure we can find it again?' Sky asks.

'They have distress beacons, but you have to be close to pick up the signal. We know where to listen.'

'What if somebody else hears it?'

'They won't. I've altered course. We're in dead space now. No starship has any reason to be out here.'

'So how come we're sneaking off to do it?' Sky asks.

Murdo glances past us again. 'The fewer who know, the better. So don't go telling anyone.'

About now, the warning sign behind him catches my eye.

'Will you shut the drive off? Or we'll be zapped.'

He grimaces. 'Best not to. The others would feel it and wonder what's going on. It's not like it'll kill us.'

I look at Sky, unsure.

She shrugs. 'Makes sense, I guess.'

Thankfully, Murdo knows his way around handling cargo, so we're not in the hold too long being fried. Using an overhead hoist we lower two of the massively heavy crates into the airlock compartment. Using levers, rollers and wedges, we sweat them into the pod. It's heavy work and even I'm shaking by the time Murdo slaps a push-panel with a red handprint on it and the access lock snaps shut. We scramble back up into the hold and Sky lets us out.

When she closes the hatch behind us . . . it's bliss!

After a breather we return to the crew compartment. We haven't been missed. Murdo carries on through to the flight deck. A minute later, the deck shifts under me.

'Did you feel something?' Anuk asks.

I look at Sky. She looks at me. We shake our heads.

7
SHANGLO BACKWATER

I don't have a problem with heights, but looking down at Shanglo makes my stomach squirm. Our freighter hangs nose-low over the moon, yet my feet stay planted on the deck behind Sky's seat and I don't fall forward. I know we make our own gravity, but it does my head in. We shifted back into real space an hour ago. Since then the freighter's been decelerating and manoeuvring us into orbit, all on automatic, while Murdo watches and tries to chew his lip off. I'd been looking forward to see the storm-like nebula again, but this close it's all spread out and too faint to see.

That's what Murdo says anyway.

Sky was funny. She had a right go at him, sure he'd flown us to the wrong system. But the star map is on his side.

We saw Shanglo's planet on our way in, a lifeless-looking grey blob. That's away to our right now. The system's half-dead sun is somewhere behind us, a red giant.

As we track over the moon's day-side, most of the surface is hidden by yellow-white clouds towering above their dark shadows. But I catch glimpses of lush green land too. Towards the far horizon I see glittering blue. Murdo says this is an ocean, which is like a really big lake.

Dodgy stomach or not, I've never seen a more beautiful sight. I could gaze at it forever.

'Okay, I want everybody out of here,' Murdo says. 'Now!'

He reckons our descent could get rough so we all need to be strapped in. With Sky being a jammer pilot too, she's in the right-hand flight seat. I've a few hours' flying time myself and have bagged the seat behind them.

Anuk herds the other kids back to the crew compartment.

I'm pulling my straps tight when Murdo summons up a graphic display of the star freighter.

'Initiating separation, in three, two . . . go!'

The flight deck shudders violently. On the graphic our freighter splits into two parts, our dropship front end shrugging off the larger dee-emm drive assembly.

'Split complete,' Sky says. 'Everything's in the green.'

Anuk yells that they're all strapped in.

Murdo rest his hands on the controls for atmospheric flight, built into the armrests of his pilot seat. On the left are the throttles to control our speed. On the right a pistol grip controls pitch, roll and yaw. He swears it's called a joystick, which is weird. These last few hours, I've never seen him so excited, and I've caught it off him. My heart thumps like it's trying to punch its way out. If we manage to offload this darkblende he says we'll be up to our necks in creds, so rich that we'd struggle to spend them all in our lifetimes.

I'd settle for never being cold, hungry or scared again.

Not for the first time I have to pinch myself that I'm not

dreaming. Days ago I was Wrath's most wanted. A hunted rebel, hiding out in holes in the ground, misery and suffering all I had to look forward to. Now this . . .

'Right,' Murdo says, giving us his most annoying grin. 'Let's see if I can remember how to fly a descent.'

'Try real hard,' Sky says.

My feeling exactly. I saw this thing when it was on its way down to Wrath. It doesn't hang about.

'I'll do my best,' he tells us. 'Hold on.'

Our drop starts smooth, but the atmosphere thickens fast and we start to be buffeted. Soon I'm glad for my wrap-around seat and my straps. I've been on wild flights in jammers back on Wrath, but they were nothing compared to this. After one particularly savage buffet rattles my teeth, I shout out to Sky, asking if something's gone wrong.

She checks her displays. 'No-o, we're go-o-o-d.'

And then, quite suddenly, everything calms down again. I can make out features below us, mountains and rivers. But they seem to be leaping up at us hellish fast.

'Hey, pull up!' Sky yells.

I reckon the dropship does it for him, but only at the last possible second. I'm shoved down into my seat so hard it's as if ten heavy men have piled onto me. My seeing greys out. By the time I can focus again we're in level flight with clouds whipping past unbelievably fast. And we're definitely not on Wrath. Shanglo's sky is a different blue, and shot through higher up with weird, ghostly tendrils of green.

Murdo gives himself a shake. 'Switching to manual.'

'Is that a good idea?' Sky says, only just beating me to it.

'You want me to wait until I'm landing it?'

A fair point that shuts us up.

He does a few shallow practice dives and mildly banked turns without any problem. Then throws it around more confidently like he's back aboard his windjammer.

A big grin splits his face. 'See, nothing to it, huh?'

'Where's this old contact of yours?' I ask.

'Cobb's a thousand klicks that way.' Murdo points in the direction we're flying. 'A compound at the edge of a great big plateau. Should be hard to miss.'

That I can believe as the surface of Shanglo flashes past beneath us. Apart from a dark smudge in the distance, all I see are flat, tree-smothered plains in every direction. Murdo noses us lower, until we're skimming the tops. These trees are way bigger than anything on Wrath.

'Fine bit of lumber here,' I say.

Murdo glances at me, as if I've said something funny.

Not long after, we arrive at that brown smudge I'd seen. The trees disappear like somebody flicked a switch. Under us now is a scarred and shattered landscape, criss-crossed with tracks, dotted with stumps where trees once jostled.

The brown stretches ahead to the far horizon.

'What the hell happened?' Sky says.

'Auto-loggers happened,' Murdo says. 'Lumber's big business. No trees left on the Core worlds, so they log it here and ship it back. Rich folk like a bit of wood.'

He cranks us round and we get a look at how the forest ends behind us in a straight line that can't be natural, before we fly on again over the devastation.

'No trees left?' I say. 'What happened?'

'Used them all up. Poisoned them. Who cares now? I reckon that'll be our rock ahead in the distance.'

A cluster of strange plateaus sticks up from the ravaged landscape. Flat-topped, sheer-sided, they look like they've been squeezed up out of the ground. Murdo's flying us towards the biggest one, which must be a good few klicks across. I can see the outline of buildings on top of it.

'Weird,' Murdo says.

'What's the matter?' Sky asks.

'Cobb's guys must see us coming, so why aren't they on the comm, demanding that we identify ourselves?'

'Why don't you give them a shout?'

Murdo sucks his teeth, not looking too keen, but then he presses a button on the joystick. 'Cobb compound, incoming free-trader is the . . . *Never Again Two*. D'you copy?'

Nothing. He calls again. More nothing.

When we make a low pass over the compound we find out why. All that's left of Cobb's compound are tumbled-down walls and burnt-out skeletons of buildings. Murdo curses, and cranks us back round in a steep turn.

It looks no better on the second pass.

Still cursing, he sets us down on an open area outside the ruins. It's not his best landing, but I'm saying nothing.

'This is dumb,' Sky says. 'Nothing's left here.'

But Murdo's already unstrapping himself. He growls that he wants to take a look around. Minutes later, all of us except for Sky are crammed on to the loading platform as it lowers.

We step off it on to the surface of another world.

ANOTHER. WORLD.

Never did I think this day would come. My head bangs with trying to take it all in. The ground feels springy underfoot, but it's just some reddish dirt. And that's when I realise gravity here must be weaker than I'm used to. I take a cautious breath and taste the air. Tingly. Rich. Painfully fresh after the scrubbed and processed stuff we've been sucking in. A host of weird smells shove their way up my nose, none of which I could put a name to. But the most amazing thing has to be Shanglo's sky, creepy tendrils of green reaching across a blue so deep it's on its way to purple.

Cam crumbles some of the red soil between his fingers.

'See this? Even the dirt looks different.'

Murdo claps his hands to get our attention. He tells me and Cam and Ravi to come with him to check out the remains of the compound. The rest are to stick close to the ship and keep a lookout. Sky's up in the freighter's nose turret, covering us. As we head off, I wave at her.

Do I get a wave back? Nah. Just a shake of her head.

Murdo asks if I have my blaster.

I pull it out and check it. 'Expecting trouble?'

'It has a habit of following me around.'

The scorched wall of the compound tells its own tale of trouble. It's obvious that no ordinary fire tumbled these massive stones. They've been smashed down.

'Somebody fired heavy-duty weapons at this,' I say.

Murdo says nothing, but the grim look on his face tells me I'm not wrong. All three of us scramble inside through one of the torn gaps. The compound must've been a sight to see once, with dozens of warehouses and storage silos. Now it's a tangle of twisted metal and charred wood.

Moving cautiously, we pick our way deeper inside.

The scars of a vicious fight are everywhere. Ragged blaster splashes. Neater holes punched by pulse-rifle shots. But rust has taken big bites too, and when I accidentally step on some wood it gives way, rotten all through.

I straighten up and let out the breath I've been holding.

'Whatever happened, it was years ago.'

Murdo grunts. 'Looks like it.'

'Who d'you suppose did this?' Cam asks.

'How should I know? Cobb dealt with mean people. Maybe he crossed one of them. Only . . . he was no pushover. Not just anyone could come here and make this mess.'

Clearly gutted that we won't be flogging our darkblende, he kicks out at some of the burnt wood.

'Could ComSec have shut him down?' I ask.

According to Murdo, Combine Security forces are the only law that reaches out this far from the Core worlds. He's been telling us stories about his run-ins with them.

But he shakes his head. 'Nah. That lot would take care of Cobb from orbit. There'd be nothing but a crater here.'

'Shush!' Ravi hisses. 'Hear that?'

We all shut up and listen.

After a while, a clang of metal on metal comes from ahead of us, where warped and rusty girders stick up from the remains of what must once have been a warehouse.

'Now would be a good time to leave,' I say.

Murdo ignores me. Next thing he's jogging towards the

sound. Cam and Ravi sneer at me before following him. I curse, and hustle to catch up. One of the stone-arched entrances is still mostly standing, and somebody's cleared a path through the rubble under it. Murdo swings wide, approaching it from the left side so he won't be seen from within. He waits there until we're all crouched beside him before sneaking a quick peek in.

Whatever he sees, he grunts and relaxes.

And then, before any of us can stop him, he's striding through the archway, showing off his empty hands.

'Hey there,' he calls. 'Can we have a word?'

Me and the other two lads swap uncertain looks, before leaping up to chase after him. We don't get far though, because Murdo comes tearing out again . . .

Snapping at his heels is the weirdest creature I've ever seen. Way bigger than a bull fourhorn, its hide is mottled orange and six massively powerful legs drive it forward. At the end of a stupidly long neck, the thing's head is no bigger than my fist. Lucky for Murdo, it's being slowed down by hauling a long flatbed wagon. Perched on this, whipping the creature along, is a white-haired old man.

'Hi-yah!' he bellows, spit flying.

Murdo flings himself aside and rolls out of the way. Ravi scrambles left and clear, Cam and me dive right.

Creature and wagon thunder past us.

'Don't let him get away!' Murdo yells, scrambling up.

How we're to do this I don't know. But now one of the wagon's wheels clips a heap of debris it's swerving round. Top-heavy and carrying too much speed it tips over and crashes on to its side, spilling a load of scavenged steel. Red dust boils up. Blaster in hand, I run towards it. At the front the unhappy creature is jammed between the pulling poles, snapping and making all sorts of hideous noises.

I'm sure scavver guy must have broken his old neck. But what do I know? He comes hobbling out of the dust.

'Look whatcha done!' he wails angrily.

Murdo curses and makes a show of knocking dirt off himself. 'It's your fraggin' fault, you old fool. If you hadn't tried to run us down, it wouldn't have happened.'

The guy's beast is full-on weird, but otherwise I've seen his like back in the Barrenlands. A shock of hair that might be white if it got washed. Straggly beard. Mouth full of broken teeth. Bent back. Calloused hands. Lined face and deep-sunk eyes that have seen too much hardship.

'Didn't mean to run you down,' he says. 'Wouldn't do that. Didn't see you, did I? No.'

He squirms, like he doesn't know how to stay still. Head tilted back, his watery eyes slide around strangely, never settling. I realise he's blind, and a bit mad.

'Relax. Nobody's going to hurt you, old-timer,' Murdo growls. 'We just want to know what happened here.'

The man twitches. 'Don't know nothing 'bout that. I'm only a blind old scrapper who minds his own business. What I don't know can't hurt me, see.'

Murdo tries again, but gets the same answer.

Cam wanders over, a length of steel pipe in his hand. 'I'll make him talk, if you like.'

Murdo tells him to leave the guy be. 'Maybe he *doesn't* know. There's a crewed maintenance platform near here, where they service the auto-loggers. We'll drop in, load up on supplies and see what they have to say.'

Cam looks gutted. 'The guy must know something.'

'You heard Murdo, we're out of here,' I say.

Now if I was the old scavver, I'd keep quiet and be glad not to get my last few teeth kicked out for nearly running us down. But not this guy. He starts pleading with us to help him right his wagon. Murdo goes to shove him aside, but gets grabbed and whined at from close range.

Nasty, with all that spit flying.

'All right, all right!'

With its heavy load shed and using a length of timber as a lever, the wagon is soon back on its wheels. It seems no worse for its crash. Neither does the beast. It heaves itself up and very nearly gets a mouthful of Ravi.

We leave the scrap metal where it fell though.

'He loaded it once, he can load it again,' Murdo says.

The old scavver feels his way slowly round the wagon, like he can't believe we did it. He mumbles to himself too, that we 'ain't Syndicate guys, and that's for sure.'

We're walking away, but I turn back.

'Syndicate? What's that?'

I tell Murdo what I overheard.

The guy licks his shrivelled lips, plainly wishing he'd kept his gob shut. And starts up again with his I'm-only-a-blind-old-scrapper-and-don't-know-nothing routine.

'These Syndicate guys, was it them who destroyed this place?' Murdo gestures around at the devastation.

Dumb if you ask me, as the blind scavver can't see him.

'Don't make us ask again!' Cam snaps.

'Okay, okay. It was the Syndicate. Who else? But you can't tell anyone I told you. If word gets back to them –'

'Relax. It won't,' Murdo says, waving at Cam to back off. 'I'm an old friend of Cobb, the guy who owned this place. Don't suppose you know what happened to him?'

The man grunts. 'Dead. Like the rest.'

Takes a while, but Murdo eventually worms the full story out of the guy. An outfit calling itself the Syndicate has blasted and slaughtered its way to the top of the many criminal gangs operating in the Vulpes sector. They'd come calling and told Cobb he worked for them now. Cobb didn't fancy that and had told them to go to hell.

'Always was a stubborn son-of-a-bitch,' Murdo says.

The scavver shrugs. 'And now he's a dead son-of-a-bitch. That's what happens when you mess with them Syndicate guys. You want my advice? Steer well clear.'

We're slogging back to our freighter when it hits me. 'Hey, maybe Shanglo wasn't a complete bust. We could flog the darkblende to this Syndicate mob.'

Murdo shoots me a glare like I'm the biggest gom ever.

'And what if it's *their* darkblende? You heard that scavver guy. They run pretty much everything now.'

'Any other great ideas?' Cam says, all mocking.

I go to snarl that we can ask our skinny prisoner, but remember in time that he's light years behind us by now, frozen inside the jettisoned escape pod with his gobby mate.

8
BLAST FROM THE PAST

With riches at stake, Murdo doesn't give up easy.

Over the next few days we set down on three more worlds. On the first his contact had been taken out like Cobb. The second made no bones about working for the Syndicate now and wanted nothing to do with our darkblende, just in case. On the third world his contact had done a runner. Frustrating as hell, but it's not all bad. We've been able to buy supplies and fill our aching bellies. Anuk had him load us up on working clothes too so we've ditched our ident-camp rags and look less out of place. Money is called creds out here too, but there's no minted coins like on the Wrath, only numbers stored in weird little plastic devices. You scan the creds on and off. We scavved some off the freighter's old crew and Murdo knew how to use them.

On Barzahk, a desolate and wintry mining world where surface temps can't be arsed climbing above zero even in summer, we get a scare. And then, at last, a break.

Our scare comes as Murdo's lining up our descent to the surface. Sky's in the co-pilot seat again. I'm watching from behind them. Our lights are dimmed and I'm drinking in the view of Barzahk below. One second Murdo's tapping away at a control panel, the next he's cursing.

'We've got incoming.' He jabs a finger at the display before him. 'It's a fraggin' warship. ComSec!'

The screen shows an outline of the planet below, with our yellow dot orbiting it. The bigger red dot that Murdo points out is closing in from our right side. I peer through the side viewport and spot a tiny speck.

'There! I see it.'

Murdo gets busy at his panel. The display dissolves, re-forming to show a brutal-looking spaceship.

'Can we outrun it?' Sky asks.

Murdo shakes his head. 'Doubt it. Too late to try. We're already well within range of their blast –'

A shrill alert from the comm system interrupts him.

'Freighter in Barzahk orbit, this is Combine Security cruiser *Nantahala*. Identify yourself immediately and make ready to be boarded for a routine inspection.'

A woman's voice. Casual. Assured.

'Crap!' Murdo thumps his head back into his headrest.

Sky lashes out at him. 'Well, *do* something!'

'Like what?' he groans.

Nantahala woman repeats her demand, curtly this time.

My racing mind comes up with a desperate idea. 'Maybe being caught by ComSec isn't so bad? We could come clean and tell them everything. Wrath, idents, the Saviour exploiting us. It's not *our* darkblende, is it? And we haven't done anything wrong. All we've done is escape.'

Murdo and Sky both scowl at me.

'Why not?' I say, as bile fills my throat.

'Because, Kyle,' Murdo says savagely, 'ComSec play rough and they wouldn't listen. They'll just hang us as smugglers. Oh yeah, and escaping from a dump world is a hanging offence too. Good luck confessing to that.'

But now Sky makes us jump by letting out a loud yell.

'The cruiser's breaking off!'

I drag my eyes back to Murdo's screen. Stabs of blue light flicker at the cruiser's bow. Thrusters? Slowly but surely it swings around and shows us its stern. Next thing, a massive flare of blue overloads our screen as it lights up its drive. By the time the screen's working again, all it shows are stars and a blue dot that's getting smaller fast.

Murdo grunts. 'Well, how about that?'

'Never said goodbye or nothing,' Sky says, grinning.

'Rude, I call it,' I croak, playing along, while relief sucks the bones out of my legs and sets them shaking.

Murdo flicks the display back to the Barzahk system. The red dot that's the cruiser streaks away from us.

'Not hanging about, are they?'

'Good!' I say. 'What do you suppose happened?'

'Might be something to do with this. I'm picking up a broadcast on the emergency comm channel.'

He taps at his panel and speaker-hiss fills the flight-deck. Amongst the buzz and crackle, I make out a new voice. Whoever he is, he sounds seriously tense.

'Mayday, mayday, mayday . . . heavy two zero zero nine out of . . . *chhhrrr* . . . inbound Thessalus six . . . *chhhrrr* . . . being pursued . . . unidentified raider . . . I say again, we are being pursued . . . *chhhrrr* . . . interstellar coordinates are . . .'

'Thought so. Distress call,' Murdo says, and kills the signal. 'Whoever those raiders are, if we bump into them the drinks are on us. They've saved us.'

'Too right,' Sky mutters.

'Wonder what will happen to the freighter?' I say.

'That call will have taken days or weeks to crawl its way here at light speed,' Murdo says, intent on his controls again as he starts our descent to Barzahk's surface. 'Whatever played out, it's all over by now.'

'So why'd the cruiser clear off?' I ask, confused.

'There might be survivors who need picking up. And they'll be looking to chase the raider down. The Combine is all about creds. They won't take kindly to losing one of their heavies, or its cargo.'

'Not our problem,' Sky says. 'Is it?'

'Guess not,' I say, as we start our bumpy descent.

We get our break at an outdoor bazaar full of blue-lipped stallholders shouting their wares through clouds of misting breath. A bundled-up Barzahk merchant woman beckons for Murdo to join her in the shadowy back of her tented stall. A wood stove glows there. We go to follow him, but her assistant – as wide as I am tall – blocks our path.

Sky's teeth chatter. 'Who'd want to live here?'

'Not me, that's for sure,' I say.

By the time Murdo reappears we're nearly frozen solid. As we stumble through the snow back to the landing field, Murdo tells us he has good and bad news. Sky being Sky wants to hear the bad first. Murdo tells us the woman isn't a buyer. Not because the darkblende could be Syndicate, more because she just hasn't got the funds we'd be looking for.

'The good news is she hates the Syndicate. Her only son had taken over her business. Syndicate guys came calling and the fool talked back to them. They gutted him. Made her watch.'

'Lovely,' Sky says, shivering. 'How's that good?'

'It means she hates them enough to want to spite them. Gave me a lead. Somebody who still does a bit of business behind their back. And he's . . . not far away.'

We both notice his hesitation.

'But?' Sky says sharply.

Murdo pulls a wry face. 'But he operates out of the Ark. It's a rough old joint. And I'm a wanted man there.'

'Wanted?' I say.

'For killing a man. It was self-defence. He cheated me. But it's worth the risk anyway. Happened when I was your age, so I don't suppose anyone will know me now.'

'You don't *suppose*?' I say.

'He's old now and ugly,' Sky says, winking at me.

'Hey, less of the ugly,' Murdo says. As Barzahk's bitter wind slices through us, there's a spring in Murdo's step. My guess is he's already spending his share in his head.

Our take-off and climb back to orbit are uneventful. By the time Murdo's set our new course I'm almost warm again. Sky's still bundled up though, and wracked by coughs.

'Why don't you go lie down?' I say. She's sick enough already and could do without catching a chill.

But all I get is glared at and told to mind my own business.

I ask Murdo if this Ark place is our best chance to sell the darkblende, or our *last* chance? He shrugs, says it's either that or we'll have to risk approaching the Syndicate. He says not to worry, that he's got a good feeling.

Sky snorts so hard she starts coughing.

Later, curled up together in the sleep bay we share, Sky sighs so loudly that she wakes me up.

'Something wrong?' I ask.

She wriggles around to face me. 'If we do manage to flog the darkblende, will you still help me find Tarn?'

'Course. Gave you my word, didn't I?'

'Yeah, well. Words are easy, and creds are tempting.'

Now it's my turn to sigh, and I make a bit of a meal of it. In the gloom we've made by rigging up a curtain, Sky's breath is warm on my face.

'Okay, okay. But what if this Ark guy turns his nose up at the darkblende like the rest? Selling it back to the Syndicate seems crazy. They'd kill us.'

'Murdo's sure it won't come to that.'

'He's not sure, he's just greedy. Creds are all he cares about.'

Hah. Murdo says Sky only cares about her sister, Tarn, but she doesn't need to hear that. Instead I share a thought that's crawled around the back of my mind for a while. 'Maybe the stuff's more trouble than it's worth. Maybe we'd be better off ditching it before it gets us killed.'

Sky coughs again, but not as painfully as before.

'How would we get to Enshi Four without any creds?'

'We sell the freighter instead. A go-fast smuggler ship like this must be worth a good few creds. With our split of the proceeds, we can do as we like.'

I feel rather than see Sky shaking her head.

'Nah. No way will Murdo or the others go for that. Even if they did, what if this is a Syndicate freighter? Who would dare buy it off us? Nobody, that's who.'

Oh yeah. Same problem. Wish I'd kept my mouth shut.

She pulls me closer. 'Guess we'll just have to hope Murdo manages to sell the darkblende on this Ark.'

'You don't believe in hope.'

'I don't believe in dying either. It still happens.'

We're out of dee-emm and back in regular space. Our instruments tell us the Ark is coming up fast, but even with my sharp nublood seeing, it's still only a small sun-licked dot compared to the giant world it orbits. Murdo's working on giving our freighter a false identity.

'How about the *Nagasaki Maru*?' he asks.

'Whatever,' Sky snaps. 'Set it before they ping us.'

This Ark space station is no half-forgotten backwater like Shanglo and Barzahk. We can't just fly in and set down unannounced. First we have to identify ourselves and satisfy their security forces we're not blacklisted.

Murdo gives his screen one last tap. 'Okay! We're now the free-trader *Nagasaki Maru* out of New Kyoto.'

'*Nagasaki Maru*!' I like the way it stretches my mouth.

The freighter's hacked comm lets us choose to show up on scans as any one of a dozen legit transports. Murdo says when we're inside the Ark's hangar we'll tuck ourselves away and nobody will be arsed to check.

Now our comm lights up red as we're hit with an identity

request from the Ark. And it stays red for longer than I can hold my breath, which can't be good.

'You sure you did it right?' Sky asks Murdo.

The light flicks green. A deep robot voice pours itself into the flight deck. '*Nagasaki Maru*, this is the Ark. Final approach authorised. Proceed to deck zero, bay eleven.'

Murdo rocks back in his seat, grins and makes a fist.

There's nothing to do now but sit tight and watch the Ark grow slowly larger ahead of us. It'll be over an hour before we make our final approach. Cam, Anuk and some other kids are crammed into the back of the flight deck again. The rest are asleep in the crew compartment. Their lack of interest in approaching a new world, or worry at what might happen if things go wrong, blows my mind.

'What's this Ark then?' I ask Murdo.

'You'll see for yourself as we get closer,' he says, leaning back into his seat, 'but the thing is big enough to be an asteroid. Half of it was already a wreck when it showed up here, but that still leaves plenty of room. They say you can live your whole life there and not walk every deck.'

I sit up straighter. 'It showed up here?'

'Who wrecked it?' Sky says.

But Murdo won't be rushed. He tells us how, forty standard-years ago, an outbound mining support ship was the first to spot the incoming spaceship. After hailing it and getting no answer, they see the damage and figure she's a derelict, either abandoned or its crew dead. 'They get all excited, figuring they can claim salvage and have her for scrap. But just as they're about to do a hard docking and cut their way inside, the derelict fires up some kind of drive system and parks itself in orbit here.'

He jabs a finger at the planet we're approaching.

'So it wasn't abandoned?' Cam says.

'That's where it gets freaky.' Murdo grins. 'It still won't answer the comm. The miners get cold feet and call in ComSec to deal with it. They turn up eventually, give the thing a going-over and get even more excited.

'Techs are flown out from the Core worlds to check it out. Historians too. Turns out this thing is an ancient spaceship from the Long Ago on Earth. They reckon it set out over five thousand standard-years ago, in the middle of the Troubles, carrying a whole load of refugees. The drive tech back then was crude, early dee-eem, crawlers compared to what we've got now. And they didn't have cryonics. I guess that's why they built it so massive – because generations of settlers would have to live and die on board before they got here.'

Sky shudders. 'Like being in the camps all your life.'

'They must've been desperate, for sure. The historians knew a few Ark ships were fired off, but this was the first ever to turn up again. Only while it's been crawling through the big cold empty of space, completely forgotten, we've survived the Troubles, improved our drive tech and spread out into the galaxy, leaving it behind. And then one day it finally catches up with us when it arrives here.'

I can't help gasping. 'But why *here*, so far from Earth?'

Murdo shrugs. 'The ComSec scientists think something happened during all the fighting that threw it off course and into deep space. Its AI was set up to scan any star system it passed for a human-habitable world, so it kept on going and going until it sniffed out this place.'

'Fighting?' I say, twitching. 'What fighting?'

'You'll see in a bit. The settlers only made it four generations into the trip, then wiped themselves out.'

'It wasn't some accident?'

Murdo lets out a grim little laugh. 'Nah. They found barricades and other obvious signs of combat. The bodies were ferried down to that planet and buried. Big ceremony. So you could say they made it to their new world.'

'Not what they'd hoped for though,' Anuk says.

'No. Anyhow, the Combine guys slapped a preservation order on it, so the mining guys got frag all and were mad as hell. There was talk of hauling it back to Earth using a wormhole jump-tug, but talk's cheap and jump-tugs aren't. In the end, they patched her up and fitted the place out as an orbital trading platform. She's been here ever since.'

The Ark looms ahead of us now. It's a weird-looking cylinder, all lumps and bumps with masts sticking out supporting arrays of flat panels. The damage is visible, great rips in the hull down at the bottom end. Mostly it just looks ancient.

Murdo slows us to final approach speed. I'm wondering how we'll find our berth when a drone vessel whips out to meet us. It spins around and projects a big glowing sign behind it.

Nagasaki Maru, Deck 0, Bay 11.

'Fancy,' Sky says.

Murdo follows it in. Hangar deck zero is the lowest of several lit-up slots cut into the Ark's hull. Immediately below it is torn metal and dark gaping holes. Murdo tells us these lower wrecked decks are called the ghost levels.

'Does anybody go down there?'

'Not since the ComSec techs left. It's open to space.'

As we close in on the Ark I realise just how immense the derelict is. It soon fills our forward-view panels.

'Huge, huh?' Murdo mutters.

For someone who hasn't flown a star freighter for years, he does a great job of sliding us inside hangar deck zero without hitting anything. The drone leads us past dozens of docked spaceships, many busy being loaded or unloaded. We arrive at our assigned berth, a gap between two larger freighters. A large circle on the deck flashes our adopted name. There's just enough room for Murdo to nudge in forward before spinning round to face out again, which seems standard. As he sets up our landing hover, the drone ship kills its follow-me sign and nips off.

'Nothing to it,' Murdo says, as he powers down his controls. But the sweat running down his face and the slump back into his pilot seat give the lie to this.

'Won't they expect us to unload our cargo?' Sky asks.

Murdo stirs himself. 'Nope. See, that's why *Nagasaki Maru*'s such good cover. Free-traders often don't carry booked cargo. If we're asked, we say we've swung by on spec, to see if we can trade what we're carrying.'

'We don't tell them it's darkblende though,' I say.

Sky rolls her eyes at me. 'Well . . . duh!'

9
CHASING THE DEAL

A few minutes later and Murdo has a fight on his hands. He's insisting on only taking me and Sky with him to track his contact down, while the rest of the kids stay on board.

'Why them again?' Cam snarls.

'For the same reason they came with me on Barzahk. They've lived outside the camps on Wrath. They know how to carry themselves without standing out.'

'We've been stuck on this crate for days,' Ravi protests.

'Yeah,' Pol says. 'We want to stretch our legs. We won't go far.'

But Murdo tells them they'll have to be patient for a little bit longer. He promises that after he's sold the darkblende he'll take them anywhere they want. It sounds familiar to me, like when he wanted us to come with him to the No-Zone, but I can see where he's coming from.

In the end he gets his way. Anuk's left in charge.

Murdo lowers the three of us down on the freighter's loading platform. Towards the rear of the hangar deck there's a guarded gateway in a barrier, and he leads us towards it. But I've only got eyes for the open slot in the side of the Ark that we flew in through. Beyond it I see swirling clouds on the planet's surface way below, which is worrying. How is it we can breathe up here?

When I ask Murdo he grunts and points. 'If you look outside you'll see a shimmer. That's an air shield. Too weak to stop a freighter, but it keeps the air in.'

'Got it.' I see the shimmer now, like a heat haze.

'What do *these* gommers want?' Sky says.

Behind the barrier, dozens of shabby-looking men and women are gathered. They're watching us intently.

'They'll be looking for unloading work,' Murdo says.

'The guards won't ID you?' This is my big worry ever since he let slip he's wanted for murder here.

But he seems cool about it. 'Relax. I've had iris implants. Cost me, but they should fool any scan.'

Anyway, it's too late to turn back. We're at the gate and the guards are giving us hard stares. One demands the name of our vessel. Murdo tells them it's the *Nagasaki Maru*, and that we're free-traders. This gets us sneered at.

I'm guessing free-traders are the lowest of the low.

'Any of you carryin' energy weapons?'

We shake our heads. Our blasters have stayed behind. Signs plastered everywhere warn that the penalty for being caught carrying them on the Ark is summary execution.

Murdo offers himself up to be checked.

One guard images his face, another pats him down. I hold my breath, but no alarm sounds. The guards fit his left wrist with a metal bracelet.

'You need this to get back in, so don't go losing it.'

I'm next up. And as this isn't Wrath, my missing little finger shouldn't mark me out as an ident. Even so, my mouth goes dry on me as I stick out my hand. But nothing bad happens. If anything, the guard's less sneery with me as she snaps the bracelet round my wrist. It tightens itself weirdly until there's no way I could prise it off, yet somehow it doesn't pinch. Sky gets hers fitted last of all. And that's when I notice she's wearing that old skin-glove of hers again, with its fake little finger. A good thing too, I reckon. Saves awkward questions about why we're both missing them.

The gate is opened for us and we're nodded through.

Straight away we're surrounded by the waiting workers. We have to shove through them as they beg and plead with us for work. This close I can see how thin and ragged and desperate they look. And the stink of them is as bad as anything I've smelt in the Barrenlands.

'I thought it'd be less shitty here,' I grumble.

Sky agrees. 'Makes our old dump world look good.'

'Every hangar deck or spaceport I've been to, it's always the same,' Murdo says. 'The higher decks where the trading houses have their offices and the merchants have their pads that'll be a lot sweeter, you can bet. Although you'd still need to watch your step. Just 'cos there's less filth, it don't mean the people up there are any less dirty.'

'Is that where we're heading?' I say, hopefully.

'In your dreams.' He frowns and peers around uncertainly. 'We're looking for a bar, but it's been so long I'm not sure I can remember how to find it.'

The solution comes racing towards us on skinny legs. A dozen young brats, all shrieking loudly that they'll guide us to wherever we want to go.

'Okay, okay. Deck three, Bar Goujian,' Murdo says.

'No problem!'

A long-legged scrap of a girl, no more than ten, starts towing him away. A bigger boy yells he knows the way too and tries to cut in. She stiff-arms him aside.

'Get lost! I shouted first.'

I trade shrugs with Sky. We hurry after them.

Murdo asks his little guide if she knows the back ways.

'Back ways, side ways, long ways, short ways, I'll take you any way you want. Only place I won't go is the ghost levels. You wouldn't wanna go there anyway.' She stops and thrusts a hand out. 'Two creds it'll cost ya. Bargain.'

'One,' Murdo says. 'And we go back ways.'

The girl pulls a sulky face, but the other kids aren't far away and I'm guessing one cred is better than no cred.

'Deal!' She drags him along again.

We weave through a vast cargo-handling area, so busy it looks like a nest of wrathmites that someone's poked with a stick. Laden carry-platforms whine down aisles between storage racks so high they fill the gap between deck and ceiling. Overalled workers scurry everywhere. The girl chivvies us inside a shadowy alcove at one aisle end, makes sure nobody's watching, levers open a flap and has a quick fiddle. A maintenance hatch hisses open. Inside is a dimly lit stairwell, its walls a mess of crude drawings. Metal stairs wind upwards. Stairs that need actual climbing. And there was me with my head full of stories of how off-worlders have clever ways of being lifted up by stepping inside special little rooms in their buildings.

We start clattering our way up.

It stinks in here too. Piss, and worse.

The girl sees my disgusted look. 'You said back ways.'

A lot more than three flights of stairs later we duck out through another service hatch and find ourselves on an elevated metal gantry, staring down at deck three.

'Looks like the Blight down there,' I say, gobsmacked.

'Not *that* bad,' Sky wheezes. 'But . . . yeah.'

Below lies a sprawl of crude and flimsy dwelling places, cobbled together from all sorts of scrap. Here and there some more substantial buildings stick up. I think I can make out some of the Ark's original bulkheads and internal divisions, but mostly they seem to have been torn out.

'What do you call this dump?' I ask the girl.

She narrows her eyes at me. 'Home.'

Glancing back occasionally to make sure we're still behind her, the girl leads us down and along a maze of narrow alleys that skirt the edges of the shanty town. We collect one or two curious glances, but otherwise the few people we see mind their own business. After a while we plunge more towards the ship's centre. It gets busier. More signs of industry. Shops selling wares. The quality of the buildings starts to look up too, which is a relief.

'Bar Goujian,' she says at last, and points.

A rusty sign hangs outside a low, windowless structure, displaying a hand-drawn foaming tankard. The stink of stale beer hangs in the air.

'Are you sure?' Murdo asks.

An old guy is shuffling past. She asks him the name of the bar. He confirms it's the Goujian, and shuffles on.

'Told ya,' the girl says.

'Deal's a deal, I guess,' Murdo says.

He pays her off, bumping one of his cred storage devices against a battered one she produces from deep inside her threadbare outfit. She does a delighted little skip and a jump as her device flashes from red to green. In credit.

'I'll wait here and show you back down for another cred,' she says, hopefully. 'You'll get lost otherwise.'

But Murdo tells her we can find our own way back.

With all the climbing and walking, Sky's cough starts up again. She fishes out her last bag of boiled buzzweed and scowls, seeing there's only scraps left. She tips it all into her mouth and starts chewing.

The girl watches. 'Sick, huh? I can get you stuff.'

Sky snarls at her to mind her own business. The girl sticks her tongue out at her and clears off.

'We'll go and find you some meds later,' I say.

'I'm fine,' Sky lies. 'C'mon, let's do this.'

'I'll get the drinks, you guys grab a table,' Murdo says.

We push inside through the swinging door and a blast of heat and smoke and loud chatter. Whatever time it is, the bar is jammed. A rough-looking lot, but nobody pays us the slightest attention. Murdo makes for a bar set up in the middle. We blink into the dimly lit gloom and get lucky for once. People are leaving and we snag their table. Good one too, in a dark corner but with sight of the door.

Murdo joins us soon afterwards, beers in hand. He looks relaxed enough, but I'm starting to get a bad feeling.

'If your guy has enough creds to buy our cargo, what would he be doing in a dive like this?'

'Nothing,' he says, draining his glass.

'So why the frag are we here then?' Sky growls.

Murdo studies his empty glass, as if disappointed. 'Top guys pull strings, but never get their hands dirty. The guy I'm looking for here is one of their fixers. The girl behind the bar says he'll be in soon and she'll point him out.'

I sip at my beer cautiously, then take a proper pull.

It's not bad, compared to the swill we used to choke down in the Deeps. Anyway, it helps the minutes of waiting crawl by. The bar looks and sounds better too. One muscle at a time, I start to unwind. I even lift my left hand from where I'd kept it below the table, and rest it next to my glass. Nobody cares here. Nobody's going to yell at me for being a twist. I could get used to this, for sure.

Sky nudges me, hard.

A tall man is being served by the barwoman. She whispers across the counter to him. He glances around, real casual. Thin face. Hook nose. Murdo, deep into his fourth beer already, nods at him. But he gets no nod back.

'Is that our guy?' I ask, confused.

'I reckon so,' Murdo grunts.

'Why doesn't he come over here then?'

'Wants to show who's boss and make me come to him.'

'Well, go on then,' Sky says. 'What you waiting for?'

But Murdo won't be rushed. He says we shouldn't look

too eager. Only when he's downed his beer does he head over. Standing beside the hook-nosed guy he orders another beer and pays. They start talking. Whatever Murdo says to the guy I'm sure I see him stiffen. Next thing, they're walking off together and disappearing through a bead-curtained doorway in the rear wall of the bar.

'I hope that's not the last we see of him,' I say, as it hits me that without Murdo to pilot us we're stuck here on the Ark.

Sky tells me to relax. 'They'll only be going somewhere private, so they won't be overheard.'

But with so much at stake, relaxing isn't easy. And an hour later, with no sign of him coming back, I've run out of nails to chew. I tell Sky I'm going to take a look. She takes a deep breath and nods. We head to the curtained-off door, but no sooner do we push through it into a passageway than two heavy-set guys stand up from their card game to block our way.

'You must be lost,' one says.

'Or looking for trouble,' his buddy growls.

Sky glances at me. I know that look; she hates being threatened. But getting into a fight seems awful dumb.

'Guess we're lost,' I say quickly.

I haul Sky back through the bead curtain before her temper gets us killed, and only let her shrug me off when we're a good few steps away. Heads are turning and she has the sense not to rage at me for grabbing her. We walk back to our table, but halfway there I see it's been taken.

'What now?' I say. 'Stay or go back to the freighter?'

Sky grimaces. 'How about one more beer?'

The young barwoman who served Murdo serves us. I swipe a

cred thing Murdo gave me. It works, but she could have charged us anything for all I know.

'First time on the Ark?' she says, wiping the counter.

Sky blanks her, but I admit it is. She seems friendly and it beats worrying about Murdo. I feed her the crap about us being free-traders. And she listens, which makes a pleasant change from being scowled at.

'Bit young for crew, aren't you?' she says.

'We pull our weight. Beats being a grubber, for sure.'

She looks puzzled. I explain that's what we call farmers back on . . . and just barely catch myself.

'Uh, back home,' I finish.

Before the woman can ask where *that* is, I ask what life's like on the Ark. In between serving, she tells us there are worse places and that she likes it up here. She's from the planet the Ark orbits, a deep-mining world where folk go months without seeing the sun. 'I mean it can be rough up here, but at least it's living, you know? Not dull like where I came from. A lifetime drilling rocks? Frag that. Ready for another beer?'

I'm tempted. Sky isn't. 'No! We'd best be getting back.'

And it's my turn to be grabbed and towed away.

I'm about to protest, but now I see what she's seen. Murdo, over by the bar's entrance.

He ducks outside and waits for us to join him.

'Well? Do we have a buyer?' Sky says.

Murdo fakes a grim look, then smiles. 'I think we do!'

10
SO CLOSE, SO FAR

Murdo has us arrange the ten darkblende crates we have left in a fan shape, out in front of the other crates that are kicking about in the hold. His buyer isn't big on trust and is sending someone to make sure our cargo is for real.

'How much is it worth?' I ask when we're done.

'Whatever we can get for it,' Murdo says. For the first time I can remember, he looks edgy.

'Roughly?' Cam says.

'It's bad luck to talk about it before a deal, but if this was legit I reckon you'd be talking . . . millions. Okay?'

'How much is that?' Anuk asks.

'Remember all those stars you saw?' I say to her. 'If each was a cred, that's how much. Plenty to go around.'

That gets everyone excited. Even Sky looks impressed.

Ravi sticks his head into the hold. 'Your guy's here!'

'By himself?' Murdo asks.

Ravi nods. 'He's . . . something else.'

Sky begins herding everybody below. Murdo doesn't want

whoever's coming to see a bunch of kids and figure we're a soft touch. He's hired four big hangar workers and had Anuk fit them out with spare crew clothing.

'I'll do the talking, Kyle,' Murdo says.

'Yeah, yeah. Whatever.'

We ride the loading platform down to the hangar floor. Our 'crewmen' are hanging about there, looking tough. And strolling towards us is a man in a dark coat so long it swirls about his legs with each step he takes.

Ravi was right – this guy *is* something else.

He's good-looking and knows it. But it's the way he carries himself, head high and shoulders back, like he owns the place. The way he moves too, like he's got oil inside him, not bones like the rest of us. When he stops in front of us and looks us up and down, I've never seen someone so clean. His skin glows. His short-cropped blond hair shines.

Next to him I feel grubby and ordinary.

Oh well. At least I could rip his head off if I wanted to.

He's wearing tinted wrap-around glasses that hide his eyes. But he takes them off now, sliding them up on top of his head, and studies us out of two different-coloured eyes. The left is light blue, the right a rich brown.

'Is this the *Nagasaki Maru*?' he asks us, real soft.

Murdo clears his throat. 'It is. And *you* are?'

'Here to assess the merchandise.'

His weird eyes flick from Murdo to me. For a moment I worry his glance lingers on my left hand. But why would it? My missing little finger means nothing here.

'Welcome aboard then,' Murdo says, and gestures for

him to join us on the loading platform.

'Your son?' he asks, as he steps on.

Murdo snorts. 'No. Somebody else's bastard.'

He hits a button. We rise up until the platform thumps to a stop as it fills the matching hole in the hold's floor.

The stranger looks at our arranged crates. And reaches inside his coat, only to freeze as I aim my blaster at him.

'Bit tense, are we?' he says, very dry.

'We call it careful,' Murdo says. He steps around behind the guy and pats him down, very thoroughly. All he comes up with though is some kind of large wallet.

I relax, take a step back and holster the blaster.

'What's in the wallet?' Murdo asks.

'My testing kit.'

Murdo throws it to me. I open it up. Scrapers. Spatulas. Empty plastic dishes. Small squeeze-bottles full of brightly coloured liquids. Some small sensor device.

I nod at Murdo and hand it back to the guy.

He thanks me politely enough, looking amused. I try not to stare at his long fingernails, painted a glossy black.

'Where shall I start?' he says.

Murdo beckons to me. The nearest crate's lid isn't nailed down. We pull it off and lean it against the side.

'There you go. Darkblende. Promethium-148,' Murdo says, gesturing at the small metal chest nestled inside.

'We'll see, won't we? Open the rest.'

As we crowbar them open, he waves the sensor thing over the chest inside. Each time it flashes red and buzzes.

Murdo mouths 'radioactive' behind his back.

Apparently satisfied, the man puts the device away. He leans into the last crate we opened, and fiddles with the controls on the chest. The over-centre clasps that hold it closed all snap open together.

Murdo takes a big step back. So do I.

'Rather you than me,' Murdo says. 'That stuff's lethal.'

The man straightens up, his amused look back. 'I'm afraid one of you will have to help me, by holding it open.'

Murdo looks at me. What a shock.

'Don't worry,' the man says, showing me his impossibly white teeth in a mocking smile. 'A few seconds of exposure won't do either of us any lasting harm.'

Can't say I'm keen, but I shuffle forward.

'Do I get a bigger share for this?' I hiss at Murdo.

He tells me to shut up.

'Ready?' the man asks, poised with scraper and tube.

I nod, lean in and heave the hinged lid up towards me. It takes all my strength. Immediately my fingers start tingling and I get this disgusting sick taste in my mouth. With the lid in the way I can't see the darkblende. Fine by me, as the guy's face glows in the blue light that shoots up out of the chest. Teeth gritted, he lunges and scrapes and then leans back, dropping white powder into the tube.

Not waiting to be told, I let the top slam back down.

Whatever was in the tube, it reacts with the powder and starts fizzing. And turns bright green.

'That good?' Murdo asks, from a safe distance.

'You'll be pleased to hear the green means it's pure.'

I'm feeling better already, but as I look along the nine

remaining crates I shudder. Lucky for me though, the man says he only needs to sample the one.

'As you wish. So what now?' Murdo says.

The man wraps up his test kit carefully and pockets it.

'That depends. I don't suppose you came by such a significant quantity of promethium . . . legally?'

'Don't suppose we did.'

'It limits the price we can offer.'

'I'll talk about that with your boss,' Murdo growls.

'That won't be necessary,' the man says, frowning slightly. 'The merchandise is as described. On that basis, I'm authorised to offer you fifty thousand creds.'

I can't help twitching. That was the Slayer reward for my capture. I mean, what are the chances?

But Murdo looks like he's been kicked in the nuts.

'Fifty thou! You're kidding?'

'Take it, or leave it.'

Murdo gets in the guy's face. 'That's nothing for this amount of darkblende and you know it. Get out of here!'

It's as if the guy's odd-coloured eyes fill up with ice.

'I think perhaps you misunderstand me,' he says, real low. 'Our offer . . . is fifty thousand *per chest*.'

'Oh,' Murdo says. 'Right.'

With ten chests, I make that . . . yeah, loads. My heart lurches inside me. It's hard not to shout out.

'A generous offer,' the man goes on. 'Especially as we suspect the merchandise once belonged to a dangerous rival of ours.'

He doesn't say Syndicate. He doesn't have to.

I glare at Murdo.

Don't be greedy, go for it!

He nods. 'Deal. Five hundred thou then, for the lot.'

With a sly grin, Murdo spits on his hand and sticks it out. And fancy guy's tougher than he looks. Spits and shakes without a frown, like he's done it before.

I'm so relieved, my legs shake.

They start bickering about payment now. Murdo wants to make sure any creds transferred can't be snatched back electronically, and can be accessed off-Ark. The man seems to be reassuring him. Words like 'encrypted' fly back and forth, mostly over my head. I'm sent to fetch drinks.

By the time I'm back with two steaming mugs of hot liquor-laced chai, Murdo seems satisfied.

'Your funds will be with you tomorrow,' the man says.

Your. Funds. I mouth the words. They feel good.

'Tomorrow then. Same time?'

The man nods, but smiles coldly. 'I'll bring two of my associates to help with the loading. They won't be armed. But a word of warning to you – my people will not be messed with. Please don't do anything foolish.'

Murdo smiles back, just as coldly. 'A deal's a deal.'

'Good. We understand each other then.'

I get stuck with taking the guy back down on the loading platform. Only takes seconds, but I swear he stares at me the whole time, that amused look on his face again.

'Oh, I almost forgot,' he says, and tosses me his cup.

I have to be fast to catch it. He nods, and puts his tinted glasses back on. It's not exactly dazzling on the hangar deck, so I figure he likes to hide his odd-coloured eyes. Without another word he turns his back on me and walks away, the long coat flicking around his legs.

When he's out of sight, I head back up.

Murdo waits until the platform seals itself into the floor of the hold before he punches the air.

'*Yes-s-s*. We fraggin' sold it! FIVE HUNDRED THOU!'

Our fake crewmen have been paid off and are gone. Murdo's told the others that the deal is on. When he shares the price we're getting I expect the nublood kids to go nuts. But they just chew their lips and swap glances.

'Do you understand?' he asks, a bit edgy.

'We do,' Anuk says. 'It's great. But will it happen?'

Murdo shakes his head, as if disgusted. 'You guys need to think more positive, you know that?'

Me, I get where Anuk's coming from. I've been through a lot since I found out I was nublood, but their whole lives have been pure misery. To imagine that in a few hours we could all be leaving here free, with more creds than we can spend in a lifetime . . . nah, it's best to count your fourhorns after they've trotted through the gate!

'How will the handover work?' Sky asks.

'They'll check the crates again. If he's happy, he'll make a call and transfer the creds. We confirm receipt, offload the crates, then lift out of here and scram.'

'Where to?' Cam asks.

'We can figure that out later. The main thing is to get clear.'

Hours drag by. Our watch system falls apart as nobody is able to sleep. A few kids play games, but only half-heartedly. Me and

Sky, we spend hours hunting for med stuff to help relieve her pain and cough. No such luck. In the one remaining escape craft we find a trauma kit, but it's been raided and there's nothing useful left. Sky says we'll have to go and buy some on the Ark.

I wince. 'Murdo won't like that.'

'Murdo can go to hell. Look, I'm out of buzzweed. Without it, I'll soon be coughing my lungs up.'

'But where would we go?'

'We can ask. Or Murdo might know.'

But Murdo claims he doesn't remember. He reckons Sky should 'suck it up' until we're safely off the Ark with our creds, when she'll be able to afford a hold-full of her own med supplies. Sky gets so mad I have to jump between them. She yells at him that she *can't* wait. Next thing, Cam's whining that if *we're* allowed to go for a wander around the Ark, he and his mates are going too. Murdo nearly has a fit. But in the end all he can do is snarl that if we're not back by the time the darkblende is unloaded, he won't wait.

Leaving him yelling at Cam, we grab some creds and head out. I reckon that we've got over ten hours. Plenty.

We've just shoved our way clear of the mob of pleading hangar workers when the same little girl who guided us before comes dashing over.

'Can you really get me med stuff?' Sky asks.

The girl nearly nods her head off. 'Sure. There's a quack up on deck five. He sells top stuff. Ain't cheap mind.'

'Is it *proper* medicine?' I ask.

'I swear it is. But if you want cheaper stuff I can sort that too. How many creds you got to spend?'

'Never you mind,' Sky tells her. 'We'll try your guy.'

A cred changes hands. The girl leads us the same way as before, but two flights of stairs higher. It's a little less squalid than deck three, but not much.

'How many decks are there?' I ask.

'Seventy, so they say. The top few are fancy-fancy, but we're shut off from them. My name's Mags, by the way.'

I hesitate. Sky doesn't. 'I'm Sky, he's Kyle.'

'Sky,' Mags says, beaming. 'That's a nice name.'

And then we're outside a shack built from corrugated metal sheets. A missing roof panel is patched with a tarp, to keep out light I'm guessing, as there's no weather here. On a rusty sign is a drawing of a winged stick, two snakes coiling round it. Waiting outside are a dozen ragged and sick-looking people.

They stare at us, dull-eyed.

Mags gestures at the door. 'These losers have nothing, so they have to wait. You can pay, so you go right in.'

'This doc, he treats them for free?' I say, impressed.

'Sometimes. When he's sober.'

'You brought us to a *drunk*?' I say, and glance at Sky.

Sky sighs that we're here now, limps to the welded-together front door and hauls it open. I follow her into the gloom, which stinks of stale sweat, liquor and smoke. Slouched in a chair beside a stained metal table is a wreck of a man. I've seen more meat on the scarebirds we used to stick in fields on Wrath, but something tells me he's not as old as he looks. He says nothing, just stares at us and takes a long drag from a tube.

The girl scuttles inside too. 'Doc, it's me, Mags!'

Yellowish smoke dribbles out of his nose and mouth. 'Brought me patients, did you, Mags? You're a good girl.'

'You're a healer?' I say, doubtfully.

With a grunt of effort, the man levers himself to his feet. 'I am indeed. Healer. Physician. Dispenser of balms. Good as you'll get on these lower decks. What's ailing you?'

Sky shoves me aside. 'It's me who's sick.'

'What seems to be the problem?'

'My lungs. They're shot.'

'Hah. You and me both then.' He cackles and coughs, takes another drag and looks her up and down. 'And you've been living with this for a while now, am I right?'

Sky scowls. 'Dying with it, more like.'

He gestures towards the table. 'I'll take a look at you.'

'No, you won't. Listen, I just need something to help me breathe and take the edge off the pain. Enough to get me through the next few weeks. I can pay you.'

'I should hope so. Wait here.' He shuffles off into a back room and returns carrying a box. Placing it on to the grubby examination table he starts counting out plastic-wrapped bags.

'What is that?' I ask.

He rattles off a fierce long name full of *di-oxy*-this and *omni*-that at me. 'It's strong,' he says, showing me his ruined teeth. 'I take it myself. You can't say fairer than that.'

'How much?' Sky asks him.

'I could do you two weeks' dose for . . . fifty.'

'*Fifty?*' I say, horrified.

'The good stuff don't come cheap.'

Between us we scrape together twenty-one. Not even a week's worth. I try to bargain. The guy laughs and shakes his head. Which makes me angry – angry enough to take the stuff and run. But with our deal looming, I know the last thing we need is trouble. So I hand twenty to the creep and tell him that we'll be back with the rest in an hour.

He shrugs. 'Take your time. I ain't goin' nowhere.'

We duck back outside again.

'You go,' Sky says. 'I'd only slow you down.'

'You'll be all right waiting here?' I ask.

She half scowls, half smiles. 'I'll try not to hurt anybody.'

Knowing the last thing I need to do now is get lost, I pay a delighted Mags my last cred to guide me again.

It's a pain, but at least we've still got plenty of time.

As we make our way down through the decks, I start to breathe more deeply. I guess it's because I start to believe. In a few hours we'll leave the Ark with enough creds to afford the best of treatments for Sky, and set us up for years. We'll even have our own star freighter to work this sector. So many nights in the lousy Barrenlands I'd stared up at the stars and dreamt of having adventures among them. With Wrath locked down, I'd never imagined those dreams might one day come true. Yet, somehow, here I am.

'This way, dummy!' Mags says, plucking at my sleeve. Too busy daydreaming, I almost got left behind.

I give myself a shake. The deal's not done yet.

But excitement is a hell of a hard thing to shake off. It sneaks back. We're *so* close, it whispers.

Back on deck zero, Mags has no bracelet to access the hangar deck, so she waits for me while I run to the freighter to fetch the extra creds. I tell her I won't be long.

A bored guard at the gate scans my security bracelet. Her scanner lights up red.

'Which vessel are you off?' she asks.

'*Nagasaki Maru*,' I tell her, impatiently. We've still got hours, but I don't need this. 'It's the free-trader over —'

I trail off, stunned.

Bay eleven is empty. Our freighter's gone!

PART TWO
TEMPTATION

11
MAROONED

No amount of protesting or pleading puts our star freighter back on hangar deck zero. The guards say they saw her lift out a few minutes before I got here. After jeering at me for being so stupid as to get left behind, they strip my bracelet off me and bundle me out through the gate.

'But what am I supposed to do?' I say, helplessly.

The man shrugs. 'Not *our* problem.'

Dazed, I stumble back the way I came. The waiting labourers have heard what's happened, or know what my despairing look means, and they leave me be.

Mags comes skipping along.

'Hey, Kyle, what's wrong?' she says, so brightly it hurts.

'Nothing,' I lie.

'Want me to take you back to Sky?'

This is when the full sucker punch of Murdo running out on us hits me. The doc's pain-meds won't save Sky from dying. I'd counted on finding Tarn and using her nublood for that. But now we're marooned here that can't happen.

'Let's go,' Mags says, tired of waiting for my answer.

She sets off again, dragging me after her. So many dark thoughts pound through my head. I remember nothing of the trip back up. But suddenly I'm standing outside the doc's shack again and Mags is frowning at me, as if she's said something. Frag knows what though. And there is no sign of Sky.

'Where is she?' I say, looking round.

Mags rolls her eyes. 'Must be with Doc, like I said.'

Sick to my stomach, I fumble the door open and lurch inside. But the only person there is the doc, slumped in his chair as if he hasn't moved since we left.

'Do you know where Sky is?'

He yawns. 'That the sick girl you were with?'

I nod. 'She was waiting outside.'

'Yeah? Well the last time I stuck my head out, I didn't see her. She must've cleared off. And don't ask me where again, because how the hell should I know?' He sneers and stands up. 'Look, if you still want that stuff, kid, it's another thirty creds. Forty if you argue. The bars are calling. I'm closing up.'

It's his sneer that does it. Rage possesses me, hot and bitter. Our freighter's gone, and so is Sky. I slam him against the wall, so hard that the whole hut shakes.

'If you've done something to her, I swear I'll kill you!'

He winces, bug-eyed and shaking.

'I ain't done nothing to your girl, I swear it.'

I slam him one last time and let him go. There's nothing to him. Even as sick as she is, if he'd attacked Sky she'd have left bits of him all over the place. His shack is a mess, but I see no obvious signs of a struggle.

'Take the meds,' the man says, backing away. 'You can pay me the rest later. Please don't hurt me.'

I feel ashamed now, which makes me even angrier. But I glance over my shoulder and Mags is watching.

She blinks. And I go from raging back to despairing.

My head pounds, making it hard to think.

'You better not be lying,' I growl.

'I'm not. Look, here you go.'

He grabs the drugs from the table and shoves them at me. I stuff them into my pockets and stumble back out.

Still no Sky though. Where the frag is she?

'Why don't we ask *them*?' Mags says, following me out.

Only ten or so years old, her head's screwed on tighter than mine. The line of people waiting outside hasn't got any shorter. Mags asks one old crone if she saw the slight girl with white dreads. And the woman nods.

'Which way did she go?' I ask, encouraged.

The woman lifts a claw of a hand and rubs her fingers together, obviously wanting to be paid.

'Tell him,' Mags hisses, 'or he'll rip your old head off.'

I fix the woman with my Barrenlands mad face. She swallows hard and tells me in a dry husk of a voice that Sky was sitting across from her when some people had walked past. She'd jumped up and limped after them.

'Was like the girl seen a ghost,' the crone adds.

'When was that?'

'Five minutes ago, give or take.'

'Can't have got far,' Mags says. 'I could find her for you. Ten creds if I bring her back here? Bargain.'

'I don't have any creds,' I sigh, too fed up to bother lying.

'You're good for it. I trust you!' She races off.

I drag myself over to where the crone said Sky was and sit in a heap. Automatically I glance up to see how far the sun has slid across the sky. Nuh-uh. No sky, no sun, no way to see what the time is. And what does it matter, with no freighter to run back to and nowhere to go?

Never thought I'd miss the Barrenlands. I do now.

Across from me the doc appears outside. He sees me sitting there and flinches, quickly pulls the door shut behind him and locks it. The people still waiting call out, pleading with him to see them before he goes. But they're wasting their breath. He scuttles off without a word. One or two get up and shuffle off themselves. Most stay where they are, not wanting to lose their place, I guess.

Or maybe they've got nowhere to go, like me.

Time trickles by. My thoughts are a thick and dirty sludge of misery inside my head. I can't believe Murdo would run out on us like this. And what was Sky thinking, taking off when she said she'd wait here? For one heart-squeezing but stupid second I worry Sky has gone off with Murdo. But I'm being a gom again. With her bad leg, no way could Sky have made it down there ahead of me and Mags.

How long do I sit there waiting? Tough to say. Long enough to decide something bad must have happened.

When Mags reappears at last, skipping along all careless, I could rip her head off. I grab her and shake her.

'Well? Did you find Sky?'

But she screws her runt face up at me defiantly and won't say another word until I release her. When I do, I get a fierce kick in the shins.

'Sky said that you'd be bad-tempered,' she jeers.

I let out a sob of relief. 'You found her?'

'Took a while, but yeah. She's down on deck three. Wants me to bring you there, to show you something.'

'Like what?' I say, rubbing my leg.

'Dunno. Says it's important, and you'll understand.'

Important? It fraggin' well better be. But at least it sounds like Sky's okay and that's something for me to clutch at.

'You coming then?' Mags says.

'If I can still walk,' I mutter.

On our way down, the girl tells me – gleefully – that she likes Sky better than me now, and how I'm a disappointment to her. 'You shouldn't have hurt the doc. He ain't so bad.'

I calm down enough to tell her I'm sorry.

She says she'll forgive me, but it'll cost another cred.

We're shoving our way along a narrow lane on deck three, full of open-fronted shacks selling foods and snacks, when I spot Sky's white dreads. She's towards the back of a crowd of people, all busy gawping at something we can't see further along the lane. As we make our way towards her, the crowd begins to break up.

'Nothing to see,' somebody calls out. 'Move along.' The shouter is a big bloke, a big bloke wearing grey military-style gear. He's shooing everybody away.

Sky's doesn't see us coming.

'Well, look who's here,' I say, low and mean.

She starts like I meant her to and spins around to face us.

'Kyle! Good. Hey, I'm sorry I wasn't –'

'You're *not* sorry. You said you'd wait there for me!'

She stiffens at the lash of my voice and scowls. But then, unexpectedly, she seizes me by the hand.

'Kyle, I *couldn't* wait for you.'

Well, I can scowl too. 'Why? Get bored, did you?'

She tightens her grip on me. 'Shut up and listen. I was hanging about when some guys walked past. And I know one of them! There were brothers, Zak and Zed, in the same ident camp as me, but a few years older. Both real nasty pieces of work. I reckon it was Zed I saw. He was the nublood.'

I say nothing, picturing the empty hangar bay.

'You think I'm making it up?'

I shrug, my mouth going dry on me. 'No. Maybe you did see him. But none of that matters now.'

She drops my hand and looks disgusted.

'Course it fraggin' matters. There he was, walking about as bold as you like. No way was he a slave. Don't you see? He'll have started out the same way as Tarn, shipped off Wrath in a cage. I figured maybe he could lead us to her!'

I grimace, knowing I should tell her that our freighter's gone and we're marooned here, but it sticks in my throat.

Her face softens. 'Look, if I'd stopped to leave a message for you with that creep of a healer, I'd have lost Zed. I figured I'd catch him up, see if I was right, and be back at the doc's before you. Only with my leg I could only just keep them in sight. Sheer luck I saw them turn down this lane. By the time I got here they'd ducked into one of the businesses. Couldn't see them anywhere and the lane dead-ends a few hundred metres on. I was waiting to see if he'd pop out again when Mags found me.'

'What's with all these Ark security guys?' Mags asks.

'Yeah, well, you weren't long gone to fetch Kyle when somebody was killed along there.'

'Killed?' Mags says, eyes wide. 'And I missed it!'

She races over to some kids who are hanging about.

Sky gestures at a finer building further along the lane where more of the guys in grey are milling about. 'People came streaming out of there, yelling and screaming. It's a drinking place I think. Anyway, I waited here to see if Zed reappeared, but he didn't. Then these guys in grey turned up. Some piled into the club. Others threw their weight around out here, asking if anybody saw anything. But nobody did, or if they did then they're not talking.'

Mags comes running back from chatting to the kids. 'My mate over there says somebody got whacked! Head blown off. Brain splashed all over the walls.' Eyes shining, she turns her hand into a gun and blasts me. 'Like that.'

'How long have we got?' Sky asks.

'Huh?' I say, doing my best gom impersonation.

'Before Murdo wants us back at the *Nagasaki Maru*, or whatever he called it. Listen, this Zed guy must still be here somewhere. If we wait, we can grab him on his way out.'

I open my mouth . . . and close it again. And I guess that's when Sky sees the anguish in my eyes.

'What's the matter?'

'The freighter's not there,' I mumble. 'It's gone.'

Sky goes very still. Her dark green eyes bore into mine.

'You sure?' she says. That's all.

I sigh and nod. 'Bay was empty when I got down there. The guards saw her lift. She's gone all right.'

Sky curses under her breath.

'That Murdo always was a stinkin' rat,' she hisses.

12
SURVIVAL

'You guys are stuck here?' Mags says, wide-eyed.

I grit my teeth. 'Looks like it.'

'Told ya,' she says. 'You shouldn't have roughed the doc up. What goes around comes around.'

I glare at her and tell her to get lost.

She shakes her head. 'You owe me ten creds for finding Sky. I'm sticking with you till you pay up.'

I nearly lose it, but don't want my shins kicked again.

'We should go,' I say to Sky.

She looks at me, all mocking. 'Yeah? *Where to?*'

I try to get my head to take a break from misery and do some thinking. 'Let's find someplace safe where we can rest up without being messed with. And we'll need to sort out water and food. I don't suppose they hand it out for free here. We blew everything on your meds.'

I dig one of the doc's packets out and show it to her.

Sky looks relieved. 'Later. I'm okay for now.'

We're the only people left standing around at the mouth of

the alleyway. Everybody else has either wandered off or been moved along. One of the grey-uniformed ArkSec guys turns and gives us a long hard look.

'Come on, let's go,' I say, exasperated.

'Zed's still here,' Sky says. 'He didn't get past me.'

'You think?' Mags pipes up. 'All these places have back ways out into the next alley over. The deck under them has more service tunnels and maintenance shafts than my brother's got spots. Your guy's long gone. Soon as ArkSec showed up, he'll have cleared off. Bound to.'

But Sky refuses to budge. In the end I give in, not having the heart to argue with her. After all, she's just been handed a death sentence. And so we wait.

Mags soon gets restless and says she's off.

'Hey, where will we find you?' I say, worried this ten-year-old is our best shot of surviving here.

'I'll find *you*. Don't forget, you guys still owe me!'

She's not long gone when the ArkSec guys finish doing whatever they were doing in the building. They load a black body bag into the armoured flitter that brought them here, and pile in after it. A lift-cell whines. The flitter rises to a highish hover before sliding away over our heads. The alley soon starts filling up with people again. I have the feeling people get whacked all the time around here.

'How long do we stay here?' I say.

'Long as it takes,' Sky snaps. 'We're in no rush, are we?'

She limps over to some overflowing rubbish bins outside an empty-looking shack and lowers herself down to sit in their shadow. From here she can watch everyone entering and leaving the alley, but can't be easily seen herself.

I shake my head and go and sit beside her. The bins stink.

'Zed's still here, I know he is,' Sky says.

'And what if he isn't?' I say.

Sky's face twists into her best scowl.

What I *don't* say – but can't help thinking – is that Sky's just putting off facing up to our dilemma. And she can't have seen this Zed. I mean, what are the odds of an ident nublood being here on the Ark and walking about a free man?

Nah. My guess is she saw what she wanted to see.

I'm asleep when Sky stirs me with her boot and wakes me up. She's on her feet looking down at me. Is her scowl the same one she had earlier, or a fresh one?

'Still no Zed?' I say, stretching.

Sky stifles a yawn and shakes her head.

I struggle up, stiff and hungry. 'So what now?'

'We do what we always do. We survive. I took some of that stuff. Bitter as hell it was. I could use a drink of water.'

Now that she's said it, I'm thirsty too. But where do we get water with no creds left? In the Barrenlands I know how to follow wildlife to find water. For food I'd scavenge for edible plants, trap and hunt. There isn't a whole lot of wilderness knocking around up here though.

It hits me suddenly how much I'm out of my depth.

Doubts must be crawling all over my face because Sky loses the scowl at last. She takes a cautious breath, manages not to cough and hangs her left fist out. 'We'll be fine. If that Mags girl can hack it here, then so can we.'

I bump stumps with her. 'You'd hope so anyway.'

'I *did* see Zed, you know.'

A lie is called for. 'I believe you. Pity you lost him. He might have been able to help us out.'

Sky sighs and gives her eyes a long rub. 'I'd be more interested in how he got here.'

'You tired?' I say automatically.

She frowns. 'I can't remember when I *wasn't* tired.'

I see she's still wearing the security bracelet from the hangar deck. It gives me an idea. 'Maybe we should go and check that Murdo's still gone? Could be something happened and he only had to clear off for a while.'

Sky looks me in the eye.

'You really think he'd come back for us?'

'No,' I admit. 'But it'd be dumb to stay here if he *is* back, the deal all settled and him looking for us down there.'

She snorts. 'Fat chance. But we should check.'

I was so dazed when Mags led me up here that I can't remember the back ways we took. It takes us a good hour or so of wandering about to find our way down again. What I'd thought was a massive double pillar supporting the deck above turns out to be two connecting shafts. At the base of each is an opening with people streaming in and out. The left entrance is guarded and everybody entering and leaving gets checked. The right entrance is unguarded.

I'm still scratching my head when Sky figures it out.

'One way is for up,' she says. 'The other is for down. You only get checked going up.'

It makes sense. 'Think we should risk it?'

'What's to lose?' Sky says, and limps towards it.

We latch on to the people shuffling inside the right-hand entrance. Nobody pays us any mind. But when it's our turn to step inside we get a shock. Other than a metre-wide grating circling the wall, the column is a huge, empty shaft. Folk in front of us head left around the grating. Still chatting away, they step out into thin air and drop out of sight.

Gobsmacked, we stop dead. Or try to. People behind us shove us further in, muttering crossly. Sky stumbles. I only just stop her from pitching headlong into the hole. Then we've no choice but to follow the people walking left.

But at least now I see what's going on. A man steps off the far side of the grating and I marvel as he floats steadily downwards, faster than a feather but not much. Even more amazingly, I see some people way below us appear to land in mid-air and walk back out of the shaft, I guess onto a lower deck.

Sky blows air out of her mouth. 'Wow.'

She goes to step off, but I pull her back and point out that the section of grating we're on is marked D-2.

'I reckon we need to step off where it says D-0.'

'Smart-arse,' she mutters.

The grating bounces under us. I peer down as we walk. It's fifty metres to the bottom of the shaft.

'See you down there.' Sky steps off, cool as you like.

Something invisible catches her and starts lowering her down. Teeth gritted, I step gingerly off after her. And it's not so bad. We float down all the way to the bottom, so my guess about the markings was a good one. A haze marks where we'll land, and I see it in time to bend my knees before I hit. It stops me and feels like solid ground. I stand there, swaying.

'Watch out!' Sky pulls me aside.

More people nearly land on top of me. A sour-faced old guy pulling an empty trolley behind him snarls at us to clear out through the exit like we're supposed to.

'Beats stairs,' Sky says, as we step out on to deck zero.

We find ourselves in the cargo-handling area. It's still frantically busy and we wander about for a good bit before we see a sign pointing to the hangar area. The gate is being besieged again by a mob of hopeful workers. We hang back and watch until a dozen or so lucky ones are picked and get let in.

'Maybe I could do that?' I say.

Sky shrugs. 'I'll see if that scumbag Dern is back.'

She limps off towards the gate. Those labourers who weren't picked shuffle away past me. I step in front of one woman and ask if I could get work here.

Dull-eyed, she looks me up and down, and shoves past.

'Forget it,' a familiar voice shrills.

I turn round and see Mags, busily rooting at her nose.

'Why's that?' I say.

She admires a snotty finger before wiping it on her grubby tunic. 'You wouldn't be picked.'

'Why not?'

'You're not full grown. Not strong enough.'

I'm about to protest that I'm as strong as anybody I've seen on the Ark – stronger with my nublood – when Sky limps back from talking to the guards at the gate. The missing security bracelet and the bleak look on her face say it all.

I ask anyway. 'No sign of him then?'

She shakes her head. 'No. We're stuck here all right.'

Three long, thirsty and hungry days later I finally manage to get my hands on one lousy cred. It's all that's left on a storage stick that somebody has dropped. We spend it at a place on deck two where a cred buys you a daily fill of a litre water bottle for a fortnight. Never has water tasted so good. Between us we drink a week's worth.

I nearly bring it back up later, when Mags takes delight in telling us how Ark water is recycled pee and sweat. She falls about laughing at our disgusted looks.

Right there I decide I can't be staying on this Ark forever. I need to drink chilled water from a mountain stream, not some processed stuff that might taste okay but has already been through hundreds of strangers' insides. Yuck!

We've a lot to thank Mags for though. In between whining at us that we still owe her ten creds, she's sorted us out with this scrape we're curled up in, a hiding place behind life-support equipment on deck three. There we can get some rest and stash what little gear we have. When she's not doing her guiding – or whatever else she does to scratch a living – she comes and finds us. Gradually, Sky gets her to tell us the tricks of getting by on the Ark with little or nothing. Leaky pipes good for a lick of free water, food-waste collection bins to be raided.

I don't kid myself the girl's doing this for me because she isn't. Mags seems drawn to Sky; she's always sneaking stares at her. Sky moans that it's doing her head in.

Fed up with rummaging through bins we're desperate to get our hands on more creds. But how? We've walked the feet off ourselves looking for paid work, and gotten nowhere. Mags was right about the labouring work. Everywhere we tried it – the hangar decks included – we're too-young faces in amongst a mob of men and women, many a head taller than us. And I can hardly shout about my nublood strength, can I?

'If we can't work,' Sky says, 'we'll have to beg or steal.'

She's busy with her knife, working on some wood she scavved. I see now that she's making herself a crutch.

'What's wrong with your leg brace?' I ask.

'Nothing, but I'll leave it behind. My bad leg and cough should pull in a few creds.'

'You're really going to *beg*?'

She stops work on the crutch and looks at me. 'Why not? Nobody's going to hire a sick-looking girl with a cough for manual labour, are they? The only thing I'm cut out for here is begging. That way we can eat until you find yourself work. And I can be keeping an eye out for Zed.'

'I don't like it. Give me another day. I'll find work.'

'We'll see,' she says. 'And don't worry – soon as you have the creds rolling in, I'll quit begging.'

She has a bit of a coughing fit and grimaces.

'Isn't it time you took your meds again?' I ask.

'Quit fussing, will you? Anyone would think you cared.'

Sky tries for her blink-and-you-miss-it smile, but another coughing fit chases it away. To be fair to the weird healer bloke, his stuff does help her. Then again, it's so strong it would bring a corpse back from the dead. To make it last while we're still broke, Sky's taking half-doses. Which is just as well. It helps her breathe and soothes her pain, but doesn't give her the massive high a full dose does. Even so, for a few hours after she's choked the stuff down I don't like to leave her alone.

When she's done coughing she chews her lip. 'Begging and scrounging might fill our bellies, but it won't buy us our passage to Enshi Four.'

'I'm too hungry to think that far ahead,' I say.

She sighs. 'Back on Wrath we'd hop a windjammer.'

'We're not on Wrath,' I point out helpfully.

'Maybe we could hop a star freighter instead. There are drinking holes all over the lower decks. Brothels too. Once we've got ourselves a few creds to rub together, we'll check them out. I bet they're heaving with freighter crews. And that way we could find out what's headed where.'

'You do the bars, I'll do the brothels,' I say.

Sky fake laughs. 'Thing is, security's a lot tighter here than your typical windjammer base. They count the labourers in and out, so we can't slip aboard that way. But maybe—'

I think I hear something, hold my hand up to shush her.

'Company?' Sky mouths.

And now I'm sure. Stealthy footsteps closing in on our refuge. Something else too. A muffled sobbing?

'Three at least. Trying to be real quiet,' I whisper.

Sky curses.

I'm wondering if we've still got time to make a break for it when an ear-splittingly loud metal-on-metal *boom* has us both ducking our heads and flinching.

'We know you're in there!' a man calls out.

'Get your thieving, gutter-deck arses out here.' Another man's voice, laying it on like he's bored. 'Give us what's left of the doc's stuff and take your beating.'

'Oh great,' Sky says.

'You got three seconds,' the first voice growls. 'If you're not out by then I'll burn you out.'

Another boom makes it tough to think. My guess is someone's bashing an iron bar on the pipes of our refuge.

But they're at the opposite end from our way out.

'Two!'

'Move!' Sky shoves me ahead of her.

I dive into the tunnel, roll on to my back and haul myself along the overhead pipes. A last big pull and I slide out, hands in front of my face, as he calls: 'One!'

I scramble to my feet, with Sky not far behind me.

Our visitors are gathered at the far end of the life-support pumping unit. Two are big lumps of brute-faced muscle who must spend half their life pushing weights around. One carries a long iron wrecking bar, the other what looks like a killstick. A third man, older and a lot less heavily built, is yanking Mags's head back by a fistful of her hair and twisting one of her arms behind her back. The little girl's face is a mess of blood, snot, tear streaks and misery.

All three men look round and start, clearly not expecting to see us pop out where we did.

'I'm sorry!' Mags wails, and chokes on her sobs.

13
OPPORTUNITY

We might have made it out of our refuge without being grabbed, but it's at the dead end of a long alleyway so that still leaves us cornered. The old guy, his hands full of Mags, jerks his head. His goons lumber towards us. They look like they're going to enjoy taking us apart.

It's the night watch on this deck so the lights are dimmed, but the banging and shouting hasn't gone unnoticed. People stick their heads out of shack windows to see what's going on. Human nature, I guess. There can't be many places where folk don't like watching other folk get hurt.

Nobody runs to help us though. Course not.

I'm dropping into the fighting crouch I was taught when Sky elbows me. 'Don't!' she hisses out of the side of her mouth. 'Make out you're scared.'

'Shouldn't be too hard,' I hiss back.

But I hear what she's saying and straighten up. We start backing away. Not that there's far for us to go before we're up against the life-support unit.

'Whatever that little shithead kid told you, she's lying,' Sky calls out to the advancing men, faking a real whiny voice. 'We never stole nothing.'

'You've got the wrong kids,' I protest.

One big guy does that dumb head-tilting thing, popping the muscles in the wedge of meat that's his neck.

'Funny how they all say that,' he rumbles to his mate.

They're on us now. The guy with the iron bar lashes it at a pipe. The massive *clang* makes both of us jump; no need to fake that. My heart skips loads of beats.

'Search 'em first,' their boss shouts. 'And I want a good look at them before you rip their thieving faces off.'

The big guys swap thwarted looks. One orders us to turn around and lean against the wall.

'And don't try nothing!'

I'm not sure about this, but Sky does as she's told. My hesitation costs me a prod in the guts from the guy with the iron bar, which doubles me up. Next thing, I'm slammed face first into the bulkhead. The guy holds me by the scruff of the neck while he pats me down. Careless. But he's a big man and I'm just some scared kid. I moan and sag into the wall, making out I'm hurt worse than I am.

From a metre away, Sky narrows her eyes at me. Which, I guess, means get ready.

'This one's carrying,' my searcher calls out.

He's found my blade and waves it at his mate. This is what I've been waiting for. I swing an elbow savagely back, aiming for where I reckon his ugly face must be. It connects and I hear a satisfying crunching sound, bone or gristle. The guy grunts. His grip relaxes. I treat him to a second and third shot, until he lets go. I spin round to see him clutching his nose, blood spurting through his fingers.

'Kyle, watch out!' Sky yells.

I leap back as the second bruiser lunges at me with his killstick. Even my nublood healing won't save me if he tags me with that. He curses and slashes at me again. But all those muscles are more for show than speed. I dodge easily, and even manage to grab my blade off the deck.

I don't need it though.

Sky launches herself at the guy from behind, slugging him on the back of his head with the weighty hilt of her hunting knife. His killstick clatters to the deck. Back arched, clearly stunned, he totters towards me like a hopeless drunk.

I take the gift, double him up with a straight kick to the belly, and drop him with a vicious spin kick.

But now I screw up, admiring my handiwork when I should be finishing the first guy. He quits clutching his face and very nearly takes my head off with his iron bar. I only save myself by throwing my hands up and blocking. The bar catches my right forearm a glancing blow. Something gives. Pain rages all the way up to my shoulder, pulling a loud grunt out of me. I drop my knife and scramble away before he can finish me.

'Here!' Sky throws me the fallen guy's killstick.

I catch it left-handed as, with blood streaming down his face, the guy lunges at me again. I don't mean to block with the stick; that's just what happens. Sparks fly. So too does the iron bar, which leaps out of his hand. He cries out, convulses a few times and tumbles to the deck.

Fine by me. Both thugs stay where they've fallen.

'Nice work,' Sky says.

We face the older boss guy, who's still holding on to Mags. His gobsmacked look would be funny any other day.

Sky spits. 'You need to get yourself some bigger goons.'

'Let go of the girl,' I snarl at him.

My hurt right arm is killing me. I want payback.

Side by side, we start walking towards him. But now he lets go of the arm he's been holding behind Mags's back and grabs her round the throat.

'Any closer and she's dead!' he yells.

We stop. Mags tries to pull free, but he's too strong.

'Hurt her, and I'll make sure you'll die screaming,' Sky says, showing the man her blade.

'Will you now?' the man sneers.

He starts backing away, dragging Mags along after him. Next thing, the girl hooks her foot round his ankle and trips him. Over he goes, flat on his back. Even before he hits the deck she's flailing and scratching and sinking her teeth into his arm. I dart forward to help, but by the time I get there she's fought her way clear.

The old thug tries to get up. I kick him back down.

'Hey, go easy,' he howls, shielding his face and trying to slide himself away from me along the deck. 'We were only doing our job. If you want to kick the crap out of someone, it was the doc who sent us after you.'

Sky limps up to stand alongside me, blade in hand.

'Did the doc beat this little girl until she told you where to find us? Or was it you, you bastard?'

'What do *you* care? She's nothing but gutter-deck trash.'

Dumb. Sky snarls something and lunges at him with her knife. I only just manage to grab her, using my bad arm. Pain spikes up it, so jagged and fierce it makes my eyes water, but before she can gut him I haul her back.

'No! The guy's scum, but the last thing we need is ArkSec hunting us for killing him.'

She shrugs me off angrily, hurting me even worse.

'We can't just let him walk away!'

'Too right!' Mags sobs. 'Beat him like he beat me.'

Tempting. But fighting him is one thing and beating him to a pulp as he grovels there another. Then again, we don't want this guy coming after us a second time.

I tell Mags to fetch me the iron bar.

'You got it.' She darts off.

The old guy curses and tries to struggle up. I plant my boot in his chest and shove him back down.

'D'you want me to do this?' Sky says, grim-faced.

I power off the killstick and tuck it into my belt. 'Nah, you'd kill him. Don't let Mags watch.'

She's back with the bar already. 'I want to.'

'Well, you can't.' I snatch it off her.

Sky grabs Mags, turns her round and pulls her close.

Feeling sick, I lean over the old man and snarl at him that if I ever see his ugly face again I'll kill him. He quits scrabbling away on his arse and glowers up at me.

'You ain't got what it takes,' he sneers.

'Oh yeah?' The iron bar is cold in my hand as I raise it.

Suddenly his tough-guy sneer disappears and he starts cringing and shrinking away from me.

'All right, all right, maybe you do.' He scowls up at me and licks his thin old lips. 'You're angry. I don't blame you. But don't go smashing my head in just yet. That little girl says you're new here on the Ark, looking for work and not finding it. Put the bar down and I can help you out.'

I hesitate, long enough to give him hope.

'It's rough at the bottom,' he rasps. 'I've been there and done that. But a tough kid like you, real handy in a fight, you could earn serious creds. If you let me show you how.'

'I can guess,' I say. 'Working for you. Collecting debts. Beating the crap out of little girls. I don't think so.'

I heft the bar again, taking aim at his legs.

But Sky steps between us. 'Wait. Let's hear him out.'

After nerving myself to break this guy's legs in cold blood, I'm less than impressed.

'Why bother? He'll say anything to save himself.'

The man props himself up on his elbows. 'I'm serious. There are places here where bare-knuckle cage fights are staged. No holds barred. Anything goes. Loads of creds change hands on who'll win. A lightly built kid like you, the odds you'd get would be crazy. I saw what you did to those losers over there. You can handle yourself, and –'

Sky grimaces. 'These fights can't be so hard to find.'

He shows her his stained teeth.

'Try it then. They're illegal. Only those in the know hear about them. You two would never find them. Even if you did, it's a fistful of creds to buy your way in, and you'd need more creds to place your wagers. Creds you ain't got. But I can sort all that. Take you to the best places, even teach your ninja boyfriend here a few ring tricks to stack the odds in his favour.'

He dabs at his mouth with the back of his hand, mopping blood away from where I kicked him.

'Look at it another way,' he continues. 'You can knock lumps out of me, but that won't stop the doc paying someone else to come after you, will it? He's mean like that. Hates being crossed. And who knows if you guys will get so lucky next time?'

'We didn't get *lucky*,' Sky says.

He winces. 'True. But d'you want to be looking over your shoulder the whole time? Doesn't have to be that way. Work with me and I'll keep the doc off your back.'

Work with me. This guy's starting to sound like Murdo, stringing us along with one of his deals.

'And you'd do that . . . why?' Sky says, and coughs.

He hawks and spits blood, his watery old gaze fixed on me the whole time. 'For a start, I don't heal so fast at my age. And then I'll be betting on you too. Win a few fights at long odds and we'll both make small fortunes. So are you going to use that iron bar on me, or can I get back up?'

Sky glances at me. 'What d'you think?'

'He's lying,' I say, but I'm less sure than I was at first. When he talks I hear his greed speak as loudly as his fear.

'Don't take my word for it – ask your little friend,' the man says. 'I'm not making these fights up.'

We look at Mags. She nods.

Only now do I see how cruelly the girl's been beaten. I tighten my grip on the bar. If ever anyone deserved a battering in cold blood, this bully at my feet does.

'So how would it work?' Sky asks him.

With a relieved grunt, the man struggles back to his feet.

'My name's Zarco,' he says, dusting himself off. 'There's a deck six bar, the Hole in the Wall. Ask for me there tomorrow night at the start of red watch. The girl can find it.'

Mags scowls but nods again.

He goes to reach inside his jacket, but I heft the bar and he hesitates. 'Relax! You guys look like you could use a bite to eat. Here are the creds the doc paid me. Think of it as a down payment. You can pay me back out of your winnings.' More slowly and carefully now, he fishes out one of those e-cred storage devices and tosses it at me.

I catch it with my hurt arm and can't help wincing.

He frowns. 'How hurt *are* you?'

'It's nothing,' I say, without thinking.

'Maybe we should make it two days from now?'

'That'd be better,' Sky says for me.

The device must sense the heat of my hand. It lights up and shows me ten creds is the going rate on the Ark for a beating, or a killing. Disappointed, I pocket it.

Zarco nods, like that means something. 'Spend it on food not drink. You don't want to fight with a sore head.'

He turns to walk away.

I pull away from Sky. 'Zarco!'

He looks back, a bit mocking. 'What?'

And I whack him across the face, knocking him down again. He's lucky I do it weak-handed. Luckier still that I only just catch him with the end of the bar. As it is, he's a long time getting up. Clutching at the side of his face, which is torn and already swelling up, he glares at me.

'What was *that* for?' he mumbles, spilling blood.

'A down payment,' I say, my voice shaking like the rest of me. 'Lay a hand on Mags again, you get the rest.'

Sky laughs, low and mean. Mags claps.

Hate burns in the man's eyes, but all he does is nod.

14
KYLE AS RINGER

'Hey, Zarco, here's your down payment!'

For what feels like it has to be the thousandth time, Mags swings an imaginary iron bar at an imaginary head.

'Will you *quit* that?' Sky snaps.

'Yeah, give it a rest,' I say. There's only so many times I can take being reminded of what I did.

'Only messing,' Mags says, and sticks her tongue out.

After Sky set and splinted my broken forearm – which wasn't a whole lot of fun – we treated the worst of the girl's scrapes and bruises. She's looking better, although that could be all the muck we scraped off her. She's lost three of her teeth. I tell her they were only her baby ones, and will grow back soon enough. It might even be the truth.

'What you looking at me like that for?' she says.

'I wasn't looking *at* you,' I say. 'I was looking *through* you. Doing a bit of thinking, that's all.'

'What about?'

'Wondering what these fights will be like.'

A lie. Truth is she's caught me feeling sorry for her being only pureblood human, like Sky. She'd heal much quicker and be sure of growing her teeth back if she had nublood pumping in her veins. Now we're no longer on Wrath, maybe being a nublood isn't such a curse after all.

After splitting the difference and paying her five creds for finding Sky, Mags is letting the two of us stay in what she calls her 'den'. Compared to that rat hole we'd been living in, this is a huge step up. A long-forgotten storage room, Mags says when she first stumbled across the place it reeked and was wall-to-wall with clinging spiderwebs. Well, it still stinks a bit, but it's cosy enough. With all the junk the girl's scavved, there's just about room for the three of us.

Best of all, it's got a back way out through a ventilation shaft, so we needn't fear being trapped again.

'Is anybody hungry?' Sky asks.

Mags looks round. 'Always. I could run and get you some food if I had a cred.'

'What happened to the creds we gave you?'

'Spent 'em,' she says, looking sly.

Sky turns to me. Left-handed and awkward, I fish out Zarco's e-cred thing. Mags holds hers out. I tap twice, transferring two creds. 'Get yourself something too.'

Her eyes go shiny. 'Kyle, you ain't such a loser after all.'

I roll my eyes at Sky. 'You hear that?'

'You're buying her food, she'd say anything,' Sky jeers from where she's sitting on a ratty old blanket.

'Won't be long,' Mags says, and clears off outside.

Sky opens her mouth, but snaps it shut again.

'What?' I say, curious. Her face has gone all serious too.

She looks at me sideways. 'If I hadn't stopped you, you'd have hurt that Zarco guy, wouldn't you?'

'What does it matter now?' I say uneasily.

'Just want to know, that's all.'

I take a breath, let it out slow. 'I guess I would have.'

'Thought so,' she says, and sighs.

'It's nothing *you* wouldn't have done.'

'No. But that's me. There was a time you'd never do that, not in cold blood anyway.'

'Yeah, well, maybe I've changed.'

Sky stretches her bad leg out. 'That'd be a shame.'

'Would it?' I say.

But she just grimaces and doesn't answer.

Gingerly, I flex my right hand. My forearm still aches, but a lot less. I run my other hand along the broken bone and it feels pretty straight. That's a relief. My nublood heals me fast, but it can't push bones back in place. If we hadn't set the bone before it healed, we'd have had to break it again to straighten it. And I can do without that.

'Want some of my meds?' Sky asks.

'No thanks. You need them more than I do.'

'Give me a break. You can buy me some more later, with our winnings from the fights.'

I look at her. 'Who says I'll win?'

As I'm saying this, Mags slides back inside.

'You'll win. They won't know what hit 'em,' she says.

Her hands are full of bulging bags, and the smells coming from them fill my mouth with drool. All I can think about now is eating. But after we're done scoffing the food, she looks at me all doubtful.

'Sure you want to do these cage fights?' she says.

'Don't worry,' Sky says. 'Kyle can take care of himself.'

Mags winces. 'That's what my dad told my mum. His last fight wasn't supposed to be to the death. But the other guy stomped him so bad he never woke up.'

'Some fights are to the *death*?' I say, horrified.

'Sure. Not all of them.'

'Where's your mother now?' Sky asks.

'Don't know, don't care. Off selling herself to score bliss. I don't have nothing to do with her. She's no good.'

I squirm hearing this. Not Sky though, she just nods like, yeah, life can be crap like that.

'Do these death fights earn bigger money?' she asks.

Mags shrugs. 'Loads more, I think.'

'Forget it,' I snap. 'I'll fight for creds, but I won't kill.'

Sky scowls. 'I was only asking. Maybe we'll get lucky and win big enough on regular fights to buy ourselves passage to Enshi Four, before . . . it's too late.'

Yeah, thanks. Like I'd forgotten you're dying.

'What's in Enshi Four?' Mags pipes up.

'We're looking for her sister, Tarn,' I say. 'Could be she's there. It's a good place to start looking anyway.'

Mags frowns. 'So you two ain't brother and sister then?'

Hard to say who pulls the bigger face, me or Sky.

'Why'd you think that?' I splutter.

'You argue the whole time.'

I'm fed up, but still I can't help laughing at this.

The girl lies back on her bed of blankets stuffed with lumps of scavved insulation, and fires a sigh up towards the ceiling of the compartment. 'I shouldn't have led Zarco to you,' she says, in a smaller voice. 'That was bad.'

Sky shakes her head. 'You did what you had to do, to survive. We understand, don't we, Kyle?'

'We do,' I say through my teeth.

Because I hear what Sky is *really* saying. If a fight to the death is what it takes to get us off this Ark and chasing after Tarn, she reckons that's a risk well worth taking.

Mags, her stomach full for once, closes her eyes and soon falls asleep. Sky starts coughing. To avoid waking the girl she swallows another half-dose of her meds.

'I've an idea,' she slurs as it takes effect. 'You'll hate it.'

'Will it get me killed?' I jeer.

She scowls. 'You're not the only one who can fight.'

'No fraggin' way!'

'Why not? I'd get better odds than you would.'

Fortunately, before we can get stuck into a full-on blazing row, Mags wakes up with a violent start.

'Bad dream?' I ask her.

The girl gives her belly a going-over with her hands, before sitting up and sighing with obvious relief.

'It was gross. I dreamt I ate so much that I burst!'

Deck six. As high as I've been on the Ark, and I like what I see. The outer ring is still slum, but as we head inboard towards the core we pass better buildings, built to last. The Hole in the Wall lives up to its name though. It looks like a right dive.

The thug working the door demands we push our hoods back and show him our faces. One look at Mags and he plants a meaty hand in her face and shoves her away.

'Come back in a few years, kid.'

We leave her outside, red-faced and cross.

The bar is dimly lit and so full of smoke and rough-looking customers it takes me a while to spot Zarco at a table. He turns and glances at us, but that's all. No waving us over to join him, or anything like that.

'What'll you have?' a grey-faced barkeep asks.

'Two beers,' Sky says, and shoves me towards the bar.

Zarco still gives no sign of knowing us, but as I'm paying for our drinks, he gets up from the table he's sitting at and slips out through a door at the back. I go to follow him, but Sky holds me back. 'In a bit. Let's not be too obvious.'

Suits me. The beer's not the worst I've tasted. I flex my right hand again, making and unmaking my fist.

'How's the arm?' Sky asks.

'Getting there.' Where the break was it's still itchy, but I don't have any pain. I reckon I could punch with it.

We give it five minutes.

Another bruiser minds the door at the back and watches us as we head over. My heart's already pounding and now it starts to race, but all he does is nod and push the door open. As we step through, he swings it shut behind us.

'You took your time,' Zarco growls.

He sucks deeply at a black tube and blows a cloud of evil-smelling yellow smoke our way. Through this I see his face is still all livid and swollen where I clipped him with the iron bar, but the torn flesh has been stapled back together. I see too that he's not alone in the small room.

A hunched old man sitting on a stool in the corner grins at us. 'This kid beat the shit out of *three* of you?'

He sounds like he needs a drink, or new vocal cords.

'Kid's tougher than he looks,' Zarco says, wincing and reaching up to feel his cheekbone.

The old guy cackles. 'He'll need to be.'

'Can we get on with this?' Sky says, dry as you like.

More sickly smoke curls out of Zarco's mouth and nose. He studies me so intently I start to worry. Have we walked into a trap? That door is the only way in or out.

But now he jerks his head at the old guy on the stool.

'Norton here isn't much to look at, but he was a top fighter. He'll tell you everything you need to know.'

Old guy struggles up off his stool.

'The Ripper, that was me,' he says. 'Ninety-three straight fights I won, and a dozen or so rigged ones after that.'

Once upon a time he'll have been a big, solidly built guy, but he's a wreck now, hunched over, limping worse than Sky. His battered old face is a mess of lumps and scars. One eye's gone. Nose is spread across his face. Ears swollen and mutilated.

I swallow, wondering what I've let myself in for.

The guy shuffles closer and peers up at me out of his one good eye. 'Zarco says your arm's hurt.'

'He's fine,' Sky says. 'We're wasting time. Line us up with a fight and we'll take care of the rest.'

But Zarco shakes his head. 'Not so fast. Hear Norton out.

To make money at this game and walk away with it, you have to win the right way.'

'Won't do to win too early, or too easy,' Norton says.

Some animal must have died in this guy's mouth from the state of his breath. It's so foul I reckon he could still win fights by blowing on his opponents.

I grimace. 'So how *should* I win?'

'We'll get to that. But first you got to not lose.'

He glances down at his right hand, balled in a fist. I make the mistake of looking at it too. Next thing, he launches it at me in a vicious uppercut. Only by instinct, luck and a big shot of nublood do I get out the way.

'What the *frag*?' I make fists of my own.

Sky's hand slides inside her jacket, going for her blade.

No need. The old fighter is done trying to slug me. He holds his hands up, palms out. 'Relax, son. Just seeing what you got. Zarco said you was fast, but I had to see for myself. Better you take a shot from a sad old has-been like me than climb into a fight cage and get yourself killed.'

My heart is still doing its level best to hammer its way out through my ribs, but I guess the guy has a point.

Unclenching my fists and my stomach, I straighten up.

Sky looks unimpressed. 'We done fooling around?'

Zarco grins. 'Get on with it, Norton.'

The old fighter glances at him and then turns back to me. 'So you're fast and can handle yourself in a fight. That's all well and good, but I'm here to teach you how to be a ringer. Hiding your skills. Taking hits. Looking like you're losing so the odds go against you. Making your win look like some kind of fluke.' He wags a swollen-knuckled finger at me. 'Not all, but a lot of the folk who go to these cage fights are low-deck scum, rough and nasty and mean as hell. They hate to be cheated. If they sniff a rat they'll lynch you.'

'And anyone betting on you,' Zarco adds.

I'm not sure I follow all of what Norton says, and my uncertainty must show on my face.

He shows me his last tooth. 'Listen to me and you'll be fine.'

For the next hour or so the man teaches me the basics of being a 'ringer'. Some is play-acting, which is easy enough. The hardest bit is learning how to roll punches and kicks, getting mostly out of the way, but not all the way. Do it right and it should look like you took the full hit. To demonstrate this he has Sky throwing punches at him.

He's good. Loads of times I'd swear she's caught him.

After that he shows me ways to take an opponent out without the crowd seeing. Eye gouges. Sneaky nerve pinches to leave a guy tottering and ready to be hit. Nastier stuff that I'm not sure I've the stomach for. Lastly he teaches me the signal. When Zarco figures I've done enough losing and the odds of me winning are long enough, he'll put our bets on and signal. Only then do I win the fight for us.

'Remember, the punters mustn't feel like they've been had. If you fight three rounds like a jerk, but then suddenly wake up and take your opponent apart –'

'Yeah, yeah,' Sky says, sounding bored. 'We got it.'

15
IN THE CAGE

Zarco hands me three little squishy dark red blobs that look like sweets and a small phial of green liquid. 'Take the green stuff now so it has time to work.'

I peer at it suspiciously. 'What is it?'

'Alco-blocker. Drink that and you can pour as much booze into yourself as you like and not get wasted.'

I down it and gag. It's like drinking bleach.

'What are those red things for?' Sky asks Zarco.

'Pop one or two in your mouth before you climb into the cage, but don't let anyone see. Bite it when you get hit and you'll be spitting blood all over the place. The crowd'll love that, and it'll send the odds our way.'

I pocket them, hoping they taste less foul.

Zarco's starting me out at a smaller cage fight in an abandoned warehouse down on deck zero, where he says my opponent won't be too tough. We're hiding round the corner from a side door minded by sharp-eyed toughs. A stream of shifty-looking people are being let in.

'Remember, watch a few fights first,' he says. 'And no matter what happens, you don't know me. Okay?'

Sky scowls at him. 'You do your job, we'll do ours.'

Zarco grunts and heads round the corner to join the line. We watch and wait until he's admitted before we slide on over ourselves. I've seen Murdo stumbling-drunk, so I fake a bit of that. And get a pleasant surprise. Sky pulls my arm around her and leans in so we weave across together. Nobody gives us so much as a second glance. A minute later and ten creds lighter we're waved inside.

'Behind the crates at the back,' door guy mutters.

He must think we're deaf or stupid. From behind a wall of stacked crates at the far end of the warehouse come roars and yells. It's like I'm back at the Peace Fair where this all began, as the mob bays and screams for twist blood.

'What's wrong?' Sky whispers, as I slow down.

'Nothing.' I take a breath and force myself to keep going.

Behind the crate wall is an arena, crude terraces built from yet more stacked crates. In the middle is the hexagonal fight cage, six walls made from sections of chain-link fencing. The noise is overpowering. So too is the smell of sweat, smoke and stale beer. If this is a smaller gig I'd hate to see a big one. Several hundred people must be crammed in here. The crate terraces heave with standing watchers. At deck level a seething mass of bodies surround the cage, all pushing and shoving and screaming instructions at the bare-chested fighters in the cage, as if they can hear them.

The two fighters circle each other warily, trading occasional punches and kicks. The smaller guy's bleeding from a badly cut eye. I don't fancy his chances.

I spot Zarco on the bottom terrace to our right. He's screaming at the fighters like all the rest, spittle flying. If he sees us he doesn't let on.

Sky nudges me and points out a woman standing on a box by a tall white pole. Her back's to the cage and she's making weird hand gestures. People thrust creds at her. She thrusts slips of paper back at them. Around the cage other women are doing the same brisk business. Taking bets, I reckon. And there's a bar set up in a gap on the far side of the cage. Kids no older than Mags squirm their way through the crowd, delivering drinks.

'Somebody's raking the creds in,' I yell to Sky.

'Somebody always does,' she yells back. 'And quit staring. You're drunk, remember?'

She's right. I let out a few feeble shouts at the fighters.

The fight doesn't last too much longer. The bigger guy wrestles his smaller opponent to the deck, and pounds him senseless with punches and elbows to the head. Long after the guy's face is meat, he keeps hitting.

The crowd love it, cheering and urging him on.

Finally, to boos and jeers, three bulky guys lumber inside the cage through a gate in one of the walls and haul the winner off him. A tall man in a fancy black outfit follows them inside. Most of the boos become cheers as he hoists one of the winner's bleeding fists up and proclaims him the victor. Cursing losers tear up and toss betting slips. Laughing winners shove their way towards the women at the white betting poles to collect. More drinks are loudly called for.

A runt kid tugs my sleeve. 'Whatchawan?'

He's off before I'm done saying two beers, back soon after

clutching foaming beakers. My eyes are already watering from the smoke, now they water even harder when the kid names a price of three creds each! Zarco's only lent us an even thirty, to be paid back from my winnings.

'Ouch. We'd best win big!' Sky shouts in my ear.

The next fight starts. I join in the yelling and screaming. Sky fakes being too drunk to shout and waves her beer around. Four fights and two strong beers later she doesn't have to pretend. The blocker's working for me, but she hasn't taken any. I helped drink her first beer, but she won't let me touch the second. I have to stop her asking for a third, reminding her we need the creds to bet with.

She belches loudly. 'Oh yeah. How about this guy then? Reckon you can take him?'

The winner of the last fight is still in the cage, strutting around and beating his heavily tattooed chest.

I chew my lip. 'Don't know. He looks –'

Mean, I was going to say. But Sky's already weaving her way towards the cage.

'You got *so-o-o* lucky!' she yells at the fighter.

I lunge and try to pull her back. But she won't be pulled, and now people start pointing and laughing.

The fighter quits posing and growls. 'Shut up, bitch!'

'Shut up, yourself!' Sky hurls the last of her beer at him. The wire stops the beaker, but the dregs get him right in his ugly face. 'Beating your big-man chest like you're so tough. But you ain't tough. My boyfriend here could take you easy.'

Swinging her right arm around like it's only loosely connected to her shoulder, she points at me.

About all I can do is glare at her.

Sky, playing the drunk girlfriend to perfection, stumbles back to hang off me. 'You can take him, can't you?'

Nobody cares what I think. Everybody's hooting and jeering. Eager hands bundle us cage-ward.

'Uh, Sky?' I say.

But then I'm face to face with the guy in black.

'You sure about this, kid?' he rumbles.

Sky pinches me, hard. I manage a nod. And then I remember to throw in some swaying on my feet. Not so it looks like I'll walk into the first punch thrown; hopefully just enough to convince him I'm not stone-cold sober.

'Like my girl said, he ain't so tough.'

He frowns. 'Folks pay to see a fight not a slaughter.'

'I'll go easy on him then,' I say, before I can stop myself.

This gets a load of laughs, and the crowd seems happy enough with slaughter. *Give him a chance*, they yell. *Let the fool kid have a crack at him!*

The guy shrugs. 'Your neck. How old are you?'

'Almost nineteen,' I lie, pulling my boots off followed by my over-jacket and my shirt.

He yanks the cage door open. 'Sure y'are. Well, you've been watching so you know the rules. One bell starts the fight, two bells stop it. Rounds are three minutes. One-minute breaks to get patched up. Your girlfriend can do that for you. No killing, but otherwise anything goes. The fight's over when one of you can't get up, or taps out.'

'You'll be fine.' Sky leans in and gives me a beery kiss.

The crowd cheers.

I'm thrust inside the cage.

The door slams closed behind me.

My bruiser opponent swaggers towards me, cracking his big knuckles and looking at me all mocking.

'Boy's got some ink,' he calls out. 'Must be tough!'

The crowd roars with laughter. He's jeering at the small blue Reaper tattoo under my left collarbone. And I guess it must look feeble compared to the intricate patterns covering his chest and right arm, done to show off his muscles.

'Tough enough,' I say through my teeth.

'You think?' he says, lip curled.

A bell clangs and the fight is on. The guy grins, bellows and makes a lunge to scare me. I leap back, forgetting the cage wall is right behind me, and clatter it hard.

Laughing nastily, he takes up a fighting stance. 'Nowhere to run to in the cage,' he says, and shuffles forward.

I say nothing, too busy concentrating. And wondering what the fraggin' hell I'm doing here.

Thanks to Norton, I know not to drop into a proper fighting crouch. Instead I copy this guy's stance, head down, fists up. He throws a big flashy jab. I block it and slip away sideways before he can trap me against the cage wall.

Worried I was maybe too slick, I fake a little stumble.

He grunts, chases me down and throws a flurry of punches this time. I duck and dodge, making him miss.

Tap him in the ribs too, because . . . why not?

And hear loud roars of approval from the crowd.

Up until now I reckon the guy's been showing off. Now he spits curses and gets serious. His next attack is vicious and tougher to defend. I cover up and try to ride the punches that get through like Hayden showed me. This goes okay, until it doesn't and he catches me high on the side of my head.

Next thing I know, I'm kissing the deck.

The crowd lets out a big *Oooof!*, like they felt it too.

I go to push myself up. No chance. He kicks me in the ribs so hard it flips me on to my back. And I'm so stunned and winded he could finish me easy.

But he doesn't . . .

Nah. The big gom's so sure of himself he stands over me, bellowing at the crowd like a beast. And the crowd? They roar back their appreciation.

Well, frag that. I'm *not* done for. Not yet.

I kick him in the leg to get his attention. And when he turns to glower down at me, I kick him in the balls. He bellows again, obviously furious and in pain.

Figuring I've bought myself some time, I go to scramble up. No such luck. Either the guy's wearing protection down there or else he's tougher than I'd bargained for.

I'm hardly up when he knocks me back down again. The rest of the round is kicks and punches and pain. Mostly pain. I cover up best I can, and squirm and wriggle away. But he's on top of me, his weight pinning me down as he pounds the hell out of me. I have to use my full strength to stop him pulling my hands away from my face. The bell must save me. I don't hear it, but the punching and elbowing stop. And now I'm over by the wire. Sky's in the cage, shoving a dripping-wet sponge at my raw face.

'Get off,' I mumble, pushing it away.

'What are you *do-ing*?' she hisses.

My left eye is swollen closed, so I can only glare at her out of my right eye. 'Losing. That's the big idea, isn't it?'

'Yeah, but you're only supposed to *pretend*.'

'I'm doing my best.'

Sky glances over her shoulder, but it's so noisy we could shout and nobody would hear. 'Can you turn it around?'

'Don't know,' I say miserably.

And now she's bundled out of the cage.

The bell clangs for round two. It's a brutal sound.

I could stay on my stool and it's over. But I can't. The pig-headed Barrenlander inside me hates being beaten, and anyway I'm raging angry now. At Sky for caring more about creds than me, at Zarco for talking me into this madness, and at myself for being dumb enough to agree.

Before I know it I've hauled myself to my feet.

The watching punters fall almost silent for a moment, as if surprised. Only when my opponent lumbers towards me does the hooting and baying start up again. Thing is though, big and strong as my opponent is, he's been through one fight already and it's costing him. He's slower on his feet now, throws fewer punches and there's less snap and spite in them when he does. I stay out of harm's way. Even get a shot of my own in, which shuts the crowd up. But none of this will shift the odds further against me winning. Cursing Sky and Zarco, I hold my breath and let one of the guy's punches catch me, or seem to. Rolling them is easier now he's tiring. I reel away, as if stunned.

I can do this ringer thing, I reckon.

But two rolled punches later, he gets lucky and catches me. Down I go again, no faking. And now he's back on top of me, dishing out more ground and pound. I'm covered in my blood when the bell saves me again. He gets a warning for hitting after the round was over. I get to keep the pain.

I'm crawling on my hands and knees to the cage wall, when Sky limps over to help me.

'Great fraggin' idea this was,' I mumble.

She leans me back against the mesh and splashes water on my face, like some cold wet will make everything okay.

'Do we bet or not?' she hisses.

Her voice sounds odd. Disappointed?

Bitterness swells inside me. 'That's your call.'

The bell sounds for a third round. I hear groans from the crowd as I struggle back to my feet. I reel to the centre of the cage and swing a tired punch. My opponent blocks it easily enough, but he's not leaping about the cage either, and sweating and blowing hard too. And now a few toughs in the crowd start scoffing at his failure to put me down.

Clearly stung, the guy curses and comes after me.

I duck one haymaker, throw myself at him and hold on for dear life. This at least stops him swinging at me. But the guy knows how to fight in a clinch. He goes low, drives short rasping punches into my ribs and kidneys.

Hurts me too, but not as badly as he might think.

And it's now or never. I cry out and fake my legs buckling, sagging into him so he's all that's holding me up. When I hear his satisfied grunt, I know he's bought it. What he should do is take me down to the deck again and pound me. But no, his type wants the showy finish. He grabs my hair, drags me to each of the six cage walls in turn to smash me against the wire mesh.

Each time the crowd that side howls with delight. And it's no fun, but it hurts less than punches and kicks. And I get to see Sky screaming for the fight to be ended, anguish all over her face.

That lifts me. Suddenly I can handle the pain.

As we get to the last panel, I let both my legs collapse under me, hanging my full weight off him. He spits curses, tries to drag me back up. I don't let him, hooking my legs round his ankles and throwing myself sideways.

Done right, I'd shatter his ankle.

I don't manage that. There's no fearful crack of bone breaking. But I *do* hurt the guy. He lets go and falls real awkwardly. I roll away and clamber back to my feet.

Stand there over him, swaying and panting.

He goes to struggle up, bellows with pain and clutches his ankle. Stays down. Guess that means I'm the winner.

Don't know. Don't care.

Teeth bared, I set about hurting him like he's hurt me.

16
ROCK AND A HARD PLACE

I wake with a start. A blurry Mags is staring down at me, so near that her breath tickles my face.

'Don't do that!' I moan, flapping at her.

She giggles and ducks back out of the way. 'I'm keeping a close eye on you, like Sky told me to.'

'That's *too* close,' I say, sitting up. 'How'd you get in?'

'Duh. Sky told me the door code.'

I groan, unimpressed. A glance around the room shows me it's just the two of us in here. 'Where is she?'

'Off looking for that Zed bloke again.'

Why did I even bother asking? Course she is. And I'm not going to sigh about it, not in front of Mags anyway.

'You all healed yet?' she asks.

'Almost,' I say, yawning and giving myself a scratch.

It's three days since my last fight. After that first one I won, I lost the next two. Got cocky, Sky reckons. Walked into a sucker punch early in the first round of my second fight, but I was plain unlucky in the third. Neither cost us, as both times I went down before she'd bet. Anyway, since then I've won three in a row, all with solid odds. I'm lots better at slipping punches now, so the few lumps and bumps I picked up in my last fight are gone already. Zarco doesn't need to know that though. So he doesn't get suspicious we've told him I need seven laying up and healing days between fights. Sky, in a rush to get after Tarn, wanted me to say five. Frag that. She doesn't take the punches and the pain.

The sigh I thought I'd stopped gets away from me.

That's how Sky is, I guess. Determined. Still, it'd be nice to wake up and find her lying beside me. But these days we hardly see each other, she's off out so much.

'You're mad you are, sleeping on the floor,' Mags says.

'What's it to you?' I say grumpily.

The kid's curled up on the big bed, watching me. How people sleep on those things, I don't know. I find the mattress thing way too soft. When Sky's not here I pull the blankets off and bunk down on the decking. Might give the bed another go tonight though. Hell, I'm paying enough for the thing and this deck-seven room around it.

Sky says it's wasting creds. Maybe so, but I earned them the hard way so I figure I'll damn well spend some.

I stick a finger in my mouth and root around. Two of my back teeth got knocked out in that last fight. Both have grown back and they feel like new.

'How come you heal so quick, Kyle?' Mags asks.

'Oh, not *that* again.'

'You can tell me. I won't tell nobody.'

'I told you already. I wasn't hurt as bad as it looked.'

Mags shakes her head, and jumps down off the bed. 'Maybe not the last fight, but you were the fight before. And the fight two before that. I got eyes, ain't I? Sky says it's because you grew up on a high-grav world, but that's crap. I've seen folk off heavy worlds. You'd be all stocky and slow-moving.' She stamps her foot. 'Look, just tell me!'

I hesitate. 'Okay, okay. I got bit, by a bug.'

'A . . . *bug?*' she says, staring, her face full of doubt.

'Yeah. A, uh, healer bug. Nasty. Orange. As big as your fist. Sting that feels like you've been shot. Most people who get stung die; only a lucky few survive.'

'And you got lucky?'

'I'm here, aren't I? Yeah, the bug's venom sticks around in your blood. Somehow it helps me heal quick.'

'You're not making this up?'

'No, no. Ask Sky when she gets back. She'll tell you.'

'Can you do other bug stuff, like fly?'

'I wish. Now clear off, I want to take a shower.'

'So take one, I won't look. Sky said that you'd feed me.'

'Oh, she did, did she?'

'What've you got? I ain't fussy.'

'There might be leftovers lying about.'

'Where?' The girl skips to the corner of the room that's our kitchen and eating area and starts poking around.

I leave her to it, stumble behind the screen to the tiny washroom, pull my clothes off and step on to the cleansing tray. The mist hits me. How it works I don't know, but no scrubbing or scraping is needed. It does all that for me in a few seconds. Dries me too, with a blast of warm air. When I step off I'm so clean it hurts. Mags says rich folk wash like this several times a day, but that would do my head in. Once every few days is fine. Too clean isn't natural.

I'm pulling my ratty old clothes back on when that mirror catches me again. I'm not used to them, so I always think it's my twin brother standing there gawping at me. But of course Colm's back on Wrath, fighting to turn the No-Zone into a rebel safe haven.

That's if the Slayers haven't caught up with him . . .

I shut the grim thought out – as if not thinking it can protect him. But it won't be shut out. A dark worm of worry and guilt, it burrows back into my head. Feeling gloomy I go to check on Mags. But as I step around the screen there's a knock on the door. Loud and impatient.

I glare at Mags. 'Have you told anyone we're here?'

'Nuh-uh. I swear I haven't.'

Whoever's there, they knock again.

One day it'd be nice to hear that sound and not have my heart climb into my throat. I grab my jacket and hunt for my knife.

'Who is it?' I call out, careful to stand to one side. Energy weapons are banned on the Ark, but so are cage fights.

'Zarco. Gonna let me in, or what?'

I slap the button. The door slides open and he slips inside.

'How'd you find us?' I ask as I close it after him.

'It wasn't easy. Had you guys down for some grubby little squat on the gutter decks, not a fancy pad like this.' He looks around, pulling an impressed face. 'Not bad. Deck seven too. Must cost you an arm and a leg.'

'What do you want?'

He smiles, but it doesn't make it anywhere near those mean eyes of his. He looks me up and down.

'You're looking well, Kyle. Ready to go again?'

It hits me that maybe I'm looking more healed than he'd expected. I make a show of limping past him, sling my jacket on the table and sit like I'm stiff and sore.

'It's not seven days yet,' I say.

'Yeah,' Mags says. 'Can't you count, Zarco?'

His sort-of-smile fades. 'Does the brat need to be here?'

I think about insisting she stay just to wind him up. Tempting, but I decide against it.

'Mags, give us a minute, will you?'

Her face goes pinched and cross, but she gets up and stomps to the door. 'Sure. It stinks in here all of a sudden.'

Zarco waits until the door closes behind her.

'Where's your skinny girlfriend?'

'Out.' I don't need reminding. 'And she has a name.'

He lowers himself on to the seat opposite me at the table. 'I saw Sky the other day, you know. Begging in one of the open marketplaces on deck six. I wondered why. You guys haven't gone and blown *all* your winnings, have you?'

Begging? I fight to keep the shock off my face.

'Maybe you saw someone who looks like her?' I say.

Zarco shrugs and pulls out his smoking-tube, but sees me glaring and tucks it away again. He scratches at his greying stubble. 'If you say so. Look, Kyle, our little game has played out well so far, but it can only last so long. Each fight we do now, the bigger the chance of someone having seen you before and calling you out as a ringer.'

'You saying we should quit?' I say, surprised.

'No. I reckon we're still good for one more fight before we lie low for a while. But if we're going to push our luck we should try to squeeze more out of it.'

I say nothing. In my experience, nothing sucks explanations out of people faster than a bit of silence.

He clears his throat. 'So far, we've been pissing about in scummy fight dens on the lower decks. On the best nights we walk away with a few hundred creds. It's good and solid, not to be sniffed at. But we can do better. I watched you at the last fight, Kyle, and you've got talent to burn. We need a fight on a higher deck, for bigger money.'

'So what's stopping us going up a few decks?'

'You make it sound easy. It isn't. To access deck ten and above we'd need permits. High-deckers don't like mixing with gutter-deck lowlifes like us.'

'So can you fix me a fight or not?' I snap, confused.

Zarco leers triumphantly. 'They can't get enough fighters on the higher decks with everyone being so soft up there, so they drop down here and scout around. Someone with high-deck connections was at your last fight. Seems you caught their eye. Anyway, they got in touch with me. For a hundred creds they'll sort us transit permits and entry to an unlicensed fight club on deck sixteen. And fifty creds each is nothing to what we could win up there. We could walk away with thousands.'

I stare at him, but he seems serious. Thousands of creds. That would buy us both passage to Enshi Four, easily.

'Do they know I'm a ringer?'

'Sure. They'll be betting on you too.' He hesitates, and then says: 'Look, it's all fixed up. We're on for tomorrow night. You owe me fifty.'

'Tomorrow night?' I blurt. 'But —'

'I know, I know,' he says, holding his hands up. 'You're still hurting after your last fight. But listen, kid, chances like this don't line up every day. She says the next fight night after this is a standard-month away. It was take it or leave it. I figured you'd be up for it. Tell you what – forget you owe me fifty. I'll cover that, as an investment.'

'Big of you,' I mutter.

'Well?' he says. 'Are you in?'

I take a deep breath, let it out slow. 'Okay. Why not?'

Relief lights up his mean face. 'Good!'

When he stands up to go, I lever myself slowly to my feet. I lay it on thick that I'm still feeling the knocks from my last fight, but won't let that stop me. Just as well Sky isn't here; she'd be making being-sick noises.

'You'll be okay?' Zarco says, sounding worried.

'Don't sweat it. I'll be fine when the bell goes. Where should we meet you tomorrow? And what time?'

He says to meet him in the Hole in the Wall an hour before midnight. 'Only you though. Not Sky.'

I stiffen for real. 'Why not?'

'Nothing to do with me. My contact says she can only fix permits for the two of us.'

'But Sky has to be there, to place our bets.'

'She can't be. I'll do it for you. Just bring your creds along and I'll bet them alongside mine. We'll split the winnings afterwards, when we're back at the Hole.'

'You only tell me this now?' I say, suspiciously.

'Worried I'll grab your winnings and make a run for it?'

I grit my teeth. 'Sky and me, we're a team.'

He sneers. 'A team, huh? I don't know what you see in that scrawny little cripple. A good-looking lad with creds to spend, you could do so much better. I know some girls who'd show you a good time. A ghetto-world kid like you can't hardly imagine. Say the word, I'll fix you up.'

I point behind him. 'See that door? Bad-mouth Sky again and I'll shove your head right through it.'

He sneers. 'Take it easy. All I'm saying is if I was your age again, I'd spread myself around, have some fun. You must get tired of being scowled at.'

I step towards him. He takes the hint, opens the door and steps out into the corridor. 'Tomorrow night then, an hour before midnight at the Hole. This is the big one. Don't be late.'

I growl that I won't be. He smirks, and walks away.

After the door auto-closes behind him I work through a mouthful of the worst curses I know. I'm still going strong when he's back and banging on the door again. Wondering what he's forgotten I stomp over and slap the opener.

The door slides open, but it's Sky standing there. She looks awful, like death warmed up. Blood runs red from her nose over her mouth and drips off her chin. Little Mags is by her side, only barely able to hold her up.

'Wha tha creep wan?' Sky slurs.

She limps inside, staggers and falls headlong into me.

17
ONE LAST FIGHT

Mags helps me get Sky undressed and into the bed. Sky tosses and turns the whole time, slurring stuff I mostly can't follow, although I hear 'Zed' a few times.

'Did Zed do this to you?' I ask her.

'Hoo di wha?' Spit dribbles from her mouth.

I wet a rag in the washroom and clean her face up the best I can. She quietens and closes her eyes. And I don't see any marks, so she hasn't been hit, but there is a cloying sweet smell on her that isn't booze or buzzweed.

'Did you see what happened to her, Mags?'

The girl gives a knowing snort. 'Sky should know better.'

'What do you mean?' I say, crossly.

Mags sighs. 'She's blissed. Hitting each wall of the corridor like a drunk she was when I saw her staggering back. The nosebleed is what happens when you first start sniffing the stuff. Can't you smell the stink of it?'

While she's saying this, I'm picking up Sky's clothes from where I threw them. Something drops from one of her pockets on to the floor – a grubby little plastic packet.

Mags pulls a disgusted face. 'There. What'd I tell you?'

I pick it up and sniff at it. Yuck! This close, the sweet and sickly smell is overpowering. My head spins. The plastic was once see-through, but it's so dirty now I can't see inside. From the squidgy feel, I'm guessing a powder.

'Oh, Sky, what've you done?' I sling it on to the table.

Her eyes flick open again. 'S'good stuff!'

'No it ain't,' Mags says, shaking her head. 'You know what else they call it? Brain burner.'

'What d'you know? Yer just some brat kid,' Sky snarls. Her head lifts off the pillow, but it seems like it costs her too much effort and it thumps back. 'Is the bess. Takes my pain 'way. Can't hardly feel nothin' now. Is . . . bliss.'

'Bliss now, but you pay for it later. Everybody does.'

I pull Mags away to the far side of the room. 'This bliss, it's some sort of drug then?' I whisper.

Knuckling her eyes, Mags sniffles and nods agreement. 'My mother does the stuff. That's why she's no good.'

I swallow. 'But Sky should be okay, right?'

'Depends on how much she's sniffed.'

A curse gets away from me. That boiled buzzweed Sky had been using was bad enough, so what was she thinking taking some new drug she knows nothing about? She squirms around in the bed, muttering to herself.

I feel horrible, helpless and useless.

'Is that what you guys say behind my back?' Mags says sulkily. 'That I'm just some no-good brat kid?'

I don't need this right now, and in my despair I come close to snarling at her like Sky did. But none of this is her fault, so I dig deep. 'No, course not. Sky's off her head, that's all. She doesn't know what she's saying. She thinks you're great. Honest.'

Slowly her little face brightens.

'How long will Sky be like this?' I ask.

'The bliss bit don't last, but she'll be sleeping it off for a day afterwards, maybe even two. And there'll be no living with her when she wakes up. Bliss lets you down fierce hard. My ma, she'd beat me and Matty as soon as look at us. We soon learnt to clear off and leave her to it.'

I stare at Sky. She seems quieter, as if asleep now.

'Sky won't be like that.'

'Bliss turns everyone mean.'

For both our sakes, I try for a smile that feels impossible. 'Sky's already mean. Maybe she'll wake up sweeter.'

Mags grins. 'All the same, I wish she hadn't sniffed it.'

'You and me both,' I say with a grimace.

Mags wasn't kidding about how long it would take Sky to sleep off her bliss hit. Hours slide by with her showing no sign of waking up. With time running out before I'm supposed to meet Zarco, I try to wake her. No amount of shaking or splashing cold water on her face will keep her eyes open. In desperation I send Mags off clutching a cred to buy the strongest kaffa she can find. Kaffa's like chai, but stronger. When I dribble some of it into Sky, this does the trick at last, although I get cursed and flailed at. While she sits up in bed clutching the steaming flask and trembling like a newborn lamb, I tell her Zarco's fixed me up with a big-money fight on deck sixteen. When I get to where she can't come with us she spits kaffa everywhere.

'No fraggin' way! You should never have agreed.'

'That's what I said,' Mags chips in.

I grit my teeth. 'Sky, if it works out, by this time tomorrow we could have booked passage to Enshi Four.'

'And what if it *doesn't* work out?'

'You weren't here. I had to make the call. Zarco reckoned it'd be a month before we got another chance like this . . .'

'I should be there, to watch your back.'

Sky sets the kaffa down, her hand shaking so badly she spills most of it, and tries to struggle up. Fails miserably though, and slumps back down with a tired curse.

I can't help sighing. 'Now who's the gom? You're in no fit state to get out of that bed, Sky, let alone haul yourself with me to deck sixteen. Look, Zarco won't pull anything. Why would he? He's on to a good thing with me. I'll be back before you know it. Mags can look after you.'

Mags shrugs. 'It'll cost ya. And not if I get snarled at.'

But Sky's not listening. She crawls across the bed to where I've piled her clothes. Starts rooting through them.

'You're wasting your time,' I tell her.

Sky stares at me, big baggy shadows under her fierce green eyes. 'Where is it?'

'The bliss? I chucked it. It's no good for you.'

You'd think I'd shot her. She glares at me, her face full of fury. 'What do you know? I *need* it!'

'What you *need* is proper painkillers.'

She goes from raging at me to sagging back. If anything I find this more frightening because it's so unlike her.

'You and your twisted blood,' she slurs. 'You've no idea. When your kind gets hurt you heal so fast you've hardly time to know what pain is. Well, you should try being a scab with a smashed leg and wrecked lungs. Every step hurts. Every breath is agony. Pain chews at me every second of every day, so bad it's all I can do not to scream.'

I swallow, hard. 'Look, I know –'

'YOU DON'T! YOU'VE NO FRAGGIN' IDEA!'

This last bit Sky pretty much screams at me, spit flying.

Thing is, I'm already wound up from worrying about the fight, and I've always hated being shouted at. Before I know it, I'm snarling back at her.

'So getting yourself whacked on bliss will make you better, huh? How can you be so fraggin' stupid? You'll only make yourself worse!'

'I – need – it,' she grates.

An ugly silence stretches out between us.

'Zarco says he saw you begging. What's that about?'

Sky laughs. Bitterly. Horribly. 'It was either that or sell myself, only nobody would want to do it with someone who looks as messed up as I do.'

I gawp at her, gobsmacked.

'And so what if I went begging?' she snarls. 'You're bringing in creds fighting in the cages; I'm fed up with staring at walls and feeling useless. Plus nobody sees a beggar, but beggars get to see everything. I . . . saw Zed again.'

I say nothing, but let doubts show on my face.

'You think I didn't?'

'Did you see him before or after you snorted the bliss?'

Just as well I'm out of punching range, but I still don't get away with my jibe entirely. Sky snatches up a water beaker I'd left by the bed for her and hurls it at me. I swat it away easily enough, but get splashed. We trade savage glares.

Then I see something I never thought I'd see. Something that dampens my anger and puts a lump in my throat.

Sky's eyes shimmer, and fill with tears.

Guilt stabs at me. I take a deep breath and sigh it out. 'Look, I've got to head off now if I'm going to make Zarco's fight. Soon as I'm back we'll go buy passage to Enshi Four. With luck we'll have enough creds left to buy you some proper pain meds too. Okay?'

Sky says nothing, but a single tear escapes her glare, tracks down her face and drips off her chin.

I take a step towards her. Can't not.

She folds her arms and turns her back on me.

And now Mags clears her throat, reminding me she's here. When I glance at her, she jerks her head at the door. Kid's right. I'm late already.

'You going to wish me luck then, Sky?' I say.

But she won't look at me and mutters some curse words.

'You sure you're up for this?' Zarco asks.

It's not the first time he's asked me that since I showed up to meet him. I don't suppose it'll be the last.

'I'm up for it,' I say. 'Quit asking.'

'This is the big one.'

'I know. You told me already, a hundred times.'

Truth is, I'm looking forward to the fight. When I've ducked and run and been hit enough to stack the odds my way, I'm planning on taking my rage out on my opponent. Whoever it is, I'll make him sorry he was born.

We're on deck ten now, heading for one of the transit shafts, to pick up our high-deck visitor permits.

'What'll you spend your creds on?' Zarco asks.

'Got to win them first,' I mutter.

He tells me I'll be fine. Then, as he leads me through the maze that is deck ten's trading area, he starts listing all the things he'll spend his share of the winnings on. A bigger apartment; fancier clothes; gifts for the women he runs around with. I nod and grunt and mumble things like 'yeah, that sounds good'. Meanwhile, a louder voice inside my head nags at me sourly. What a shame, it says. Zarco gets to blow his winnings on luxury. I get to blow mine on a flight in some grubby freighter to Enshi Four. And the rest will go on some hopeless chase after Sky's sister.

The way I see it, we'd be better off spending our creds on proper treatment for Sky. Surely there's some healer up on the higher decks who could cure her? And after that we could finally live some kind of life together?

Nah. Sky would never go for that.

I think maybe I let a groan slip out. Zarco stops and turns to frown at me. He looks worried.

'You sure you're –'

I growl at him to leave me be. He clamps his mouth shut and heads off again. A minute or so later we arrive at a busy market area. Fancy-looking stalls. Merchants calling their wares. At the far side of it are the openings of a transit shaft. As always, the going-up side is heavily guarded.

We work our way slowly towards it, pretending like we're checking out the goods on offer, until Zarco stops at a red-canopied stall selling electronic devices.

The merchant behind it, face on him like a fed-up rat, greets us like long-lost friends.

'Gentlemen, anything catch your discerning eye?'

We leave there clutching a small plastic tag each. Seconds later we hand them to a guard to be scanned.

'Reason for visiting deck sixteen?' she asks us.

Zarco spins her some crap about his company providing cleaning staff. I'm the stand-in for somebody who's sick.

'Hiring kids these days?' she asks.

'Sure. Why pay more for old and slow?'

She laughs, hands our tags back and lets us past. I follow Zarco inside and around the grating. At the D-16 marker, he steps off into space without breaking stride. Stomach squirming, I step out after him. As soon as my foot lands on that slight shimmer in the air I'm swept upwards. Before we're allowed out on to deck sixteen, our tags are rechecked and Zarco has to spout his lies all over again.

As we emerge, a man wearing expensive clothes that don't go with his cheap face steps forward to meet us.

'One of you Zarco?'

Zarco nods. 'That's me. We're –'

'You're late. Let's go,' the man snaps, cutting him off. He turns away and sets off at a fast walk, not looking back to make sure we're following him.

'High-deckers are such arses,' Zarco whispers.

'Looks like it,' I say, busy gawping at my surroundings.

I'd thought the better parts of deck seven pretty flash compared to the crap I was used to back on Wrath. This deck isn't as show-off extravagant as the Saviour's palace, but it's impressive in its own way. For a start it's clean. Even the deck under our feet is. No litter or muck. You could eat your dinner off it without dying, my foster-mother Rona would have said. And there are no shanty shacks fouling up the place either. Every building is made from metal and glass so shiny I see myself reflected. It smells good too, like the air is softer.

But I don't stay impressed. The guy leads us away from the bright lights and glittering steel of the centre, out to a darker and meaner warehouse district at the rim.

'This where the fights are?' Zarco asks.

'It's not far now,' is the only answer he gets.

Makes sense, I guess. Even up here cage fights are illegal. The people staging them need out-of-the-way places that can hold a big crowd. A warehouse is just about ideal. Something *is* odd though – hardly anyone else is around.

I catch Zarco by the arm and whisper: 'Are we the only people going to this fight, or what?'

He frowns. The guy ahead of us looks back.

'They're already there. Like I said, you're late.'

And now it seems we've arrived. The way ahead dead-ends in a shutter. Set into that is another door. Our guide bangs on it and a small camera swivels to point at us.

'Smile,' Zarco says through his teeth.

The smaller door swings open. Our guide waves us through it into a short, dimly lit tunnel, steps in after us and swings it shut behind him. At the other end is an identical metal shutter. From behind this I hear the muted but familiar hoots and jeers of a crowd watching a fight. When he opens the door-within-a-door at the far end, the roars and yells almost deafen me.

My heart pumps. My knees feel loose.

But this is the big one. I don't wait for him to sneer and wave us through. I shove roughly past him and go inside.

And grunt with shock.

Because there's a big open space like I'd expected.

But no crowd. No cage. No fight.

Just one man, who greets me with a mocking smile. Short-cropped blond hair. Ankle-length black coat. It's the guy who came aboard to check out our darkblende cargo.

He holds up something in his left hand. Presses it with a flourish. The invisible crowd shuts up.

All I can hear now is the thrashing of my heart.

'Hello, Kyle,' the man says. 'We've been looking for you.'

18
AN UNEXPECTED OFFER

I glance behind me, figuring to make a break past the guy who led us here. No chance. The door I barged in through slams shut. Three more men step out of the shadows to back him up, hoods hiding their faces. Two brandish the short, weighted clubs we call wasters on Wrath. The third guy has a blade. Zarco, still staring open-mouthed at the blond guy who greeted us, hasn't seen them.

'What is this?' he snarls.

It's the last thing he'll ever snarl.

Knife guy pulls Zarco on to his blade, driving it deep between his back ribs. His eyes widen and blood spills from his open mouth as he stumbles back into his killer's arms.

I'm shocked, but not so shocked that I can't move.

With a yell I launch myself at the nearest guy, and knock him down. But I lose my balance doing it. As I'm recovering, a waster connects with my head. The deck leaps up and smashes into me. A kick in the guts curls me up.

Somebody laughs nastily.

'Hey, Kyle, how've you been?'

Both the laugh and the voice are familiar.

Wheezing, I peer up at the guy with the blade who's standing over me. He pulls his hood back – and sure enough it's Cam. Cool as you like, he wipes the bloodstained blade on his trouser leg before sheathing it. The other guys lose their hoods too, but they're strangers.

I go to struggle up.

'Not so fast.' Cam shoves me back down with his boot.

The blond man joins him now in staring down at me. Those two weirdly different coloured eyes of his bore into me, as if searching for something.

'Your friend not with you, Kyle?' he asks.

I put my best Barrenlands dumb face on. 'Huh?'

'Sky,' Cam says. 'Your little scab girlfriend, remember?'

The man grimaces. 'Where is she?'

It's like a cold hand squeezes my guts. But if he's asking then he doesn't know. That's something, I guess.

'How should I know?' I say, trying to sound bitter.

'Don't be a fool. We both know she was at your last fight.'

I shrug, able to draw breath at last. 'We broke up after that. Bitch had been spending my winnings on bliss. I don't know where she is. Honest.'

Cam shakes his head. 'He's lying.'

'Are you, Kyle?'

'I'm not. You could ask Zarco, if you hadn't killed him.'

The blond man shifts his gaze from me to where Zarco lies stiff and dead in a puddle of his own blood. His face tightens and he shoots a bleak look Cam's way. 'I thought I made it perfectly clear you would wait for my signal?'

I have the small satisfaction of seeing Cam squirm before I'm grabbed, tied and gagged, and hauled away.

Never have I seen such a weird room. White floor. White ceiling. Impossibly smooth white walls without a single window. I know roughly where the door is, because I was dragged through it, but I can't see it now. I'm slumped on one of only three pieces of furniture in here, a white fur-covered couch the match of the one the blond man is sitting on. Between us squats a low table made out of what looks like glass. On it is a fancy-looking pot and two tiny glass cups. Away to my right by the wall a sort of column hangs vertically down from the ceiling. A metre off the floor this swells out into a squashed globe shape. Inside this, flames leap and flicker, but I can't feel no heat from it and I can't smell smoke. I guess it's only for show.

'We haven't been introduced,' the man says, an amused smile playing with his lips. 'I'm Rhallon.'

I quit rubbing the soreness out of my untied wrists, sit up straighter and try to meet his gaze as steady as I can.

'What do you want with me?'

'We'll get to that. But first, how about some cloud tea?'

Without waiting for an answer, Rhallon bends forward to lift the pot and carefully pours what looks like green steam into the two glass cups. He slides one towards me.

'I'm not thirsty,' I say, even though I am.

He slow-blinks. 'Neither am I. But this isn't mere water, to be drunk because you are dry. I drink cloud tea for the taste, and because I can afford the luxury where others can't. You haven't had any luxury in your life, have you, Kyle?'

'Not much,' I admit. As in . . . no fraggin' luxury at all.

'Treat yourself then. This is one of the finest and most expensive drinks in our galaxy. The airborne plant that produces it flowers just once every thousand years, and only then can its buds be harvested. Imagine!'

He sips from his cup. I watch as his odd-coloured eyes squeeze closed. He sighs loudly, clearly loving it.

I decide my tea can wait.

While he's sighing, I scan the wall for the door and wonder if I should make a break for it. Still can't see it though. And it's bound to be locked.

Rhallon's eyes flick open again.

'So tell me, Kyle, where are the last two crates?'

I fake confusion. 'Crates?'

He frowns, looking pained. 'We met when I was checking out your freighter's cargo. You were selling darkblende, remember? Only it wasn't yours to sell, was it?'

I say nothing, reckoning that's safest.

'*Was* it?' he repeats, firmly.

'That wasn't my idea,' I say. Sounds lame even to me.

To my surprise, Rhallon nods. 'I didn't say it was. But the fact remains, Kyle, that both the freighter and its precious darkblende cargo belong to my organisation. Perhaps you've heard of us? We call ourselves . . . the Syndicate.'

Figures, but I can't help shivering.

'I've heard of you,' I croak. 'Who *hasn't*?'

'And I've heard all about you, from Cam.' He smiles, and sips delicately again at his tea. 'Naturally we're glad to have our freighter back, even if it is missing its crew . . .'

He pauses, looks at me, eyebrows arched.

But I'm not about to hold my hand up for that, so I keep my face blank and my gob shut.

Another sip of tea, another wry smile from Rhallon.

'Never mind the crew. If the fools were weak enough to let you escape, you did the Syndicate a favour by disposing of them. But sadly they're not the only things we're missing. You see, each trip to Wrath ships back twelve crates of darkblende. Yet when we seized the freighter and unloaded it we found only ten. One of the ship's escape craft is also missing. A coincidence? I doubt it.'

He says all this so soft, almost friendly. But his weird, odd-coloured eyes drill into me, diamond-hard.

'Where are the last two crates, Kyle?'

'I – I don't know,' I mumble.

Why lie? Hard to say. Maybe I remember Murdo banging on about the jettisoned crates being insurance in case things went wrong. Or maybe it's just my Wrath instincts – always lie first and only tell the truth if you have to.

'Don't you?' he snaps. 'Cam said you would.'

For a second, Rhallon's mask slips and I see the anger behind it. I put my best indignant face on and shake my head.

'Cam's a gom. If anybody knows, it'll be Murdo. He's –'

'Not talking. A stubborn man.'

'He's still alive then?'

Rhallon's mask drops back into place. He smiles and nods, all pleasantness again. 'Your friend is a guest of ours. Cam tells me he helped you stow away on the freighter?'

I lick my dry lips. If I cough up about the crates, then Murdo'll be no more use to them. Just as well I lied then.

And lies are best hidden among truths.

'He did, but we're comrades not friends. We fought together. After we broke out of the cage, me and the other kids were just passengers. Murdo's a starship pilot who got marooned on Wrath, so he did the flying. If crates went missing, it'll be his doing. He always was greedy.'

Rhallon stares at me long and hard. 'Maybe we should find your scab girlfriend and see what she has to say?'

My heart sinks, but I manage a shrug.

'She'd tell you the same.'

He grunts, and slides my untouched cup closer to me. 'Your tea will be getting cold, Kyle.'

I still don't want it, but figure I'd better play along. Lifting the cup, I gaze at its contents. It looks more like dense green smoke close up, but swills about like a liquid.

I take a cautious sip. And start. It tastes like . . . sunshine.

'Good, isn't it?' Rhallon says.

It takes all my willpower to put the cup down again. The sensational taste hangs around for a good few seconds before I'm back to tasting bile in the back of my throat.

'What happens now?' I ask. 'To me, I mean.'

'That depends, Kyle.'

'On what? I still don't know where your crates are.'

'So you said.' Rhallon hesitates. For the first time I see him look less self-assured. 'Cam tells me you stowed away on that freighter deliberately. Is that right?'

I shrug. 'We did. It seemed like a good idea at the time.'

'Risky though. Why do it?'

My mind races. 'Murdo didn't tell you?'

Rhallon frowns. 'He's only told us why *he* stowed away. But why did you do it? That's what I want to know.'

I take a deep breath, frantically wondering where to start, what to tell him and what to leave out.

'How much has Cam told you about Wrath?'

'No more than I knew already.'

And now Rhallon blows my mind like Sky once did. Starting at his wrist, watching me the whole time, the man peels the skin off his left hand. Only it's not skin: it's a tight skin-coloured glove that comes off, the fake little finger cunningly arranged to follow its neighbour.

I gasp, as his five fingers become four.

'You're nublood!'

He smiles, holds his hand up and inspects it.

I shake my head, like I can shake the confusion out of it. And it works. Things suddenly make sense, like his goons taking me down so easily in the warehouse. They were nubloods too, I bet. Rhallon ignoring our warnings and opening up the darkblende. Of course! He knew he could take the radiation exposure, just like I did.

He rubs at the stump of his missing little finger, the mark of the ident. 'I was your age when I was shipped off Wrath. Started out like we all did, sold as a slave on Enshi Four. Did three long and vile years of that before the Syndicate came looking and bought me out. I've worked for them ever since. You see, Kyle, they appreciate our unique abilities.'

Our abilities? I stare at him, wondering.

'But enough of me. You and your scab girlfriend deliberately hid among the prisoners being shipped out on our Wrath freighter. Again, *why* do that?'

I pull myself together. 'Desperation.'

Rhallon settles back on to his couch. 'Do tell.'

I think quickly. What to tell, what *not* to? One thing's crystal: I can't let on I'm the Saviour's son, in case he decides to sell me back for a tidy profit. So I start in on how I'd been fighting for the ident resistance, but that it had begun falling apart. I don't say why though. I lay it on that we fled to the No-Zone in Murdo's windjammer because we figured this was the last place Slayers would look for us, only to stumble accidentally across their secret spaceport, and witness crates and cages being carried off by a lockdown-busting dropship.

Not once does Rhallon frown, which is a relief.

'And?' he says, when I pause.

'It was only a matter of time before the Slayers hunted us down. Seeing that dropship lift got me thinking. It seemed like our only way out. Sky was up for it too. She saw the caged prisoners and had this crazy idea her nublood sister would've been shipped out that way too.'

'Not *such* a crazy idea, was it?' Rhallon says.

'Guess not.' I tell him how Murdo helped us break into the prisoner cage, before being thrown in with us unexpectedly, and busting out to avoid being zapped any more by the leaky drive. Then I skip lightly through Murdo's failed quest to sell on the darkblende cargo.

'And that's how we ended up here, on the Ark.'

'So you did,' he says, and smiles.

'The merchant woman on Barzahk set us up, didn't she?'

'And she will be rewarded for her good sense and loyalty. The Syndicate believes in rewarding loyalty.'

Loyalty, my arse. They killed the Barzahk woman's only son in front of her, just for talking back to them. She'll have betrayed us out of fear, not loyalty.

But even I'm not dumb enough to blurt that.

'That's some story,' Rhallon says. 'I'm impressed.'

I grimace, heart pounding in my chest like I've swallowed a steam hammer. 'So how does it end?'

Rhallon's smile twitches, but stays put. 'It doesn't have to end. Perhaps this could be a new beginning for you.'

He leans forward, staring at me so intently that I squirm.

And makes me an offer I can't refuse.

19
INITIATION

It's well past the middle of deck seven's night when I get back to our rented room. I lean my buzzing head against the door, swaying on my feet from the booze, wishing I'd thought to take the alco-blocker. Too late now. I fumble in my pockets for my keycard, but can't find it.

No need. The door swishes open.

'Where the frag were you?' Sky snarls, blade in hand.

I shove past her. 'I'm fine, thanks for asking!'

She sticks her head out to make sure I'm on my own, then closes the door behind me. I stumble to the kitchen, pour myself some water and glug it down. When I look round she's on the bed, putting the blade away.

'Well?' she says.

'The fight was a Syndicate trap. Walked right into it.'

Sky could at least look shocked. Or concerned. But no, all I get is her sideways look.

'You don't believe me?'

'Trapped in a bar, were you? You stink of liquor.'

I guess maybe I asked for that. 'Listen, Zarco's dead. And it was Cam stuck the knife in him.'

This wipes the sneer off her face. '*Cam?*'

I rub at my tired eyes. 'Shift over and I'll tell you.'

Sky makes room. I weave my way over, throw myself down beside her, and start in on what happened.

'So Murdo didn't clear off with the freighter after all?'

'Nuh-uh. They grabbed it back. And they're holding Murdo somewhere, trying to make him tell them where he stashed those two darkblende crates.'

'You didn't tell them?'

'Course not. Murdo'd be a dead man.'

Sky shrugs, as if this wouldn't be the end of her world.

I carry on with my telling.

'He's a nublood!?' Sky hisses, when I get to *that* bit.

Maybe it's the shock that does it, but her cough comes back now with a vengeance. Grabbing a rag she hacks away into it. It ends up flecked with blood. I put my arm around her clumsily, but she shrugs me off.

'So what else happened?' she wheezes.

I grit my teeth. 'Turns out Rhallon's not the only nublood in the Syndicate. He's asked me to work for them.'

Sky pulls the rag from her mouth. 'What did you say?'

'Yes. I figured no might be the last thing I ever said. Cam and the rest of the nublood kids have all signed up too. Anyway, Rhallon took me to a bar then, to celebrate. Cam wasn't there; Anuk and some of the others were. She told me what happened. Seems Cam had slipped off by himself after we did and come back looking real shifty. And guess who was on guard when the Syndicate guys hit the freighter? Our good friend Cam. She reckons they must've grabbed him and he agreed to betray us.'

'Wouldn't put it past him,' Sky says, scowling.

'They fought, but it was hopeless. Murdo did a runner, but didn't get far. The hangar guards were nowhere to be seen. Bought off or cleared off, she doesn't know.'

'What happened to the freighter?'

'Flown to another hangar up on deck eight.'

Sky grunts, and chews at her lip viciously. 'So that's the end of your cage fighting, is it?'

'Rhallon says I work only for the Syndicate from now on.'

'So that's fraggin' that. We're stuck here!'

I hang my head. If we'd done what she wanted and made for Enshi Four in the first place, none of this would have happened. Then again, who knows what would have happened there?

'We're not *stuck* here, just delayed.'

Sky gives me a look, like 'what's that supposed to mean?'

'I get paid for each job I do for the Syndicate.'

'Yeah? How much?'

'I didn't dare ask. But the Syndicate guys were chucking creds around like they had plenty. It'll beat humping crates around on the gutter decks for three creds a day, that's for sure. And Rhallon says if I prove myself and work my way up I can earn more than I did cage fighting.'

'Rhallon says this, Rhallon says that,' Sky says, pulling a mocking face. 'You seem pretty taken with him.'

'I'm just telling you what he told me.'

Truth is though I *am* impressed.

'So what are these jobs?' Sky asks suspiciously.

I suck my teeth. 'Don't know. But Rhallon says . . . well, the first job is some kind of test, to see if I can handle Syndicate work. They'll let me know where on this.'

I show her the comm device, a stiff sliver of plastic about the size of my palm. It'll buzz when a message comes in and is synced to my touch so that only I can read it.

Sky checks it out, then throws it back at me. 'What happens if you don't get the job done?'

I draw my finger across my throat . . . like Rhallon did.

She has another coughing fit. Not as bad as the first, but still tough to watch. I fetch her some water.

She drinks it down and sighs. 'I need to get my hands on more of that bliss stuff.'

'No, you don't. You need proper meds.'

'Proper meds cost. Bliss is cheap.'

I figure now isn't the time to argue about this.

'By the way, you were right about that Zed guy. He was at the bar with us, so he's Syndicate too. I only found out when someone called his name.'

'Did you get to talk to him?'

I shake my head. 'Nah. It was awkward, being the new guy. I talked to Anuk and Ravi mostly.'

Sky takes a careful breath. 'What about me? I could work for the Syndicate too. That way we could earn twice as fast.'

'It's, uh, not that simple,' I say, wincing.

'Why not?' Sky growls.

I stand up and step out of kicking and punching range. 'Look,

I'm just telling you what Rhallon told me, so don't get mad. But they only hire nubloods.'

Sky lets loose with some choice curses. 'I'll talk to him.'

'That's a *really* bad idea.'

'You think I'm too sick, that I can't cut it?'

'Course not!' I take a deep breath. 'It's just . . . he hates pureblood idents. You should hear the guy. He won't use your name, kept calling you my "scab girlfriend". Seriously, you need to keep away from him.'

'But he's nublood. What's his problem?'

'I've no idea. He asked where you were. I said we'd bust up and gone our separate ways. Not sure he believed me, but he let it slide. For now anyway.'

Sky grunts and looks sceptical. She's about to snarl something, but is stopped by a loud *buzz-buzz-buzz*. My Syndicate comm card is calling.

I scoop it up from where I'd thrown it on the bed. The buzzing quits and a message slowly materialises. I did some more learning of my letters at the Deeps so I'm better now, but still slow.

'Deck four . . . uh . . . Tandee District.'

'Show me,' Sky says, and snatches it out of my hand. 'Rocannon's Bar at midnight,' she reads out, needing only one glance. 'You reckon you'll be sober by then?'

My heart sinks. 'Hope not.'

'You'd best get some sleep. I'll go and find Mags.'

'Mags? What for?' I say, confused.

'Oh, so you know where this Rocannon's Bar is then?'

Fair point. For a few creds Mags can guide me so I don't get lost or show up late. Which wouldn't be good.

'Want me to come with you?' I mumble.

'Why?' The look of scorn Sky gives me could strip paint.

I sleep the whole of the day away, but when I wake up Sky's still not back. Two mugs of strong kaffa clear the last of the drunkwebs out of my head, but my mouth still feels like I've been chewing sawdust. The room lights turn that hint of red, so it's night-time again. Still no Sky. I'm pacing and starting to panic when the door hisses open at last.

But it's only little Mags.

'Where's Sky?'

'Dunno. Off scoring more bliss? She said you'd pay me three if I got you to Roc's by midnight.'

'You mean Rocannon's?'

'Yeah, yeah. I know the place. It's a dump.'

Part of me is gutted Sky can't be bothered to be here, but the last thing I need right now is another argument.

'So whatcha going there for?' Mags asks.

'Never you mind.' I grab my jacket. 'Let's get moving.'

Half an hour later I'm looking at a crudely hand-daubed sign in the distance. B-A-R, it says. Nothing about it being Rocannon's. This is deck four's outer rim and we've picked our way to it through a shanty area that wouldn't look – or smell – out of place in the Blight. The bar itself is a shabby little one-storey dive, and looks dead as anything.

My stomach squirms. 'You sure?'

Mags yawns. 'Yup. That's Roc's all right.'

I pay her the three creds. 'Wait here until I come out.'

'No way. I got things to do.'

But the promise of another three creds soon changes her conniving little mind. I tell her to stay out of sight, and make for the battered and rusty metal door. There's no handle that I can see. I push it. But nothing doing: it's locked.

'Over here, you fool,' a voice hisses.

I look around, and see Zed beckoning me from the corner of the building. Relieved I'm in the right place I hustle over. He steps back out of sight of the door and I follow. Zed's not much taller than me, but built heavier. Shaven-headed, he has that kind of face that sneers without trying.

He looks me up and down and spits. 'So you're Kyle?'

I nod and tell him I got his message.

'Well, no shit,' he drawls.

What was it Sky said about him? Already a nasty piece of work back in his ident-camp days. No change there then. But I've been around bullies before and bite my tongue. Despite the late hour there are a few other people around, but they don't look at us, slogging past with their heads down. Wherever Mags is I can't see her, which is good.

'Time to prove yourself,' Zed says.

'Yeah? How?' I say, getting a bad feeling.

He shows me his teeth, but I wouldn't call it a smile.

'Inside this bar, sleeping off his last fix, is a gom called Doohan. He's one of our dealers. But he's been holding out on us. And we can't have that, can we?'

I clear my throat. 'Guess not.'

'Rhallon wants *you* to make an example of him.'

He holds a blaster out to me. Snub-nosed, old and well used. A brutal weapon. And what can I do but take it? The mag says it's good for one shot only. So that's my test: have I got what it takes to kill for the Syndicate? And it's more than just a test. Kill for them, and they've got me.

'This Doohan, what's he look like?' I croak.

Zed grins. 'I'll point him out.'

He leads me back to the bar's door and taps some sort of signal on the metal. After a while I hear movement inside. A small shutter opens. Bleary eyes peer out through it. Zed shifts so what light there is catches him. I hear a breath being sucked in. Chains rattle. Bolts scrape back. The door swings inwards, oil-starved hinges squealing in complaint.

Zed shoves his way inside, growling at me to follow.

Behind the door is the guy who let us in. He cowers as we step past him, and then scuttles outside. Fast on his feet for a fat guy. He must know Zed is Syndicate.

It's fierce dark in here, but Zed hits some switch and lights the place up a bit. A smoke haze hangs in the air, thick enough to cut with a knife. Through it I see a long bar hugging one wall. It's the only furniture in here. Tattered mats lie scattered on the floor. On a dozen or so, sleepers are stretched out, crude hookahs bubbling away beside them. And now the sickly sweet smell of bliss hits me in the back of my throat. I get it. A bar in name only, this shack is actually a flophouse for bliss-heads.

The light has a few of the dopers blinking up at us. Zed uses his boot to stir the rest.

'Want to live?' he snarls. 'Tell us where Doohan is.'

A baggy-eyed young woman, the leavings of bliss, jabs a shaking finger towards an open doorway.

'First room on the right,' she grates.

'Wait here.' Zed slips through the doorway, fast but quiet. I hear a scuffle. Then he's back, hauling a ragged little man by his hair. He forces him down on to his knees in front of the bar and glances at me. 'Not much to look at, is he?'

I shake my head, not sure I can talk.

Zed steps away and stands so he's blocking the entrance. The little guy looks from him to me, all wild-eyed.

'Please don't,' he whimpers.

A string of dribble spills from his slack mouth. And I cringe as I see the front of his trousers turn dark with wet.

Him or me, him or me, I chant to myself.

Zed tut-tuts, like a parent with a naughty child. 'Oh, Doohan, what *are* you like? You deal for us. We supply and protect you. In return, we take our cut from what you make. Simple, isn't it? You win, and the Syndicate wins too. That's how it works. But you were greedy, weren't you?'

'I'll pay what I owe,' Doohan gasps.

Zed grimaces. 'We're past that.'

Doohan's head drops. Big sobs shake him.

The trapped dopers stay rooted to their mats, as if turned to stone. The only things that move are their eyes, as they slide their dull stares from me and Zed to Doohan.

'So, Doohan,' Zed says. 'You know what happens when you mess with the Syndicate, don't you?'

The guy mumbles another, 'Please don't.' More drool spills from his quivering mouth. He sobs and stares at the floor beneath his knees as if there's a way out for him there.

Zed sneers, and gives me the nod.

I raise the blaster, but a shake has got into my hand and the fraggin' thing wobbles all over the place.

'What are you waiting for?' Zed snarls. 'Waste him!'

The room fades around me. I'm back in front of a cage, staring at the monster inside while a bully called Nash yells at me, wanting me to torture the creature by zapping it with the electric prod I'm holding. But the creature in the cage *wasn't* a monster, was it?

Zed curses loudly, and I'm back in the room.

I grit my teeth. One of Zed's hands is tucked into a jacket pocket. If I don't show willing, I'm guessing he'll pull out another blaster to fry me *and* Doohan. And with me dead, Sky's as good as dead too. So I tell myself that this guy cowering before me *is* a monster. A lowlife bliss dealer who's wrecked more lives than just his own.

Bile fills my throat, but I know what I have to do.

I jerk the trigger home. The blaster kicks back into my hand. The fake-wood bar explodes, shards of plastic flying everywhere.

But Doohan's still kneeling there, not a mark on him. Somehow, I've missed the guy!

From the door, I hear Zed make a strangled noise full of disgust and disbelief. Before he can pull whatever weapon he's got, I chuck him the empty and useless blaster.

Instinct makes him reach out and catch it.

By now my hunting blade is in my hand. Not daring to look at Zed, I set off towards Doohan.

'You won't get lucky twice, creep,' I snarl at him.

The guy lets out a low moan, scrambles up and flaps at me weakly, trying to fend me off. Yeah, right. Without breaking stride, I drop kick him backwards, sending him crashing into the blaster-shattered bar. The countertop gives way. He tumbles over and down behind it. I vault the bar and drop on to him.

One short punch to the temple snaps his head around and he goes limp. Which is good for both of us.

I grip my knife tighter . . . and do what I have to.

When I'm done I'm spattered with blood, none of which is mine. I stagger back up, breathing heavily, and gaze at the dripping blade in my hand. Zed arrives. He leans over the blasted bar to check my handiwork.

What he sees wipes the sneer off his face.

'Happy?' I say, like I knife people to death every day.

20
A LUCKY BREAK . . . OR NOT

'You're not much use with a blaster then?' Rhallon says.

'I'm handier with a blade.'

'Yes, so I hear.' Before I know what he's doing, he's licked a finger and is dabbing at my face. I twitch and pull back.

He laughs. 'You've still got his blood on you.'

My stomach flips. 'It won't kill me.'

His touch lingers long enough that my face goes hot. Across the room Zed watches and scowls. Anuk reckons that he's got a thing for Rhallon, but Rhallon's not interested.

'You did well,' he says. 'I'm impressed.'

I wince, wishing that I was anywhere but here.

Here is a big room in a safe house on deck eight, full of Syndicate guys all laughing and drinking and smoking. I'd give anything to scuttle back to Sky, scrub Doohan's blood off and curl up with her. But Zed says I have to be here.

A woman comes over and whispers in Rhallon's ear. Next thing I know he's handing me his wine glass to hold.

'I'll be back.' They leave the room together.

I'm left standing there like a dummy, my hardly touched beer in one hand, his wine glass in the other. And sick with worry about what this woman might be telling him.

Fortunately Anuk's here too, and comes to my rescue. Well, sort of. Before I can stop her, she's snatched Rhallon's glass and knocked back half of it.

'Hey, go easy! You'll make yourself drunk.'

'That's the fraggin' idea,' Anuk says sourly. 'You think he likes you, don't you, Kyle? Because he looks you in the eye and smiles. Well, I've been watching him, and guess what? Rhallon dishes that crap out to everyone. That's part of how he gets his way. Gommers like Cam, they lap it up.'

I glance around nervously, hoping nobody's overheard. 'I'm not Cam. And I wasn't born yesterday.'

She frowns at me, and then sighs. 'Yeah. Sorry.'

I hadn't known what to make of Anuk, but she's growing on me. Just shows, as Rona used to say, that judging someone by what they look like is dumb. This girl's tough, but no way mean. Not like Cam and some of the others. After what she's suffered in the camps, that's impressive.

Looking at her now though she seems lost.

'Are you . . . okay?'

She takes a breath, lets it out shakily. 'No. Not really.'

I sip my beer without tasting it, guessing that I'm not the only new Syndicate recruit who's been tested today.

'We did what we *had* to do,' I whisper.

She starts, spilling a bit of the wine. And then drains the glass, almost savagely. 'But now we have to live with it.'

I don't know what to say to this.

To our right, Cam, Stitch and Ravi are chatting with some of the younger guys. Cam's face is flushed with drink. He looks happy, and like he belongs here.

Me, I feel like an outsider. Some things never change.

Anuk looks over at them too. 'Before you got here, Cam was taking great delight in telling me how he knifed your cage-fighting friend in the back.'

'He's an arse. Don't let him get to you.'

She grunts. Neither of us say much for a while.

Then suddenly, the words spilling out of her, Anuk tells me she was handed a blaster and told to kill a shopkeeper. 'Poor guy had missed some payments. For protection, or something like that. He pleaded with me, said it wasn't his fault, business had been bad.' Her voice catches. She can't look at me.

Rhallon returns to the room, chatting to a man I haven't seen before. They're both laughing about something.

A good sign? Fraggin' hope so.

'You said we're not monsters,' Anuk mutters.

'What?' I say, distracted.

'That's what you told us back on the freighter, that we'd been lied to, that we're *not* monsters.'

I look her in the eye. 'It's true. We're different, that's all.'

'So why did I kill that shopkeeper then?'

'You'd no choice.'

'Didn't I? I could have blasted the Syndicate guy making me do it . . . or turned it on myself.' She goes to drink from Rhallon's glass again, but finds it empty and curses.

Too loudly. Heads turn.

I widen my eyes at her, lean in and whisper, 'There are no

monsters, only bad people and good people and everybody in between. Think about it – if we really *were* monsters, we wouldn't regret having killed, would we?'

She doesn't look convinced. 'Cam doesn't regret it.'

I shrug. 'You're not Cam. He's a bully, like Zed. And we've both seen pureblood humans do worse. Tearing innocent children from their parents and sticking them in camps. Making kids slave down mines.'

Anuk takes a deep breath and gives herself a little shake.

'Maybe I *am* a monster, just no good at it.'

'Sky says the same about me.'

'Where *is* Sky?'

I hesitate, reluctant to answer, not wanting to lie.

She sees this. 'Forget I asked. She's lucky though, not to be mixed up in this. Last time I saw her, she didn't look so great.'

'Sky was sick before she stowed away on the freighter. That drive exposure made her worse.'

Anuk winces. 'She must really care for her sister to risk what she did. My sister Lotte would never do that for me.'

I open my mouth . . . and close it again.

'What?' Anuk says, looking at me all sad-eyed.

'Thing is,' I say, 'if we do catch up with Tarn, her blood could heal Sky.' I rattle quickly through how this works, and how I used my nublood to save Colm.

Her eyes go from sad to startled. 'What? Seriously?'

'Seriously.' I swig my beer, only it goes down the wrong way and chokes me.

Across the room Zed thinks this is hysterical. 'What's wrong, Kyle? Can't handle your beer, huh?'

I should know better, but turn and glare at him.

Big mistake. Straight away he's shooting his mouth off to his mates about how I missed Doohan from point-black range with a blaster. They roar with laughter. Encouraged, he pulls a snarling face, grabs the nearest guy and mimes knifing him, over and over. The guy plays along, crying out.

'Shame it wasn't *him* you stabbed,' Anuk mutters.

'Thought crossed my mind.' I turn my back on Zed. 'D'you think we'll have to do more killing?'

'Not for a while, I think. See pretty boy over there?' She points out another Syndicate guy chatting to two young women. 'His name's Logan and he was hitting on me big time before you turned up. Trying to sympathise his way into my bed. He says after we're initiated, they'll start us out as runners.'

I nearly choke again. 'There's *more* initiation?'

'Relax. Rhallon makes a speech, that's all. Then we get our gloves, to hide our missing fingers. And some creds to buy smarter clothes with. If we're representing the Syndicate, we can't be looking like tramp-freighter crew.'

'What's a runner do?'

Anuk shoots me a warning look.

Rhallon's on his way over to join us. He arrives with his usual smile, but that soon fades to a frostier look as his eyes take in the empty glass in Anuk's hand.

'Runners,' he says, 'run errands. Delivering messages. Collecting payments. That sort of thing.'

'I'll get you another drink,' Anuk says quickly.

But before she can scuttle away, a guy arrives bearing a metal tray laden with glasses. He holds it out to Rhallon first, to select one. He takes his time. Then it's our turn, but we just grab the nearest. Rhallon taps at his glass with a long black-painted fingernail, making enough of a ringing sound to get people's attention, and waves Cam over.

Ravi and Stitch stay put, looking jealous. I guess they're yet to be tested.

The room falls silent. Don't know what I'd been expecting, but Rhallon's speech is mercifully short and to the point. First off he asks us in turn if we want to join the Syndicate. Surprise, we all say yes. Next he asks the guys who came with us on our tests whether we'd proved ourselves. Zed screws with me, pulling a face like he's not sure, before grudgingly admitting I had.

He gets the laugh; I get to taste bile.

Rhallon lays out the rules. Follow orders. If you get caught, don't be a squealer. No fighting or cheating among ourselves. And the penalty for screwing up is death.

Sounds like Gemini all over again. Sort of.

He wraps things up by welcoming us in turn to the Syndicate and presenting us with a small, neatly wrapped packet. We raise our glasses and toast, 'the Syndicate!'

After that, the serious drinking starts.

Cam, Stitch and Ravi come over and join me and Anuk.

'If I ran things,' Cam declares, 'new guys would have to cut the head off their kills and bring them to show us.'

'You're sick,' Anuk says. 'You know that?'

'Let's get out of here,' I say to her.

'Oh, what?' Cam says. 'You two a couple now?'

I get in his face. 'You're pushing your luck, you gom.'

He steps back, like he's shocked.

'Wind your neck in, Kyle. Can't you take a joke?'

We push past him. I think he spills his drink. Sad that. But leaving is easier said than done. Two big Syndicate guys are standing by the door. They see us coming and block our path. Their smiles are friendly enough, but we're going nowhere. One looks past us into the room and signals.

Rhallon excuses himself from the conversation he was having and crosses the room towards us. 'Calling it a night, are you?'

'If that's okay?' I say, past a gulp in my throat.

'Been a long day,' Anuk mumbles.

'Of course,' Rhallon says, nodding. 'But Kyle, I wonder if you could help me out with something, before you go?'

'Sure,' I say, but my heart sinks.

Anuk shoots me a sympathetic look before she clears off.

Rhallon leads me out through the rear of the compartment, along a twisting, dimly lit corridor, and then stops in front of a rusting metal door. It's dingy and smelly and cold here, and I can hear a steady *plunk-plunk-plunk* of dripping condensation. We must still be up on deck eight, but it looks and feels more like the gutter decks. I get the mother of all bad feelings.

Rhallon pounds on the door and it swings inwards.

'Well?' he asks the man who opened it.

The man shakes his head.

Rhallon hisses out a sigh, but then turns to me and smiles. It's not his best. 'Your pureblood friend is testing my patience to its limits, Kyle. We still don't know what became of those last two crates of darkblende.'

'Murdo?' I say.

'Who else? Maybe you can make him see sense.'

'What should I say to him?'

'Whatever it takes. Find out and we'll be very grateful.'

Yeah, I bet. And Murdo will be dead. Me too, if Rhallon finds out I've been lying about not knowing.

'This way,' the other guy says, and beckons.

I follow him into a cramped chamber. One plastic chair. A round hatch set into the middle of the floor. And it stinks in here. Blood and sweat and . . . worse. I go to glance back at Rhallon, but Murdo's jailer clangs the metal door closed behind me with a grunt of effort. I see that his knuckles are caked in dried blood. He lumbers from there to the hatch in the floor and heaves it up and open. The rungs of a ladder lead down into gloom.

'Bang on the hatch when you want letting out,' he says.

I wonder. But if Rhallon wanted me locked in with Murdo, I'd have been dragged here. So I grit my teeth and start clambering down. And almost get my head banged as he closes the hatch over me, plunging me into pitch-darkness. Cursing him, I have to do the rest of the climb by feel. But as my boot reaches the bottom rung, a puny light flick-flickers on at last.

'Go to hell! Leave me alone,' a voice croaks.

I look around, and suck my teeth. Murdo is hanging by his wrists from chains hooked to the ceiling, dangling like a piece of meat, his toes just reaching the floor.

'Murdo. It's me, Kyle!'

Ever so slowly his head lifts.

'Kyle?' he wheezes. 'They got you too?'

Except for his long, greasy blond hair, I'd hardly know him. His face is a mess of cuts and bruises. One eye is swollen closed, the other flooded with red from a burst blood vessel. I'm gobsmacked he can see me . . . or talk.

'They've got all of us now,' I tell him.

My wandering eye spots something in a corner. I jog over and find it's a water bottle, still half full. My guess is it belongs to the thug upstairs. Dishing out beatings must be thirsty work.

I show it to Murdo. He nods eagerly, tips his head back and opens his mouth. Wincing, I slop some water in. He swallows greedily. Another mouthful and I thumb the bottle closed again. From the state he's in, it's a while since he's had water. More will just make him throw up.

'How come you don't get chained?' he says.

'I work for the Syndicate now.'

He frowns. 'Didn't have you down for a gangster.'

'Yeah, well, needs must.'

I take a look around at this pit we're in. It has to be part of the in-between deck, which I know is riddled with inspection and service tunnels. Another hatch in the floor beneath the ladder leads further down. Equipment cabinets stamped with numbers are fastened to the walls. No sign of any cameras watching us, or microphones listening in. Then again, not seeing them doesn't prove anything.

Murdo shifts, rattling his chains. He goes to say something.

I figure I'd best get in first.

'Listen,' I say, frowning at him real hard, praying there's a brain left inside his smashed-up head. 'Rhallon reckons that when they grabbed the freighter back, two darkblende crates had gone missing. Is that right?'

He fixes me with his good eye, blinks, says nothing.

I swallow, relieved.

'Tell me where they are and I'll get them to let you go.'

Murdo laughs, or tries to. 'And there was me thinking you came down here to bust me out.'

'Your only way out of here is if you tell me where those crates are. If you don't, then I can't help you.'

He sneers. 'Now where have I heard that before?'

I look around the pit again and shiver at how grim it is. Never did I think I'd feel sorry for Murdo, but I do now. If I was him, I'd have told them where the crates were for a quick death.

'You should've stayed on Wrath,' I say miserably.

Murdo has another go at a bitter laugh. 'I've been in worse fixes. I'll think of something, you'll see. I'll cut a –'

His head slumps down.

For one awful second I think he's died on me.

But when I take a closer look I see he's breathing. Gently, I tilt his head back and dribble some more water into his torn mouth. He swallows, and starts coughing. His eye flickers open. Seeing me so close, he somehow conjures up his annoying grin.

'If you ain't dead,' he mumbles.

'You're still alive,' I sigh, finishing the saying for him.

21
BUST UPS, BUZZING SKULLS

It's still early, but Sky was already up when I finally dragged myself back to our room. With her coughing fits, she struggles to sleep these days. The lack of it has painted dark circles beneath her eyes. I'm catching her up with what happened after I was summoned and expect the full scowl and rolled-eyes treatment for missing Doohan with my blaster.

But not a bit of it, Sky just nods.

'I had to finish him with my knife. It was . . . grim.'

She looks at me, real cold. 'Yeah? How grim?'

'What d'you mean?' I say, confused.

Sky stands up and starts limping around the room. If she had a tail it'd be lashing behind her. And when she whips round to face me, I see her face is scrunched up and furious.

'How could you?' she yells. 'A no-good dealer, and you risk everything to let that loser live. ARE YOU MAD?'

I gasp. 'How'd you know?'

See, Sky's not wrong. I *didn't* kill Doohan. I only made it look like that. My blaster miss was deliberate. So was shoving him behind the bar so that Zed couldn't see what I was up to. Knocking the guy out with one punch was lucky. The rest was acting and bursting two of the fake-blood capsules Zarco had given me for the cage fights.

'What if they find out he's still alive?' Sky snarls.

My face burns. 'They *won't*. Doohan's bound to keep his head down now. He'd be crazy not to.'

Sky clutches her head. 'Wrath give me strength. The guy's a bliss-head. He thought he could hold out on the Syndicate and get away with it. He *is* crazy!'

I open my mouth. Shut it again.

Truth is, I've had the same cold, sweaty thoughts myself. That's why I was sweating when Rhallon got called out of the room, terrified that I'd been found out.

'So I took a chance. I *couldn't* kill him, not in cold blood.'

Sky groans. 'Your fraggin' conscience will get both of us killed!'

We trade glares, until I remember that she still hasn't answered me. 'Who told you?'

'I was there! One of those lying on a mat. I got Mags to take me to Rocannon's before I sent her back to fetch you.'

That staggers me. 'Mags? She never said.'

'For ten creds she'll forget anything.'

'But what were you doing there?'

'Figured you might need backup. By the time I realised what you were up to, it was too late. You'd done your big stabbing act and cleared off. Then what was I supposed to do? Jump up and shout at you to get back in there and kill the guy for real this time? I don't think so.'

My next breath is a long time coming.

'You weren't fooled?'

Sky sighs. 'Even *you* couldn't miss from so close.'

I let myself fall backwards on to the bed and stare up at the ceiling, despairing. But it's not long before I sit up again.

'Okay, I screwed up. But it's not too late. If we get to Doohan before the Syndicate finds out, we can –'

'Kill him?' Sky hoists her eyebrows. 'Let me guess, I get to do it while you look away.'

I hang my head. Silence stretches out, so taut and uncomfortable I have to say something. Anything.

'There's something else. I saw Murdo.'

Sky sniffs. 'Yeah? What did he have to say for himself?'

Miserably, I tell her how Murdo had been imprisoned and beaten to a pulp. 'Rhallon wanted me to get him to tell where he stashed those darkblende crates. He wasn't best pleased when I came back with nothing. Look, I know you don't like Murdo, but he didn't abandon us here and he's in a desperate state.'

'Should've flown us to Enshi Four, shouldn't he?'

Dismayed, I get up and make for the kitchen area. I figure I might as well make myself a mug of kaffa. While it's brewing, I tear open the packet Rhallon gave me earlier. There's a cred-stick inside, two hundred already pre-loaded. And that glove thing with the fake finger. Rhallon says we have to wear them whenever we're out and about on the Ark. Makes sense. Otherwise ArkSec would know to look out for kids with missing little fingers. Gingerly, I pull it on. As I do, the damn thing sort of sinks into the flesh of my hand. I curse, loudly.

This gets Sky's attention. 'What's the matter *now*?'

I show her my hand. It's impossible to tell the extra finger is fake. It bends with the next finger, and feels likes real skin to the touch. A-mazing. Looks weird though. I guess I've grown used to not having the little finger.

Sky grunts. 'Great. Listen, while you've been off with your Syndicate mates, I looked into passenger flights to Enshi Four. Even gutter class ain't cheap. And we'll both need fake IDs and transit passes. There's a guy on deck six who can sort them. All-in, it's ten grand. Each.'

'Twenty grand? You're kidding?'

'Wish I was. Maybe Zarco's cage-fight scam could've earned us those kind of creds, but between my begging and your Syndicate work it's going to take us forever. And I don't have forever.' She reaches out, swipes my mug of kaffa and chugs it. 'But maybe there's another way . . .'

I grit my teeth. 'Like what?'

'You said that the freighter we flew in on is hangared up on eight. I say we grab it back and fly ourselves to Enshi Four.'

It's lucky she nicked my drink or I'd be spitting kaffa.

'Oh sure. And you'll fly it, will you?'

'Murdo will. After we bust him out of that hole.'

I give Sky my best *you can't be serious* sneer. 'That's mad!'

She narrows her eyes in a way that makes me glad she doesn't have a blade in her hand. 'What's so mad about it? Trying to flog that darkblende was mad. I said we should have gone straight to Enshi Four. But no, you and Murdo wouldn't listen. You got greedy. And now when I come up with a way off this wreck, all you do is sneer again!'

'Flogging the darkblende wasn't *my* idea!' I snap back at her.

'Went along with it though, didn't you?'

'You want to second-guess everything? Well, I can do that too. Maybe I should've stayed with Colm on Wrath.'

'Maybe I'd be better off if you had.'

She glowers at me until she's doubled up by another coughing fit. Grudgingly I fetch her a glass of water, sit her down on the bed and help her to sip it in between coughs. With a rag, I wipe away the stuff she's bringing up. It's nasty, shot through with blood.

Wheezing curses, she pushes me away.

'I need another hit.'

'No, you don't. That bliss'll only screw you up worse.'

Eyes streaming, she glares at me. 'Take a good look, Kyle. In case you ain't noticed, I'm already screwed up. Bliss is all that keeps me breathing.' She struggles up, grabs her jacket off the floor and limps towards the door.

'You're in no state to be going anywhere,' I say.

Sky tips her head back and sighs, before shooting me a mocking look. 'Fine. You go score my bliss then. I'll tell you where my dealer hangs out, shall I?'

Something snaps inside me.

'Fine. You want that crap, you can get it yourself,' I growl. Turning away, I pull some of the bedclothes off the bed on to the floor and throw myself down on them.

Silence. For several long seconds. I won't look at her.

The door hisses open and closed.

When I do look, Sky's gone.

And I'm glad. That's what I tell myself anyway.

I'm dog-tired, but can't sleep. I toss and turn in the darkness for what feels like hours. If I'm not thinking angry thoughts about Sky, I'm sweating about Doohan showing his ugly face and getting me killed. And then, when I do finally manage to fall asleep, it's only so nightmares can screw with me.

In the worst I'm staring up in horror at an enormous Rhallon. Ten times my size, he holds Doohan in one hand, a little wriggling man-doll.

'Look who I found!' big-Rhallon booms.

His giant teeth are all filed into sharp fangs, the way some Reaper warriors do back on Wrath. In his hand, Doohan quits struggling and looks down at me.

'I don't know him,' I say, my voice weedy and shrill.

'Yes you do, yes you do,' Doohan chants. 'You were supposed to kill me, but you didn't.'

I scream at him to shut up. He laughs. A haunting laugh that stands all the hairs up on the back of my neck.

'You disappoint me, Kyle,' Rhallon booms.

'I'm sorry,' I say, falling to my knees.

'Do you know what I do to those who disappoint me?'

I shake my head. It's not the only bit of me that's shaking.

'This!' Somehow Rhallon has morphed into a giant bellowing Sky. Scowling, she lifts Doohan up and bites the poor guy's head off. A chomp and a chew, and she spits his bloody skull out so that it lands at my feet.

I leap back, gagging, as it starts buzzing at me.

Frantically, I try to kick it away, but can't –

That's when I wake up, tangled in a sheet, flailing and fighting to get free. The ceiling glowtubes sense me moving and light the room. Sky's still not back. And it's my Syndicate comm card that's buzzing.

Cursing, I reach for it.

The message is a summons to the safe house on deck eight. It's warm in here, but I shiver. Has Doohan been fool enough to show his face again? Will Rhallon and a bunch of Syndicate toughs be waiting to pounce when I show up? Or is this my first job? I've no way of knowing.

No choice neither – I'll have to go and hope for the best.

I check the time readout on the wall and start. I've slept the best part of a day away and it's late, deep into the third watch. Throwing the sheets off me, I struggle up and rub at my eyes miserably. I know we argued, but I wish Sky was here. A scowl would be better than nothing.

'Where the hell are you?' I mutter.

Silence answers me and I feel a sharp stab of loneliness.

I've an hour before I have to be there and it's only one deck up, so there's no great rush. I take my time showering and change into the cleanest clothes I can find, listening out the whole time for the hiss of the door opening.

But Sky stays gone. And time marches on, relentless.

My guess is she's slumped somewhere, off her head again on that bliss crap. I can't wait any longer, but it's hard walking out of that door not knowing if I'll ever come back.

What the frag was I thinking, letting Doohan live?

A few minutes later I've hauled myself up to eight and am standing outside a plain metal door at the back of a cleaning supplies shop. The droopy-eyed guy behind the counter nods at me, and presses a button.

The door slides opens. Holding my breath I step inside.

Two different guards from the last time I was here are waiting to check me out. One peers at my comm-card message. The other pats me down, finds my blade and tosses it with a clatter into a box with other weapons. Their hard faces give nothing away, other than boredom.

'Rhallon's expecting you,' one says.

Up a short flight of stairs and I step back into the compartment where we had the initiation drinks. Zed, Cam and half a dozen other young toughs I don't know are lounging about on couches. When they see me standing there, all I get is glared at. Dread fills me up and my legs want to turn and run. Somehow I step forward.

A concealed door in the compartment's far wall swishes open and Rhallon sweeps inside.

'Kyle, there you are,' he says. 'Good.'

Zed, obvious anger pinching his face, hauls himself to his feet and jabs a finger at me. 'Sorry, boss, but what the hell is *he* doing here? This ain't no job for a kid.'

I can't help glancing at Cam, who's no older than me. Unlike me though, Cam sucks up to Zed big time.

'I'll be the judge of that,' Rhallon snaps, then flicks his gaze my way, as if reminding himself what I look like. 'I'm told you're handy in a fight, Kyle. Is that right?'

'I can hold my own,' I say, feeling hugely relieved.

Zed screws his face up into a big sneer. 'He must fight a whole lot better than he shoots then.'

His mates laugh, loving this.

'What kind of job is it?' I ask, my face hot.

Rhallon shakes his head. 'All you need to know for now is that you'll be off the Ark for two weeks at least. Pack your gear accordingly, but keep it light. We'll lift out tomorrow morning.

Everybody needs to be here, ready for boarding, an hour before the end of red watch. Okay?'

We all nod, and despite not knowing anything about what we'll be doing, I feel a twinge of excitement. But Zed still looks unhappy and is shaking his head.

'Do you have a problem with that, Zed?' Rhallon asks.

'I do. If we bring that kid along he'll get in our way, or get himself killed. Why not Hossein or Kerrie, or Oskar?'

'Zed's right,' one of his mates rumbles.

Rhallon lets out a frustrated-sounding sigh.

'Very well. How about he shows us what he's got? I'll bet you ten creds you can't take him down, Zed.'

Zed snorts. And then grins. 'Ten? You're on.'

I stare at Rhallon in dismay.

He shrugs. 'This job is the big time, Kyle. Pull it off and there are riches to be made. Frag it up, we'll all swing. They've a right to know that you're up to it.'

Couches are shoved back to clear a space in the centre of the room. Zed strips his jacket off. And I wince as I see how massively built he is. This'll be lots of fun, I don't think.

Then again, it's not lost on me how this mysterious job could well be the miracle Sky and I need. With luck, my share could buy us passages to Enshi Four. First though, I've got to stop Zed from ripping my head off. Let's hope my six months of daily Gemini combat training will give me an advantage over his bulk and his viciousness.

We square up in the cleared space.

Zed's stance is upright. Careless. A big target.

I have him down for a lunger, and he doesn't disappoint. After a bit of circling around each other, he makes a grab at me. For a built guy he's fast, I'll give him that. But so am I. Fast enough to skip sideways and leave him clutching nothing but air.

Rhallon laughs, and does me an accidental favour.

Zed is riled. Red-faced and snarling he comes after me again, swinging his big fists. But my cage fights have honed my ducking and weaving, and it's not hard to avoid his punches. He puts so much power behind them that he loses balance and stumbles. Right into my counterpunch. I catch him with a hard left in the throat that chokes and staggers him. While he's busy bulging his eyes, I take him down with a simple hip throw.

And step back, not even breathing hard. Bounce around a bit on the balls of my feet, for show.

'What did I tell you, Zed?' Rhallon calls out.

He gets up again, cursing. 'Kid got lucky, that's all.'

Now he's more careful, more dangerous. Doesn't change anything. All he's got is strength and the willingness to hurt, no empty-hand fighting skills to speak of.

I start to enjoy myself. And 'get lucky' again. This time he hits the deck awkwardly and stays down for long enough that I worry I've done him real harm. But he's only winded.

Rhallon steps between us. 'Enough!'

Zed slumps back, panting. Glares murder at me.

I wink down at him. Dumb, I know, but I can't resist it.

22
MARAUDERS AND SCREAMERS

When I get back to our room, Sky's turned up. Sort of. She's scored more bliss and is so smashed and dopy I'm not sure she follows when I tell her I'll be away for a while. Her head nods, but there isn't too much going on behind her eyes. In the end, all I can do is make her comfortable, and run around buying two weeks' worth of food for her to eat while I'm gone.

Luckily Mags shows up. I tell her to watch out for Sky the best she can. Twenty creds it costs me. That girl could bargain rings round Murdo.

I make sure I'm back at the safe house in plenty of time. Nobody says very much, which suits me.

When everyone is here, Rhallon leads us back down to the lower decks. And then lower still, down a hidden maintenance shaft, until we must be deep inside the ghost levels. We emerge in a dimly lit area that's been patched up and repressurised. It's cold and dank. Condensation drips from rust-streaked walls. And pretty much filling all of the available space is the bulk of a starship. Behind it, stars shimmer through an air shield.

A ramp is down and waiting. Rhallon herds us all aboard. A bearded guy in overalls is waiting. They bump fists.

'Masson,' Rhallon says. 'Good to see you.'

'Been too long,' he says. 'I'll get your guys settled in.'

Squashed in is more like it. The crew quarters on that freighter we stowed away on were measly, but this is a fraggin' joke. I end up with a length of corridor, to be trodden on and cursed.

Hatches clang shut. Lights flicker, and I feel and hear a deep thrumming. We're on our way. Not long afterwards my skin feels scratchy as we shift into dee-emm.

Not good, but I console myself that I've had worse.

We're fed in two shifts, half of us taking turns to be crammed into the one compartment big enough.

Rhallon joins us from the flight deck. He waits until we're mostly done stuffing our faces, then stands and stabs an elegant finger at the portable display screen he's holding, like a scaled-up cleverbox. 'Listen up. This juicy red dot here is a Combine heavy transport by the name of *Le Roi Batti*, inbound to our part of the sector. Our sources tell us that it's heading for a cargo drop on Arawak Nine.'

The other guys around the table look real interested. Zed is practically licking his lips.

'What'll she be carrying?' he asks.

Rhallon smiles. 'Their last stop was at the Grey Drift, an asteroid field in the New Ceres cluster. They picked up a big load of viridium. Don't ask me what the stuff is for. All I know is it's a precious metal and as rare as loyalty. We've already got someone gagging to buy it off us.'

I swallow hard, remembering the faint distress call that pulled the ComSec cruiser off us in Barzahk orbit. So that's what this job is . . . we're going raiding.

Of course. It was always going to be the Syndicate.

Rhallon powers the screen down and gestures at the bearded guy. 'Masson here is my second-in-command. He'll brief those of you who haven't been on a raid before. Pay close attention to what he has to say.'

With that, he heads back to the flight deck.

Masson has one of those deep, rumbling voices that booms around the confined space. He tells us this ship we're on is a stolen and stripped-down assault ship fitted with an enormously powerful drive, capable of easily chasing down any regular space freighter. With its go-faster mods it might even outrun the fastest ComSec cruiser. 'We call it our screamer.'

'Because it's so fast?' Cam says.

Some of the experienced guys laugh and swap looks.

'Not just that. Somebody had the bright idea of stripping out most of the shielding to save mass. When our pilots wick it up to full power, it gets pretty grim in here.'

Oh great. I groan out loud.

Masson rumbles on about how dee-emm exposure is nasty, but won't kill us. We're heading for our intercept point at cruise setting, so shouldn't feel too bad. Only if our quarry runs will Rhallon order full power.

'Will they run?' somebody asks.

'Some try to make a deal. But they all run in the end.'

Heavy freighters like *Le Roi Batti* are no pushovers, Masson goes on to explain. They'll carry security guards for protection during loading and unloading. Many will be ex-military or ex-ComSec. Past their fighting best, but still dangerous. We could come up against def-bots too, little flying drones they can stick on us. One touch and you're dead or stunned, depending how they're set. With us being raiders, he reckons they'll be set to kill. Any fighting will be hand-to-hand; energy weapons are too risky in case they cause a hull rupture. We'll have the edge of nublood speed and strength. They'll have prepared defences. He tells us how, on the most recent raid, the target's guards trapped some of our fighters in a compartment and let the air out.

'You lucky lot are their replacements.'

'Fresh meat to the Syndicate grinder,' Zed says.

Lastly, Masson assigns us to various assault squads. Each squad leader will take us through what's expected of us over the next few days. He answers a few questions, then leaves us to chat, mostly about what the spoils might be, and how they're shared out. I nod and smile, making out I'm listening.

But I'm not. This set-up feels so horribly familiar. I'd thought the Syndicate was at least doing some good by offering nubloods a way out of slavery. Nah. Like always it's only so we can be used again. Back on Wrath, nubloods were forced to slave down the Saviour's darkblende mines. Cheaper than machines, able to survive the fierce radiation. It's the same deal here. With our fast healing we're the ideal crew – the *only* crew – for an unshielded raider ship. With our speed and strength we're ideal assault troops for a fight where you daren't use energy weapons.

And if the Syndicate lose a few of us, so what? They can ship more of us in from Wrath.

It's tough not to look as sick and gutted as I feel.

Later we're given body armour and killsticks. The weapon is

the length of my forearm, an insulated grip at one end. When I ask the woman who hands me mine how to switch it to stun, she gives me a hard stare. 'Why bother?'

'I just want to know.'

Grudgingly, she shows me how.

'Too soft to kill?' Zed says, and sneers.

I show him my teeth. 'You're not *still* sulking?'

We face off again, although I don't suppose he'll start anything with everyone around. And I'm right. But now he leans in close so only I can hear. 'When we board that freighter, there'll be fighting. It'll be confusing. If I tagged you with my killstick, nobody would know.'

'That cuts both ways,' I say, and shove past him.

But for all my trying to act tough, I'm shaking as I crawl into my sleep bag in the companionway. And that's gutting. After all I've been through, I thought I'd be braver by now. I try telling myself that bullies like Zed are all snarl and no teeth, but can't quite believe it. No three ways about it – I've made a dangerous enemy. The guy's capable of anything.

Closing my eyes, I wish Sky was here. She'd know how to deal with Zed, or could watch my back.

I fall asleep still cross at her, but missing her more.

In the days that follow, as we make our way at quarter speed to where the freighter will pass, Zed does his spiteful best to wind me up, bumping into me, whispering jibes. But I reckon Rhallon has had a word with him, as it could be worse. I pass the time by sleeping mainly. Until Rhallon remembers he wanted me to pass on some of my empty-hand fighting moves. So now I spend hours in the compartment behind the flight deck, instructing.

I'm helping a guy up after showing off a reaping leg throw when Rhallon asks how it was I hooked up with the Gemini ident resistance and got my combat training.

'What d'you mean?' I stall.

'I assume you were sent to the Facility, the same as the rest of us. Did you escape? I've been meaning to ask you.'

The other guys all look interested.

I think quickly. Admitting I didn't grow up in an ident camp could lead to awkward questions. 'I never made it to the Facility. Gemini forced down the Slayer windjammer carrying us there. That's how I joined the resistance.'

'Taking a chance, weren't they? What if you'd all been killed in the shoot-down?'

'After what I hear about the Facility, I'm not complaining. Anyway, a few months later, we took the place out.'

Rhallon starts. 'You destroyed the Facility?' He sounds almost disappointed.

I'm nodding when the hatch to the flight deck bangs open. A jumpsuited young woman sticks her head out.

'Contact,' she yells. 'A heavy transport.'

'*Le Roi Batti*!' Rhallon's face lights up with a savage joy.

'Looks like it.' The girl ducks back into the cockpit.

And I'm surrounded by bloodthirsty roars and cheers.

'Shut up and listen!' Rhallon shouts. 'Soon as we're in range, we'll order them to cut their drive and prepare to be boarded. If they run, we'll have to chase them down. That means full power for as long as it takes. I promise you though, the misery will be worth it after we've taken her. For now, I want you all wearing your armour and in position to board.'

With that, he follows jumpsuit girl on to the flight deck.

'Move yourselves!' Masson bellows.

I hardly hear him. My heart is pounding and I stare at the flight-deck hatch. That girl in the jumpsuit, who stuck her head out and shouted to Rhallon. Her hair was dark and long, but the shape of her face and those fierce green eyes . . .

23
A HARD DOCKING

The freighter chooses to run. Course it does.

Rhallon orders max thrust and we give chase. The light goes feeble in our compartment and it fills with a deep thrumming sound I feel more than hear. My skin quits itching, but only because it starts crawling off me. Even though I knew it was coming, the dee-emm exposure is a sucker punch. I cry out and fall to my knees. This is agony and torture and poison all at the same time, ten times worse than anything I felt on the old freighter. And I'm not the only one cursing and groaning.

But my nublood starts to fight back. Little by little, breathing gets easier. I go from wanting to howl to wondering if I can stand up. Others beat me to it, climbing back to their feet. Yeah, well, they'll have been through this before. Gritting my teeth I listen as Cam asks Masson what happens if the freighter we're chasing calls for help.

'They can call all they like,' he says. 'Won't do any good. Comms only limp along at light speed, so it'll be ages before they're heard. By then we'll be long gone.'

It still messes with my head just how unimaginably IMMENSE the gulfs are between worlds.

But what I want to know is . . . *was that Tarn I saw?*

'Guys!' Masson calls out. 'Quit bitching and moaning – we've work to do. You know the drill. Armour up and get into position ready for boarding.'

He pushes past, heading off to tell the rest of the crew.

I grab his arm as he goes by. 'That girl who stuck her head out of the flight deck. What's her name?'

Masson snorts, shrugs me off and keeps going.

Cursing, I peer through the hatch and into the cramped cockpit. All I can see from here though are the backs of two big flight seats, with Rhallon leaning between them. Beyond him a screen shows the wriggling blackness of dark matter. In the middle is a red symbol for a spaceship, obviously fleeing. A box beside it has numbers counting down.

'Move yourself!' Zed snarls, pulling me after him.

I shove him away furiously. 'Let go of me.'

But this isn't the time to charge into the flight deck. Rhallon would kill me. Guess I'll have to wait until after we've taken the freighter. Assuming I survive. So I grit my teeth and stumble and squeeze back through the ship. My assigned position is in the corridor outside the docking chamber.

Kragg snaps at me to hurry up and get my armour on.

'Yeah, yeah.' I'm not in the mood to be snapped at.

I'll be fighting alongside Kragg, a man called Rat and a woman called Una. After the hard docking, where we clamp our screamer to *Le Roi Batti*'s hull and cut our way inside, we'll be the second assault squad to board. Once in, our job is to secure the freighter's drive chamber.

That's if we can find it . . .

I struggle into my armour and check my stick is showing orange for stun. Una sees this and sneers. Her weapon of choice is a long iron bar. She calls this her 'wrecker'.

After that it's waiting and suffering.

Rat curses as his nose starts dripping blood.

I suggest he tilts his head forward and pinches his nose. He tells me to drop dead.

We get a few short breaks from our torment as we alter course. Turns out starships can't manoeuvre while in dee-emm; inertia would rip them apart. They have to shift into regular space, alter course and then shift back. *Le Roi Batti* must be ducking and weaving as they try to get away, and we'll be matching their every move. See, that's another advantage we've got. Nublood pilot, nublood speed and reactions. They stand no chance of shaking us.

Suddenly there's an ear-splitting *tzzzummm* sound. The starship staggers beneath me, sending me sprawling.

'Are we hit?' I say, startled.

Kragg looks at me like I'm the biggest gom ever.

'Relax, kid.' Una says. 'That was just the shockwave from our dee-emm drives clashing and spitting us both back out into regular space. Which means they're done running now. As long as we keep real tight to them they won't be able to shift again. Won't be long before we board them.'

It seems she's right.

I hear cheering. Rhallon appears, in full body armour.

'This is it!' he calls out.

Despite myself, I feel a stab of excitement.

As he passes me, he thumps my shoulder reassuringly. Or maybe he's just shoving me aside. He ducks inside the docking compartment to join his lead assault squad, already crouched round the big airlock hatch in the floor.

Kragg nudges me. 'See the guy with the plasma lance?'

I do. On my side of the airlock a guy is dressed head-to-boot in protective gear, dark goggles dangling around his neck. He'll do the cutting-in after we've hooked the freighter, and has only seconds to finish it, so the defenders don't have time to take up defensive positions.

'What about him?' I ask.

'Last guy who did it burnt his foot off. Kept going though, and finished the job. Good effort, I thought.'

I'm not too sure if I believe this, but wince anyway.

Someone shouts to hang on, that during final approach things could get rough. I copy Kragg and wedge myself across the narrow corridor. Only just in time. Next thing I know I'm being sat on by a dozen invisible fourhorns and crushed down into the decking. All around I hear the screech of tortured metal and the crashes and bangs of stuff that hasn't been secured properly. After that we get flung this way and that. Several times it's all I can do to stop myself being pitched head-first into the opposite wall. I smell the sharp stink of dust and debris being shaken out of their hiding places. Now we all go light and float up. The up is easy, but the slamming back down is hard.

Somebody lands badly and cries out in pain, but after a dull metal-on-metal clang, everything settles down. A speaker in the ceiling howls, making me jump.

'Guys, we're locked on and driving the docking tunnel in. Start cutting on my mark. Three . . . two . . .'

The voice could be Sky's.

'One. Get cutting!'

The assault crew don't hang about. Two haul open the hatch in the floor. The guy with the plasma lance swings his legs over the edge and drops out of sight. There's a blinding blue flash as he fires the fierce tool up. Next thing, thousands of sizzling golden sparks fountain out of the hole. I smell burning metal, like when I was welding. And I start worrying about crawling through a tunnel with space outside after it's been peppered with hot metal fragments.

'Hey, Kragg, shouldn't we be in spacesuits?'

He laughs scornfully. 'Hold your breath. It's what I do.'

Not funny. But the others think so, and snigger.

A loud metal crash and a gust of equalising air pressure tell us our cutter is done. We're in.

'Go! Get in there!' Rhallon yells.

Fair play to the guy, he's the first to follow the plasma-lance guy into the tunnel, swinging his legs over the raised hatch rim and dropping down out of sight. The rest of the first assault team are close behind him.

But I'm too busy gawping and not following Kragg.

'Move it, Kyle!' Una's shove gets me going.

Clutching my stunstick, I stumble after Kragg into the docking compartment. From below us I hear the scuffles, grunts and thumps of hand-to-hand fighting. We rush to our places around the hatch. A glance shows me it's one hell of a long drop. From the stacked crates down there, we've cut our way into a cargo hold. One of our guys lies sprawled below us, his leg folded impossibly under him.

'Hold this!' Kragg shouts, chucking me his killstick.

Vaulting into the hatchway, he slides down a ladder on the side, not bothering with the rungs. It's a few metres from the bottom to the deck below, but he lands okay and straightens up. I drop his stick to him, then mine, and follow the same way. Blister my fingers and nearly land on the guy with the bust leg, but it's quick. And nobody takes a whack at me on my way down, which is good.

Kragg throws me my stick. 'You help the rest down. I'll watch your back.'

This is what we've practised. I catch the next guy's stick so that he's got both hands free for the ladder. While he's sliding down, I risk a glance around and see a shiny head-sized sphere smack into one of our guys. There's a bright flash and he rag-dolls backwards. Loads more of the deadly little def-bots whine about. Our first assaulters, led by Rhallon, are struggling to fight them off.

Una's next down. Grabbing her wrecking bar off me, she charges past Kragg and swings at one of the bots.

Bang! A blinding flash. The heavily dented drone spirals away, trailing sparks and smoke, smacks itself into a bulkhead and clatters lifelessly to the deck.

But these things are smart. Another one speeds around in a wide circle before flashing in to attack her from behind.

Kragg leaps. He knocks it down with his killstick.

'Sneaky little fraggers!' Una yells.

As more of us get stuck in, the last def-bot is turned into

a battered and smoking wreck. Three of our guys are down though. None look like they'll be getting up again.

Kragg shouts for us to follow him and sets off at a run towards a hatch on the far side of the hold. Before we reach it, it bangs open.

Body-armoured guys pour in through it. A grim-faced lot, they're carrying clear plastic shields and killsticks.

Kragg doesn't hesitate. With a roar, he springs forward and starts swinging. Tags one too. The man cries out and crumples. Before I know it I'm at his shoulder and swinging away too. Now that I'm fighting I'm not scared any more. The guards' shields make it tricky to tag their bodies, but when they swipe back at us it exposes their arms. One guy has a go at me. I block with my armoured left forearm. Before he can pull his arm back I use all my nublood speed and tag him in his unprotected armpit. I feel the *tzzziiip* as the stick discharges. He drops like a slaughtered goat.

Rat, one of our bigger guys, doesn't bother with his stick. When the guard he's facing tries to force him back with his shield, he grabs it and yanks it off him.

Una smashes away at them with her wrecking bar.

Rhallon and the survivors of his team come running. We're too strong, too fast, and too many. It's all over in seconds.

A few scramble back through the hatch and leg it. The rest decorate the decking with their stiff bodies. The three I've tagged will be unconscious. As for the others – well, I don't look closely, but my guess is they're all dead.

'You're hurt,' Kragg says to Rhallon.

I see now how Rhallon's left arm hangs by his side.

'It's nothing,' he says. 'Secure the drive. I'll take care of the flight deck. Kyle, you're with my squad now.'

I nod and follow as he pounds off along a corridor.

Our way to the flight deck is blocked by a bulkhead and a locked hatch. Through a clear panel set into it, I glimpse fearful-looking crew watching us from the far side. Rhallon bangs on it and they twitch, but they're not about to open it.

We don't let that stop us. Hatches like this were designed to keep space or a fire out, not determined raiders. Rhallon waves one of our squad forward. She produces a big old bolt-cutter with insulated grips and uses it to hammer open a panel in the hatch. A look at the wires inside and she cuts something. Lots of sparks. The hatch sighs open. And there's no fight in the guys on the other side. As we swarm through they surrender.

I should feel glad, as it saves them from being killed. But it seems so pathetic, I feel ashamed for them.

That's when a lone def-bot comes streaking in.

I only just catch the glint of it out of the corner of my eye, but instinct kicks in. It's a metre away from taking Rhallon's head off when I whack and deflect it with my stunstick. I don't catch it hard enough to take it out, but at least it misses him. Agile as any hunting bird, it turns and hurls itself back at us. One of Rhallon's guys steps up and smashes it out of the air with his killstick. It lands at my feet, big licks of flame coming out of it.

'Bind them,' Rhallon says, as if nothing had happened.

We snap-tie the prisoners' hands behind their backs before Una herds them to the hold. Further on a few braver guards have one last lunge at us. We swat this lot like bugs too.

By now, even though I know what we're doing is wrong, I

can't help feeling a raw and fierce satisfaction.

But it doesn't last long.

The flight deck's hatch is locked, and this time there's no handy panel with wires inside to be cut. Rhallon has a simple but brutal solution. He has one of the captured guards fetched. Meanwhile, Kragg bangs the butt of his stick on the hatch to tell whoever's hiding inside that we're here. When the prisoner is brought, Rhallon holds a blade to the man's neck and waves at the hatch's built-in camera.

'Open up,' he snarls, 'or watch me slit his throat.'

The hatch . . . stays shut.

Rhallon slits the guy's throat, and drops him like a rag. Another guard is fetched, a woman this time. I can't keep the horror off my face.

Kragg sees, and grins. 'Took three last time.'

So I'm massively relieved when I hear heavy-duty bolts grind back, and see the hatch start to open.

Still smiling, Rhallon drops the ashen-faced woman by slamming the knife's hilt into the back of her neck. She crumples to the deck like someone's stolen her bones.

Kragg ducks inside, leading with his killstick.

'Clear!' he calls back to us.

We pile in after him, Rhallon first. With this being such a big transport I'd expected a big flight deck, but it's not all that much bigger than our screamer's. A pair of fancy sculpted seats face loads of control screens. Between them stands a tall woman in a blue and green uniform. Her lined face is pale with fear and blotchy with anger.

'This freighter operates under ComSec authority and

protection,' she growls. 'When we don't turn up at —'

Rhallon lashes out and shuts her up. She staggers back, eyes bulging, clutching at her throat. Hits the back of the seat behind her and slides down it.

'Reckon she's in charge?' Kragg asks.

'Not any more she isn't,' Rhallon replies, smiling.

24

A HARDER CONVERSATION

The fighting is over. A last few def-bots have been shut down remotely from the flight deck. Ten minutes after hard docking our way in, *Le Roi Batti* is ours.

'Can you manage here?' I ask.

Rhallon has left me and a guy called Lexy guarding the flight deck. He's off somewhere checking the cargo manifest to see where the precious viridium is stowed.

Lexy, always chewing on something, frowns. 'Why?'

'I'm busting for a leak.'

'Be quick then. If Rhallon finds you gone he'll skin you.'

I tell him I'll be quick, and clear off. But it isn't a pee I'm desperate for. Ever since the fighting stopped I've had only one thing on my mind – Sky's sister, Tarn. Those dark green eyes. That voice. If I'm right, this changes *everything*.

Even just thinking about it makes me breathless.

Mustn't bump into Rhallon though. That'd be BAD. But I can't be sneaking about either, so I decide to act all cool, like I've been ordered back to the hold. Which goes okay until I run into Una, Cam and another two of our guys prodding a dozen or so captured crew along the corridor towards me. Hands bound behind their backs, the prisoners stumble past looking miserable and scared. I don't blame them. Our lot are treating them brutal as hell.

'Where you taking them?' I ask Una.

'To the escape craft. Fire 'em off and forget 'em.'

Cam grins and winks at me, clearly enjoying himself.

The prisoners shuffle past as I step aside. One of them, a freckled young redhead girl who can't be much older than I am, shoots me a pleading look. I turn my face away, ashamed, and hurry on. After that, my luck holds and I find my way back to the compartment we hacked into. A quick peek inside shows me Rhallon isn't here. Conscious that I daren't be away from the flight-deck for too long, I clamber inside and jog towards the ragged hole in the ceiling. Somebody's shifted a crate so it's under the hole. A wire ladder hangs down.

I'm clambering up on the crate when a pack suddenly drops from above, very nearly hitting me. And now the ladder is lashing about, because somebody's on it.

Damn it. Jumping clear, I wait impatiently, glancing around and praying Rhallon doesn't show up.

When I look back, the climber's down.

'Tarn?' I say, startled.

Her messed-up, glossy black hair is different. No tattooed teardrop drips from her left eye. But still, there's no three ways about it: I'm looking another Sky in the face.

'I'm busy.' She grabs the pack and goes to push past me.

Not thinking, I grab her arm. 'Wait!'

She yanks it free. 'What's your problem?!'

One thing's for sure, thanks to her nublood she's loads stronger than Sky. I step back, hold my palms up and try not to look threatening. Or like I'm some nutter.

'Sorry. Listen. I'm Kyle. And we *need* to talk.'

Tarn sneers. 'I don't think so! What I have to do is find this old freighter's flight deck and get it moving again.'

With that she shoves past and makes for the open hatch leading forward. I hustle to catch up with her.

'Sky's been looking for you,' I call out.

That stops her and stiffens her back. She swings round and fixes me with a scowl I know only too well.

'What – did – you – say?' she asks, real low and slow.

I take a deep breath. 'Sky and me, we've chased after you all over Wrath. Thought we'd found you too, in the No-Zone, but you'd already been hauled off-world.'

Tarn sways visibly. '*Sky?*'

I try for a smile. 'Your twin sister . . . remember?'

'And what if I don't want reminding? Or to be found?'

I open my mouth. Close it again.

Without another word, Tarn turns her back on me and stomps off along the corridor.

I sigh, grit my teeth and run after her.

'Look, I know you two don't get along, but she –'

Tarn whips round. Catching me by surprise, she grabs me and throws me up against the corridor wall. All I can do is stare bug-eyed as she holds me there.

'Leave me alone,' she hisses.

'But she's your sister,' I say. 'And she's in trouble.'

Tarns peels her lips away from her teeth in a grimace that would scare a Reaper, and shoves me so that I bang my head against the hull. 'In trouble? Good! That bitch is nothing to me. Serves her right for all the suffering she brought me. You can tell her that from me, why don't you?'

And she may be Sky's twin, but I see now that she's a stranger – a cruel and mean and spiteful stranger. Being an ident myself, this shakes me to my core.

'You don't understand,' I say.

Tarn laughs. She actually laughs. 'Don't I?'

Who knows what would have happened next? But a clatter of boots on deck plates warns us somebody is coming. Tarn lets me go and we spring apart. A second later some of our guys appear. Leading them is Zed, not a mark on him. A shame that.

'Tarn,' he calls. 'They're waiting for you.'

'Yeah, yeah. On my way, aren't I?'

One last glare at me and she squeezes past them.

I'm so gobsmacked and disappointed I just stare after her, shaking my head. Big mistake. Next thing I know, Zed's mates surround me and he gets in my face.

'Well, look who's here – Rhallon's little pet,' he growls.

'Ha ha.' I step around him.

One of his thug mates shoves me roughly back.

'Not so fast,' Zed says. He flashes a sly look at each end of the corridor, making sure that nobody else is about. His hand dips and reappears clutching a laser-knife.

I quit raging at Tarn and wake up to the trouble I'm in.

Four of them, one of me.

'You don't want to do this, Zed.' I back away. Reach for my

stunstick, but it's not there. Course not. It's on the flight deck, where I left it. Hadn't thought I'd need it.

'I think I do.' Zed grins, and powers up the blade.

I shake my head. 'Rhallon saw me after the fighting was all over. He knows I wasn't hurt. Stick me with that thing and how long will it take him to figure out it was you?'

'You know what? I'll take that chance.'

He twitches the green blade at me, making me jump.

'With you dead,' says Zed, glancing back at his mates, 'that's one less to share this raid's loot between.'

'Sounds good,' one of them says.

Only now, when I least expect it, my odds improve. One of the other guys slips around him. I think he's coming *at* me, but I'm wrong. He gets between us, hands out to ward Zed off.

To my astonishment . . . it's Cam.

'Leave him be, Zed! He ain't worth it.'

Zed bares his teeth at him. 'What the frag are you doing? Get out of my way. Or do you want gutting too?'

But fair play to Cam, he holds his ground. 'You heard him. Do Kyle now, and Rhallon'll kill you for defying him.'

'Yeah!' I say, and wish I hadn't – it sounds so lame.

'Shift yourself,' Zed says to Cam.

'No.' Cam steps back beside me instead.

Two against three now. I like these odds better.

Rage turns Zed's bully face purple and blotchy. His eyes narrow at me, a sure tell that he's getting ready to lunge. I drop into my fighting crouch, fists clenched.

But the lunge doesn't come. Like most bullies, Zed's no fool. Either he thinks better of taking the two of us on, or the worry of what Rhallon might do to him kicks its way into his head at last. With a curse, he powers the blade down.

'We're not done here, Kyle,' he growls. 'Don't think we are. And Cam, you'll pay for crossing me.'

I keep my gob shut, not wanting to push my luck.

Cam mumbles something feeble about *not* crossing him, just saving him from himself. Zed sneers his ugly face off at that and pushes between us, before stalking off down the corridor and ducking into the hold. A second later, when they realise they're being left behind, his other two bully mates go to shove their way between us too.

Nah. I've been shoved enough. I snarl and make like I'm going to throw a punch. Startled, they both leap back. One trips and ends up on his arse. Serves him right, I reckon. If there's one thing I hate more than a bully, it's a bully's sidekick. I make a point of stepping over him before he can get up.

'Wait up!' Cam calls, scrambling after me.

I wait until the corridor curves round enough so that we're out of sight, then stop and turn to face him. 'And there was me thinking you hated me worse than Zed does.'

'Who says I don't?'

That tells me. 'Yeah, well, thanks.'

He scowls. 'Don't thank me, thank Anuk.'

'*Anuk?*' I say, very nearly spitting my teeth out.

'She, uh, asked me to look out for you.'

I stare at him. 'Anyway I owe you.'

'You do. The next time you see her, you could tell her?'

Letting out a breath I hadn't realised I was holding, I tell Cam I'll be glad to. And mean it. He nods. We end up looking at each other almost shyly. It's . . . awkward.

'Look, I've got to get back to the flight deck,' I say.

'Not keeping you, am I?'

I turn to go, hesitate, then look back.

'You heard what Zed said. Maybe we should stick together from now on, and watch each other's backs.'

Cam grunts. 'Might be a smart move, all right.'

I shove my fist out. We bump stumps.

'It still don't make us mates though,' he says, grinning.

'Never said it did,' I say. 'Come on, let's go.'

On our way to the flight deck I hope my absence hasn't been spotted. And wonder what I should say to Tarn to make her listen to me. But when we arrive, its hatch is closed.

Lexy is lurking outside, clearly fed up.

'You took your fraggin' time.'

'Wasn't missed, was I?'

He shakes his head, and I can breathe again.

'What you doing out here?' I try the hatch. It's locked.

'Waiting for you. The pilot says that we can go.'

'Thin girl? Black hair?'

'That's her. Cross as hell about something she was. Wouldn't talk to me, just threw me out.'

I decide talking to Tarn had better wait.

'So what now?' Cam asks.

Lexy has us follow him to the crew quarters. There, it seems we can take it easy for a while and lick any wounds that need licking. Suits me. I'd thought we'd be put to work transferring that viridium stuff to our screamer so we can clear off with it, but Lexy puts me right. Our screamer's too small, so we're keeping the *Le Roi Batti* as what he calls a 'prize' ship. We'll fly it to the nearest dark market and offload the cargo there. With luck, we might find a buyer for the freighter itself.

'Screamer rides piggyback. Gives the crew a break,' he explains from where he's stretched out on a couch.

But I'm only pretending to listen.

Zed, I reckon I can handle. I'm less sure about Tarn. In my head I play back what happened . . . and feel like puking.

'What's wrong?' Cam asks, looking at me.

'Nothing,' I say, startled.

But that's a lie, of course. Just about *everything* is wrong.

25
THE PLEASURE ZONE

Le Roi Batti's drive has graphene shielding a metre thick so I only know we're 'shifting' through the back door of dark matter because a display says we are. Cam swears he can feel a tingling in his toes, but I tell him that's got more to do with him not washing his feet. With nothing to do but kill time by sleeping or playing dumb games, time crawls by. When I can I hang out by the flight deck, hoping to catch Tarn by herself. But either the other Syndicate pilot is in there, or the hatch is shut.

It's three days before Cam's toes quit their tingling and the freighter finally shifts back out into regular space.

Rhallon gathers us in the compartment where we gobble our meals. A bulkhead-mounted screen shows the star-spattered view ahead. Front and centre is a world wrapped in clouds, and we must be closing on it fast as it's bigger each time I look.

Everybody's buzzing with excitement so it's fierce loud in here. Kragg stands and bellows at us to shut up. We do, but only after Rhallon comes in.

He makes straight for the screen and stands before it.

'Okay, listen up,' he says. 'We're about another hour from orbit, so the good news is it won't be long before you can stretch your legs and have some fun.'

Lots of whoops and cheers from the room.

'It's not my legs I want stretching,' Cam whispers.

I pretend I didn't hear him while Kragg works on shutting everybody up again. The rumour is that as a reward for taking the freighter we're being treated to some downtime in a pleasure hub, whatever that is.

'But first we need to offload our cargo,' Rhallon continues. 'We'll hold position out here while we do that. Kragg will organise you into working parties. I expect you all to put your backs into it. The faster we unload, the faster we'll be down there.'

He jerks his head at the cloud world behind him.

It hasn't got any bigger since he started talking so I'm guessing we've shut our drive down. And now I see what look like sparks floating up from its surface. Dozens of smaller freighters swarming spaceward to meet us.

'What's this place called?' I ask Una, but she won't tell me.

'Duh! If you don't know, you can't spill,' Cam jeers.

I don't rise to it. Three days we've mucked about together and he's not getting easier to like. Anyway, I get it. Life in the Syndicate means secrets and lies, just like Wrath.

Six hours later, my back's breaking and my arms feel stretched long enough to drag on the floor. But we're done, and *Le Roi Batti*'s six holds are empty. I listened while I was slaving away. These small freighters will smuggle our captured cargo to the far reaches of the Vulpes sector, for sale on various illegal dark markets scattered about.

The last of them has undocked. Rhallon looks pleased. With good reason, according to Una who saw the cargo manifest. Seems there was more viridium than we'd thought, so this could be the Syndicate's richest raid yet.

'That should be good for *all* of us,' Cam says to me.

The cloudy world fills the screen now. Once we've slotted into our orbit we'll be met by a shuttle and ferried to the surface below. Heavy freighters don't do atmospheric descents, not without breaking up.

'Good,' I say, fiddling with my fake-finger glove. We're all wearing them again. Rhallon's orders.

'You don't sound sure,' he says. 'We've got one hell of a result here and we're still alive. So why the long face?'

'I've just got a few things to figure out.'

'What sort of things?'

'Nothing-to-do-with-you things!'

'Okay, okay.' He takes the hint and shuts up.

A few things to figure out. Doesn't sound so hard, said like that. But the truth is I'm still reeling from Tarn's reaction and worried I won't be able to talk her round. I can only hope that when she hears her nublood can save Sky from dying . . .

I think I sigh out loud because Cam rolls his eyes.

He has a point. When I was down about something back in the Barrenlands, Rona would say: 'Worrying won't get you anywhere, just do the best you can.' And she was right. It got us through some tough times anyway. So I give myself a shake. I'll talk to Tarn again. This time, I'll *make* her listen. And if she won't offer Sky her blood, then I'll damn well take it from her!

But how to catch her alone?

Una's at the next table over. I slide along my seat and tap her on the shoulder. 'Una, you got a second?'

'No. Get lost.'

The woman's always saying things like this, so I don't blink. 'Do we all go down to the surface?'

'Of course. Why? Don't you want to?' she says.

'What about our pilots?'

She grins. 'Taken a fancy to one of them, have you?'

I nearly spit my teeth out. 'Well?'

'Tarn, is it? Yeah, she's cute.'

'Do they, or don't they?'

'Relax, Kyle. Yeah, we all get to go. Another crew is incoming to take this thing off our hands.'

Cam has big ears. 'What will happen to it?'

'It'll be sold on. Or flown to a wrecker world and carved up there for scrap. That's my guess. Harder to trace.'

I zone out, because I've heard what I wanted to hear. Tarn *will* be joining us on the cloud planet.

And I'm not about to give up on Sky.

Somewhere down there, I'll have to take my chance. . .

No three ways about it, this pleasure hub is the most mind-blowing and beautiful place I've ever seen. A vision of steel and glittering glass, the lower three-quarters is like an upside-down tower. Narrow at the bottom, it spreads out to support a vast aerial platform. On this, reaching for the sky, is a vast open-topped structure. Its walls – and that's no way cool enough a word for what I'm looking at – are massive overlapping petals of glass, so the whole thing looks like a flower opening up to greet the sun. Within the tinted petals I glimpse a column with loads of stacked decks or levels. Walkways wind gently up and down between them. The platform and the inside of the flower dome are green and lush, with lakes and grassy areas, trees even. And all this hovers in mid-air above the clouds.

Unlike dropships, this orbital transfer shuttle has viewports either side of its passenger compartment. Speed and sharp elbows won me a seat by one. I'm getting a good look at the hub as we spiral down towards it.

'My turn,' Cam whines.

I press myself back into my seat.

He leans across me and does that weird sucking-in whistle of his. 'Wow! I like it here already.'

It does look good. Better than good. I so wish I could let myself go and enjoy myself here. But I can't. I've got to get close to Tarn and talk her around, if that's possible.

We put down on a weird landing deck that sticks out a hundred metres or so from the side of the structure. Weird, because apart from a few yellow-painted lines, it's clear and see-through. When I peer down uncertainly from the end of the ramp, clouds scud by beneath my feet.

'What are you waiting for?' Rhallon says, stepping boldly on to it. 'If it can support the shuttle, you'll be fine.'

For sure, the men and women lined up on it to welcome us don't look bothered. Their smiles are as impossibly white as their uniforms. They wave so enthusiastically to us you'd swear our arrival had made their day.

Now I don't know what's scarier, them or the platform.

Cam steps down, wobbles, and grins. Not wanting to be last,

I join him. Wobble myself. Laugh out loud.

Delighted, I glance back. And catch Tarn looking away.

Next thing I know I'm being led away by one of the smiling women in white. She says her name is Andrea and hopes to make my stay here a pleasure. For the next half hour she shows me around, while I fight to keep my mouth from hanging open at the wonders I see. My tour ends with her showing me my vast room, and all the zillions of gadgets and things it can do. Amazingly, I have it to myself. It even has an outside sitting-and-gawping-at-the-clouds area she calls a balcony. I'm blown away, well and truly.

'I'll leave you alone now,' Andrea says, switching on the smile again, bright as a welding arc. And then she looks me in the eye. 'Unless you'd prefer company?'

An invisible blowtorch heats my face. Not trusting my voice, I shake my head.

Does she look vexed? Amused? Hard to say.

'Very well. I wish you a very pleasant stay with us. If you want anything, *anything at all*, just call my name.'

I manage a strangled 'thank you'.

She bows and leaves. And for a good few seconds after the door swishes closed, I could kick myself from here all the way back to Wrath. If Cam finds out, he'll die laughing.

Groaning, I shower and have a scrape at my face, then change into clothes Andrea has laid out. Softer and smarter than I'm used to, I feel uncomfortable in them, but Rhallon doesn't want us wandering about all this loveliness in our battered spacer-gear. A wince into a mirror shows me I look all right.

When I finally find my way down to the platform-level bar we're supposed to meet up in, I'm not the first. Rhallon's chatting to Rat and our other pilot.

No Tarn yet. Maybe she chose not to be alone?

Rhallon waves for me to join them. As I sit, a man appears at my shoulder and offers me a fancy red drink on a tray.

'What is it?' I ask, uncertain.

'Won't kill you,' Rat says.

'You might even like it,' Rhallon says.

A beer would be more my thing, but I take it anyway. They've all got the same and raise their glasses.

'To the Syndicate,' Rhallon says, 'and a job well done!'

We drink. As the stuff burns its way down my throat, I can't help glancing around to see if the waiter heard.

Rhallon notices and tells me to relax. 'Whatever we say or do here, it stays here. That's the deal at these places. But that doesn't mean we should shoot our mouths off either. Okay?'

We all nod. As more of our guys drift in, I listen and learn some more. A pleasure hub like this is illegal in space, or on a planet's surface. But as long as it floats about in the atmosphere, ComSec have no authority to shut it down.

'Hey, look,' somebody calls out. 'The sun's setting.'

It is too, and what a sunset! As it sinks below the horizon, orange and red spears of light seem to shoot up into the fast-darkening sky. For a while the cloudscape beneath us turns into a windswept sea of silver and gold.

It's so beautiful I wish Sky was here to see it.

Out of the corner of my eye I see Tarn come in. But she's with two other guys and stays on the far side of the room.

'I never thanked you, Kyle, did I?' Rhallon says, his face turned gold by the sunset.

'What for?' I say, nervously.

'For saving me from that def-bot. I wouldn't be sitting here now if it wasn't for you. So, thank you.'

Not knowing what to say, I say nothing.

Rhallon smiles. He tells me I did well on the raid, justifying my selection. 'And it won't be long before you get your reward. The Syndicate always rewards those who do well and show loyalty. You *are* loyal, aren't you, Kyle?'

For once I think before I speak.

'The Syndicate is the best thing that's ever happened to me.'

He likes this, I can tell. But as our leader, he has to spread himself around. He excuses himself, and moves on to another group. I sip my drink, which I can't say I like. And very nearly spill it when Cam thumps himself down beside me.

'You're not wrong,' he says, clinking my glass with his.

'About what?' I try not to be irritated. And fail.

He necks his drink and grins. 'What you said just now, when you were sucking up to Rhallon. About the Syndicate being the best thing that's ever happened to us. Well, course it is. Nobody gave us nubloods anything, all pureblood fraggers ever did was take from us. So why shouldn't we use our strength and speed to take what we want.' He snags two more drinks from a passing waiter's tray. 'The way I see it, we're owed!'

I said it because that's what I figured Rhallon wanted to hear. but hearing Cam echo it back at me, I wonder if it's true.

Pretty much everyone is here now and the party cuts loose. The music thumps louder. The main lights dim, others fire up like strobes in all sorts of colours, pale pinks and greens that remind me of the shimmering lights we'd sometimes see in the Barrenlands' night sky. Waiters with bottles glide around the room making sure our glasses never go empty. Some people get up and start dancing. I steer well clear of that. And now, mingling in among us, are brightly dressed young men and women, all about our age. All of them friendly and good-looking.

I concentrate on my glass and getting drunk.

The rest of the party I don't remember exactly. Or, when I wake up a long time later, how I got back to my room.

Luckily, there's way more to this hub than partying and getting slaughtered. There are games rooms, trails to be walked, and views to be gazed at. The food is amazing, and you can have as many helpings as you like. I know I should be seeking out Tarn, but there are just so many distractions.

Tomorrow. I'll track her down tomorrow . . .

Three days slide by, in a blink.

Much of my time, I spend watching the snow leopard. At least five times the size of the scrawny little felines we have back on Wrath, her thick fur is smoke-grey on top with darker spots and rings, but whiter on her underbelly. Four massive paws, and an incredibly long tail. The most beautiful creature I've ever seen. Feeding time's the best. She gets excited and paces back and forth until they lob in a hunk of meat. When she eats, the bone-crunching power of her jaws is astonishing.

But it's her unblinking cat eyes I stare at the most. A paler green than Sky's, they're the colour of sadness. I could stare at them forever.

It's the middle of the fourth day and I'm leaning on the rail of the observation platform, peering down at the big cat. She's sprawled on her favourite flat rock, panting. Her eyes are half closed and her massive, heavily furred paws twitch.

Footsteps. Tarn joins me at the rail.

'I wonder if she's dreaming about hunting?'

I stay very still, scared that if I make any move I'll spook her and she'll clear off.

'Or escaping?' I say.

Tarn flicks me the quickest of glances. 'D'you know I thought of buying her with my raiding creds. Ship her to a planet where there's loads to hunt. Set her free to roam.'

I risk a look at her now. 'Yeah? So did I. But we couldn't afford her. Kragg says on the dark market she's worth her weight in darkblende a hundred times over. Because she's one of the last of her species and protected by ComSec, or something like that. Anyway, she'd still be alone, the only snow leopard.'

'Cats don't need company. They're like me.'

I take a deep breath. 'What about Sky?'

Tarn's face pulls tighter, but at least she doesn't slam me into a bulkhead and start raging.

'What *about* her?'

I cut to the chase. 'She's dying. Only you can save her.'

26
A WALK AND A TALK

Dying. A little word that carries a big fraggin' punch, you'd think. That's how I'd imagined it anyway. Tarn looking shocked. Tarn gasping and reeling back.

Nah. Tarn just looks at me. Doesn't even blink.

'Did you hear what I said?'

'I'm not deaf.' She turns to stalk off. Stops. Curses. Looks back. 'I'm going for a walk. Want to join me?'

'Want' is too strong a word, but all I say is: 'Sure.'

The snow leopard stirs, yawning and lifting her head to glare up at us, as Tarn heads off again. I shoot the big cat a last wistful glance, before hurrying after Tarn. The path she takes winds its way through an impossibly perfect meadow.

As I catch her up, Tarn stops to pull her shoes off.

'What are you doing?' I ask.

'What's it look like? This grass is cloned from old Earth grass. We're paying for it, so we might as well feel it underfoot. The shrubs and trees and flowers, they're clones too. Can you smell the blossom? Lovely, isn't it?'

Seconds ago I told her Sky was dying. I stare at her, wanting to snarl, knowing I daren't.

'Now who's deaf?' she says, and sighs. '*Do you smell it?*'

'Yeah, lovely,' I say, grudgingly, sniffing so my nose fills with the sweet scent. 'If you like that sort of thing.'

Her smile struggles. 'Why don't you go barefoot too?'

'I spent half my life barefoot.'

'This is different. A pleasure. As close as you'll ever get to walking on old Earth. You should treat yourself.'

'Why not?' I bend and pull my shoes off.

'There's a place I like,' she says. 'We can talk there.'

She steps off the path on to the lush green grass and sets off, arms swinging, shoes dangling from her hand, as if she hasn't a care in the world. I roll my eyes at her back and follow her. Earth-cloned or not, the grass feels deliciously cool and damp against the soles of my feet.

'Walk beside me,' Tarn says. 'I won't bite you.'

I'm not so sure, but I speed up until we're side by side.

Cutting through some trees that she tells me are Earth oaks, Tarn leads me to the bank of a little pool. A wooden hut with a thatched roof stands on stilts a metre or so out from the shore. A thickish plank spans the gap. We pull our shoes back on and cross over. Inside, a woman in white is waiting. Smiling another impossibly perfect smile, she bows and asks us if we require anything from the hut's bar.

'*Require?*' Tarn mimics. 'Oh, I like the sound of that.'

'No. Thanks,' I say.

The woman bows again and leaves. We have the hut to ourselves. The side facing the pond is open, with a guard rail.

Tarn leans on this and gazes out at the water.

'I hear you saved Rhallon's life.'

'So what?' I lean on the rail beside her.

'Rhallon's got his eye on you. Says he thinks you might have what it takes to be a top Syndicate operator.'

This is big news, but it can wait. 'Let's talk about Sky.'

Tarn sighs, as if I'm boring her. 'You talk, I'll listen.'

'She's dying,' I say, a sudden lump in my throat. 'Darkblende poisoning. Her lungs are shot. The trip out from Wrath on that crappy old freighter made her worse.'

Still Tarn just stares out at the pond. Unbelievable.

'A month is all she's got left,' I say. 'At best.'

Finally Tarn turns to look at me. 'You've got her stashed on the Ark somewhere, haven't you?'

I'm so stunned, my next breath is a long time coming.

'Who told you?' I gasp.

But I'm hardly done asking when the answer hits me. Of course! My new mate Cam spent time with Sky. As soon as he'll have seen Tarn – even with her dark hair and slightly fuller face – he'll have guessed. And squealed.

'Cam!' I hiss. 'I'll wring his fraggin' neck.'

'Harsh,' Tarn says. 'So Sky risks everything to chase after me? I suppose I should be touched.'

I've been fighting a scowl. It gets away from me now.

'You *should* be! Ever since your last Peace Fair, Sky's thought of nothing but you. Avenging you when she thought you were dead. Saving you after we found out you might be alive and a slave. You're *all* she thinks about.'

'Do I look like I need saving?' Tarn says, sneering.

'No,' I growl. 'But Sky *does!*'

She shrugs. 'So buy her some doctoring then.'

I shake my head. 'She's too sick. They don't have the med tech on the Ark. Like I said, only you can save her.'

'Me? What can I do?'

'You're nublood. She's your sister.'

'My *scab* sister, you mean?'

Tough to let such a cheap shot slide, but somehow I manage it. 'All she needs is some of your blood. Your blood will heal her the same way it heals you.'

I hold my breath.

Tarn's face twists itself into knots. 'Are you crazy?'

'No. Look, you said you'd listen. Hear me out.'

'The hell I will.' She goes to push past me. I block her path. We trade glares. But I've been glared at by Sky.

'There's something you don't know. You were held at that Facility place, weren't you? Working their mines?'

'And so what?' she snaps.

'So you were one of the lucky ones. After we raided it we found out there was other nasty stuff going on. In the domes kids were being experimented on. The Slayers' techs were trying to make our healing ability work for them. But guess what? They found it only works for blood relatives, like sisters.'

I stop, the memories of my time in the Facility too grim.

Tarn looks at me sidelong. 'Bullshit.'

'Is it? My brother was blasted in the chest. Nothing our Gemini healers could do to save him. We had nothing to lose, so we tried it. Less than an hour after we got some of my blood into him, he was out of danger. Made a full recovery too. I'm telling you, Tarn, it was like a miracle.'

She opens her mouth, shuts it without saying anything.

'Look, I know you blame Sky for ending up in the camps. But she was a child, and we all make mistakes. Sky's whole life since then has been about trying to make it up to you. Isn't it time to let that hurt go? It's not like I'm asking you to kiss and make up. Just say you'll save her.'

Do I see Tarn's face soften? Can't be sure because she turns her back on me now, looking back out over the pond. There must be fish, because something splashes.

I breathe real soft and wait.

And wait some more, my heart thumping inside me like I've been in a cage fight. I look at her hands. Her fingers are clenched so tightly round the guard rail the knuckles turn white.

A good sign? Or bad?

'At least tell me you'll think about it,' I say desperately.

Her shoulders lift with the breath she takes, sag down as she lets it go. She turns to face me.

'What's it worth?'

I don't think I've heard right. 'Worth?'

'To you?' she says. And now I see the sly look on her face. 'Cam told me you and Sky are hooked up. That true?'

I stare at her, not buying it. All this tough-girl uncaring crap, it's got to be some kind of act. 'We were once. Maybe we still are. It's been tough with her so sick.'

Tarn smiles, a twitch of her lips. 'What do you see in her?'

'We went through some tough times together.'

'Who doesn't on Wrath? That's not what I asked you.'

I squirm, tempted to tell her to mind her own business. Feel a sting of guilt too at having wondered the same myself these past few months. What *do* I see in Sky? I try some answers out in my head. They all sound dumb.

'We just get along,' I mumble.

'You feel sorry for her,' Tarn jeers. 'Is that it?'

That snaps my head up. 'Sorry? For Sky? You're kidding. Either that, or you don't know your sister. She's a warrior. The toughest fighter I've ever met. She has heart. And you know what? The two of us, we *get* each other.'

I stop, wishing I was better with words, like Colm is.

'Aw, that's sweet,' Tarn says, her sneer going nowhere. 'Won't do you any favours with Rhallon though.'

'What won't?' I ask, confused.

'Being hooked up with a scab like Sky. He hates scabs.'

Scabs. The word still makes my skin crawl. And now I remember Rhallon calling Sky my *scab* girlfriend.

'What's his problem with . . . them?'

Tarn shrugs. 'Rhallon hates all purebloods, but scabs most of all. You should hear him when he goes off on one. Purebloods are the past; we're the future. And we *are* loads faster and stronger, you can't argue with that.'

I groan, thinking of guys like Zed. 'So what? That doesn't make us better people, does it?'

'Course it does,' Tarn says, glaring at me like I'm a fool. 'Rhallon says that's why we should be in charge. He has it all figured out. First we take over the Syndicate from within, then we take this sector. After that . . . who knows?'

Part of me feels sick; the rest wants to laugh out loud.

'You *do* know that's madness?'

'The future, you mean?'

I snort and throw my hands up in despair.

'Oh sure, some future that'll be. Did nobody ever tell you what happened back on Wrath? Back in the day, there was a nublood uprising or attempted takeover, according to who you listen to. After that, the Twist War. And guess what? We lost. Didn't work out so well for us nubloods, did it? Our beloved Saviour and his Slayer thugs in charge. Ident camps. Peace Fairs. You make purebloods fear us again and they'll fight back. There are hardly any of us and you want to take on the might of the Combine? They'll crush us like we'd crush a stinkbug.'

Tarn's head shakes tell me I'm wasting my breath. But then, to my surprise, suddenly she's all smiles again. She leans forward, and pokes me in the chest almost playfully.

'You know what, Kyle? I could get to like you.'

All I can do is stare, gobsmacked.

She steps even closer, lifting her face up to mine.

'If I *liked* you, Kyle, I wouldn't tell Rhallon what you've just told me. All that defeatist, anti-nublood crap, I mean. I've a feeling he might be less than impressed.'

This close I can smell liquor on her breath. Still drunk from last night's party? I wouldn't be surprised.

'Forget Rhallon. Will you heal Sky, or won't you?'

Tarn's sly look is back again. 'Make it worth my while.'

'How?' I say reluctantly.

'I get your share of the split from this last raid.'

'All of it?' I say, my voice climbing.

'Every single last cred,' she says. 'Do we have a deal?'

I hesitate, holding my breath and faking a frown like Murdo

would, as if I'm thinking about it. But I'm not. Sky's life against creds I've never seen. It's a no-brainer.

'Deal.' I stick my fist out to bump stumps and seal it.

But Tarn ignores my outstretched hand. Instead she frowns, cocking her head. 'Hear that?'

'Hear *what*?' I say impatiently, my heart sinking, sure she's messing with me again. But now I hear it too. A faint buzzing. No, make that two buzzing sounds. With a start, I realise one lot is coming from my right-hand jacket pocket. I reach in, half expecting a trapped bug. I fumble out my Syndicate comm card. The buzzing quits as soon as I touch it, but the urgent message in red keeps on pulsing away.

Return to quarters. Be ready for immediate departure. Rhallon.

I look at Tarn, wondering. She's flicking her comm card with a finger and looking out over the lake. I look too, suddenly worried that the ComSec cruiser we ran into before has tracked us here and we'll have to run. But the only things hanging in the sky are harmless wisps of cloud.

'We should go,' she says. 'When Rhallon shouts jump, it's best to jump.' And she goes to push past me . . . again.

But I block her path . . . again.

'We made a deal, right?'

She smirks. 'Did we?'

'You said it yourself, my share from the raid.'

'Not a bad *offer*. We can talk more about it later.'

Just like that, she snatches back the deal I thought I had.

I stare at the gloating look on her face in disbelief. Horror even. Rage plucks at me too, as she doesn't try to hide her delight at raising my hopes then dashing them.

'So this is how it's going to be, huh?' I choke out.

She acts all surprised, tells me she doesn't know what I'm talking about. Reminds me that we need to get moving. I sway like I'm the one who's been at the booze, but step aside before my rage gets the better of me.

'Good boy,' she says, and stalks past.

Guess she figures she can ride me all she likes. Without her blood, Sky is doomed. She knows that now.

At the hut entrance she looks back. 'You coming?'

I make a show of turning my back on her. Childish, but I can't help it. I hear the plank creak as she crosses it. Raging, I stare out at the pond, but see only darkness.

When I do look around, Tarn's long gone.

A moment later, the serving woman reappears at the entrance. I'm a bit slow wiping the despair off my face.

'Is everything all right?' she asks, real motherly.

'No!' I bolt out past her, along the plank. Feeling drained and helpless, I drag myself back up to my room in the tower.

And make myself a grim promise.

If Tarn lets Sky die, then she dies too. Because I'll kill her.

27
SOME NASTY SURPRISES

I guess I left my door unlocked. I'm stuffing a last few things into my pack when Cam bursts in.

'You're Rhallon's pet. He tell you what's going on?'

He throws a pack on to my bed, which has made itself since I went out, like it always does.

'I'm *nobody's* pet. And I've no idea.'

I sweep his pack off the bed on to the floor.

'Hey, what's biting *you*?'

For a crazy few seconds I'm tempted to tell him, but stop myself just in time. Cam can't help. Nobody can.

'It's nothing. You could've knocked!'

Cam rolls his eyes in fake outrage. 'Give me a break.'

'How about your neck?' I mutter.

'Ha ha. C'mon, let's go find Rhallon or Masson and see what's going on? Beats hanging about here.'

I hardly hear him though. My head pounds, but not from the drink last night. Tarn's words are still haunting me.

What's it worth?

Next thing I know, his fingers are snapping in my face. 'Kyle, wake up. Are you coming, or what?'

I knock his finger-snapping hand away, annoyed.

'You told Tarn about Sky being on the Ark.'

He shrugs. 'Yeah well, I bumped into her on the screamer. Asked her if she had an ident sister called Sky. She gave me this big old scowl and stomped off. But then that first night in the bar here, after you'd wandered off somewhere, she collars me. Asks me how come I know Sky. I told her. So what?'

'But you couldn't be arsed telling me, huh?'

'Tarn said not to. *Ordered* me not to.'

'Oh sure,' I say, sceptical.

'It's true,' he protests, grinning. 'But what are the odds, I thought? You bumping into your sca–' He sees me stiffen and chokes the word off. 'I mean your girlfriend's sister like that. Except it wasn't so unlikely, was it? Rhallon's been rounding up as many of the nublood kids shipped off Wrath as he can. We make good Syndicate raiding crews. Tarn was one of the first he rescued and signed up.'

'Who told you that?' I say. But it makes sense.

'Tarn did,' Cam says. 'Tell you what, she likes Sky even less than I like my brother, and that's saying something. She can hardly bring herself to say Sky's name.'

I sigh. 'Tell me about it.'

He looks at me, obviously hoping for some gossip.

I'm not in the mood. 'Let's go find out what's happening.'

As we grab our packs and head for the door it bangs open again. This time it's Kragg who sticks his head in.

'Playtime's over, lads. Move it. We're out of here.'

More of our Syndicate lot mill about outside in the corridor. Kragg bangs on doors until he's dug out everybody on this level. Everybody's bitching, but nobody has any solid word on why our stay is being cut short. A few white-clad men and women who've been looking after us up hang about in the background, watching. They look as surprised as we are that we're leaving.

Ten minutes later we're a few levels lower and gawping through a barrier at that see-through landing platform. The orbital shuttle that brought us here – or one very like it – is settling down on to the pad. The bright blue glare of the drive cuts off. Hissing white coolant vapour billows up.

'Pity,' Una says. 'I liked this whole being-spoiled thing.'

Nobody disagrees with her.

Me, I'm thinking this brings me a few days closer to being back on the Ark and having to tell Sky about Tarn. The good news is I found Tarn. The bad news is that your sister says you're not worth saving. Sorry. I swear I *did* try . . .

Bile rises in my throat and I shake my head.

A crewman disembarks, runs over and has a word with Rhallon. Rhallon's face goes tight and unhappy. Masson is summoned. He tells us the shuttle has a slight problem that will need to be checked out before we board.

Only Cam is dumb enough to cheer, but if he thinks we can go back to boozing and living it up, he's wrong. Hub staff come running and smiling. They bow and scrape us to a nearby waiting room. Drinks are on offer, but they're the healthy fruit-juice kind. Tarn's not here. And neither is Rhallon or Vitali, our other pilot.

An hour later we're still stuck here, told nothing.

Sick of sitting and worrying, I ask Masson if I can go for a wander. He says fine, as long as I don't go out of shouting distance. Ignoring my scowl, Cam tags along.

'Let's find out what's wrong with the shuttle,' he says.

I doubt they'll let us near it. And I'm right. Even when Cam lies his face off to the man guarding the barrier, saying we're apprentice engineers, for the first time since we got here we're told no. It costs the guy in white to say it, and he's sorry, but there's nothing he can do.

I pull Cam away, mid-protest.

'No means no,' I say. 'Let's just wander.'

This low down the floating hub's platform is less fancy than up top. I'm guessing this is where all the work gets done, out of sight and mind. It's hotter too. Maybe that's why the hatch has been left open. I glance inside and see white-clad figures gathered before a wall-mounted screen.

'. . . *scene of the attack . . . no survivors found yet . . .*'

Quietly I slip inside.

A few seconds later, Cam joins me. 'What's the deal?'

I shush him, but too late. We're spotted. A sweaty-looking older guy waddles towards us.

'Sorry. You're not allowed in here. Please go away.'

No chance. Shoving past him, I step closer to the screen. A man's face fades away, replaced by a view of star-spattered space. Debris floats around in the foreground.

'What's happened?' I say.

The woman in front of me starts and looks around. It's Andrea, who looks after my room, her neat white uniform a bit undone, off-duty maybe. 'Sir, you shouldn't be –'

'What attack? Look, just tell me.'

She winces. 'A starship arrived in orbit. They'd picked up a transmission from a ComSec cruiser. Another freighter has been attacked. No survivors again. Terrible, isn't it?'

It's as if an icy hand grabs my guts.

'No survivors?' I croak.

On the screen a bright light suddenly flicks on and lights up the floating debris. And it's not debris. These are bodies. A dozen or so, none suited up for space. Looking frozen solid as they tumble slowly through the big cold empty.

Andrea's hand flies to her mouth. 'Oh no!'

A flexible metal arm swings into view and extends towards the nearest body, a young woman. Long red hair floats around her head, set free by the zero gee. The grabber on the end of the arm takes four goes to snag her. The hair comes alive, swirling about with the contact. The woman stays stiff and dead though; hard vacuum has sucked the life out of her. The robot arm gathers her in. Just before she disappears from view her face slides past the camera. Eyes wide open, staring at nothing. Horror on her freckled face. Bloody froth frozen around her mouth.

And I cringe inside. This is the frightened girl from that freighter we captured. To be fired off in an escape craft, that's what Una had said. Another fraggin' lie.

'Who could do such a wicked thing?' somebody wails.

A man near me shakes his head. 'To kill those people in cold blood . . . you'd have to be some kind of monster.'

He's right.

Cam catches my eye.

As the arm goes after the next body, we clear off.

*

Una shrugs. 'Okay, so I lied. What was I supposed to say, with them listening? If a fourhorn figures it's being led to the slaughterhouse, it'll panic and kick.'

'But *why* kill them?' I say, my face burning. 'Why not just shove them in an escape craft, like you said?'

She twists round in her seat and fixes me with a hard stare. Behind her head, through the viewport, we burst free of cloud into a bright blue sky the opposite of my mood. We're aboard the repaired shuttle, climbing back into high orbit.

'Because I'm Syndicate, and follow orders,' she growls.

'Too right,' Cam says, nodding.

He swears he wasn't part of shoving them out of the airlock. Says too that moaning won't bring the girl – or any of the freighter's crew – back to life, so why bother?

But I can't be so cold. 'They'd surrendered!'

Una curls her lip at me. 'That don't make 'em blind. They saw our faces. They could identify us.'

'Not now they can't,' Cam mutters.

'Exactly.' Una turns away. We're done talking.

I close my eyes, but not for long. The dead girl stares her dead stare at me, out of a cloud of red hair.

'Are you crazy?' Cam whispers. 'What's done is done.'

I growl at him to go to hell.

When we reach orbit, I get another nasty surprise. The word going round was that we'd be transferring to a commercial transport for our ride back to the Ark. Nah. Hanging there ahead of us is the brutal-looking Syndicate screamer.

We transfer back aboard.

After the hub, it feels even more horribly cramped than

before, as if it's shrunk. The others scramble for favourite places. I let them, too fed up to be bothered. As we get underway Rhallon squeezes us into the tiny compartment aft of the flight-deck. Our two pilots stand in the open hatch.

Tarn winks at me. What a bitch.

'Change of plan,' Rhallon calls out. 'Sorry to cut your leisure time short, but I promise I'll make it up to you. First things first, we've got some more work to do.'

Work? Raiding and killing. Spacing innocent crews . . .

Smiling, he tells us an unexpected opportunity has come up. A big transport called the *Karachi Dawn* was dumb enough to relay *Le Roi Batti*'s distress call. Our loitering screamer picked up their transmission and was able to fix the transport's location and course. Their reward, Rhallon jeers, will be us relieving them of their cargo.

The other Syndicate guys go mad cheering. Not me. Dark thoughts stomp through my head again.

Rhallon waits for the cheers to die down. 'One more thing. We picked up another transmission, from the ComSec cruiser that's been sniffing about. They've been to the scene of our previous attack, so they'll be hunting for us.'

He pauses to let this sink in.

Kragg clears his throat. 'Shouldn't we be running then, boss, not tearing after another freighter to hit?'

Hope stirs inside me. I could almost hug the guy.

But Rhallon just smiles. 'That, Kragg, is exactly what the captain of that ComSec cruiser will expect us to do. I say we disappoint him. Do the *un*expected. Way I see it, he's got himself a dilemma. Does he guard all the freighters in this area?

Impossible with only one warship. And where's the glory in playing nursemaid? No, my bet is he'll be trying to chase down *Le Roi Batti*. And while he's off doing that, we can be greedy and knock off another prize.'

Greedy. He says it like being greedy is good. And judging by the cheers he gets, this lot agree.

28
TIME TO CHOOSE

Rhallon's in a hurry this time. Full power for six hours straight. I'm way past wanting to scream as the dee-emm exposure rips at me. By now I just want to die.

'Still alive up there?' Cam moans.

He's lying on the deck. I've scrunched myself and my sleep bag on top of pipework recessed into the wall. We're inside some sort of service tunnel.

Cramped and hot, but it beats being trodden on.

'If you call this living,' I moan back at him.

He shifts below me, muttering a mouthful of curses. 'Do you think we still need to be watching out for Zed?'

I groan. With everything else weighing my mind down I'd forgotten about him.

'So *this* is where you've been hiding?'

I start so violently I bang my head on the pipe above me. But it's Tarn squatting at the tunnel entrance, peering in.

She growls at Cam to make himself scarce. He grumbles, but

drags himself past her and clears off. Not far enough it seems. She has another growl at him.

Meanwhile, I struggle out of my recess and flop down on to the deck, propping my back against the wall. Grit my teeth and try hard to wipe the hurt off my face.

'Shouldn't you be up front doing pilot stuff?'

Tarn smiles. How? I couldn't, not feeling this lousy. I guess being the screamer's co-pilot she's used to putting up with the drive-pain. Or else she's just tougher than I am.

'Relax, Vitali has it covered. Won't be long now. Figured I'd stretch my legs before the fun starts.'

'Fun?' I can't help wincing.

She shrugs. 'You'll be glad to hear the *Karachi Dawn* will be a pushover compared to the last one. Looks like the crew have bailed. They fired off an escape craft.'

I'm still squirming in agony, but instantly I can bear it more easily. No crew means no killing.

'So it's stopped, has it? The freighter, I mean.'

'Course not. It only dropped out of dee-emm to fire the pod off, then shifted back in and kept running. It'll be on autopilot, so we have to keep chasing after it.'

I must look puzzled. Tarn sighs.

'Takes us away from the pod, doesn't it? So the losers inside can get away. Otherwise we'd scoop it up, before we do the freighter. Those escape craft fetch big creds.'

She looks at me, like she's waiting for me to say something. But I can play that game too.

I keep my mouth shut. I won't beg. Not yet.

She frowns, and pulls a pouty, fake-thoughtful face. 'What

was it we were talking about, Kyle? D'you remember?'

I have to count to ten before I answer. Even then there's an edge to my voice I can't help. 'We were making a deal. I give you my share from the last raid. You save Sky with your blood. We were about to bump stumps on it.'

I shove my left fist at her.

But no. Course not. Tarn glances at it like it's some kind of mildly interesting bug. Her left hand stays where it is.

'Were we?' She wrinkles her forehead.

This is when I know, deep in my gut, that no amount of asking, pleading or begging will persuade Tarn.

She's not here to be persuaded. Only to twist the knife.

But knowing's one thing, giving up's another.

'My share of *both* these raids,' I say through my teeth.

She looks me in the eye, for longer than is comfortable. Her smile still lurks, but it's an awful thing.

'What *wouldn't* you give, to save Sky?' she says at last.

'Nothing . . . I'd give anything.'

'You're just saying that.'

'Am I?' I say defiantly. Sweat from the heat in here gets in my eye. It stings, and takes some blinking away.

Tarn straightens up. 'Wow. Sky's got her hooks into you deep.'

I'm opening my mouth when the shock wave from our target's dee-emm drive hits, pitching me across the tunnel. Tarn staggers, but somehow stays standing.

I pick myself up. 'Look, just tell me what you want!'

Tarn still stares at me, her eyes burning with a green fire. 'You really are dumb, Kyle, aren't you? You've already given me what I want, what I've *always* wanted.'

Despairing, I shake my head. 'What's that then?'

She sneers. 'Figure it out. I'd best be getting back, before Rhallon starts yelling.'

Next thing, she's scuttling away down the corridor.

'Wait!' I call, scrambling after her, but by the time I've crawled out of the tunnel she's long gone.

Cam's heading my way, curiosity all over his face.

'Don't ask,' I growl.

Only later, as I crouch miserably in my body armour, watching as our plasma-lance guy finishes cutting into the hull of the grappled freighter, does it finally hit me.

What have I given Tarn? Revenge on Sky. That's what.

Zed's dead. With the *Karachi Dawn*'s crew having bailed we hadn't figured on any fighting. Some def-bots swarmed us, but we soon swatted them. And then cut our way out of the cargo compartment we'd hard docked into.

That's when they'd hit us.

Zed was first through the hatch. He fought hard from what I've heard, but not hard enough. Turns out the escape craft that cleared off was only carrying a few of the top-ranking crew. The lower ranks were left behind, together with twenty or so passengers, all of them miners. Mad at being abandoned, tough like space-miners have to be, and with nothing to lose, they put up a hell of a fight. By the time it was over, Zed's one of five guys who won't be getting back up again.

I got off lightly, with little more than a few bruises.

Rhallon's happy though. Word is that in among the *Karachi Dawn*'s cargo of ore-processing gear, he's found a big consignment of energy weapons. Nothing sells so well on the dark market, Una reckons, as weapons.

'Someone always needs killing,' she says.

I keep quiet, dreading what will happen next. More than half of the crew and passengers who fought us are dead already. They're the lucky ones, I reckon. The rest we've gathered together and shoved up against a bulkhead. Those who can lift their head stare at us, hate in their eyes. They know what's coming too.

'What the hell are *they* still doing here!?'

Rhallon's back from checking out the cargo. If he's happy, he hides it well. Una, who'd been bandaging a cut leg, scrambles to her feet. 'Sorry, boss. We'll take care of them.'

Masson whispers something to Una. My guess? Where the airlock compartment is. I step back, not wanting any part of this. Yeah, right. Kragg shoves me forward again.

'You and Cam, bring up the rear. Keep 'em moving.'

Next thing, we're escorting them through the freighter. Kragg and Una get the less hurt ones to drag, carry or help those who can't walk by themselves.

One guy with a hurt leg falters. Cam bangs the deck behind him with his killstick, showering the guy with sparks. The guy flinches and limps a bit faster.

'Sorry-looking losers, huh?' Cam says, and smiles.

I ignore him, picturing a different set of prisoners shuffling past me, the pleading look from the redhead girl who ended up a cold floating dead thing. Cam knows what we're doing, yet still he can grin. What is wrong with him?

Or is it me? Am I being weak when I should be strong?

We stop. Una's clearly lost. She has Kragg drag one of the

crewmen aside and asks him something. Life-support fans thrash noisily so I can't hear what he says. But I'm guessing it's not helpful. She threatens the guy with her wrecking bar.

Fair play to the man, he just bows his head. That takes guts. The kind of guts I wish that I had.

But Una won't be denied. Cursing, she hauls a second crewmember over. A woman hurt so bad I doubt she knows what's happening. She readies her wrecking bar . . .

The guy talks.

'Pity,' Cam says beside me.

'You're sick,' I say. 'You know that?'

Not long after, deep in the bowels of the freighter, we shove and prod the prisoners into a circular compartment. A massive hatch set into the deck is the freighter's main docking airlock. At intervals around the walls are three smaller hatches. One displays a flashing red sign.

HAZARD. NO ENTRY. POD DEPLOYED. HAZARD.

Blinking orange signs above the other two declare the pods behind them are unserviceable. It figures. Otherwise this sorry lot would've made a run for it too.

You'd think seeing the airlock would make the prisoners restless, but no, they all stay quiet. My head bangs. I can't look at them. Instead, my mind's eye shows me others waiting to die, back at that Peace Fair I attended. A twist is about to be purified. The rope is put around her neck. Her face wears exactly the same stricken and hopeless look, right up to when the trapdoor beneath her feet *thunnkkkks* open.

Flashing lights and the shriek of a siren pull me out of my memories and back into the compartment.

Una swears and hits something on a control panel.

The siren cuts off, but the lights keep on strobing their warning. Metal grates on metal, and a hole appears in the centre of the hatch in the floor as overlapping blades slide sideways. As these draw back into recesses in the hatch collar, the opening gets bigger. Like a giant's eye reacting to the sun coming out from behind a cloud. When it's fully open, I see the airlock chamber below. In the floor of that is another hatch. Beyond it will lurk the big cold empty of space.

'Get down there,' Una calls out to the prisoners, stony-faced, tapping her leg with her wrecking bar. 'Now!'

But they just stare.

'Move yourselves!' Kragg snarls.

An older guy sobs and shuffles towards the open hatch.

That sob, it reaches deep inside me. It claws and plucks at my heart. It shames me for standing and watching.

A cold rage possesses me.

'No!' I say, to myself as much as anyone.

Lexy's the closest. A jab in the kidneys with my stunstick and he arches backwards. Even before he hits the deck I'm swinging at Kragg. Catch him a solid whack on the side of his big ugly head, but my stick can't have recharged because it doesn't drop him. He staggers, bellowing in pain, before lashing out at me wildly with his killstick.

I duck it. Before he can swing again, I spin kick him.

Still the bastard won't go down. I kick him again. He stumbles backwards, falls into the open airlock.

A dull thump follows as he hits the outside hatch.

'What the hell are you doing?' Una shouts, eyes blazing.

To my left, Cam stands frozen.

'Help me,' I yell at him. 'This ain't right.'

Stupid. I should be watching out for Una. Her wrecking bar blurs towards my head. Would've taken it off too, only I just manage to block with my stunstick. It shatters. The shock of the impact numbs my forearm. I reel back a step, clutching the broken remains.

Una grunts in satisfaction. 'I always knew you didn't have it in you to be Syndicate.'

'Go to hell,' I growl.

She has another swing at me. I duck it this time, and throw myself at her. Close in – where her long wrecking bar's less use to her – that's my only chance.

Using all my strength, I knock her down.

As we hit the deck, she grunts. The iron bar flies from her hand. Rolling away, I grab it and scramble to my feet. Una's slower getting up. Much slower. Her face is pulled all tight with pain and she's clutching at her side. I see why; my broken stunstick spikes out from between her bloody fingers.

'Get Rhallon!' she hisses past me.

I risk a look. Cam's by the open hatch to the compartment now. He swallows so loudly I hear him.

'Don't!' I shoot him my best pleading look.

Yeah, right. He clears off, yelling loudly for Rhallon.

Disgusted, I look back at Una. She yanks my stunstick from her side. Red splashes from the wound onto the deck. She totters, and waves the jagged, blood-slick end at me.

'Rhallon'll make you wish you were never born!' she snarls.

I swish the wrecking bar at her, driving her backwards. My

rage is chilling fast and fear flutters about, waiting to take hold, but I cling to a desperate thought. There's only one way into this compartment and the hatch isn't that big. They'll only be able to rush me one at a time. With Una's bar I reckon I can pulp a good few Syndicate heads before they take me down.

I drive her back towards it. She grits her blood-framed teeth and flails weakly at me, but can hardly stand.

'Kill her!' one prisoner calls out.

'No!' I force her out of the compartment, stepping in the blood trail she leaves behind – just as Rhallon and the rest come running.

Una mumbles what I've done and then collapses. Rhallon steps over her without a glance. Says nothing, but I can see the promise of a cruel and vicious death in his eyes.

'This is cold-blooded murder!' I shout.

Rhallon smiles. He actually smiles. 'I think of it as mere slaughter. They're only purebloods after all.'

I glare at him. 'You make me ashamed to be nublood.'

His smile fades. 'You've spent too much time with scabs and pures, Kyle, and that's made you . . . weak.'

I picture Sky, so fierce, so determined. And know that I'm stronger for our short time spent together, not weaker. Anyway, caring's not weakness, it's strength.

'Come on then,' I growl back, clanging the frame of the hatch with the iron bar. 'I'll show you how *weak* I am.'

Rhallon nearly takes my bait, but Masson drags him back before he can charge, then hefts his killstick.

'I'll take care of him.'

'No, wait!' Rhallon snaps.

He reaches behind his back and produces a blaster.

I take one look at it and step back, like that'll save me. 'You'll breach the hull!' I say. Pathetic.

He aims it at me. 'Well, wouldn't that be . . . terrible?'

As he pulls the trigger, I hurl myself aside.

Not far enough.

The blaster roars. It's raging blast clips my left shoulder, spins me around and rips a scream out of me. I end up on my knees, clutching burnt flesh, waiting for a blast to kill me.

Only it never comes.

I hear a whistling. Curses. Shouts. A loud bang. The whistling changes pitch to a painful shriek. My ears pop big time.

Somehow, I manage to lift my head.

Rhallon's shot has blown a hole in the freighter's hull. This widens further as supersonic air tears through it. Now there's a wind in here bigger than any I've ever felt on Wrath, only it's sucking at me not blowing as the compartment depressurises.

Rhallon's mouth works as he shouts something at me. All I catch though is 'die with your pureblood friends!'

Then he slams the hatch closed, sealing us all inside.

PART THREE
REDEMPTION

29
SUCKING ON EMPTY

It's like being in the middle of a windstorm. All sorts of debris whirls up and out through the tear in the hull.

Could I block it with something? Nah. It's too big. Already I can feel myself panting. My heart races as it fights to make do with less air and my blasted shoulder feels like a nightrunner is chewing on it.

I slump to my knees. Defeated. Sad.

'Into the airlock,' a man's voice yells. 'Hurry!'

Lifting my head takes all my strength. The crewman who defied Una is frantically trying to herd the other prisoners towards the airlock hatch in the floor of the compartment. He sees me looking and shouts.

'Give me a hand here – we've only got seconds left.'

'What's the use?' I yell back.

'Stay here, we die. In the airlock, we –'

But the rest of what he yells is lost in the shriek of escaping air. Doesn't matter though. A desperate hope lights up his bearded face and it's catching. I scramble up and lurch my way through the maelstrom towards him.

'Tell me what to do!' I shout.

'Get into the airlock. I'll pass 'em down, you catch 'em.' He grimaces at my shoulder. 'Can you do that?'

Without thinking, I nod. It's a long drop into the airlock, with no ladder, not that I can see anyway. Cursing, I sit on the edge, swing my legs inside and push off.

I land hard, right beside Kragg.

He's very dead. His neck's broke so bad that his head has folded underneath him. Yeah, well, tough.

A few of the less hurt prisoners tumble in after me. I catch them the best I can with only one arm. The bearded crewman lowers another guy, too hurt to help himself. We grab his legs and lower him the rest of the way. But soon I'm working on my own. The others slump and stay down. I'm wheezing myself, an iron band tightening around my chest.

'Hurry!' I half yell, half gasp.

No answer. All I hear is a *thump* up top.

Panic rips at me. The crewman was figuring to save us, but didn't say how. Without him, we're still screwed.

I call again. Still nothing. Frag it!

How to get to him, one-armed and without a ladder?

Shock is kicking in. I'm struggling to think and my seeing is blurry. No wonder. The shriek of escaping air is back to a whistle there's so little left in the compartment.

But maybe there *is* a way . . .

I suck as big a breath as I can into my tortured lungs and hold it. Back up. Run. Leap at the airlock wall and kick upwards. Somehow my right hand closes on the rail around the hatch frame. Leaning back, I manage to walk my feet higher. That gets me closer. Close enough to throw my upper body and left arm upwards. By luck more than judgement my left hand closes on the rail.

Howling at the pain, I pull myself up and out.

Bearded bloke is on his knees, fighting to drag an injured woman to the hatch but losing. I stagger over, drag her the rest of the way. Lower her one-handed into the airlock as far as I dare, before dropping her. If she breaks something, I can't help that. Back for the guy. Same for him.

My lungs feel like I've swallowed fire.

One last passenger. A girl. Unconscious. Helpless.

Only now I hear the grating sound behind me. Different in the thinner air, but the airlock hatch is definitely closing.

If I go for the girl, I'll be trapped. I dive and slide head first into the opening that's left. Kragg does me a favour he'd never do if he was still alive and mostly breaks my fall. I still hit hard though, and my wounded shoulder explodes in agony. Next thing I know, the hatch slides fully shut over me and the hiss of escaping air cuts off. To my left, beardy's recovered enough to be messing with a control panel on the airlock wall.

He gives it a last slap, and slumps down.

Stupidly, I try to breathe, but I'm sucking on empty.

My seeing, already blurry, goes grey around the edges. Dimly I think I hear a softer and gentler hissing.

Is this what dying sounds like?

No. Suddenly I can breathe again. Deliciously cold air fills me up and my seeing clears again. It's not all good though, as the pain from my shoulder comes raging back too.

Bearded guy grunts with obvious relief.

'I left a woman behind,' I croak.

He winces. 'I *had* to close the hatch. Another few seconds and we'd all be dead. We saved as many as we could.'

I guess so, but still I hang my head.

He struggles up and starts seeing to the other people in here. I slide over to the nearest wall, lean against it and have a gawp at my shoulder. It's bad. A charred flesh wound so deep that bone shows. Crisped skin hangs off in tatters. Just looking at it is eye-wateringly painful.

I watch him as he tends to the others. Three have cuts and bruises, four are more battered, two look grim. He makes these as comfortable as he can, then comes over. Peers at my wrecked shoulder and tries not to grimace.

'I'll need help binding it,' I say, through my teeth.

'Sure.' One of the less hurt men offers up an undershirt. Could be cleaner, but we can't pick and choose. He tears it into strips and bandages me up. Does his best to be gentle, but even so it hurts like crazy.

'I was in the military,' he says. 'Seen men blasted before, but never seen anyone jump back up like you did.'

'Yeah, well, what do we do now?'

'Not much we *can* do. We're stuck here until someone lets us out. But at least your raider friends can't get at us, with the evacuated compartment in the way.'

'Surely they'll think we're all dead?' I say.

'Better hope so. Otherwise they can remotely open this outer airlock door we're sitting on.'

We all look down.

The 'floor' is one big hatch. This finger's width of metal is all that's between us and the big cold empty.

It stays closed for now.

A woman asks whether we'll show up as being in here. He tells her only if they look at the right display, not likely if they think we're dead. And then he clears his throat.

'But that's not our *biggest* problem.'

He explains that, for safety reasons, airlocks have independent life-support systems. It's a big pressurised tank, capable of filling the lock with air maybe half a dozen times from empty. When it gets low it can be refilled from the main starship system. But tank refills can only be done from outside the airlock.

'With all of us gobbling air, we've got a day. Two at best. And that's only if we conserve it.'

'How?' one guy jeers. 'By not breathing?'

'We keep our activity down. Sleep if we can.'

Nobody says anything. I guess we're all thinking the same dark thoughts. Taking refuge in this airlock hasn't saved us, just shoved back our dying by a few hours. Either we'll run out of air and suffocate, or Rhallon will find out we're still alive and flush us out into space. . .

Beardy clears his throat. 'Listen, thanks for standing up for us back there. I'm Ryan.'

'Kyle,' I mutter.

We shake hands. Hurts me more than him.

'Why'd you do it?' he asks.

I take a deep breath, then remember I shouldn't. 'Let's just say I signed up for raiding, not killing in cold blood.'

'Don't they go hand in hand?'

'Found that out the hard way, didn't I?'

The lights flicker and I hear a low throbbing sound.

Ryan grunts. 'They're firing up our drive.'

He gets up again, limps to the control panel and does something. A display shows the view outside the airlock, nothing but a mess of stars. Then the throb deepens and the stars start to wink out, replaced by the eye-sucking darkness of dee-emm. I look away quick. The last thing I need now is to see spooks oozing and sliding around.

'Any idea where they'll be heading?' Ryan asks.

'Not really. I'd guess the nearest place they can offload and sell on whatever you're carrying.'

'He knows all right,' jeery guy spits. 'He's one of 'em!'

I could tell the jerk I was only a grunt so got told frag all. Or I could go and shut him up. Tempting that. More air for the rest of us then. But I can't be bothered.

'Whatever,' I say, and squeeze my eyes shut.

Dark thoughts fill my head again. What the frag was I thinking? On Wrath I'd moaned at Sky about the big picture, how the survival of our nublood species was more important than our lives, or saving her sister. Yet here I am, wading in to help some purebloods I don't even know.

And for what? Nothing. I just get to die with them.

Should I have followed orders and survived? Could I have talked Tarn into giving Sky some of her blood? And what about Colm? If he's still holding out in Wrath's No-Zone, I could've tried to get help for him. If ComSec knew what was going on, surely they'd intervene?

Should've, could've . . . didn't.

Without Tarn's blood, Sky will die a lonely and painful death on the Ark. The Syndicate will go back to Wrath for more darkblende. They'll help the Slayers take the No-Zone and its spaceport back, and Colm will die too.

All thanks to me . . . and my gommer conscience!

A woman who's all smashed up inside is the first to die. We move her body over by Kragg's. Doing this leaves us all gasping. Soon after, Ryan says it's time to swap the air out. He vents the stale stuff out into space and fills us up again with fresh. It takes about a minute and we have to hold our breath until he signals we're good again.

Three purges and fills later, two more bodies are over there. Only seven of us left now.

We've been stuck in here the best part of a standard-day. My shoulder is less agonising now, but it's hard to be glad. The airlock's tank is empty. We've had our last fill.

'Maybe we'll get to wherever your mates are taking us before the air goes too bad,' he says.

'How does that help?'

'With this airlock inaccessible they can't dock, so they'll have to land somewhere. We can bust out then.'

'Is there anywhere that close?'

He hesitates. 'Dunno. But I'm not a navigator.'

Just for a second I share his desperate hope. But like Sky says, hope is for losers. Chances are we'll suffocate long before we get anywhere. And even if by some miracle we do manage to bust out, what then? Blaster shots in the back as we run, I reckon. Ryan doesn't need to hear that though.

Time goes by. Breathing gets steadily tougher. One good thing, it finally shuts jeering guy up.

I close my eyes again and wait for the end.

Soon my head aches like Zed's been using it for kicking practice. I feel dizzy too, and want to puke. Ryan *does* puke, all over himself. Then it becomes a struggle to keep my eyes open. I pass out for a while, but my nublood won't let me die so easy. I wake up with a fierce start, face pressed to the deck in a puddle of my drool.

For a few seconds I'm confused, not knowing where I am. Then the knowing comes rushing back, and with it fear.

Wheezing, heart racing, I push myself back up.

I'm alone. Or might as well be.

The rest of the guys in here lie about where they've fallen. Why I bother I couldn't tell you, but I drag myself around like I'm a thousand years old and check pulses.

All are still alive, but only barely.

The screen still shows the eye-sucking black of dee-emm. I prop myself against the airlock wall and gaze into it.

Stare blindly at the spooks.

Somehow they show me Sky's face. Sadness and strength. And now her blink-and-you-miss-it smile lights it up like the flare of a struck match. Did I ever tell her how much I loved her? I don't think so. And now I never will.

I lose the feeling in my arms, my legs.

Each breath is torture.

Knowing I'll never see Sky again is worse though.

Tears of regret sting my eyes.

But then, through them, I see lights. They glitter and dance, like hanging lanterns on a windy night.

I blink the tears away, fight to focus.

Not lights . . . stars.

Which means *something*. But what? I can't remember.

And then I can.

We're back in regular space!

I keel over slowly, and the deck clobbers me.

30
TELLING AND SHOWING

If this is the long forever of being dead, it's not so bad. I'm warm and comfortable. Breathing's easy, and . . .

And I open my eyes.

To figure out pretty quick I'm *not* dead. If I was, my hands wouldn't be cuffed together. I wouldn't be in a room with white walls. There wouldn't be guards either side of the hatch. Or a uniformed woman whose no-nonsense face reminds me of a younger Rona, holding a syringe-gun thing in her hand.

I sit up, too fast. My head spins.

'Take it easy now,' she says. 'You're hurt.'

'No shit,' I mumble.

'How do you feel? The med-bot's shot you as full of pain relief as it can, but we need you awake.'

'I'll live.' My shoulder hurts less fiercely, but still gnaws at me. I'm lying on my back on a padded table. Somebody's nicked my clothes, but thankfully I'm covered by a sheet. Suspended above me is a vicious-looking piece of tech, lots of bladed arms and grabbers. It brings back ugly memories of

Slayer medics harvesting my nublood. Not good.

'What's with these?' I show her the cuffs.

The woman gives no sign of hearing, just shakes her head slowly. 'Remarkable. Already lifting your injured arm. And I was so sure our med-bot was wrong not to take it off.'

I glance up again. And shudder.

And then I see the patch on her sleeve.

C-O-M-S-E . . .

Oh. Crap. Combine Security!

My relief at being alive takes a kicking, remembering how Murdo was so down on them.

'Where am I?' I say. 'Who are you?'

She glances a question at someone behind me.

I twist my head to look, but he's already walking around to join her in front of me. An older guy, he wears a ComSec-grey uniform too, but with more insignias. That, and the way he carries himself, yells he's the boss here. Close-cropped greying hair. A savage scar that curves over his ear and down his right cheek. Whatever once tried to rip his face off must've had claws like a nightrunner. And I see his right hand now, a mix of plastic and metal.

He scowls, with the half of his face that works. 'Keep staring at me, and you could hurt my feelings. And trust me, you *don't* want to do that.'

I drag my eyes away, reluctantly.

'Tell him,' he says to the woman. 'Make it quick.'

She clears her throat. 'You're in the med-hub of the ComSec cruiser *Nantahala*. Two days ago we responded to the *Karachi Dawn*'s distress call, made contact and gave chase. As we closed in, your friends disengaged their raider vessel and fled. We were about to pursue, but detected life signs and investigated. Luckily for you. With your trauma so severe, the med-bot put you into an induced coma. I'm First Lieutenant Laghiri, and this is Captain Turyakin.'

Scar face glares at me.

'So the Syndicate's recruiting kids now?' he growls.

I shrug. Doesn't sound like they know we're all nubloods. But they *do* know where I fit into the freighter raid. My stomach feels full of ice-cold stones.

'Kyle, isn't it?' Laghiri asks, more friendly.

Startled, I nod. Then I remember telling that crewman my name. 'The others in the airlock, they survived too?'

'Most, but not all.'

'Did they tell you I tried to save them?'

'They did. And perhaps we can take that into account.'

Right. Like whether to hang me, shoot me, or just chuck me out of the nearest airlock. That sort of account.

My mouth goes dry. 'I can explain.'

Neither of them looks particularly convinced.

'Membership of a proscribed criminal organisation,' Laghiri says, counting my crimes off on her fingers. 'Space piracy. Absconding from a secure containment world.'

I despair, but I'm confused too. *Containment world?* Is that some fancy name for Wrath?

Turyakin's deep voice pulls me out of my wondering.

'Let's get to the point, shall we? As captain of this ComSec warship I have the authority to execute you, without trial, for any single one of these offences. However, Lieutenant Laghiri tells me that your actions undoubtedly saved lives, and she would have me show you mercy.'

I dart her a pathetically grateful glance.

'Yet more lives were lost than saved,' he goes on. 'I can't ignore this. And your Syndicate raider is still out there . . .'

So I might not be the brightest, but I get the hint.

'I know stuff,' I say quickly. 'Names. Places. Maybe I could help you track them down.'

'Only *maybe*, Kyle?' he says. And smiles bleakly, showing me a glint of metal teeth in line with his scar.

'Where will the raiding ship make for?' Laghiri asks.

I try to think, but my head's full of mush. And while it's tempting to blurt out everything I know in the hope it'll save me a stretched neck, something stops me.

She sighs. 'You owe the Syndicate nothing, Kyle.'

Some of the mush clears, but still I hesitate. It's not the Syndicate I'm worried about, or willing bastards like Rhallon and Masson. It's kids like Anuk, caught up in it like I was. If I cough them up, will they face execution? What about Tarn? Like Sky, she's not the surrendering type. She may not be willing to help, but if it comes to a fight and she dies, that's Sky's last chance gone. 'It's . . . complicated,' I say miserably.

Turyakin snorts. 'You're already in a storm of trouble. Don't make it any worse. If you won't talk voluntarily, we'll *make* you talk. And then you'll be hanged for your crimes. It's really very simple.' His metal-plastic hand clenches, making an unpleasant crunching sound.

I swallow, wishing I hadn't woken up.

'But it doesn't have to be that way, Kyle,' Laghiri says. 'Tell us where your Syndicate raider operates out of. If you help us, then we can help you.'

Does a very fine earnest look too, as if she means it.

That's when the last mush clears from my mind at last and it hits me. Need can cut both ways. They need information; I need them not to execute me. And where there's need, as Murdo likes to say, there's a deal to be made!

I breathe deep. 'Okay, I'll tell you what you want to know. But I want something in return.'

Laghiri frowns. Turyakin's face darkens.

'You're in no position to make demands,' he snarls.

'Please, just hear me out. There's a girl. A good friend of mine. She's not Syndicate. She's sick, dying from darkblende exposure. I want her looked after, that's all.'

'Darkblende?' Laghiri says.

Turyakin's scar writhes as he grits his teeth. 'Very well,' he snaps. 'We'll do what we can for her. Now talk!'

It's as good as I'll get.

'The Ark. That's where they'll head to. If not straight away, then later on. It's where they're based.'

His eyes drill into mine, then flick back to Laghiri.

She's already lifting a hand-held comm device to her lips. 'Control, this is Laghiri. Alter course for the Ark spacestation. Max drive speed. I say again, max speed.'

Next she nods at me. 'You've done the right thing.'

Hope so, even if hope is for losers. But I guess time will tell.

Next day I'm still stuck in the med-hub, but at least I've been given a grey jumpsuit to wear. Laghiri's here, having another gawp at my wound.

She shakes her head, not for the first time.

'What?' I say, like I don't know what's bothering her.

'Yours isn't the first blaster wound I've seen,' she says, frowning. 'Or the worst. But it was bad enough. By rights, the shock alone should have killed you. But now look!'

I've looked already, angling a mirror.

The wound has closed up a lot, so no bone is showing. Everything's still blistered and ugly and sore, but the healing itch is crazy and almost as bad. I won't be throwing left hooks for another day or three, but it's healing well. And impossibly fast, if you've never seen nublood healing before.

No wonder Laghiri shakes her head.

'How's this happening?' she says, staring.

'I'm just hardy, I guess.'

'Don't get smart with me, Kyle. I can have those cuffs put back on you as easy as I had them taken off. Okay?'

Laghiri cut me that break for answering their questions. Fed me too, when my stomach grumbled. Names, descriptions, locations. I reckon I gave them everything they wanted. Wore my finger down jabbing at a fancy tri-D map of the Ark's insides, pointing out Syndicate safe houses.

But I don't know what to say now, so I say nothing.

'This is something to do with Wrath, isn't it?'

I start, gobsmacked. 'How'd you know I'm from Wrath?'

'We took a blood sample.'

'So you know I'm nublood then?'

'We found your gene tag, if that's what you mean.'

Laghiri pulls one of the med-bot's screens so we can both see.

In the background, charts and numbers mean nothing to me. In the foreground, a message flashes red.

Origin: Wrath. Category: Containment. Status: Locked down.

'I don't get it,' I say, confused.

'Before anyone is contained on a world like Wrath —'

'Dumped, you mean?'

She frowns. 'Before anyone is . . . *dumped* . . . their blood is altered with a special genetic marker, which is passed down from parent to child. You were born with it.'

I glance at my missing little finger, the mark of the ident. This'll be like that, only inside me.

'Is there anything you *don't* know?' I say, helplessly.

'Plenty. Like it must have been hard for you growing up on a con . . . on a world like Wrath. Tell me about it.'

'It's a long story,' I mumble.

'We've got time,' she says. 'Even at maximum drive speed we're still two standard-days out from the Ark.'

I consider. What to tell, what *not* to? But suddenly, it's like I ache to tell her everything and be done with it.

I mean, what the hell harm can it do?

But with so much to tell, where do I start? Weirdly, this impossibly clean med-hub room hands me that. Not one grain of dust lurks anywhere. So unlike the Barrenlands back on Wrath, where the dust is part of your skin.

Yeah, the Barrenlands is as good a place as any.

I've just started the telling with me and Rona scraping a hard living, when Turyakin shows up.

'Kyle's filling us in on Wrath,' Laghiri says.

Turyakin hoists his eyebrows, which does awful things to his scar. 'Good. I look forward in particular to hearing how you escaped from a containment world . . . something that isn't supposed to be possible. And how your girlfriend was exposed to darkblende.' He folds his arms and leans back against another of the med-hub's tables. 'Carry on.'

Nervous now, I lick my lips, and start the telling again. Barrenlands. The Saviour and his Slayer army. Idents being hated and feared. The Peace Fair. Being blasted by Reapers, healing, and finding out I'm a twist.

Up to now Turyakin listens stony-faced, and Laghiri asks the questions to make sure she understands.

Now both start and stare.

'You healed *then* like you're healing now?' she says.

I nod, tip my head back and point at my jaw and neck. 'The wound was right here. Took me longer to mend back then. I heal much faster these days.'

'Where's the scar?' Turyakin says, fingering his.

'Gone. Won't be a scar here either, after my shoulder's done healing. On Wrath they hate us for that, and persecute us. They call us twists and say we're monsters. But we're not, we're just different, that's all.' Do I tell them we're faster and stronger too? Nah. That can wait.

'Twists?' Laghiri says.

'On account of our blood being twisted,' I say. 'We hate that name though, so we call ourselves nubloods.'

They both look at me long and hard.

No shit. Sitting in this compartment, so far from the grim reality of Wrath, it must sound far-fetched. But they can't argue with my healing shoulder. And they don't.

I tell them the rest now, being betrayed, on the run with Sky, hooking up with Gemini. And once I've started, I don't hold anything back. Tears sting my eyes as I live the horror over again. Discovering to my horror that I'm the Saviour's son. My role in the Facility raid. But it's only when I tell them about the mines we found there that their eyes light up.

'Promethium on a containment world,' Turyakin says. 'That shouldn't be possible.'

'Maybe the survey missed it?' Laghiri says.

When I describe the alien ruins we stumbled across in the No-Zone, they swap looks again. This is news, and clearly a big surprise to both of them.

'And they managed to miss this too?' Turyakin says.

Laghiri considers, and then shakes her head. 'More likely somebody on the survey team got greedy. As a former Zhang world, Wrath should be strictly off limits to *any* human operations such as mining or dumping. But if they reported it as suitable for containment use only . . .'

Turyakin grunts. 'It gets used for that. And then, after it's locked down, they can sneak back to mine the promethium in secret for sale on the dark market.'

He glares at me now, like this is all *my* fault.

Quick as I can, I wrap things up with Sky and me stowing away on the dropship. How we took it over and our doomed attempt to sell on the darkblende, only to end up being grabbed and forced to join the Syndicate. I leave out about Rhallon and the others being nubloods. Doesn't look good. Makes us look like the monsters I say we aren't.

'You're sure you were *forced*?' Laghiri asks.

I scowl at her. 'You don't say no, if you want to live.'

Her left ear buzzes. She reaches up, taps at it, and listens intently for a few seconds. Then she tells Turyakin that the ship's long-range sensors have picked up an ore-freighter inbound to the Ark. 'Do we intercept?'

He nods. 'Call it tight-beam. Say it's only a routine stop and search. We don't want them squealing.'

What's all *that* about?

But I'm just a kid, and a prisoner. I don't get told.

31
RETURN TO THE ARK

A week or so later and my shoulder's fully healed. Chucked out of the med-hub, I'm bunking down in a makeshift little cell on the cruiser's lower deck. Ryan and the rest of the *Karachi Dawn*'s survivors are here too. The difference is they're not locked in during sleep time.

I'm let out at meal times and Ryan makes sure I have someone to talk to. As well as being ex-military, he's ex-ComSec too, so he gets on well with the lower-deck crew. He's good at finding stuff out, less good at keeping it to himself. Over a bowl of lukewarm stuff I wouldn't feed to a dog he tells me the latest word that's going around.

'We're standing off the Ark, in range of our sensors, out of range of theirs. Waiting for the raider to show.'

'Where does the ore freighter fit in?'

He spoons something out of his soup, peers at it and plops it back. 'They've commandeered it, taken it over.'

'Can ComSec do that?' another guy asks.

Ryan shrugs. 'This isn't the Core. Out here, Turyakin can do as he likes. And it's a shrewd move, I reckon. Soon as the Ark spots us, the Syndicate guys will be tipped off and run. But if we send our marines in on the freighter, we can catch the rats by surprise. The first thing they'll know about it is when their doors are kicked in.'

'We shouldn't be talking about this with *him* here!'

Jeery guy glares at me across the table. I still don't know the gommer's name, which suits me fine.

I wink, to wind him up.

He goes to snarl at me, but a klaxon sounds.

Ryan grins. 'Hear that? All crew report to action stations. The Syndicate raider must've shown up at last.'

Around us, ComSec crewmembers are scrambling up from their tables and racing out. Our minder comes running to shepherd us back to our quarters. We drag our feet and ask her what's going on, but she's not saying. Course not.

'Not *him*! Kyle's coming with me.'

A hand grabs my arm. When I look round I see it belongs to Laghiri. She's wearing full body armour.

To my surprise, I end up aboard the ore carrier.

Turyakin's already there. So are squads of tough-looking ComSec marines, all armoured up too and busily checking their weapons. The hatch has hardly closed behind me when the deck plates shudder under my feet. My guess is that's us undocking from the cruiser.

Laghiri shoves me towards a crate. 'Stay here.'

She dashes off towards Turyakin. Meanwhile the soldier nearest me, Corporal Keo on her name tag, quits messing with a stubby pulse rifle and gawps at me.

'Hey, kid, what are you doing tagging along?'

'Wish I knew,' I say.

Laghiri returns. 'Kyle's ex-Syndicate. He'll be helping us identify the prisoners you bring in. So, Keo, tell your squad not to shoot them in the face. Got that?'

Keo rattles the ammo-slide on her weapon.

'Whatever you say, sir.'

Laghiri sits next to me. She loosens her body armour to make herself comfortable and glances around at the dingy cargo compartment we're crammed into. 'Our cruiser would do the run into the Ark in half an hour, but this old crawler will take three at least. Then again, it *has* been shifting ore between worlds for well over a hundred years.'

I could believe two hundred years just as easy. Its pitted hull plates wouldn't look out of place on one of our cobbled-together windjammers back on Wrath.

'You sure this thing can keep space out?' Keo asks.

Laghiri laughs. 'It's keeping the air *in* you should worry about. Relax. Ore draggers were built to last.'

I think of something. 'Do I get body armour?'

'Nah. You're expendable,' Keo says, grinning. She stands up and wanders back to her squad.

Laghiri gives me a stare. 'Do you even need it?'

I sigh, real loud. 'Look, us nubloods might heal faster than you guys, but that don't mean we're indestructible or feel any less pain if we get hurt.' The last bit is a lie, but I don't want to be the only loser here without armour.

She says she'll think about it. Frowns. Drops her voice. 'About your nublood. Keep it to yourself, okay?'

I almost laugh. 'It's not something we shout about.'

'Good.' She pulls out my old cuffs.

'Oh, no way!'

'Be a good boy and you can wait until we reach the Ark before you stick them back on. Turyakin's orders. He's worried you'll make a break for it.'

With that, she drops the cuffs in my lap.

'What if I won't?'

'Then I've got thirty marines that'll do it for you.'

She leaves me pulling faces at the hateful things. Comes back with Keo a few minutes later though, and a few spare bits of armour. She even helps me into them.

'Do I get to bring Sky in?' I ask.

'You'll stay here. We'll send a squad to collect her, but only after we're done grabbing the Syndicate guys.'

'You know they'll fight?'

Keo laughs. 'We've been up against Syndicate toughs before. Your friends have a kicking coming their way.'

'They're *not* my friends!' I snap. 'Never were.'

But neither of them is listening. Keo's already walking away. Laghiri's peering at a hand-held device.

'Relax,' she mumbles. 'My marines can handle this.'

Can they though? Sure, her marines look tough, but fights aren't won by those who *look* the toughest. They won't have been up against our nublood strength and speed before. I suddenly regret not warning them.

'Listen, this Ark lot,' I say, 'they're –'

'Tell me later,' she says, and walks away too.

*

Laghiri's 'later' never comes. For the rest of our ride into the Ark she's always busy. And watching Keo's marines get ready, they *do* look like they can handle anything.

I close my eyes and try to get some rest.

How long have I been away from Sky? Hard to figure out exactly. All I can do is hope she's still clinging on, and hasn't been hitting the bliss too hard.

To distract myself I listen to the crap being talked by some of the marines. It's like being back in the Deeps, listening to our resistance fighters. The louder, boastful guys will be less battle-hardened. The quieter guys more experienced and more dangerous. And then we're back in regular space and on final approach to the Ark.

Turyakin switches his comm to speaker mode so we can all listen in. Whoever's on the flight deck does a great job of sounding like a bored ore-carrier pilot.

We're assigned a docking slot. Deck one, bay sixteen.

The marines do one last gear check. Squad leaders flip down helmet-mounted displays in front of one eye. These will guide them to their objectives on the Ark.

The deck lurches under us and Turyakin's comm buzzes.

'We're in. Ten seconds to ramp down.'

Turyakin acknowledges this and signals for his marines to take up their assault positions either side of the loading ramp, where they'll be hard to see from outside when it drops. Two of them have pulled grubby jumpsuits over their combat gear. At a glance, they look like ordinary ore-carrier crew. It seems Turyakin doesn't trust ArkSec and their job is to take out the guys guarding the hanger exit, using force if necessary.

Laghiri elbows me. Hard.

'Okay, okay.' I slip the cuffs on.

She tightens them as the ramp grinds down, sounding like it's a century since it was last oiled. The two marines in crew camo quit standing up straight and slouch down it, out on to the hangar deck. And even though our ore carrier's air isn't any more real, I can smell the familiar stink of the Ark now.

It reminds me they're going up against nubloods!

'Hey, Laghiri,' I call out.

'Not now!' she hisses.

Turyakin's comm buzzes again.

He listens, and then nods. 'Exit's secured. Go!'

The rest of the marines clatter their way down the ramp.

Two take up firing positions just outside. Turyakin, Laghiri and a comm tech stay with me in the hold, manning their command post. Screens show the marine snatch squads as dots moving through a tri-D map of the Ark. There are vid-feeds from the soldiers' helmet-cams too.

It all goes pretty slick. The marines' blue dots blip steadily closer to the red squares that mark their targets. The vid-feeds show us wide-eyed Arkers scrambling aside.

Comm reports start crackling in.

'Delta Squad in position.'

'Alpha Squad going in now!'

One feed shows a marine crouching by a hatch. He shouts, 'Fire in the hole!' and ducks to one side. There's a bang. The screen flares and overloads. When it recovers, the hatch is open and smoking, with marines piling through it. The view jerks about then as whoever's wearing the cam follows them inside.

There are several bright green flashes, and I hear the *t-t-tump* of a pulse rifle set on burst fire.

'Get down! Hands where we can see 'em!'

The view shows a smoke-filled room. A body stretched out. People kneeling, covered by other marines.

'Delta Squad, target secured. Three taken.'

Turyakin glances at me. 'Well?'

I peer at the screen. 'The tall guy on the left is Syndicate for sure. I don't recognise any of the others.'

He nods, and presses his comm. 'Delta, man on left is confirmed. Tag and bag, then move to secondary.'

Tagging is zapping their prisoners with stunsticks. Bagging is a weird gun that wraps their legs and arms in a web of stuff that can't be cut. It also glues them to the floor, where they'll stay put until they're collected.

More reports crackle in as other squads attack their primary targets. More kneeling prisoners. Turyakin opens a channel to ArkSec. He identifies himself, informs them his cruiser is inbound and orders them to seal all hangar decks with immediate effect. Whoever he's talking to passes the comm to his boss. She sounds very unhappy, especially when Turyakin tells her ComSec marines are already aboard the Ark and conducting 'ongoing operations'.

Incoming ComSec cruisers aren't to be messed with though. In an icy voice she agrees to Turyakin's demands and promises ArkSec cooperation.

And that's when things start to go wrong.

So far, the marines' comm messages have been clipped and precise, but now one channel goes crazy. I hear yells and agonised screams from it. The rasp of blaster fire.

'Command, this is Alpha. We're taking hits. We –'

The man's frantic voice is cut off, leaving crackling behind. Laghiri chants into her comm, trying to raise him again. But still the channel stays crackly. Alarms start going off. She checks one of her displays, and curses loudly.

'Bad?' Turyakin growls.

Laghiri nods, a grim look on her face.

The marines have telltale med-sensors built into their armour. That screen shows Alpha Squad, and it's lit up red and dead.

Alpha was tasked with grabbing Rhallon.

'Damn it!' Turyakin spits. 'Who's the nearest?'

'Gamma's two minutes away. Charlie in four if they bust their guts,' Laghiri tells him, and curses again. 'Frag it. So much for taking these bastards by surprise.'

She glares at me. I stay very still.

'Send both,' he orders.

Laghiri gets busy on her comm, firing off orders.

But she's wasting her breath. Things go from bad to worse. More alarms sound. Red and orange telltales flick on across Laghiri's displays, a rash of death and hurt. More frantic comm calls flood in. Gamma Squad have two marines hit and have had to fall back. Bravo, Keo's squad, is pinned down in a massive firefight. Charlie's squad has run into trouble too and gone worryingly quiet.

'This can't be happening,' Laghiri mutters.

Turyakin's seen enough. 'All units fall back to the carrier,' he snarls into his comm. 'I say again, fall back!'

He rips his headset off and hurls it away. The comm tech winces, waits a few seconds and hands him a new set.

'Any word from the *Nantahala?*' Turyakin barks at him.

The tech shakes his head.

The next few minutes are all about helping the marines to disengage. One orange telltale turns red, otherwise things go quiet. Turyakin stands there, stony-faced.

Suddenly tech guy twitches. He holds a hand to his headset. 'Sir! *Nantahala* reports a vessel leaving the Ark.'

'I ordered hangar decks sealed!' Turyakin rages.

The tech listens some more. 'It launched from lower down on the Ark. Must've been hiding out in the wrecked areas.'

Ouch. Something else I could've told them.

'Tell them to get the hell after it!'

What's left of Bravo Squad limps back into the hold soon afterwards. Keo's the only one not wounded. Laghiri comms ArkSec, demanding they send medics immediately.

'What the frag *happened?*' Turyakin says.

Keo yanks off her helmet and has a scratch at her sweat-soaked hair. 'We got our asses handed to us, that's what. Went in fast and hard and caught them by surprise, only they kicked back faster and harder. It was like shooting at ghosts, they were so quick. I shot one and the fragger didn't even go down. I've been a marine half my life, but I never seen nothing like it. It was mad.'

I take a deep breath and hold it.

'Some were just kids, no older than *him*.'

They all turn to look at me.

'I tried to tell you,' I say. 'But you wouldn't listen.'

Turyakin bares his metal teeth at me. 'Tell us . . . what?'

'Thank you, corporal,' Laghiri says quickly. 'You did your best. Go take care of your squad now.'

Keo gives me a stiff look before moving off.

'Well?' Turyakin demands.

I swallow, past a lump in my throat. 'Some of the Syndicate guys your marines went up against are nubloods like me. The Syndicate is putting them to work as enforcers because they're such good fighters. The toughest kids from those ident camps I told you about. Some are willing, but most of them will have been forced into it like I was.'

Laghiri scowls. 'Then why not surrender to us?'

'Oh, come on!' I blurt out. 'Their door gets blasted off its hinges. Guys in body armour rush in, shouting and waving their pulse rifles. Of course they fought back.'

'What *I* want to know,' Turyakin growls, 'is how they tore their way through my space marines?'

I wince, knowing I should've warned them.

'Because we don't just heal faster, we *are* faster. And stronger too. It wasn't a fair fight.'

Turyakin snorts. 'That's . . . ridiculous.'

'Is it?' I say. And lunge at him using all my speed. I've ripped the blaster free from his shoulder-holster and turned it on him before he or anyone else can even move.

The look of shock on his face . . .

Next thing I know I've got at least three pulse rifles being levelled at me as Keo and the other marines react.

'Put that blaster down!' Laghiri yells.

Turyakin and me trade stares over the blaster's sights.

He breathes deep, frowns and then nods.

Slowly, so as not to get my head blown off, I hand him his blaster back. He holsters it and gestures at the marines. They lower their pulse rifles and I get to breathe again too.

Laghiri clears her throat. 'Sir, it's my fault. Kyle *did* try to tell me something. I'm afraid I didn't listen.'

I dart her a grateful glance.

'We'll discuss it later,' Turyakin says, looking bleak.

It gets busy now as yet more beaten-up marines straggle back. ArkSec medics arrive with their kit on a hover-lifter and get stuck into treating them. A handful of prisoners are dragged in too. Among them, Cam. He goes bug-eyed when he spots me, like he's looking at a ghost.

I turn my back on him as he's dragged past.

'What about Sky?' I moan at Laghiri.

She's slow to look up from the screen she's peering at. Can't say I blame her. If I was her, in trouble with my commanding officer, with dead and injured marines to worry about, I reckon I'd just tell me to go to hell.

'Keo! Get yourself over here,' she calls out.

The woman marine grabs her rifle and slogs over. 'Sir?'

'A deal's a deal,' Laghiri says with a sigh. 'Go on then. Tell Corporal Keo where to find her.'

I'm gobsmacked. Where I come from folk use any excuse to slither out of deals. I was sure I'd have to plead.

'I could go with her,' I say, encouraged.

'Wind your neck in, Kyle. Just tell her where, okay?'

'Okay.' I tell Keo how to find our rented room.

She listens, looking me up and down. 'You're another of those fast-and-nasties we went up against, aren't you?'

No point denying it, so I nod.

'And your girlfriend?'

'No. Sky's pureblood, like you. And she's sick.'

Keo grunts. 'Slow *and* sick, huh? That's a relief. I don't need my butt kicked again today.'

I say nothing, hoping Sky plays it cool. For Keo's sake.

32
FROM BAD TO WORSE

Corporal Keo goes off with two marines. Comes back with Sky, Anuk, Mags and a marine with a broken nose.

'Least it's not *your* nose,' I tell Keo.

Mags snorts a laugh.

Keo scowls. So does the marine clutching at his face.

'Told the guy not to touch me,' Sky slurs.

Anuk and Mags are holding her up. Always slight, Sky's even more skin and bone now. Her eyes have big grey bags under them. Her wrists don't fill her handcuffs, even though they're tightened down. And she reeks of bliss.

But she's alive, and relief fills me up. Until I remember what I have to tell her about Tarn.

Sky's gaze slides slowly around the hold, before fixing itself on me. She sways and looks disappointed.

'They got you too then, Kyle?'

'Looks like it,' I say, showing her my cuffed wrists.

Her look becomes a frown and then a disgusted scowl. 'You told them where to find me, didn't you?'

'I did what I had to. Like you and your bliss.'

Sky nods, real slow. 'Wow. I thought you weren't coming back, but I never figured you for a squealer.'

That stings. 'I wouldn't have left you. You *know* that.'

'Can't this wait?' Anuk says, rolling her eyes.

She nods at Mags. Working together, they help Sky limp to the nearest crate and then lower her down onto it.

I go to follow, but Keo grabs my arm.

'You must be dumber than you look, kid. Your girlfriend's a bliss-head. That won't end well, you know that?'

I shrug free angrily. 'She's had it rough.'

Turning my back on her, I head over to where Anuk is fussing over Sky, making her comfortable. Sky won't look at me.

'Didn't expect you to be brought in too,' I say to Anuk.

'She's been staying with us,' Mags says.

Anuk plants herself down with her back against the crate and huffs a big breath out. 'Not long after you cleared off, news of that pirated freighter reached the Ark. It didn't take much figuring to know that's what all those whispers of a big job were about. That settled it for me. I'd already had my fill of killing for the Syndicate and wanted out. I remembered you'd shacked up with Sky someplace. Took a while, but I found her.

'Sky agreed to hide me and I helped Mags look after her. I've been there since, trying to figure myself a way off the Ark. Until your ComSec friends came calling . . .'

'I bit one of them,' Mags says.

'She did. You should've seen her. Look, Kyle, I don't blame you for squealing on the Syndicate. I'd have done it myself if I thought ArkSec could be trusted. But why the frag did you have to tell them we're from Wrath? Sky says that's a hanging offence, escaping from a dump world.'

'I *didn't* tell them. They knew.'

Sky looks at me at last, swinging her head around as if it's lead-heavy. 'How could they?'

'Quit scowling and I'll tell you what happened.'

Mags glowers at me. 'It'd better be good.'

Good? Hardly. I tell them anyway. From feeling cool about our first raid to chilling out on the pleasure hub. I leave Tarn out though. When I get to me snapping, unable to stand by and watch as our prisoners are spaced, Sky groans.

'Gommer. Will you *ever* learn?'

I wrap it up with Rhallon blasting me, taking refuge in the airlock and waking up on a ComSec cruiser.

'So you squealed on the Syndicate to save yourself,' Sky says. 'Sure, I get that. But why turn *us* in?'

'I squealed,' I say slowly, 'to stop innocent people being slung out of airlocks. Or guys being beaten to death on places like the Ark because they're behind on their payments. Mostly though I squealed to try and save your life.'

Her sneer fades. 'We both know I'm past saving.'

'Do we? This cruiser has a med-hub. Laghiri, the woman over there, she said it could cure you.'

Something sparks in Sky's eyes. Hope maybe?

Whatever it was, it's gone next blink. 'Course she did.'

'It's worth a try,' I growl.

'Is it? Cure me, just to hang me?'

But now we have to shut up as Laghiri comes over, clutching a large hand-held display. She has a quick play with it, and then turns it around so I can see its screen.

'The man tagged in red. Is that Rhallon?'

The screen shows the aftermath of a firefight. The marine wearing the camera must be wounded as the view is from deck level and I hear agonised breathing. Rhallon, outlined in red, emerges from behind a shot-up barricade. Sprawled in front of this is the body of Vitali, the screamer's senior pilot, a ragged hole in his forehead. Rhallon stalks forward, rolls the unfortunate marine on to his back, casually finishes him off with a blaster shot.

I reckon we all jump. It's like being shot ourselves.

Another Syndicate fighter joins Rhallon now, and glances down at the body. Sky curses.

It's Tarn, no three ways about it. Frag it!

'Is that Rhallon?' Laghiri snaps.

Somehow, I manage a nod. 'It's him all right.'

'And the girl?'

'Never seen her before.'

I'm terrified that Laghiri will spot the resemblance, but the footage is grainy and she's already hurrying away.

I let out the groan I've been holding in.

'You *knew*, didn't you?' Sky croaks. 'You fraggin' knew Tarn was with the Syndicate and never told me.'

'No! I swear I didn't. We only bumped into each other aboard the Syndicate raider a few days ago.'

But Sky glares at me even more furiously. 'So you didn't just squeal on me, you squealed on my sister too? After all the crap we've been through, how could you do that?'

Anuk has to hold her down. 'That was your sister?'

'What?' Mags squeals.

I try for a swallow. Fat chance. Too guilty, too angry, too dry. 'You don't understand. There's more to tell.'

Sky's rage nearly chokes her.

'If she's dead, I'll kill you! You hear me?'

'Take it easy over there!' one of our guards calls out.

'Tarn *isn't* dead,' I whisper. 'She's piloting the screamer. That's what she does for the Syndicate. The only other pilot was that dead guy with the hole in his head.'

Sky glares at Anuk until she lets go.

'So Tarn dies when that ComSec cruiser catches up?'

'Maybe it won't.'

Sky shakes her head, slumps back down.

A few uniformed ArkSec heavies show up now. I overhear Laghiri ordering some unhurt ComSec marines to go back out with them. They're off to run joint patrols and check out abandoned Syndicate safe houses.

I start, and nearly swallow my tongue. 'Murdo!'

Corporal Keo looks around and frowns. 'Now what?'

But my big gob's already got me into a world of hurt, so I hesitate. Murdo escaped from Wrath too, and is no fan of ComSec, what with being wanted for murder on the Ark. But if all the Syndicate guys have fled, he'll rot in that stinking hole. I stare at her in an agony of indecision.

Laghiri comes over. 'What? Out with it.'

'Tell them,' Sky says. 'You've told them everything else.'

I stare at her, stunned.

'If you don't,' she says, 'I will.'

Confused, I give in. 'Murdo's the pilot guy who helped bust

us out of Wrath. He's being held prisoner by the Syndicate. Or was. He needs rescuing.' I list the twists and turns it takes to find the deck eight compartment.

Laghiri turns to Keo. 'Might be worth bringing him in. Get some ArkSec guys to do it.'

'Sir.' Keo salutes, and hurries off.

I wait until Laghiri goes back to studying her screens before I turn to Sky. 'So now who's squealing, huh?'

'You were always going to tell them,' she says. 'I just gave you the hurry-up. That's all.'

'Why though?'

Sky gives me a scornful look, shakes her dreadlocked head and lowers her voice. 'Dern's a loser, but he'll fight with his back against the wall. With him, Anuk and me, maybe we'll get a chance to make a break for it.'

'And me!' Mags hisses, doing her best fierce look.

'What about me?' I say, and wish I hadn't.

Sky sneers and shrugs, like *why the hell should I care?*

An hour later, some ArkSec heavies drag in what's left of Murdo. They grab his matted blond hair and pull his head back so Laghiri can see.

'This him?' she asks me.

'Yeah, that's Murdo,' I say, and jump up to help.

'Where are you going?' Keo holds me back.

Laghiri jerks her head my way. The ArkSec heavies dump Murdo at my feet, like he's a piece of meat.

'Arseholes,' I say, to their faces.

They glower, but Keo sends them packing. She chucks me a

green packet. 'My medkit. It comes with pictures.'

I kneel one side of Murdo, Anuk the other. We roll him on to his back. He looked crap the last time I saw him, but looks a whole lot worse now. Gently as I can, I examine him. Fractured jaw. Broken ribs. Two broken legs. A lot of savage bruises. He's had the mother of all beatings.

Sky's watching us out of half-closed eyes. 'Will he live?'

'He's a mess. But yeah, he'll live. Be a while before he can walk by himself though, let alone fight.'

Murdo's eyes flicker open. They wander about at first, and then fasten themselves on me.

'You!' he says, in a ghost of his voice.

'Me,' I say, nodding. 'You've been through the wars.'

'Tell me something I *don't* know.' He grimaces, rolls his head left and right and looks around.

'Oh great. ComSec. My favourite security forces.'

I tell him to give his mouth a rest, and he must be hurting real bad because he does as he's told. With Anuk helping, I use Keo's medkit and clean him up the best I can. Fixing his jaw will take cutting, so that'll have to wait. We splint his legs with bits of wood we scav from a crate.

'Where'd you learn to do all this?' Anuk asks.

'My foster-mother, Rona, was a healer back on Wrath.'

I glance at Sky, but her eyes are squeezed shut. She gives no sign of hearing, but I reckon she did.

Anuk sees me looking.

'It's the bliss,' she whispers. 'She'll come around.'

I sigh, can't help it. 'You reckon?'

A shrill buzzing fills the hold. Turyakin pounces on a nearby panel, swatting at it like a cat swats a mouse. Then he shoves some kind of comm device in his ear.

'*Nantahala*, this is Turyakin. Pass your message.'

He tilts his head back and listens intently to a buzzing in his ear, as everybody watches.

Everybody other than Sky. She glares at me instead.

Turyakin stiffens visibly. 'Copy that. Return to the Ark. Stand-off and send the shuttle in to extract us.'

He fumbles the comm from his ear.

'Sir?' Laghiri says.

He ignores her, turns a grim-faced stare on me instead.

'First our marines are taken apart,' he growls. 'And now a Constellation-class cruiser, one of the fastest starships in the fleet, is outrun by your raider vessel. I'm getting sick of these surprises. What else should you have told us!?'

I sigh miserably. 'It's got a massive drive and all the shielding's been stripped out to make it go faster. It's only because we're nubloods we can survive the exposure. But I swear I didn't know it was faster than your—'

Turyakin's too angry to listen.

'Get these prisoners out of my sight,' he bellows.

Tarn's got away, but no thanks to me.

'Lucky for you,' Sky hisses. Her eyes are green spikes.

33
HARD NEWS ALL AROUND

Our home for the next few hours is a gloom-filled shack at the back of the hangar deck. From there we're shuttled aboard the *Nantahala*, which has returned to stand off the Ark as Turyakin ordered. We're uncuffed and thrown into individual barred cages. Sky's to my left, Murdo to my right, Anuk and Mags beyond him. Six more cages hold Syndicate prisoners who must have surrendered. I know none of them by sight, and they're not saying much.

Neither is Sky. She curls up as far away from me as she can get, turns her skinny back and starts coughing.

'I'll sort you out food and drink,' Keo says, heading off.

'What about Sky's treatment?' I call out.

She looks back and shrugs. 'That's not my call.'

And then she's gone. The hatch swings closed behind her with a solid-sounding *clang*. Gritting his teeth, Murdo props himself up against the bars between us. His battered face works at an expression I haven't seen it wear before.

'Kyle, that marine who came to get me, she told me you

sent them. Thanks. Things were getting . . . rough.'

I sigh. 'They could get rougher.'

'Sure. But whatever happens, I owe you.'

'Whatever,' I say, but inside I'm glad.

'So what's gone on while I've been away?' he asks.

Leaving out Tarn, I tell him how I ended up a Syndicate raider, and how it didn't work out so well. When I get to the marines getting their asses kicked on the Ark and the Syndicate raider escaping, he dabs at his torn mouth and grins.

'ComSec must be raging mad.'

The hatch bangs open again and Keo's back with the promised food and drinks. Food comes in small blue plastic containers with a prise-off lid. Drinks are in a plastic tubes where you squeeze one end into your mouth.

She slings one of each of them through the bars at us.

I pull the blue lid off and peer doubtfully at the brown sludge filling the box. 'What is this?'

'You tell me. Eat it with your eyes closed, that's what we all do. I'll send someone for the empties.'

'If you don't want yours, I'll have it,' Mags calls out.

'What if we need to . . . you know?' Anuk asks.

Keo grins and points out a small hole in the decking at the corner of each cage. 'Listen, don't go shoving your arm down there. Or anything else. Whatever goes in there is zapped and turned into nothing. You hear?'

Anuk wrinkles her nose and nods. 'Got it.'

And now Keo looks at me, hard-eyed, her grin gone.

'I lost good mates back on the Ark. Would've been good to know what we were up against.'

'I'm sorry. But I tried to tell Laghiri, honest I did.'

'Maybe you could've tried harder.'

'Not just maybe,' I say, and hang my head.

Silence. Then Keo clears her throat. 'I'll have a word with Laghiri. Remind her about your girl there. Our wounded will be treated first, but I'm sure we can fit her in.'

But they must have lots of wounded marines, or it takes Keo a while to do her reminding. Hours go by. Nothing happens. Without bliss to ease it, Sky's cough gets worse.

Nobody gets any sleep, least of all her. She doesn't complain, but still won't talk to me.

Finally the hatch opens and Keo comes in looking pleased with herself. I quit the press-ups I'm doing and watch as she taps some sort of electronic key thing against my cage door. It clicks and springs open. She does the same for Sky and orders me to help her up.

'Where are we going?' I ask.

'The med-hub. Lieutenant Laghiri will meet us there.'

Murdo rattles his bars. 'Hey, what about me?'

'Don't panic, blondie. We'll get to you.'

Warily, I step into Sky's cage.

'Hear that, Sky? We're going to get you healed.'

She just glares. 'Go to hell. I don't want their lousy healing. Not the way you *bought* it.'

'Nice,' Keo says. 'Ungrateful little bitch, isn't she?'

The marine steps into the cage. Before I know what she's intending, she tags Sky with a stunstick.

Sky slumps to the deck.

'Hey! You didn't have to do that!'

Keo shrugs. 'Shut up and carry her, I'll lead the way.'

I pick Sky up as gently as I can. She feels all loose in my arms, like I'm carrying a bag of water. Her head flops back and her white dreads hang down. A maze of corridors later, I'm back in the med-hub and carefully lowering Sky onto the table I woke up on. Above us, the creepy med-bot lights up.

Laghiri appears, shoves me aside without a word and fusses over Sky, making sure she's lying flat on her back, arms by her side. Satisfied, she taps at a panel. The med-bot twitches, spreads its manipulator arms wide and starts its descent.

'Come with me.' Keo grabs my arm.

The last thing I see before she hauls me away is the bot settling down onto Sky, like some big metal parasite. I shiver, glad that I'd been out cold when it messed with me.

We wait in a small anteroom with a table and some uncomfortable seats. I flop into one of them and try not to hope too hard. Keo stands by the closed door, blocking it.

Laghiri paces for a while, before stopping to look at me. 'Shame that raider got away. A good opportunity wasted. They'll be warier now, harder to catch. Captain Turyakin isn't happy. This won't reflect well on him.'

I say nothing. What's there to say?

'Kyle, is there anything else you haven't told us?'

'What d'you mean?'

Laghiri's jaw tightens. 'You were aboard that screamer. Maybe you saw or heard something you weren't meant to, something that could help us track it down?'

I screw my face up like I'm thinking so hard it hurts.

'No. Sorry. Look, I was only a grunt. Rhallon was always tight-lipped. If I knew anything I'd tell you. Honest.'

'Would you though?' she says carefully. 'Perhaps you're glad the raider gave us the slip?'

I look her in the eye. 'Rhallon tried to kill me, remember? Like you said, I owe them nothing.'

Laghiri studies me, her face one big frown.

'So if you catch the raider, what then?' I ask.

'They'll be given the opportunity to surrender. If they reject that offer they'll be destroyed.'

'If they surrender, what happens to them?'

The woman's frown becomes a scowl. 'Let me make something clear, Kyle. Don't think your actions on the *Karachi Dawn* and leading us to the Ark will be enough to save you and your friends. If our assault had gone better . . . maybe. But it didn't. Your only hope of mercy now is to deliver us that raider!'

I get the gist, even if she says it all fancy. And go cold.

'Sir!' Keo says from the door. 'Med-bot's done.'

Laghiri shoots me a last hard look before she heads back into the hub. I give my head a shake to clear it, scramble up off the seat and jog after her.

Please, please let Sky be healed . . .

The med-bot is retracting itself into the ceiling, its weird arms and probes folding themselves back to their standby positions. Underneath it, Sky lies stretched out on the table as we left her, still and pale and helpless-looking.

Laghiri heads to a display and studies it.

'Well? How is she?' I say, my voice up and down.

She holds her hand up to shut me up. Studies the panel some more. And sighs heavily.

The deck shifts under my boots. 'What's wrong?'

Laghiri glances my way, her mouth a thin line. 'Med-bot, audio report, summary only,' she says.

'Huh?' I say. But she wasn't talking to me.

'I'm – sorry,' a synthetic female voice says, dripping with sympathy. 'Prognosis – terminal. Palliative – care – only.'

My next heartbeat is ages coming.

'What's that mean?' The words buzz in my throat.

Laghiri is slow to answer. 'Our med-bot can't save Sky's life. All it can do is make sure she doesn't suffer.'

'But . . . you said it would heal her!'

'I said it *might* be able to.'

Maybe the woman says something else. Don't know, don't hear, don't care. Blood pounds inside my head like a herd of bull fourhorns are charging through it. I stagger back.

Keo grabs me and holds me up.

'It's a mistake,' I say, desperately. 'Check her again.'

'There's no point. The med-bot doesn't make mistakes. Your friend is so far gone that a full Combine Medical centre might struggle to save her now.'

Might. I clutch at that. 'Where's one of them?'

She frowns at me big time. 'Weeks away, *if* we headed there at max drive. But that's not an option. Our duty is protecting commerce out in this sector. I'm sorry, Kyle.'

'You're just going to let her die?'

'If we could save her we would. But we can't.'

For a few mad seconds I teeter on the edge of rage.

Laghiri clears her throat and looks pained.

'The bot has given Sky medication. When she wakes up,

breathing will be easier and she'll feel more comfortable. It'll also stop her craving that drug she was taking. But she can't stay in the med-hub. Your friend Murdo will be seen to next, and we have wounded marines who need ongoing treatment. I'll arrange a hover-lifter for –'

'No!' Before they can stop me, I've hoisted Sky's unresisting body off the metal slab. Laghiri hesitates, then nods. Keo leads the way back to the prison compartment, lets me back into the cage and helps me lower Sky onto her blanket.

'Want to stay in here with her?' she asks.

I nod, not trusting my voice.

She ducks out of the cage, locks the door behind her and steps over to Murdo's cage. 'Don't go anywhere – you're up next. A hover-bot will be along soon to fetch you.'

Murdo scowls. 'About time.'

'Kyle, how'd it go?' Anuk says from two cages away.

I stare down at Sky, choke, shake my head.

Silence from them. The shocked kind, that's like a shout.

A few of Sky's snow-white dreads have fallen across her eyes. I lean over and push them back with the rest. She stirs slightly, but is still out of it from the stunstick, or whatever meds have been shot into her. Her breathing does seem easier though. That's something, I guess.

'Too bad,' Murdo mutters.

The hover-bot arrives for him and he's taken away.

I sit there, wondering if Laghiri did string me along about the med-hub healing Sky. Nah. I don't believe it. So the only hope for Sky is still Tarn's nublood. Which is no hope at all.

I let my head thump back against the bars.

'You can't blame yourself,' Anuk says.

I look around, to see her and Mags watching me from the cage they share. 'You reckon? Who *should* I blame then?'

Anuk shrugs. 'The Saviour and his Slayers. They stuck us in the camps to work the darkblende.'

'Wha zat?' Sky slurs.

Her eyes are open and she's moving, but only feebly. I help her sit up, lean her back against the bars. It's not long before she's fully conscious again and able to scowl.

'What are *you* doing in here?'

I let go and retreat to a safe distance. 'Looking after you.'

But she's not listening. She takes a cautious little breath. Another one, deeper. And then even deeper, as if tasting how it feels. Her head jerks up and her eyes go wide.

'I can breathe again! Am I . . . cured?'

For an awful few seconds I wish I was anywhere else but here. I don't know what to say. But Sky deserves better than that. If things were turned around, she'd tell me straight. I owe her the truth, and so much more.

Toughest thing I've ever done is to look her in the eye.

'You're *not* healed, Sky. The med-bot checked you out, but you're too sick. It can help you with your breathing and make sure you don't suffer, but that's all.'

She nods. Once. And looks down into her lap. 'Oh well. ComSec will hang me for escaping Wrath, so it makes no difference. Either way I'm screwed.'

'We're *all* screwed,' I say.

Sky lifts her head, and shakes it. 'No. Tarn got away.'

*

Murdo's back with us. The crude splints on his legs have been swapped for exo-skeletal braces, like the one Sky wears. With these he can shuffle along stiffly. Two marines help him back inside his cage, before locking him in.

'See y'around, *Murdoch Verne*,' Keo says with a grin, before ushering her marines out of the compartment.

Murdo, a face on him like thunder, spits curses.

'What did she call you?' Anuk asks.

'That fraggin' med-bot!' he snarls, and slams the bars of his cage with the flat of his hand. 'Couldn't just sort my bust legs, could it? No. The bastard thing went and found my iris implants and stripped them out!'

'Is that bad?' I say, squirming.

More curses again, even nastier this time around.

'Bad? Turns out that cheapskate who did my implant didn't slice the old irises out like I'd paid him for, just slid the fakes in over the top. The med-bot scans me without them, pings up my real name and how I'm wanted for murder here.'

'Ouch.' His eyes *do* look different.

Murdo – or Murdoch – slides himself down the bars into a heap on the floor and puts his head in his heads.

'You might as well have left me in that stinking hole.'

34
HANGING OR BAIT

Mags acts the innocent and talks her way out of the cage she was sharing with Anuk. Keo even lets her bunk down with her marines. Soon she's the cruiser's good-luck mascot and has the run of the ship. Which is good, because she brings us our meals now and tells us what's going on.

'You wouldn't believe what I hear,' she's always saying. 'It's like they don't see me, or think I can't understand.'

Our cruiser prison has been chasing its tail around the Vulpes sector for two weeks, sniffing out likely places the Syndicate raider might be based and finding nothing. But today Mags brings grimmer news. Another freighter has been hit, and more dead bodies found floating in space.

'Right under their ComSec noses,' she says.

Anuk tuts. 'You make it sound like it's a good thing.'

Mags sits cross-legged outside our cages, watching us push the latest slop around our plates, and shrugs.

'The word is that they'll have to bunch bigger freighters together and escort them.'

Murdo grunts. 'Convoys. Makes sense, but the owners won't like it, not one bit.'

'Why not?' I say. 'Beats losing freighters.'

'Sure. But it's still bad for business, having to slog around together, visiting worlds they don't need to instead of flying direct. That'll cost time, and time is money.' He stands up and paces carefully round his cage, still cautious on his powered leg braces. 'Turyakin will hate it too, forced to play nursemaid with his precious cruiser.'

He pauses, looks thoughtful and mutters.

'That's all good though.'

At least, that's what I think he said.

'I overheard something else,' Mags says. 'Laghiri was telling one of her officer mates that if Turyakin doesn't catch the raider soon there's a good chance that he'll be relieved.'

She pulls a confused face.

'But why would he be *relieved*? I don't get it.'

In two weeks of Sky dying slowly and scowling at me like it's my fault, I've forgotten how to laugh. But it comes back to me now. 'That's just fancy talk for him being fired.'

Murdo quits pacing, looks through me.

'What?' I say, but he just grins.

'Hey, Mags, any news about our executions?' Sky asks.

Mags goes wide-eyed. She shakes her head.

'Why ask?' I snap. One laugh, and she has to ruin it.

'Because I want to know, that's why!'

We're about set for another squabble when Murdo claps his hands so loudly that he makes us all jump.

'Maybe there won't be any executions,' he says.

'No? Why not?' I ask.

'Let's just say I reckon Turyakin is going about catching that Syndicate raider all wrong. After all, you don't catch fish by chasing after them, do you?'

Anuk leans into her bars. 'You know a better way?'

'Maybe I do. Hey, Mags, make yourself useful, will you? Run and tell Turyakin or Laghiri that if they want to catch that raider they need to talk to me.'

'Huh?' Mags looks uncertain.

'Think you can make some sort of deal?' I ask Murdo.

He grins. 'No harm trying.'

Sky's face is stony, but she can't keep the worry out of her eyes.

'My sister's on that raider,' she growls.

Murdo stares at her. '*What?* Are you serious?'

'Kyle?' Sky says.

'It's true,' I confess. 'Tarn's the co-pilot. We, uh, bumped into each other when I was aboard.'

Murdo considers this, but then shrugs. 'Well, that's not my problem. I'm more worried about saving *our* necks.'

Sky's lips draw back from her teeth.

'Yeah, yeah,' he says, before she can snarl at him. 'I know. If I get your sister killed, you'll kill me. Tell you what, I'll worry about that if and when the time comes. Okay?'

'What should I do?' Mags asks.

'Ignore him!' Sky snaps.

Anuk stands up. 'Sorry, Sky, but I'm with Murdo.'

Hope is sharper than a blade and cuts me in two. I want to yell at Mags to run to Turyakin, but I know Sky will hate me if I do.

So I say nothing, like the hopeless gom I am.

'Mags!' Murdo says. 'You'll be saving all of us from being executed. You want to save your friends, don't you?'

That does it. Mags races off.

I can't look at Sky, but I hear her curse and the bang as she kicks our cage's bars. Murdo scowls at her.

'Listen, Sky, your sister won't die, not the way I figure it. If it works out, she'll only be captured.'

Sky blows a fierce sigh. 'And *then* executed.'

'Not necessarily. If I was Turyakin I'd be getting desperate. If he is, then anything will be up for grabs.'

Sky doesn't look convinced.

But less than five minutes after Mags hurtled out of our prison compartment, Keo is back with two of her marines. They make straight for Murdo's cage, and let him out.

'Now we're talking,' he says, winking at me.

Between them, they hustle him from the compartment.

'He's been gone ages,' Anuk whispers.

I shrug. 'Is that good or bad?'

We're both whispering because Sky's asleep. All the meds they're shooting into her does that. It's what the med-bot means by comfortable. As in knocked out most of the time.

'If his plan was dumb he'd be back already.'

'Unless they thought it was so dumb they got mad and spaced him. We'll have to wait and see.'

'Do you rate Murdo?'

I consider. 'I do. Making deals is what the guy does.'

'If he's right and Tarn's captured, then she could save

Sky like you once saved your brother.'

I glance nervously at Sky, but she's still asleep.

'I wish it was that simple, but it isn't.'

'Why not?'

I hesitate. 'If I tell you, you have to promise you won't tell Sky. It'd kill her to hear it.'

Anuk nods. 'I won't, I swear.'

I take a deep breath. 'When I bumped into Tarn on that screamer, I told her Sky was fierce sick and how only she could save her. Want to guess what she said?'

'What? Just tell me.'

'She said *what's it worth?*'

Anuk's eyes widen. 'No way!'

'For a while I thought I'd got Tarn to agree to trade her blood for my share in the first raid. Then it went up to my share from both raids. I said fine, whatever. But she was just messing with me. In the end, she made it pretty clear she'd rather see Sky die than give her even one drop of her blood.'

'She wouldn't save her own sister?' Anuk says, appalled.

'Ssshhhh! Keep your voice down!'

Too late. Anuk glances past me and winces.

I turn round. Sky's sitting up. From the crushed look I see on her face it's clear that she's heard everything.

'You tell Anuk, but you wouldn't tell me?' she croaks.

I go cold, then hot. 'I couldn't.'

Sky plays my trick. Says nothing, and just waits.

'I thought our luck had changed at last,' I say, with a sigh. 'But it was just like you told me – Tarn still blames you for all those years in the ident camp. Even so, I never thought she'd refuse to help you. I figured she was winding me up, or something.' A sob catches me out, almost choking me. 'Nah. Tarn *won't* help you. She's full of hate and spite and . . . and it felt too cruel to tell you.'

Sky's face sort of crawls as she struggles to take this in.

'It *was* my fault,' she mutters.

'No! It was a mistake. You were only a child.'

'You should've told me!'

I hang my head. 'I know. I hoped the cruiser's med-bot could heal you – and then when it couldn't, I figured I'd best keep it to myself. That you were better off hating me, than finding out your sister doesn't –'

'Doesn't care? You think I didn't know?'

I risk a look at Sky.

The crushed look is gone. Fire is in her eyes.

Anuk snorts. 'It's none of my concern, but why should you care what happens to Tarn? If she's captured, I'll hold the bitch down while we suck her blood out and pump it into you.'

Sky darts her a look that could do serious harm.

'You're right. It's *none* of your concern!'

Where the anger comes from I don't know, but it explodes inside me now like a bomb going off. One second I'm sitting down, the next I'm on my feet, raging.

'We're only trying to help you!'

'Help yourselves more like!' Sky snarls.

I throw my hands up, frustrated. 'And why not? Why should we all die just so Tarn can live?'

Sky opens her mouth. Snaps it closed again.

'Tarn couldn't care less that you're dying,' I go on. 'No, it's worse than that. She *wants* you dead. She *smiled* as she told me it serves you right. Frag it, Sky! WAKE UP!'

Sky stares. Shakes. Starts coughing. She's still hacking away when Keo brings Murdo back and shoves him into his cage.

Anuk jumps up. 'Well?'

He grins at her, and then at me. 'We're on!'

'How will it work?' I ask. 'What deal did you cut?'

But Murdo won't be rushed. First he strips his jacket off. Next he bunches it up against the back of the cage as a sort of cushion. Lastly he sits himself down and squirms until he's satisfied that he's comfortable.

'Turyakin buys my way of taking that raider,' he says, 'and we all get full pardons, with documents to prove it.'

I trade sceptical looks with Anuk.

'What? Just like that?'

Murdo wriggles, as if his jacket cushion isn't quite doing it for him. 'We only get our pardons if we deliver.'

Sky mutters something real nasty.

Murdo grins. 'Remember what I said about how you don't catch fish by chasing them. That Syndicate raider is a fish swimming about in space. Which is hellish big, so it's hard going on impossible to find it. And even if they *do* find it, it's so fast it can swim away from them again.'

'Cut the crap and just tell us, Murdo!' Anuk growls.

'Okay, okay,' he says. 'So you lure a fish with a baited hook and you catch it with a rod. Turyakin and his ComSec cruiser are the rod. Have a guess what *we* are?'

I groan. 'The baited hook.'

I've only ever seen a few cats on Wrath – our wildlife had a habit of eating them – but I've heard one purr. The way Murdo's carrying on, I half expect him to do likewise.

'A pardon's no use if we're dead,' I say.

He looks round. 'There is that. But, hey, at least we'll have died fighting, not thrashing at the end of a rope.'

Then, gleefully, he tells us what he's signed us up for . . .

35
SUICIDE SQUAD

A heck of a lot can happen in three standard-days if ComSec decide that it has to. Turyakin has commandeered a small free-trader that won't be missed. It's alongside, being refitted for our mission, whatever that involves. Meanwhile, we've been training hard in how to use our secret weapon.

It's been tough, but at least we're out of those stinking cages. Now we bunk down in a dorm room of our own, one hatch along from Keo's marines. We even have our own washroom, with hot water. There are strict limits to how far we can wander about the cruiser though.

Me, Anuk and Mags are playing a dumb card game. Murdo's off learning the free-trader's controls.

'Wanna know what everyone is calling you?' Mags asks.

'Heroes?' I say, pulling a face.

'Duh. Turyakin's suicide squad!' she says.

'Great,' Anuk says. 'Thanks for sharing. Real cheery.'

I glance across at where Sky's lying on her bunk, staring up at the ceiling. It's like she's hiding inside herself, or shutting the real world out. She can't even be arsed scowling any more. It's like all the fight has gone out of her.

I'm worried she's just waiting to die.

Corporal Keo sticks her head in through our hatch. 'Okay, suckers, it's time to go. Grab your gear and follow me.'

She's coming along on the mission, with four of her squad. With so many marines dead or still recovering from their wounds, they're all Turyakin can spare us.

'What about Murdo?' I ask.

Keo tells me he's already aboard.

I throw my losing hand down and stand up. So this is it. I thought I'd be more scared, but mostly I'm relieved the wait is over. Also, deep in my belly, I feel a savage eagerness at going after Rhallon. A bit of payback sounds good!

'Let's go. Hurry up,' Keo shouts.

'Hang on.' I head over to where Sky's lying on her bunk. She sees me coming, levers herself up on an elbow and glares so hard I stop short. 'Look, Sky,' I say. 'I —'

Her mouth twists. 'Yeah, yeah. You want to live.'

I'd been going to say I was sorry how things have worked out before she interrupted. But she's not wrong.

'Is that so bad?' I say, a bit sharp.

She sighs, and shakes her head. 'No. I don't blame you.'

It's a straw and I clutch at it gratefully.

'Sky, I swear I'll do whatever I can to bring Tarn back alive. And I'm sure she'll . . . hey, what are you doing?'

I say this last bit as she swings her legs off her bunk and starts lowering herself down.

'What's it look like?' she says. Shoves past me, limps over to

Keo and tells her: 'I'm coming too.'

Keo looks surprised, but shrugs. 'It's your neck.'

'Sure about this, Sky?' I say.

The look she darts me could freeze water.

Mags shouts out that she wants to come too, but Keo says a very firm no. We leave her peering and waving after us.

After a maze of narrow and unfamiliar corridors, Keo ushers us into a sort of viewing chamber. It's dimly lit, which lets us see outside through a clear wall. Instead of stars or writhing dark matter, a grey rock-strewn landscape stretches away to be lost in haze. A hundred or so metres off our right, a shabby little star freighter squats down on its landing gear. Bulky-suited figures are working on top of it. Laghiri's over by the clear wall, watching what's going on.

As we clatter inside, she turns to greet us.

'Behold,' she says. 'Your Trojan horse.'

Anuk looks at me. 'Huh?'

I blow air out of my mouth and shrug. 'No idea.'

The freighter looks as ancient and battered as that old ore carrier we rode into the Ark. But that's all part of Murdo's plan, so no great surprise. The rest, if I understand it right, has undercover ComSec agents selling the Syndicate information about a Combine trading company's scheme to avoid further attacks. A scheme involving dummy cargo being shipped aboard a heavy freighter called the *Orion*, while the real cargo is shipped in secret, aboard a recently acquired tramp freighter . . .

Sounds crazy to me, but Murdo swears it'll work, as long as Rhallon isn't handed it too easy and smells a rat.

About now, Laghiri sees Sky. 'What's *she* doing here?'

Keo frowns. 'Sky wants in on the mission.'

'She's sick. I don't think –'

'Then hang me now!' Sky interrupts, turning her fiercest scowl on the woman. 'My whole life I've been a fighter. So let me die a fighter, that's all I'm asking.'

Her bony hand seeks out mine and squeezes it.

'Let her,' I blurt out, without thinking. 'Even sick, Sky's tough. And the more there are of us to fight, the better chance we have of pulling this mission off.'

I doubt Murdo would agree, but he's not here.

Laghiri can't help glancing down at our held hands.

'Very well,' she says, and sighs. 'But you should both know there are no med facilities aboard that freighter. You could be stuck on it for weeks. We can't know how long it will take before the raider takes the bait.'

'I'll take that chance,' Sky says.

I give Sky's hand a soft and cautious squeeze. She doesn't squeeze back, but neither does she pull away.

'Can we take any meds with us?' I ask Laghiri.

She orders Keo to see to this, then tells us that before we board the freighter we must first report to the med-hub.

Anuk asks why, but we don't get told.

'You heard the lieutenant,' Keo snaps. 'Move out!'

You'd think we'd signed up to be ComSec marines. But there's no point arguing, so we let ourselves be herded back out of the compartment and along more long corridors.

Sky soon tugs her hand free again.

I glance at her, disappointed. 'I didn't think you'd be up for this mission. Because of Tarn.'

Sky's jaw works. 'You were wrong then, weren't you?'

I try to look her in the eye, but she turns away.

In the white-walled med-hub Keo turns to face us. 'Okay, who wants to be first?' she says.

At her nod, another marine holds up a weird-looking pistol with a small disc slotted into its extra-wide muzzle. Carefully he peels a protective cover off the disc, exposing some very nasty-looking little spikes.

'What the frag's that?' I say.

'A precaution. I trust you, but Turyakin doesn't.'

Keo explains that each of us will have a 'loyalty' disc shot into our necks. It's capable of taking our heads clean off if triggered. She taps a small clicker device clipped to her body armour, which must be the trigger. And then lists all the safeguards built into the disc so there's no chance of ripping it out. Murdo's already had his fitted apparently. Only after we deliver the Syndicate raider will they be removed.

Anuk scowls. 'I don't like it. What if it breaks?'

Keo shrugs. 'No disc, no mission. And you know what that means. So like I said, who's first?'

Sky mutters something crude and shoves past me. She tilts her head left, pulls her dreads aside and exposes the side of her neck to the waiting marine. 'Okay, do it.'

'This might hurt a bit,' he says, with a big grin.

Tump! The gun kicks back. Sky tries to hold a groan in and fails. So there's no 'might' or 'bit' about it. As he pulls the gun away, she claps a hand to her neck.

'Let's see it,' Keo says.

Teeth gritted, Sky pulls her hand away. A dim green light

flashes at the centre of the implanted disc. Keo unclips her clicker and passes it nearby. It buzzes.

She nods and looks satisfied.

'Who's next?' she says, like she's handing out sweets.

I step up, only because if I watch it done again I'll lose my nerve. Or maybe because Sky is watching.

And, yup, it hurts like hell. I mean I'd take it any day over being blasted, but I can't keep from groaning too. Only Anuk is tough enough to take it and not make a sound.

I finger my disc. Gingerly.

But Keo shakes her head. 'Don't.'

Next thing she does is gather together a medkit, lobbing bits and pieces into a big plastic box for me to carry.

The other marine hands Sky something called an inhaler and tells her to suck on it if her cough gets bad. 'It's got a month's worth of gas. If you're still struggling, you can give yourself a shot of this.' He holds up a thin red tube. 'Only one shot at a time though, okay? You'll feel invincible. But take too much of the stuff and you'll crash. You could even die.'

He hands Sky a small box of them.

'Will we be issued with weapons?' I ask Keo hopefully as she leads us out of the med-hub.

'Once we're on board. Body armour too.'

In another compartment, a heavily armoured vehicle that looks a bit like a Slayer landcrawler is parked at the top of a ramp, clearly waiting for us. So are Captain Turyakin and Lieutenant Laghiri. I brace myself to be speeched at.

Fortunately, Turyakin keeps it short and sweet. 'Like I told your pilot friend, deliver me the Syndicate raider and you will get your lives back. Full pardons, slate wiped clean. Hell, we'll even drop you off wherever you want. How's that?'

And we all nod our heads off.

Except for Sky.

I guess it isn't much of a deal for her.

Laghiri asks if we have any questions, but we don't.

'Good hunting then,' she says. 'Corporal Keo, we've fitted the freighter with a secure comm link. A word of warning though. We'll be a long way behind you, well out of civilian sensor range, so there will be a significant time delay. If the screamer shows up it's possible our warning won't reach you before they do. So stay alert!'

'Sir!' Keo salutes, and calls for us to follow her.

And that's that. We all pile inside the vehicle and the rear door clangs shut behind us. When it opens a few minutes later we clamber out into the freighter's dirty little hold. I go to help Sky, but she waves me away and jumps down, landing lightly on her exo-braced leg.

'I can manage,' she rasps.

Keo leads us out of the hold and forward into the freighter's cramped crew quarters. 'Welcome aboard ComSec Auxiliary Vessel, the *Whydah Gally*.'

'Why the what?' I say, and get groaned at.

Large plastic crates are labelled with our names. One's even been put together for Sky. I prise mine open to find some bedding, washing stuff and body armour. No weapons though. I guess we'll only get them later.

Meanwhile, Keo's experienced marines grab the few bunks to be grabbed. The rest of us will have to make do with the hard deck. Sky limps to a likely looking corner, dragging her box of stuff behind her.

I head that way too. 'Mind if I join you?'

She looks at me at last. 'Sure you still want to?'

Keo saves me from having to come up with an answer to that. She shows us around some of the mods her ComSec techs have made. Armour plating on the walls, designed to stop blaster rounds. An inflatable pressurised refuge. It's small now, but if the hull is breached we can inflate it and crawl inside. It's good for an hour with all of us in it.

A marine closes the hatch between us and the hold.

An alarm sounds then as the hold starts adjusting its pressure to match the atmosphere outside. Through a clear panel set into the hatch, I watch as the freighter's loading ramp thumps down and the transfer vehicle that brought us here crunches down it and heads away. The ramp grinds slowly back up again.

Not too long after that, Murdo lifts us off the surface.

36
THE BAIT IS TAKEN

Nueva Cadiz is the trading outpost where we fake picking up the 'precious' cargo. Keo locks us in the crew compartment. A bunch of crates are loaded aboard and then we launch out of there fast.

'Were we seen?' Murdo asks her afterwards.

Keo shrugs. 'There were some shifty-looking guys hanging about the port as we loaded. Then again there always are.'

Our third day out from Nueva Cadiz I'm sitting on the flight deck with Murdo, idly watching the marines in the compartment outside doing their daily exercises.

Murdo shifts in his seat. 'I still wish Sky hadn't come.'

Ever since he found out she's aboard, he's been moaning on at me about it, threatening to tell Keo that Sky's sister is one of the raider's crew. Sky's desperate he doesn't, certain Keo won't let her fight if she knows. I've only kept him quiet until now by reminding him he owes me for saving his life.

I groan. 'What harm can she do?'

Murdo grunts and mutters something along the lines of harm being what Sky does.

'Cut her some slack,' I say, for the hundredth time.

By now I've told him about Tarn's jeering refusal to save Sky, and even he had seemed shocked.

It doesn't stop him moaning though. 'I don't want her screwing things up to get revenge on her sister.'

'She won't,' I say. 'I'll make sure of that.'

'Yeah? You'd better.'

I figure it's time to change the subject and jerk my head at the marines. 'Keo works them fierce hard, don't she?'

Murdo twists round to look.

'I get tired just watching them. Glad they're here though. Without them I wouldn't fancy our chances.'

'You reckon we'll have to fight then?'

'Bound to. A few bits of tacked-on armour plating won't keep us safe for long. But that's not what I mean.'

I roll my eyes at him. 'What *do* you mean?'

'Well, let's say this all goes to plan and your Syndicate screamer shows up and grabs us. We grab them back using the grapples they've fitted, so they can't get away. And then try to hang on long enough for the *Nantahala* to come steaming in and save us. Maybe that armour plating will keep them out, maybe it won't. But one thing's for sure, your Syndicate guys won't roll over and surrender. So Turyakin will have to board and take them out hand to hand. Only that didn't go too well on the Ark, did it? So why make the same mistake again when he could just stand off and nuke both ships?'

Finally I get it. 'Only you think he can't now, because

he'd be taking Keo and her marines out too?'

'*Can't* is too strong a word. I don't *think* he would. Anyway, that's why I insisted, and why I'm glad they're here.' Murdo rubs at his stubbled chin and chuckles softly. 'Never thought I'd be saying that about ComSec!'

I glance back at the marines. And decide I'm glad too.

Later on though a worry worms itself into my head. What if Turyakin sends his marines in and they're beaten back? He'd *have* to use his cruiser's firepower then or risk the screamer getting away again. No, hiding and hoping in our armoured compartment won't cut it. We'll have to take out any Syndicate boarders ourselves, or at least do enough damage so that Turyakin's marines can handle the rest.

I collar Keo and blurt this all out to her.

'You're not wrong,' she says.

'What are our chances, d'you think?'

Keo smiles grimly. 'Marines are paid to fight not think.'

By now Sky has shifted from the crew compartment to bunk down in the hold. I've shifted there too. She hasn't told me to get lost, so I figure she's okay with that.

We're still not talking much though.

So when a day later I'm woken from a light doze by a kick to my leg, it's a surprise to see Sky clutching her rag of a blanket around her like she's cold and looking down at me.

'Tarn will never surrender to ComSec marines,' she says. 'So we'll just have to get to her before they do.'

I sit up, fighting a yawn that could get me killed.

'How do you figure on doing that?'

'When the Syndicate board us they'll expect a few scared

crewmembers. They'll get a hell of a shock when Keo and her marines get stuck into them. In the confusion, you, me and Anuk will board the screamer and grab Tarn.'

I stare at her. 'Are your meds messing with your head?'

Her lip twitches. 'Wasting my breath, am I?'

'No,' I protest. 'Just . . . let me at least think about it.'

'Why? There's no other way to be sure Tarn is taken alive. I thought that's what you wanted.'

I get that feeling of cold sweat. 'I do. Course I do.'

'So what's to think about?'

'After what Rhallon did to me, I wanted a crack at him.'

'You'd rather kill him than save Tarn?'

'That's not fair.'

We argue for ages, but in the end Sky talks me around. Not that I want to put myself more in harm's way, because I sure as hell don't. But how else do we save Tarn?

Not that she deserves saving.

I tap the disc clinging to my neck. 'What happens when Keo sees us clearing off into the screamer? She'll think we're deserting. I reckon we'd best clear it with her.'

Sky shakes her head. 'She'll say no, or try to stop us.'

'You don't know that.'

'No! We're only doing what should be done. Attack is the best form of defence – didn't they teach you that in the Deeps? We'll give the marines more time to deal with the first wave of boarders. Keo will thank us afterwards.'

'If there is an afterwards,' I mutter. And shake my head. Even sick, Sky's still so fierce and sure of herself. I wish I knew how she does it.

'Anuk was up for it as soon as I asked her,' Sky says.

I'm wondering how true this is when a siren sounds and makes me jump. Next thing, Murdo's disembodied voice booms from a speaker in the ceiling.

'Looks like we're in business. Long-range sensors show a contact heading our way on an intercept course.'

I scramble back to my feet.

Sky bares her teeth and struggles up too. 'About time.'

'Incoming comm now,' Murdo says.

There's a loud pop, and then: '. . . trader *Whydah Gally*, shift out of dee-emm and prepare to be boarded.'

The voice is deep enough to be Masson's I reckon.

And now we hear from Murdo again. 'Vessel calling *Whydah Gally*, please identify yourself.'

He lays on just the right amount of worried.

We both duck back into the crew compartment, in time to be winked at by Keo and hear from the raider again.

'*Whydah Gally*, you know who we are and we know what you're carrying. If you cut your drive and cooperate you've nothing to fear. Call for help or keep running and I will see to it that you all die roaring. Is that clear?'

We wait breathlessly for Murdo's comeback.

'Syndicate raider, *Whydah Gally*,' he says, in the shaky voice of someone who's fearful but trying to be brave. 'My captain says to go screw yourself. Is *that* clear?'

The buzz from the comm link clicks off.

A few seconds later, a grinning Murdo sticks his head through the hatch to the flight deck. 'That told 'em. I've triggered our distress beacon, changed course for the nearest world and pushed the drive to emergency max.'

This is what we'd agreed. Rolling over too easy would only make Rhallon suspicious. Better to run.

'How long?' Keo asks him.

Murdo ducks back into the flight deck. When he returns he looks grudgingly impressed. 'Tell you what, that screamer doesn't half shift when they wick it up. I make it two hours before they're on us. A lot less if this old crate's drive blows, which it might. I'm seeing coolant alarms already.'

Keo's armoured chest rises and falls as she takes a deep breath and lets it out. My heart starts hammering.

'Okay, guys,' she calls out. 'We know what's coming and what needs doing. Check your gear.'

Me, Sky and Anuk are given our weapons at last. Orange-banded stunsticks, instead of the marines' red-banded killsticks. Keo clips on a shoulder-holstered blaster.

'Hey, thought we daren't use energy weapons,' I say, 'in case shots go astray and breach the hull.'

She grimaces. 'If things go against us, it won't be a *stray* shot. I'll make sure we take our attackers with us.'

Didn't think my heart could hammer faster, but it does.

'Sounds good, I've had my fill of Syndicate hospitality,' Murdo says. 'Where's *my* weapon?'

Keo shakes her head. 'You don't need one. Lock yourself on the flight deck and be ready when I shout.'

Murdo gives her a stare, clearly unimpressed by this.

But Keo doesn't blink. 'Get moving!'

'Yeah. Yeah. I'm going.'

Before he does though, he heads over. Hangs his fist out.

Smiling, I hang mine out. We bump.

Murdo grins. 'Here goes nothing, huh?'

I try to keep my voice cool. 'Beats being hanged.'

He turns to Anuk next and they bump fists. For a second I think Sky will snub him, but I'm wrong. They shoot each other a bit of a hard stare, but when he hangs his fist out she sighs and gives him a solid bump.

And then he's off, striding towards the flight deck.

We've set the cargo hold up to give cover, as this is the most likely place they'll hard dock into. I join Sky in the shadows behind a big lashed-down metal shipping crate stamped Combine Agriculture. Anuk curls up behind the next crate over. From there she gives us a quick thumbs up.

'Sky, I'm sorry it came to this,' I whisper.

She looks at me. In the gloom her eyes look black.

'So am I,' she says quietly.

'It's easier to be mean behind someone's back,' I say, hesitantly. 'Might be different when Tarn sees you.'

Sky bares her teeth. 'Guess we'll soon find out.'

'I don't get it. You knew she hated you – what did you think would happen when you finally caught up with her?'

Sky shifts, and lets a long silence stretch out.

'I *didn't* think,' she whispers at last. 'Maybe I just grew up wanting to make amends. I'd ruined Tarn's life, but I could make it right between us by saving her from being a prisoner, or slaving, or being experimented on.'

'She doesn't deserve saving,' I mutter.

'Who are you to say that?' Sky snaps. 'You didn't live most of your life in a fraggin' ident camp, being beaten and abused. You didn't have to stand on a stage to be cut, facing a mob howling and screaming that you're a monster. Knowing you'll die if you've healed too fast. Tarn *did*!'

'Yeah? So did you. So did Anuk, and lots of other kids. And it made you hard and angry. But if things were turned around, you'd give Tarn your blood. I know you would.'

Sky stays silent for a while. 'Maybe.'

'There's no *maybe* about it.'

Silence again. When she speaks at last, her voice is sad.

'I've been . . . harsh with you, haven't I?'

I start, and take my time answering too. 'Maybe.'

'Ha ha. Shut up and listen, you gom. And don't stare at me or I'll punch you. Which would mess up telling you what a good and true friend you've been.'

I swear that my jaw comes close to landing in my lap.

Sky sighs. 'Look, I know I've been hard to be around. Too quick to scowl and snap and call you weak, like when you didn't kill Doohan. You're *not* weak, just strong in your own way. The way Rona raised you. But all my life I've been hurting and angry and . . . I guess what I'm saying is, if we could do it all over again then I'd do it different.'

Next thing, Sky's pulling me to her. She tucks her face under my chin. Her ragged breath warms my neck.

'But we can't,' she says. 'Here we are, and –'

'I've missed you,' I say, and put my arms around her.

'Me too.' She coughs gently into me.

'Hey, at least I don't have to worry any more about Doohan showing up,' I say, to say something.

'You never did.'

'What?' I pull back, try to see her face.

But she won't let me, and pulls me back closer again.

And I get it now. Sky will have cleaned my mess up for me. Killed Doohan, to save my life.

She sniffs. 'He didn't suffer. I made sure of that.'

I nod, shocked, but not really shocked, and mainly grateful. But I don't know what to say, so I just hold her tighter and hope that says what I feel better than any words.

'Um, I can't breathe,' Sky says.

I relax my hug guiltily.

'Sky, I'm really sorry about Tarn. I really am.'

She looks at me, so close that she's a blur. 'Don't be. Just watch my back like I watched yours. I'll take care of Tarn.'

For a second I think about kissing her.

But before I can, Sky pulls away.

I look round and Anuk's watching us. I see the flash of her smile. She mimes dabbing tears from her eyes. And now Murdo's voice booms through the hold again.

'The raider's speeded up. Contact now in *one* hour!'

'One is good, two is evil,' I mutter.

Sky leans back against the crate, eyes closed.

The hour crawls by, horribly slow, because that's what hours do when death lurks beyond them.

'Contact in five minutes.'

The marines check their weapons one last time. I check my stick's power telltale. In the green. Fully charged.

One minute to go.

Blood pounds in my ears, like someone's hammering at the inside of my head. And now I hear that ear-splitting *tzzzummm* sound as our freighter's dee-emm drive overlaps with the screamer's, causing a shock wave. It's a big enough hit that the freighter lurches and Sky is thrown into me. I'm helping her sit back when our drive cuts out.

Everything goes horribly quiet. Until, with a massive *clang* of metal on metal, the deck shudders beneath us.

'Contact!' Murdo calls.

'You think?' Sky growls, through her warrior scowl.

I dart a look over at Anuk. Her face is drawn, but determined. When I look back, I see Sky clutching three thin red tubes in her hand. She plunges them into her arm.

'Sky, don't!' I snatch them away from her.

Too late. They've shot their load.

'Didn't you hear that marine? You'll overdose!'

Sky rocks back. Veins bulge out either side of her thin neck, like cords. But even as I'm about to lunge and grab her, she recovers and waves me away.

'I need it,' she rasps. 'Or else I'll only slow you down.'

Before I can shout anything else, there's a loud bang and a crackle above me. I start and look up.

A hot rain of sparks are showering down.

Shit! That's a plasma-lance cutting though our hull . . .

37
TRAPS, TWISTS AND TURNS

Whoever's doing the cutting, they don't hang about. Seconds later a ragged circle of metal drops, smashing down on to the floor of the hold. It barely misses the crate Keo is hiding behind. The ear-splitting *clang* could wake the dead.

Ropes drop through the hole.

'Kyle!' Sky hisses, yanking me down.

It's torture not being able to see what's going on, but I hear it all. Rhallon urging his Syndicate raiders to, 'Go, go, go!' and Masson's deeper roar of, 'Get in there!' The hiss of hands sliding down ropes. The thump of boots hitting the deck.

I try to count. Five. Six. Maybe seven raiders.

Off to our left is the hatch that leads forward to the crew compartment. As arranged, two of Keo's overall-wearing marines burst through it now, into the hold. They fake panicked looks at what they've come face to face with, turn and scramble frantically back out again.

'Don't let them shut that hatch!' Masson bellows.

But our guys slam it closed before two of the raiders reach

it. One of them bellows with frustration and smashes at it with his killstick, showering sparks.

The hatch doesn't care, and stays closed.

Keo springs our trap. 'Do it, Murdo!' she yells.

Several loud *crump-crump-crump*s sound from outside the hull, as our grappling cannons fire cable-trailing rock anchors into the raider ship, binding us together and making sure they can't get away. That's our signal too. We jump up from our hiding places and show ourselves. Masson stares around, his face contorted with shock and rage.

Recognises me. Bares his teeth. 'You!'

I save my breath for the coming fight. As well as Masson, I recognise Una and Ravi and that big lump called Stitch. No Rhallon. They all look gobsmacked.

'Drop your weapons!' Keo yells at them.

The hatch reopens. Our other two marines leap back inside again. Masson sees and his lips pull back further from his teeth. Not in fear, but to make sure we see his scorn. I can almost hear him doing the odds in his head and liking them. Eight of us, but only two nubloods. Seven of them, all nubloods, with backup waiting above to be called in.

'What's keeping Murdo?' Sky whispers.

I'm wondering the same.

'What's going on?' Rhallon yells from above.

'It's a trap!' Masson roars. And launches himself at me.

I step forward into his charge, block the swing of his killstick with my stunstick and slash back at him. But this guy's as fast as me. He leaps back and I miss. Ravi and Stitch come running to help him. Una yells for backup and leads the other raiders in a charge at Keo's marines.

But Murdo must find the right button at last. I go from standing to floating. He's killed the synthetic gravity. We're weightless now, like in a windjammer pushed nose down.

Our secret weapon.

And it works. Instantly our opposition start flailing about helplessly, cursing and panicking.

We've trained for zero-gee combat. They haven't.

Keo and her marines don't hesitate. They launch themselves at the disoriented raiders in long, impossible-looking dives and start swinging their killsticks.

I'm tempted to go for Masson, but . . .

'Let's go!' Sky yells in my ear.

She pushes off the deck with her braced leg and shoots up towards the hole cut into the hold's roof. Anuk's close behind her. Cursing, I clip my stunstick to my belt and leap after them. What I don't count on though is one of the raiders accidentally floating up and getting in my way.

We crash into each other. I try to push him aside, but he grabs hold of me. We both end up tumbling in mid-air.

Luckily we tumble into one of the dangling ropes. I grab it and try to haul myself towards the hole. The fool hanging off me tries to pull me back. Yeah, right. Because we're in zero-gee, this makes him shoot upwards. Holding on to the rope, I jackknife inverted, plant both my boots in his chest and thrust him away, breaking his grip on me.

'Kyle, hurry!' Anuk shouts, from beyond the hole.

The rope's doing crazy things after our struggle, lashing around all over the place. Takes me a good few seconds to pull myself along it and into the hard-docking tunnel. One last tug and I shoot towards the far end.

And get a fierce shock as I go heavy again.

Our freighter's gravity field is switched off, but the screamer still has one. Fortunately, momentum is on my side. Before I fall back, I stretch and grab the lip of the docking hatch. After that it's a quick scramble up and inside.

Barely in time. The hatch slams closed behind me.

I'll worry about that later. Three raiders lie scattered on the deck, dead or unconscious. Sky's being hard-pressed by Rat and another raider. Anuk's fighting off Rhallon, but looks in desperate trouble. The girl's right arm hangs limp by her side and she's having to defend herself left-handed.

I grab my stunstick and charge at Sky's attackers.

The nearest guy sees me coming. He turns from Sky to launch a stupidly wild swing of his killstick that would take my head off if it connected. Stupid, because when I duck under it he's so off balance he pretty much falls on to the point of my stunstick. I just drive it as hard as I can into the gap under his chest armour. The stick kicks back as it discharges into him.

He doubles up and crumples.

But the gommer takes my stick with him. Caught in his armour, it's pulled right out of my sweaty hand.

Not good. Next thing I know, Sky's down and Rat is lunging at me. I dodge his first swipe, but have to block the second with my armoured forearm.

Sparks flare. The shock of the hit staggers me.

'I'll make sure you stay dead this time,' Rat growls.

Cursing the loss of my weapon, I back up. Only for my heel

to hit the lip around the closed docking pit. I trip and go over backwards. Before I can scramble back up, Rat's plunging his killstick at my unprotected face.

Somehow I manage to grab his wrist, but the man's twice the size of me and much stronger. Even as I strain to stay alive I know I'm outmatched. The blurred tip of the stick edges closer and closer. Behind it I see his brute face blotchy with effort and split with a sick grin. I make one last fearsome effort to stop him that tears the muscles in my arms. He snarls with frustration, slams punches into me with his free hand, but my armour makes me hard to hurt. So he gives up on the punching and goes to gouge my eyes out instead.

Tzziipp! I'm showered with hot sparks.

Rat grunts. His whole body spasms, and then he goes limp. His full weight lands on me.

I hear a scream. Sky?

With shaking arms I push Rat off. No. Sky's all right. Back on her feet, panting, stunstick in her hand. It was her who saved me. But as I jump up, Anuk falls, twitching viciously, sparks from Rhallon's killstick hit writhing all over her.

Rhallon sees our horrified looks. Drops to one knee and drives his killstick into the already-dying girl again and again, baring his teeth at us while he does it.

Sky curses and launches herself at him. I haul her back, before she can get herself killed.

'He's mine,' I shout. 'Give me your stick.'

'Like hell I will.'

Frag it! But Rat is still holding his killstick. I lunge and prise it free from his death grip.

'Watch out!' Sky shouts.

I spin round, expecting Rhallon to be lunging at us.

It's worse than that. He's got a blaster.

Instinctively I leap aside so he can't get both me and Sky with one blast. But Rhallon doesn't shoot. He seems content just to threaten us while he backs away to an open hatch in the bulkhead behind him. With his free hand he operates a comm device clipped to his chest armour.

'Ditch the tether!'

A tinny version of Tarn's voice issues from the comm device. 'Why? What's going on back there?'

'Do it!' Rhallon bawls. 'Then get us out of here.'

Sky shoots me a glance and starts edging closer to him.

Rhallon swings his aim to cover her. And starts, maybe getting a good look at her face for the first time. But he's quick to cover his shock with a mocking smile. 'Well, look at that. Tarn's scab sister, trying to look tough.'

Sky scowls and edges still closer.

'Take it easy, Sky,' I say, readying myself for a lunge.

'Sky?' Rhallon says, stepping backwards into the open hatch now. 'Of course it is. The sick girlfriend that Kyle here was so anxious I shouldn't meet.'

'Drop the gun, Rhallon,' I say. 'A ComSec cruiser will be here soon. You can't get away, not this time.'

But I'm hardly done talking when I hear a dull bang.

Rhallon smiles bleakly. 'You think? That was the sound of Tarn unhooking us. By the time your ComSec cruiser arrives, we'll be long gone. As for you . . .'

Tarn's voice crackles from Rhallon's comm, interrupting

him. 'Tether's gone, but I can't break us free.'

'Use full power, you fool!'

'I *am*! Hang on, I'm getting a visual. Shit! That's why. They've shot their own fraggin' grapples into us.'

The blood drains from Rhallon's face. He staggers.

Sky must figure this is our chance. She lurches forward to tackle him, but there's no way she'll be fast enough. Without thinking, I fling Rat's killstick at Rhallon's head to try and distract him, then hurl myself at him.

But you don't get to be a Syndicate boss by being soft.

Ducking the stick, he meets my rush with a punch that sends me reeling away, blood spilling from my torn mouth. Sky has a swing at him with her stick. He blocks her with his armoured forearm and then smashes her in the face with his blaster, so viciously that she's thrown backwards into me.

I catch her, hold her up.

Only now do I see the fearful combat gloves the guy's wearing, spiked with heavy metal knuckles.

He could blast us both now easy, but still doesn't. Instead he swings the gun towards a tank plastered with red hazard signs. 'Our fusion unit,' he says, a mad gloating look on his face. 'Think of it as a little sun held prisoner in that box. Safe if contained, a vengeful monster if set free. One shot from me and . . . *boom* . . . both ships are dust spreading in the big cold empty.'

Sky shrugs free of my grip. I watch in horror as she limps sideways so as to block Rhallon's aim.

His lip curls. 'Was it you who sold us out, scab?'

Sky scowls, but says nothing.

'It was me,' I say, and spit a broken tooth.

Rhallon turns his glare on me now. 'For what? Revenge? A pardon? Spared the rope to live as a ComSec sheep?'

I glance at the fusion unit. It's big enough that even with Sky in the way Rhallon can't miss.

But it's weird – I'm not scared any more.

'I did what I had to,' I say. 'What the Syndicate does is no less evil than what the Saviour did to idents back on Wrath. You're as bad as he is and needed to be stopped.'

Rage distorts Rhallon's face until I hardly recognise him.

'And you call yourself a *nublood*?' he spits.

Teeth bared, he aims around Sky at the fusion unit.

But he doesn't fire.

I watch, gobsmacked, as his eyes bulge and a bloody mist spews from his mouth. He drops the blaster. Collapses slowly to his knees, and then face-plants the deck.

Tarn stands over his body, a blade in her hand.

I go for the blaster.

So does she.

But I'm closer and beat her to it.

I shove the gun in her face. 'Stay back!'

She freezes. 'Or you'll kill me? A bit ungrateful that.'

I take a breath and lower my aim. 'A blasted leg will stop you as easy. But thanks for taking care of Rhallon.'

'Don't kid yourself I did it for you,' she says, and sneers past me at Sky. 'Or for *you*! Fool would've killed us all.'

I waggle the blaster. 'Drop the knife.'

And now a loud pounding comes from the closed hard-docking hatch behind me. I hear faint shouts too.

'Sky, see if you can open that.'

She makes no move, as if she hasn't heard.

Just as well too, because I go cold, realising I can't know who won that fight, Keo or the boarders.

Hang on. If somebody's pounding, that means the hatch can only be opened from our side. And the abandoned plasma-lance is right there in front of me. So even if it's Masson's lot doing the pounding, they *can't* get at us. Which means we can hang out in here, nice and safe, until Turyakin comes to our rescue!

The enormity of the moment is like a slap to my face.

Against all the odds we've gone and done it. Turyakin will take out the Syndicate in this sector. We'll get our pardons. With Tarn a prisoner, and the *Nantahala*'s med-bot to do the blood transfusion, Sky won't die.

I'm close to sobbing with relief.

But I daren't relax. Tarn's still a threat with that knife. I tell her again to drop it.

She narrows those green eyes at me, so like Sky's, and snarls at me, 'You want it, you come and get it.'

A noise behind me.

Something jabs me in my back.

Tzzziiipppp! A spasm of agony. And then every muscle in my body turns to mush. My legs fold under me.

Not even able to groan, I pour myself to the deck.

38
A FINAL BETRAYAL

As I lie there helplessly, unable even to move my eyes, cold fingers check the pulse in my neck.

A hiss of breath. Relief?

Sky limps slowly past me now. The stunstick she must have zapped me with clatters the deck as she drops it. I watch out of the corner of my eye as she faces her long-lost sister.

Tarn laughs. 'He didn't see *that* coming.'

'Shut up!' Sky snarls. 'If you don't want to hang, or spend the rest of your days rotting in a ComSec cage, then get back to your pilot controls and be ready to scram out of here.'

'What about the grapples?'

'I'll take care of them. Just do as I fraggin' say for once.'

'Why?' Tarn asks, so low I barely hear.

But Sky doesn't answer. Instead she quickly prises the blaster out of my nerveless fingers, pockets it and starts dragging me backwards along the deck.

I want to scream at her: 'What are you *doing*?'

But of course I can't.

She dumps me by the boarding hatch. Hunts frantically for something. Finds it with a small, satisfied grunt, and then drops to her knees by my side. Her white dreads fall around my face, as she kisses me.

'I'm sorry, Kyle,' she whispers, 'but I have to do this.'

Then she's on her feet again, reaching for whatever she found. A hiss of hydraulics and the hatch starts sliding back. As soon as it moves, Keo shouts from below.

'Look out, it's opening.'

A man yells that he's got it covered. But Sky shouts down to them, loud and urgent. 'Keo, it's me, Sky! Don't shoot! Kyle's been hurt real bad. I'll pass him down to you.'

With a big effort, she tumbles me into the open shaft.

I guess she was counting on the gravity still being switched off in our freighter. But it isn't, and I find that out the hard way, falling all the way through the tunnel and into the hold. Crates have been piled beneath the hole in the *Whydah Gally*'s hull. I land heavily on the top one, but not squarely enough to stay there. Still completely limp, I roll off the side and fall the rest of the way. Two marines try their best to catch me. I end up tangled with them on the hold floor, hurting, and looking at a line of bulging body bags.

Sky scrambles down next, drops the last few metres and lands next to me, her exo-brace taking the shock.

As the marines pick themselves up, Keo comes running. Before she can say anything, Sky's shouting again.

'Listen, Keo, we got Rhallon. Killed him. But the pilot has rigged their dee-emm drive to overload and blow. They're trying to take us with them. If Murdo doesn't cut them loose and get us the hell out of here, we're all dead!'

She lies well, spraying the words at Keo as if in a panic.

Keo's face pulls tight. 'We can't do that.'

But Sky wasn't shouting loudly just for her benefit.

'On it!' Murdo's speaker-voice says.

'No, wait!' Keo yells.

Too late. Through the deck, I feel a series of slight shudders, which I'm pretty sure is Murdo firing the charges to sever the hyperalloy cables from our grapples.

Setting the screamer free.

Keo curses and yells at her marines to board the raider. They fling themselves up the crates, only to come tumbling back down, screaming as the pain hits. I'd scream too, if I could. My skin feels like it's being ripped off in sheets.

And then, just as suddenly, the pain is gone.

I get to feel relief for about as long as a blink takes. There's a massive bang, followed by the screech and howl of air in a tearing hurry. Dust and debris shoot up towards the hole cut in the roof of the hold. Horrified, I realise the screamer must have torn itself free from the docking tunnel. The hold is decompressing so quickly and violently that I feel myself rising up.

What saves us are the piled crates. The lid is sucked off the top one, flies up and partially blocks the hole.

'Get out!' Keo yells.

Sky drags me into the next compartment. Keo's last out, staying to check nobody's been left behind.

Her marines slam the hatch closed.

The storm cuts off. All I hear now is relieved panting.

Until Keo stomps over to Sky, curses, and backhands her hard across the face. Sky takes it with the slightest of staggers and glares back defiantly.

'Cuff her,' Keo orders.

A marine binds Sky's arms behind her back. He pats her down, finds her blaster and chucks it to Keo.

Sky doesn't resist, just scowls.

Another marine shoves a stinging needle through my sleeve into my arm. Slowly my muscles remember how to work again. Meanwhile, I listen to what's being said around me. Thanks to Murdo's zero-gee trick, the fight against the boarders was one-sided, with only one marine killed. That agony we all felt was the screamer firing up its dee-emm drive to get away. With the two spaceships so close, we caught the full brutal whack of it.

I'm struggling to my feet like a newborn lamb, my tongue feeling like it's somehow grown fur, when Murdo is dragged in struggling and protesting.

'How was I supposed to know Sky was lying?'

'Save it for Turyakin,' Keo snaps.

She has Murdo and me cuffed too, before heading forward to the freighter's flight deck to comm the incoming cruiser and let them know what's happened.

Murdo slumps against the bulkhead at his back. 'Well done! Our last chance and you let her blow it.'

I open my mouth, close it again.

Sure it was him who panicked and let the screamer go, but if Sky hadn't been with us, it wouldn't have happened.

Oh, Sky, what have you done?

'Don't blame Kyle,' she calls out. 'Blame me. He had nothing to do with this. I tagged hi—'

Her voice cuts off with a weird choking sound.

I look around. Too fast. My head fills with nasty flashes.

Sky takes a few tottering steps towards us, then collapses to the deck. Next thing she's moaning and thrashing around, like she's having a fit.

I run to her, but my hands are cuffed behind my back.

'Do something!' I yell.

A marine shoves me aside, drops to his knees by Sky and holds her down to try and stop her hurting herself.

'What's wrong with her?' Murdo asks.

Shit! I remember Sky injecting all three red tubes of boost-juice and shout that out to the marine holding her.

He grimaces and shakes his head.

'Uncuff me!' I shout.

But nobody's listening. A marine shouts for Keo and she comes running back from the flight deck. Together they shove me and Murdo aside and hold us there. All I can do is watch helplessly, my heart breaking, as Sky gives one last awful shudder and goes horribly still.

The marine tears Sky's chest armour off, leans over and has a listen. And then looks up, grim-faced.

I struggle to get past Keo. 'I know healing, I can help.'

She wrestles me back again.

'Cool it, Kyle! Rytag knows what he's doing.'

Gritting his teeth, the marine yanks a stubby white tube from his sleeve, gives it a practised twist and stabs it into Sky's neck. Then he starts leaning two-handed on her chest, trying to shock her stopped heart into going again.

I can hardly bear to watch.

He takes a break after a while and checks Sky again. Sighs, shakes his head and starts over. When he rocks back, obviously knackered, a second marine takes over.

But Sky stays limp, showing no signs of life.

They change over again. One of them accidentally knocks Sky so that her face flops towards us.

Her eyes are open, but the shine's gone from them.

The marines sit back on their haunches, panting and sweating. One gives Keo a little head shake.

'She's gone, I reckon.'

For a few seconds I just stand there, dazed and crushed.

Keo lays a sympathetic hand on my shoulder.

'NO!' I roar, twisting away.

I yank my wrists apart, not caring how much it hurts. And maybe the cuffs weren't done up right, or I'm just too nublood strong. Anyway, a sharp snap and I'm free.

'Come back, Kyle!' Keo shouts.

But I'm already by Sky's side, frantically checking for even the faintest pulse. Nothing. Her skin feels horribly clammy to the touch. I go straight into what the marines were doing, shoving my full weight down through the heel of my hand into her chest. Two a second, count to thirty. Tilt her head back, pinch her nose and blow two breaths into her mouth, for about a second each. Blood from my torn wrists covers her.

Do it again. And again.

On the fifth rep I'm pretty sure I crack at least one rib. Doesn't matter though. Ribs will heal.

And again. Sweat starts to stream down my face.

I check her again, but still nothing. Not even a flicker.

'Give it up, Kyle,' Keo says. 'You tried.'

But I see her shoulder holster and remember Rona saving somebody once using an old Barrenlands trick.

I gesture wildly at her. 'Your blaster, I need it.'

She looks at me like I'm mad.

'Just the mag then!'

The look on my face must convince her, I guess. She draws the blaster, ejects its magazine and chucks it to me. A glance shows me how the contacts are shielded. A few well-aimed blows on the metal deck exposes them.

'What the hell?' Keo says, stepping back.

I rip Sky's tunic open, needing skin. A spit on the broken blaster mag's exposed contacts for luck, and I grind it into where I reckon her heart is. That's if she has one.

The mag sparks into her. I get a shock that blisters my hand. Sky gets the full zap though and arches upwards.

The mag goes flying. So do I.

I'm scrambling back to her when I swear she groans.

Shaking, I lift her up. She groans again, more loudly this time, and I feel her cool breath on my face. Life creeps ever so slowly back into her beautiful dark green eyes.

I lay her carefully back down, suddenly afraid.

Her eyes squeeze closed.

She takes a breath. And another. And then another.

Until I can breathe again too.

Keo picks up and inspects the remains of the blaster mag.

'Well, I'll be damned,' she mutters.

One of her marines offers to bandage my blistered hand and torn wrists, but I shake my head. That can wait.

I won't let go of Sky, scared she'll slip away again.

Around me, the marines start settling down and tending to their cuts and bruises. Murdo, clearly worried about the consequences of cutting the screamer free, asks Keo what the latest word is from the *Nantahala*. She tells him that it's in pursuit, but he shouldn't hold his breath.

He slumps down near us.

'What the frag was Sky thinking?' he snarls.

And what can I say? I'm thankful she's not dead, but other than that I'm as confused and gutted as he is.

We were *so* close. Now, because of Sky, we're screwed.

Even as I think this she stirs in my arms. Her eyelids flutter open and she stares at me.

I shake my head. 'Why'd you do it?'

She blinks. Opens her mouth, closes it again.

'With her blood I could've saved you. You know that!'

But still Sky just stares at me.

'You think you owed her, is that it?'

That gets through. She scowls and says something, so quiet I can't hear. I bend lower. And she grabs me, pulls me closer with strength I wouldn't have thought she had.

'Now we're quits,' she hisses, her face so close to mine that she's a pale green-eyed blur. 'Don't you see?'

I curse. Can't help it.

'That worth dying for, is it?'

She swallows, or tries to. 'We all got to die sometime.'

Behind me, Murdo mutters angrily that we'll all hang for the mess she's made if the raider gets away.

But Sky pushes me away gently, shaking her head.

'No you won't,' she croaks, and then coughs. 'Blame it on me. You guys knew nothing about it. Hell, you'd even be telling them the truth for once. How's that for a laugh?'

But nobody's laughing, least of all me.

And now her cough comes back for real, ripping her up.

I'm fetching her water when Keo comes back. With bad news. Outpaced again, the *Nantahala* has given up chasing the raider and is on its way here.

'Shit!' Murdo bangs his head against the bulkhead.

I get a few sips into Sky. It settles her coughing down, but her eyes are closed and she's grimacing with pain.

'What was that?' she slurs.

'Sounds like Tarn got away,' I say.

She nods. Coughs again, bringing up blood. Then clutches at my arm, spilling the water. 'Kyle, listen.'

'Don't talk, Sky,' I plead. 'It'll make you cough.'

But when did Sky ever do what I told her? Her eyes flicker open. She pulls me closer again.

'Don't be mad at me, Kyle,' she whispers. 'I'll sort it with Turyakin. The man's no fool. He can't blame you.'

Can't he? I'm not so sure.

'You should try to rest,' I say.

'Came a long way together,' she sighs. 'You and me.'

Tears sting my eyes. 'A fierce long way.'

She smiles. Or tries to, but she's in too much pain. And then her head falls back and she's passed out again.

Keo walks over. 'How's she doing?'

'Hanging on, like always,' I tell her. 'Sky's a fighter.'

39
FROM DARKNESS INTO LIGHT

Nineteen days scratched into our cell wall now. Eighteen since a furious Turyakin tried us for our crimes. Sky's sentenced to death for screwing the trap up. Murdo too, for his part and for the Ark murder he committed years ago. Me, I've got life on a hard-labour world, with parole possible in thirty standard-years, if I'm good. Even Keo's been punished, busted down a stripe to lance corporal for letting it happen.

I have Sky, and the discs they stuck in our necks, to thank for being spared. I'd lied my head off that she hadn't known Tarn would be there and panicked. But she insisted on telling them the truth. And those discs record stuff – which settled it.

That all feels like a long time ago now though.

Murdo and me, we're back in our cages on the *Nantahala*. Sky's in a stasis pod somewhere, being kept alive. And little Mags is gone, transferred aboard an Ark-bound freighter. Without her, news is tough to come by.

All we can do is scratch the passing days on to the wall.

I'm making the twentieth mark when our compartment's

hatch opens. But it's Lieutenant Laghiri who steps through it, instead of the usual marine who brings us our rations.

Breathing suddenly gets hard.

Is this it? Will Murdo be taken off to have his neck stretched? Will they switch off Sky's pod and let her die? Or haul her out so they can hang her beside him?

But the ComSec officer is on her own. And she's smiling.

'I've got good news,' she says.

'Like what?' Murdo says, low and calm.

I'm impressed. If I said anything, I think I'd squeak.

Still smiling, Laghiri tells us. And it is not just good news. It's *amazing* news! When she's done she unlocks the cage and says we can return to the quarters we had before the mission.

'What about Sky?' I ask.

Her smile fades. 'Yes, Sky too. Only –'

Only it might not change anything. Yeah, I get that.

But the woman has a heart. She takes me to Sky, steps out into the corridor and leaves us alone. Heart pounding, I crouch by the stasis pod. Through the frosted top I can make out the vague shape of Sky. I try to rub it clear over her face to see her better, but can't. The frost is in the plastic.

Just as well maybe. They say people look grim in stasis.

'Sky, it's me, Kyle,' I whisper. 'Don't suppose you can hear me, but Laghiri's told us we've been pardoned, you included. No hangings. No hard labour. How about that, huh?'

I look around. Laghiri's still outside in the corridor. I can't see her, but she's muttering into her comm.

'The screamer showed up, Sky. Tarn abandoned it in orbit around some agri-world. We're there now. Word is she ragged it too hard getting away, which blew its dee-emm drive. They found its escape craft on the planet's surface, but no sign of Tarn. There are loads of transports out of there and they reckon she took one. Laghiri says there's little or no chance they'll catch her now, with the head start she has.'

I lay my forehead on the pod, and sigh.

'You got what you wanted, Sky. So did Turyakin. He's put a stop to the raiding and crushed the Syndicate in this sector. His ComSec bosses are so happy they're bumping him up a rank to Commodore, or something. That's why he's letting us –'

A throat is cleared behind me.

Laghiri's back. I jump up, a bit embarrassed.

'We're about ready to open fire on the raider vessel,' she says. 'Captain Turyakin wondered if you'd care to watch?'

I glance at Sky's pod. 'Sure. Why not?'

A few minutes later, she plants me at the back of the Nantahala's command and control compartment, with Keo to mind me and strict orders to keep my mouth shut.

Turyakin looks round and gives me the tiniest of nods.

The compartment is packed with watchers. The far wall is a huge screen. An arc of blue and green world fills the bottom, and hanging above it is the Syndicate screamer.

A white box around it turns red.

'Locked on,' Keo whispers.

Three red streaks leap at the raider vessel. When they slam into it, stuff flies off. It shudders, but stays intact.

I glance a question at Keo. She says to keep watching.

A blindingly bright explosion overloads the screen. Weirdly, there's no sound to go with it. When the display sorts itself out again, the screamer is gone. In its place is a vast glowing cloud, which I'm guessing is red-hot debris.

Keo grins. 'More fun than scrapping it, for sure.'

'Wouldn't have minded seeing that myself,' Murdo grumbles later, when I describe it to him.

'You weren't invited,' I say, to wind him up.

While he's deciding what to do with us, Turyakin says we have to pull our weight now like everybody else aboard. They've been down to the planet and picked up a load of fresh vegetables. We've been put to work in the galley, peeling, slicing and stowing them in the freezers. The pile of vegetables facing us looks likes a mountain. It'll take us fraggin' days.

And we both know they have machines for this.

'Beats hanging,' Murdo says, but he doesn't sound sure.

I grunt and set about losing myself again in the mindless work. My relief at our unexpected reprieve doesn't stop me feeling sick about Sky. It's like there's light at the end of a dark tunnel I've been crawling through my whole life. But if I scramble out into it I'll be leaving Sky behind.

'Damn it!' Not concentrating, I've cut myself. Badly.

'You did that deliberately,' Murdo shouts after me, as I'm led off to the med-hub, trailing blood.

When we arrive, Laghiri's showing some hard-faced civilians around its facilities.

She sees me clutching my hand. 'Kyle?'

'Cut himself,' the marine explains for me. 'Accidentally.'

'Is this the . . . *nublood*?' a woman asks Laghiri.

Laghiri frowns, and nods.

I see how richly dressed this lot are now. Beside them her ComSec uniform looks shabby. I see too the logo on the metal case the woman is carrying. Three words, printed fancy.

COMBINE MEDICAL – RESEARCH.

My dark tunnel closes up around me again.

The woman smiles at her colleagues. 'And wounded too.'

'Perhaps,' one of the men says to Laghiri, 'he could explain what we found in the escape craft?'

I look at her, wondering. 'You said it was empty?'

Laghiri frowns. 'That's what we were told. It came down outside a medium-sized settlement, and it was a few days before it was found. One of its stasis pods was in use, so they thought they had a survivor on their hands. But when the medics they fetched opened it up, they found –'

'Blood,' the ComMed woman says.

But Tarn hadn't been hurt, not that I saw. 'Blood?'

'Two units, in proper storage bags,' the man behind her says. 'A few nights before, one of our night-shift medics had an unpleasant encounter. A dark-haired young woman with a blaster forced him, violently, to take her blood and bag it. Now why would this girl, on the run from ComSec we hear, go to so much trouble to leave her blood behind to be found?'

The suited strangers stare at me, almost hungrily.

'Where's the blood now?' I croak.

'Here,' the woman says, holding up the metal case.

EPILOGUE
SIX STANDARD-MONTHS LATER

We were sent in – inserted Keo calls it – yesterday. A stealthy little ComSec scout ship dropped us off in the dead of a No-Zone night. Our job is to be boots on the ground and do visual recon before the main landing. And it was just as well that Keo brought us along. A few minutes after sunrise we ran into Reapers. In our camo and body armour I guess we looked like Slayers. A marine was hit with a spear. It could've ended very badly, but I shouted out who we were. And then proved it, by showing my face and my clan tattoo.

An hour later I'm in a hideout dug deep into the ground, hugging my brother Colm, and shedding happy tears.

Not for long though; Keo needs him to brief her on whether the spaceport is secure for dropship landings. Colm says it is, but only barely. The wrecking-cable trap that once kept windjammers out of the No-Zone has been destroyed, a suicide attack using a transport packed with explosives. Slayer ground troops, supported from the air, are closing in.

'How close are they?' Keo asks him.

'Next valley,' Hekki says, in her thick Reaper accent.

I study Colm while he's talking. We're easier to tell apart now. I'm taller by a finger's width, maybe down to spending time in lower grav. His skin is a lot darker, sun-burnt from living the life of a nomad Reaper. And he's fearful lean, from being half-starved. But a month of Wrath sun for me, some food for him, and we'd be back to being almost identical.

Keo commed in her report. Since then we've hunkered down while Slayer windjammers slid in for their morning prowl. One dropped some incendiaries.

The marines laughed out loud. 'That all they've got?'

After the all-clear, Colm takes us to see Squint, the scavved carry-bot we rebuilt to be our pet. When he sees me he waves a scorched leg feebly, all he can manage. Colm says he was carrying ammo when a Slayer warjammer nailed him.

'We haven't got the tools or the parts to fix him.'

I scratch Squint between his fake ears. 'Maybe ComSec does.'

'That'd be fantastic. The kids adore him.'

We move on to Colm's headquarters, another hole, but roomier and with charts. There, I tell Colm and Hekki our story since we left Wrath. Fleur's not here to be told. Sadly she's been dead a while, killed in a Slayer raid. Keo and her marines are down at the spaceport now, checking it out. Their ears not being here makes the telling easier. I'm nearly done now, at the point where Sky zapped me so Tarn could get away.

Colm can't keep from making a small disgusted noise.

'Lucky it was only a stunstick,' Sky says.

She's standing over by the chamber's entrance, chewing on some root-thing that Hekki gave her. She gives us a wink and then squeezes herself outside.

'Guess some things never change, huh?' Colm says.

I let that slide and tell him about our reprieve when the screamer turned up abandoned, with Tarn long gone. But when I get to the Combine Medical lot showing up on the *Nantahala* with a case of Tarn's blood, Colm interrupts.

'Maybe they *did* catch Tarn, and made the rest up?'

Startled, I glance around. But Sky's still safely outside. And then I think back to the look on the ComMed woman's face, and what was said. 'Nah. She got away, all right. They looked too disappointed. Anyhow, what's it matter?'

'Doesn't. It's just . . . you said Tarn hates Sky.'

'She does, believe me. It's not like she hid it. But Sky saved her, so I guess Tarn returned the –'

Hekki shuts me up with a warning hiss.

I glance at the entrance and Sky is clambering back inside.

'What?' she says, as she sees us sitting there in silence.

'Kyle was, uh, telling us how fast you recovered when the medics shot you full of Tarn's blood,' Colm says.

'And now look at her,' I say. 'Good as new. Well . . . almost.'

We watch awkwardly as she limps over to join us.

'Don't all cheer at once,' she says.

Even Colm manages a smile.

'Your leg,' Hekki asks. 'That hasn't healed?'

Sky shakes her head. 'No. The damage was done too long ago and it's healed by itself, as much as it could. Kyle reckons it's a shame, but I don't. It's kind of who I am by now.'

'Were the ComMed guys impressed?' Colm asks.

'Blew their fraggin' minds,' I say.

All that's left to tell is how we ended up back here on Wrath. I start with my least favourite bit – ComMed and ComPharma wanting to test the hell out of us.

Colm pulls a grim face. 'Doesn't sound like fun.'

'It wasn't. ComSec wouldn't hand us over, but they let Med and Pharma run their tests at one of their bases, under their supervision. Strength. Speed. Some intelligence tests even, but they don't think nublood helps with that.'

'They'd never seen scores so low,' Sky jeers.

'Not true,' I say. 'And I got cut a lot to see how I healed. But, to be fair, they made sure it didn't hurt. Much. And didn't hang me when I healed real quick, just made loads of notes.'

'Did they test Murdo too?' Colm asks hopefully.

Poor Colm. When Murdo didn't return that night we stowed away, my brother assumed we'd been caught and executed.

I shake my head. 'Nah. Murdo was kept aboard the *Nantahala*. Protective custody, or something like that. He's still stuck up there now, twiddling his thumbs. Anyway, there was Sky and me, hating life, when Captain Turyakin finally shows up again. Says testing's over and takes us back aboard. What a relief, I can tell you! His ComSec bosses want Wrath shut down as a dump-world, because of the darkblende deposits.'

'And the Zhang ruins,' Sky says.

Which I could see from here, if I stuck my head out.

Colm mutters something, which could be, 'And nublood.'

I wince. 'Keo says the Combine only cares about one thing. Making itself richer. But they do have rules and regulations. I say we worry about that later. The Slayers have had it. ComSec will be here soon, and in force, to take them out. That's why Turyakin grabbed me and Sky, to help with recon.'

Hekki stirs. 'What becomes of us afterwards?'

I don't have an answer. But even if I did, Keo's upside-down head appears now at the entrance.

'Our assault ships are on their way down. Want to see?'

The landings are over. The battle, if it can be called that, has been won. As the sun drops behind the No-Zone's eastern peaks, smoke rises up from where three counter-attacking Slayer windjammers were shot from the air. Occasional distant thumps of pulse-rifle fire are ComSec marines and their combat drones doing some last mopping up. All Slayer ground forces are in full retreat. Below us, Reapers and rebels are going crazy, jumping about, whooping and cheering.

Why not? They've fought so hard and for so long.

'You should get down there,' I tell Colm.

'I will, in a bit,' he says.

It was Sky's idea to sneak up the ridge to watch the sunset. It *wasn't* her idea for my brother to come with us. But I shot her a pleading look and she held her tongue. I was impressed. At her patience, and with how well she managed the climb. Her lungs are clearly so much better, and all the training she's done seems to have paid off. She almost looked like she enjoyed it.

The view from here is amazing. We sit there, taking it in.

'Tell Colm about the snow leopard,' Sky says.

I grimace at her. It's such a precious and fragile hope. I don't like to speak about it, in case that jinxes it.

'If you don't, I will,' she says.

'Okay, okay.' Grudgingly, I tell him about the lonely big

cat from Earth I came across on the pleasure hub, and how I hadn't thought ComSec would do anything about it. 'But they did. Seized it, tried its owners and executed them, as well as the dealer who supplied it. See, rare animals like that, the only ones of their species, they're protected by laws. Harsh ones.'

Colm scrunches his face up at me. 'So?'

'So there's an organisation that got those laws passed ages ago. They still keep an eye on things, to make sure they're obeyed. And somebody tipped them off about Wrath and us nubloods. My guess is Laghiri. Anyway, now they're shouting that nubloods should have the same sort of protection.'

Colm looks at me sideways.

'Well you never know,' I say, cross.

He shrugs. 'I guess it doesn't hurt to hope.'

For a long while after that none of us says anything. Our breath starts to mist as the temperature drops. Beyond the jagged peaks the darkening Wrath sky turns from blue to the red of blood. A fluking breeze lifts the harsh smells of Wrath up from the valley below. Overhead a few sky lizards soar in lazy circles, their whistles drifting down.

Finally Colm stands up, his leg bones clicking.

He smiles. 'Listen, Kyle, Sky, thanks for coming back. I was never so glad to see anybody. We all were. Hekki's Reapers are already singing songs about how you two saved them.'

Sky groans. 'Kill me now.'

We all laugh.

Then Colm sighs. 'How long are you staying?'

I glance across at Sky.

'Until the Slayers are beaten,' she says.

After that the *Nantahala* will go back on patrol. And we'll be on it. Turyakin's dropping us off at a transit world called Angel's Drift, with creds for a few months' living and a ticket to anywhere in this sector. Our two crates of darkblende should still be floating where we left them. Murdo insists we leave collecting them for a year, until we're sure we're not being watched and the Syndicate is a bad memory. Meanwhile, he'll line up a buyer. With what we make, we'll set up as free-traders.

But I tell Colm none of this. Sky made me swear not to.

'Come with us,' I say, knowing he won't.

He shakes his head. 'Thanks. I'll stick around here. There's Hekki and . . . yeah. Maybe one day I'll come looking for you. Or you guys could swing by here again?'

'You never know,' I say.

'What about Tarn?' Colm says.

'What about her?' Sky says, real sharp.

I jump in. 'We won't be looking for her again, if that's what you mean. And I can't imagine she'll come looking for us.'

We turn to Sky. She makes us wait, then nods.

I'd worry, except I've only said what she's been saying since she woke up. Even after I'd told her, reluctantly, how Tarn's blood had saved her. Me, I reckon Tarn's done it out of spite, to keep Sky in her debt. Sky maintains it was more about remorse. Whatever. Thankfully, Sky doesn't kid herself she wants to see Tarn again. Maybe deep down she knows I'm right.

'I'll see you later,' Colm says.

We bump stumps and he clears off.

I let out a breath I feel like I've been holding for months.

Sky lets one out too, and leans into me so our shoulders are touching. 'So, Kyle, how's it feel to be sung about?'

I shiver. 'Horrible. And cold.'

She slips an arm inside my jacket and around my waist. Her lovely green eyes twinkle up at me. 'Is that better?'

I put my arm around her. 'Always.'

These last few days Sky has been the happiest I've ever seen her. That's how I know she's let Tarn go. There's a lightness to her, and it's made me fall in love with her all over again.

I'm wondering if she'd like to be kissed, when she frowns.

'You don't *have* to come with me, you know.'

She says it so solemn I laugh.

'Now who's the gom, huh? I *want* to be with you.'

So many things to be unsure about, but this isn't one of them. I tip my head back, to see if any stars are showing. A few are. Suns with worlds I might visit one day. The thought tugs at my heart, pulls a sigh out of my mouth.

'What?' Sky says, her breath on my neck.

'Nothing.' I give her a squeeze. 'Not used to being happy, that's all. Looking forward to being back up there.'

And I really am. I've finally found where I belong.

I point out the cluster of tiny lights above us, tracking across the purpling sky. One will be the *Nantahala*. But now something blots them out. More ComSec assault ships?

No. I hear the faint whistling cries.

Only a sky lizard, flapping back to roost for the night.

THE END

HIGH VOLTAGE YA READING FROM ELECTRIC MONKEY

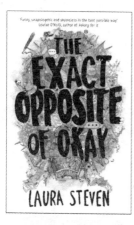

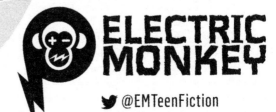

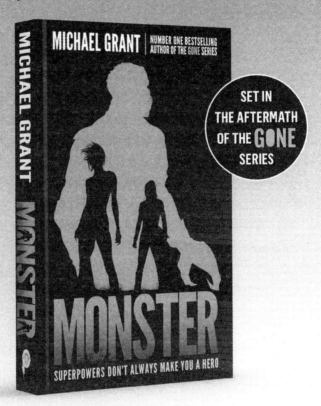